Sunstroke

Sunstroke

JESSE KELLERMAN

sphere

SPHERE

First published in the US in 2006 by G. P. Putnam's Sons

First published in Great Britain in 2006 by Sphere
This paperback edition published in 2007 by Sphere

A CIP catalogue record for this book
is available from the British Library

The author gratefully acknowledges permission to quote
from 'Can't Fight This Feeling Anymore' by Kevin Cronin,
copyright © 1984 Fate Music. All rights reserved.
Used by permission.

ISBN 978-0-75153-819-9

Papers used by Sphere are natural, recyclable products made
from wood grown in sustainable forests and certified in accordance
with the rules of the Forest Stewardship Council.

Typeset in AGaramond by M Rules
Printed and bound in Great Britain by Clays Ltd, St Ives plc
Paper supplied by Hellefoss AS, Norway

Sphere
An imprint of
Little, Brown Book Group
Brettenham House
Lancaster Place
London WC2E 7EN

A Member of the Hachette Livre Group of Companies

www.littlebrown.co.uk

TO GAVRI

In the heat of the day
visions did tempt me

The Book of Odd Thoughts, 1:3

ONE

Take care of things when I'm gone.

The earthquake began at three twenty-four A.M. and ended seventy-three seconds later. By four in the morning, Gloria Mendez had determined that her apartment had suffered no serious casualties.

There wasn't much to damage. In this she differed from many of her single friends, who had, without warning, begun accruing evidence of their solitude: framed photos of Mickey Mouse-eared nieces and nephews; a few too many leather miniskirts; mementos from three different ski trips with two different men. Siamese cats named The Fonz, or Jon Bon Jovi, or after imaginary daughters. *Alexis. Samantha. Claire.* Items you could accumulate safely, content in the knowledge that there wasn't some crazed toddler out to scratch them, shatter them, choke on them, soak them in regurgitated formula and half-digested carrots.

By contrast, Gloria's apartment looked empty. She didn't even have a mirror in her bedroom. To check her reflection, she had to go into the bathroom, stretching over the counter if she wanted to see how her Levi's fit.

She never bothered, because they always fit fine.

Spartan didn't quite describe the place. She preferred to think of it as *untethered*. By not weighing herself down with sentimentality, she was free to make changes to her life; free to accommodate another person, or two, or three. She believed that life forked for unwed women over thirty-five; you could either be hopeful or resigned. Resigned was halfway to dead, though, so Gloria chose to be hopeful.

Besides, these days women were having kids later than ever. Barb Oberle's cousin had had twins at forty-six. It was like something out of the Old Testament.

Untethered, buoyed by possibility. When Gloria gathered with friends for coffee, she sometimes imagined herself as lighter than those around her, hovering an inch or two above the crowd.

Owning almost nothing carried the added benefit of making it easier to keep the place clean; she liked things complete, tucked in.

About the walls, Barb Oberle said *For crissake, put something up. It looks like a Kubrick film in here.*

Barb had a better sense of humor than the others. It probably had something to do with the fact that she was married, but Gloria was unsure which was cause and which was effect.

The rattle of an aftershock sent Gloria scurrying to the doorway. She waited for it to pass, then went on surveying her kitchen. For once she felt thankful for the poor quality of her cabinetry. The door that stuck saved all her glassware from a lemming-like fate. She swept up a vase and sponged the viscera of high-diving jars. Beneath the sink, bleach had spilled; in cleaning it, she took care to keep it away from the Windex. Mixing the two created poisonous fumes, and if she was going to die this morning, she at least wanted to straighten up first.

The radio was calling it a humdinger. CalTech hadn't released the verdict, but "armchair seismologists" (whatever that meant) had pegged its Richter in the high sixes. Expect closure of roads and government offices. Expect power outages. Expect disruptions in cable service, phone service, Internet connections. Cell service providers are having trouble due to damage to transponders; be patient, keep trying, and maybe the grid will unclog. Do not leave your house—except if there's a gas leak. In that case, don't stay inside your house. County law stipulates that all buildings five years or younger must have an automatic gas shutoff valve; if you don't know the age of your home, it's recommended that you check. Just in case, use flashlights, not candles. Be aware that aftershocks can be as deadly or worse than the original quake, given the weakened state of—

She switched it off.

She tried to call around to see if people were okay, but the landline was out. Contrary to the radio's bleak assertions, however, her cellphone was working; Reggie had left a voicemail. He wanted to make sure she was all right. He was busy, he said, and he'd try her later in the day, when he could afford a minute to talk.

She tried him back: all circuits were busy.

Going back to bed was out of the question. Once woken, she couldn't convince her body that it had been given a second chance. She was about to run a bath when Carl's note popped into her head.

Take care of things when I'm gone.

The figurines.

She had a banana, put on some clothes, and set out for the office.

A FEW PEOPLE were out on the curb in bathrobes and slippers, smoking and twiddling dials on transistors. A man clutching a guitar sat shirtless in striped pajama bottoms atop the hood of his Volkswagen. He wore a necklace of wooden beads and was entertaining his girlfriend with a throaty rendition of a tune Gloria remembered as popular six months ago.

As she passed, they gave her looks like *What the hell are you doing dressed?* She waved and continued on her merry way through predawn post-disaster.

She had never walked the two and a half miles between her home and work. She passed from commercial zone to residential and back again, moving through alternating pockets of hysteria and catatonia. Near the Beverly Center the alarms of several dozen retailers caterwauled in unison. Dopplerized arias flared up and flamed out as emergency vehicles raced down Wilshire in search of hydrants-turned-geysers and electrical fires. She enjoyed this view from the ground, playing that rarest of roles: a pedestrian in LA.

She decided to take a detour and look in on Barb.

The Oberles lived on Camden in south Beverly Hills, in a pristine two-level Spanish with lacquered tile lining the front walk. Gloria was always struck by the evenness of the lawn. It was as though each blade of grass had been individually selected for freshness. Kenny Oberle sold luxury cars, and there was often something new and roundish in the driveway.

This month it was an Infiniti, in the champagne color he favored. He was nothing if not consistent, Gloria thought. The attitude was catching. Since marrying him, Barb, too, had become a creature of habit—albeit one who could laugh at herself.

"Next time we're going to go *hog wild*," she'd say. *"Gray."*

Nobody answered the front door, so Gloria let herself in the side gate and trod lightly across the back porch, a trapezoid of artificially weathered brick. She tapped a nail against the kitchen window, and heard something clatter inside.

Muttering: *Jesus . . .*

A queasy-looking Barb pulled aside the back door's little curtain, mouthed *Gloria?*, and disappeared behind the snap of fabric as she turned the deadbolt.

Gloria checked her watch guiltily. It was four forty-five in the morning. She hadn't realized; she felt so alert that it could have been Saturday noon, time to start shopping or have a sandwich.

The first thing Barb said was, "Why are you here?"

"Are you okay?"

"We're fine. Amanda's in bed with Kenny. Jason's picking up the books in his room. What are you *doing* here, Gloria?"

"I couldn't sleep."

Barb goggled at her, then began to laugh. "Okay."

Gloria had to smile. It *was* absurd. "My apartment's totally dark," she said. "I wanted to get out of the house."

"Well," Barb said, "come on in. We're having a party."

They sat at the kitchen table: candles and used spoons, as though Barb had just held a séance.

"I can give you lukewarm coffee or dry cereal. Your choice."

"No thanks."

Gloria's visions of her domestic future rarely resembled the Oberle household, whose only apparent source of friction was an overdeveloped sense of irony that Barb and Kenny shared and had somehow made heritable. (At age five, Jason had told Gloria, "You look good. For your age.") Gloria admired their daily seamlessness; everything ran like a German appliance. But since she had never lived in such a family, she had a hard time imagining herself in one like it.

Not that she wanted to reproduce what she'd grown up with.

She was sure her family-to-be would strike a middle chord. Not quite so blistered as her past, but not quite so *normal* as this.

"Actually," Gloria said, "I'm on my way to the office."

"Honey." Barb sat down across from her and took her hand as though she was about to explain how babies were made. "There's no work today. We just had an earthquake."

"I know."

"And even if there hadn't been an earthquake, you couldn't go to work because it's five in the morning."

"I know, Barb."

"And even if it was time for work, aren't you on vacation this week?"

"I'm going in to make sure everything's okay. Carl's figurines—"

Barb's smirk sufficed to reply.

"He loves them," Gloria said. "If they're broken—and look, the place is probably a disaster."

"That's what happens during a natural disaster. Things look like a disaster."

"I've got nothing better to do," Gloria said.

Barb shrugged. "You should be the president."

"Of the company?"

"Of the United States. There's nobody else in the city going to work right now; we could use that sort of dedication in our elected leadership."

"It's important. To Carl."

"I bet."

Gloria supposed Barb's intentions were good; she was "helping a friend move on," or however *Redbook* would describe it. It drove Gloria nuts. There was nothing to be "gotten over." There was possibility, and possibility was to be embraced.

"He's in Mexico," Gloria said.

"Safer there than here." Barb went over to the fridge and began replacing all its dislodged magnets. "He went alone?"

"Yes."

"You didn't want to tag along?"

"You're in some mood," Gloria said.

Barb straightened up, holding a report card. "Well, it is

five in the morning after a *tremor*. But you're right. I'm harassing you."

"Please don't."

They both turned toward the sound of flip-flops.

"Mom—oh, hey." Jason didn't seem at all fazed to see Gloria. In the candlelight, she could see smudges on his glasses. He was wearing briefs and nothing else. His chest was slightly sunken, a gift from Kenny's side of the family. Exposed, he looked younger than his nine years; dressed, he had an air of tweedy assurance that gave Gloria the impression he was about to go up for tenure.

"The lamp broke," he told Barb.

"Which one?"

"In the office."

"I told you not to go in the office, Jason. There might be glass."

"There *is*," he said patiently. "The lamp broke."

Barb flashed Gloria a look: *see?* "Close the door and don't go back in there. Put your shoes on. Go finish cleaning your room."

"It's done. Can I play PlayStation?"

"The power's out."

"Can I try?"

Barb nodded and Jason exited, scratching his shoulder as he left.

"He's half-asleep," Gloria said.

"Yes." Barb looked at her and said gently, "About Carl? I didn't mean to. It's strange, that's all. You're going over to the man's office like you're his . . ."

She didn't finish. Gloria wanted to supply: *wife? slave?*

"This is the nineties, after all," Barb said.

"No it isn't."

"I know. But it's easier than saying the oh-oh's. And"—Barb sighed—"I wish it was still the nineties."

"I don't see what that has to do with my going over to the office."

"You can get a date. You don't have to run around like his—I mean, he's old enough to be—"

"Barb."

"Go online. Or—Kenny's got friends—"

"I'm leaving now."

Barb escorted her through the backyard. They could hear sirens and helicopters, but everything else—everything organic—had run for cover. There were no crickets, no birds, no rustling leaves. A floodlight at the side of the house came on; its cold rays stood Gloria's hair on end.

"Don't go in if the building looks unsafe," said Barb.

"I'll call you soon," Gloria said.

As the gate closed behind her, she felt cut adrift, alone in the dizzy dance of a city staggering to right itself. For a moment she considered going home. The office could wait. The night was sinister and humid with God-knew-what mayhem. Looters? Prowling gangs of rapists?

Silly, she thought. It wasn't After the Bomb; it was early-morning shell shock.

And the prospect of going home depressed her. There wasn't anyone waiting for her. No son asking childish questions, no husband shushing a frightened girl in the other room. At least at work she could surround herself with tasks.

Along Charleville she could hear the creak of her sneakers. At Lapeer, Olympic Boulevard was deserted for miles in either direction; she laughed, realizing that she was waiting for the signal to cross.

Nasty cracks in the exterior stucco made her hesitant to enter the complex where Caperco kept two rooms. She strolled around the perimeter of the building, observing broken windows on the third floor directly above their suite. The parking overhang had shat berry-sized chunks of plaster. Otherwise, it looked okay. She remembered driving through the Valley after the Northridge quake and seeing housing complexes sunk at one corner, à la Pisa. On one such building, someone had graffitied *for rent $5/year.*

Comparatively speaking, the office looked safe. Aside from the cracks. It was a modern building, undoubtedly retrofitted since 1994. They had laws nowadays.

Of course, you could never tell. What appeared sound could be, beneath its skin, an antiquated, code-defying mess. Gloria was no expert on these matters, and she did not pretend to know more than she did.

She completed her circuit, coming to the alley adjacent to the building's west side, where she felt a rush of worry for the homeless guy who lived in the Dumpster.

Then she remembered.

Carl was fond of the man—who went by Buck—and often poked his head into the alley to bring him an extra bagel or donut. They would chat for a few minutes, Buck telling Carl that he had come up with a plan for converting oxygen into nuclear energy.

Carl would nod. "Sounds like a good idea."

"I'm still working out the kinks," Buck would say.

Last week Carl had found him blue and breathless. If he hadn't been dead already, he certainly would've been by the time the paramedics arrived, close to an hour later. Gloria and Carl watched them zip him up into what appeared to be a garment bag. As though he were defective, and they were returning him to the store.

It happened the day before Carl left. He'd said nothing about it to her, but she could read his thoughts: *Get me away from here.*

She hadn't been to the office since then—officially, she was on vacation, too—and had not processed Buck's absence. She resolved next time to bring a muffin and lay it on the spot in his memory.

She went inside.

The lights in the stairwell were off. She negotiated using her hand, listening for portents of structural collapse.

Get in, get the figurines, get out. That was the plan. Her presence here went far beyond the call of duty—justifying, she supposed, the many "World's Best Secretary" cards Carl had given her over the years. Justifying a whole different sort of card. But they didn't print cards that accurately described what she had with Carl: ten years of working alone, in close proximity, their intimacies unspoken and undeniable. He'd never voiced it aloud; still, she hoped, and as long as she had hope, she had reason to be here.

Oh please, she heard Barb say.

"Shut up," she said. Her voice echoed in the empty stairwell.

She found the hallway and groped past neighboring

suites. A heavily bejeweled Israeli named Oded dealt stones and metals from 205; next were a collectible poster dealer (207) and the offices of Gerald Goldblum, CPA (209–213). She had seen other tenants come and go, witnessed the accretion of paint that the superintendent ludicrously referred to as "refurbishment," heard the constant march of foot traffic as it slowly destroyed the garish purple carpeting. Never had she met the poster people; Goldblum and his cronies either. Oded came by once in a while to borrow rubber bands.

None of them were here now. And they *owned* their businesses. She was risking life and limb to retrieve—

Not the invoices. Not the W-2's.

The figurines.

Because Carl loved them, and if she knew him—how could she not?—they, above all else, would be the things he'd choose to rescue.

The darkness was making her moody and lonely.

She reached their suite, let herself in, and beheld the chaos.

An entire bookshelf had fainted forward into the edge of the desk, stopping four inches above her computer. Boxes had arced across the room, vomiting sheaves of stickers; bells; psychedelic tops; bubble wands; snap bracelets; keychain compasses; 99-cent magic tricks; themed erasers, their pencils gone far astray. A hailstorm of doodads Carl filed under PB&J, for Plastic Baubles and Junk. Tiny paralytic soldiers—their rifles hairy with the imperfections of molded low-quality polymers—skirmished around leering jack-o'-lantern Hacky Sacks.

Then there were the masks. They had tumbled from their hooks, landing everywhere. Heads of state, monsters, film icons, star athletes, cartoon heroes. Heaped in orgiastic piles, producing unlikely and downright revolting couplings. Jesus nibbled Marilyn Monroe's ear. Flattened atop William Jefferson Clinton, Spiderman drew a covetous stare from Bush père. Behind the dracaena, Magic Johnson and a vampire engaged in tonsil hockey.

But to her eye, the biggest problem was the slime. Green goo clung to the watercooler. Red goo bubbled up like tar pits. A column of yellow sludge wobbled atop the latex face of Fat Elvis, toppling and running across the carpet as she approached with a tissue bunched in her palm. Trying to wipe it up, she succeeded only in squishing the crap deeper into the fibers. Some toys she would never understand. It seemed about as enjoyable as slinging cranberry sauce.

Which, she realized, probably sounded *very* enjoyable to most children.

On several occasions she had begged Carl to clear the samples out of the office, but he liked having them around. It reminded him of the fun in their job, fun often obscured by the fact that they spent the day pushing paper, sending faxes, arranging shipments of toys that they never got a chance to play with.

Karma was kicking them in the ass. As much fun as they'd had together, the cleanup job she now faced presented its precise inverse: a plunging curve of un-fun.

Overwhelmed by the magnitude of the mess, she began picking things up, at once forgetting her goal. Carl's one nod to arrogance—a framed diploma from Pepperdine—

had leapt to freedom and ended up a shattered pile. Extricating the paper, she swept the shards into her hand and deposited them in a plastic bag that she hung on a doorknob.

After a while she tired of the silence. Buried in her desk was the battery-operated radio that she'd used before Carl replaced it with an expensive Bose Wave (useless for now because of the outage). She let KFWB keep her company. Normally straight-shooting, the newscasters had slipped into the repetitive, shoulder-chucking informality engendered by widespread chaos.

You know, Lisa, they say the most dangerous part of an earthquake can be the aftermath, cause it's then that life-support systems can get to critical points, and people don't take adequate care to mind where they're going.

Absolutely, Dick. Buildings can collapse. And you know what else—

She learned that a power line had gone down on Pico, constipating the entire West Side. LAPD was ordering all nonemergency vehicles off the street, and had closed the sidewalks for a two-mile radius near Carl's house. Warning of broken air conditioners and heat stroke, they told people to stay indoors and cool. An elderly lady in Encino had died.

Oddly, it pleased Gloria to hear news of substance. She had gotten out of the habit of checking the radio in the morning; normally, all it offered was Hollywood gossip. The list of that day's five-minute marriages; weekend grosses; hurricanes of mournful reportage over the state of an aging starlet's breast implants.

An hour and a half later, Gloria had used up three rolls of paper towels and ninety percent of her patience, and the place was still a mess. At least now it was a manageable mess; she had cleared aisles and created zones for UNHARMED, FIXABLE, and THROW OUT. She went to right a stack of old Caperco catalogues that had slumped, their identical back covers fanning into a kickline of Carls. He was bewigged and in face paint, his tongue fully extended and his eyes crossed. From his mouth ballooned speech:

CARL PERREIRA, DOCTOR OF GOOFOLOGY, SEZ:
I GUARANTEE . . .
FREE SHIPPING AND HA! HA! HANDLING!

The picture always made her laugh, because it was so unlike him.

She seized the humerus of the skeleton he had propped up in the corner and used its elbow to massage herself.

"Thanks, Bill."

When Carl had first gotten the skeleton, he'd put it in a hallway closet, hoping someone would come looking for the circuit breaker, scream, and get the pun. Nobody did, so he brought it back into the office, impaled it on a broomstick, and affixed it to a hot-water pipe, where it next morning scared the bejesus out of the UPS guy.

What are you going to name it? she'd asked.

Anne O'Rexic.

Without a trace of a smile. This was Carl's joking face— the gravest he owned.

I think it's a man. Look at the hips.

Then what would you name him?

She'd pinched its mandible. *Bill Emia.*

And so he became.

She appreciated that about Carl: he listened. Nothing obligated him to solicit her opinions, yet he consulted her as though she were the company oracle. Whether born of boredom or genuine interest in what she had to say, his questions elevated her. He was the only person asking.

She passed into the second room. Wedged between the loveseat and the wall, the end table where Carl kept the figurines had not moved. The figures themselves, however, had congregated in a mound on the carpet. Some had lost limbs. The lower portion of Saint Joseph had rolled away from its governing half.

She felt sick.

She spent another hour in triage, freezing with dread at every aftershock. Sixteen survivors. Six chipped. Eight maimed. Four Humpty-Dumpties calling for a whole weekend of delicate crazy-gluing, and one obliterated.

It impressed her to see how many had accumulated. If she kept making them for him at this rate, they'd have to get a bigger office.

And it depressed her to think of the task she had ahead of her. She had to reassemble them before Carl returned; otherwise, he'd be—there was no other word for it—crushed.

The greater she imagined his disappointment to be, the more reassured she felt. Because she interpreted his affection for her gifts as a translation of what he could not express directly.

"You should license them," he'd say. "Mass production. They'll be huge in Italy."

She'd smile and go back to recording checks.

Speaking of.

She was here already. There was nothing to do back home. She decided to get a little work done.

She could almost hear Carl yelling *For the love of all that's holy, take a vacation!* He liked to call her Señora Worcolica, a name she pretended to bristle at but really found flattering. She had been home for a week, and already was clawing at the walls. Even before last night she'd intended to come in this morning to check the messages.

And maybe to log some time with Quicken.

The watercooler needed to be cleaned, too. . . .

In past years, when Carl took his trip, she came in. Someone had to be behind the desk, answering the phones. The business wasn't going to run itself.

This time, however, he had insisted that she take a few days off, too. She had protested: they would miss orders; they'd tick off more than a few clients.

"I don't care," he'd said.

Talk like that made her wonder if he was planning on retiring. He brought it up every so often as a joke. Lately, though, the jokes had taken on a more determined cast, and she had begun to suspect that she'd soon be out of a job.

What then? She didn't know. She'd take care of herself, as she always had.

Or maybe Carl—she—they—

There was hope.

She sighed and said, "What else?"

The answering machine *(Heh-heh-heh-heh-hello!, you have reached Caperco Mask and Novelty)* had left its home atop the sill, ending up behind Bill Emia's foot. Luckily, the backup battery was still fresh, and the ten messages still intact. She grabbed her pen and pad, and let her finger hover momentarily over MAILBOX 1.

The first two messages were orders from retailers: a party supply on Robertson and an eclecticana dealer in Westwood called Wowie Zowie, which catered to stoned UCLA students. She knew the numbers by heart but took them down anyway. Then a telemarketer. Then a question from Jorge, one of the managers at the warehouse. Then Jorge again, saying never mind.

She scribbled, feeling derelict.

The next message was from five days ago, at two in the afternoon. It was Carl.

His cell was supposed to work in Mexico, but evidently "work" meant something different to the phone company: a steady, flatulent, electrical pulse marred the connection. She hit STOP.

Why was he calling her here? He knew she was at home. Probably, she thought, he assumed I'd come into work. He was right, of course. Here she was.

Señora Worcolica!

She smiled and hit PLAY and tried to hear through the static.

"Gloriazzzzzzzzt's me"

A twinge in his voice made her sit up. She put the pen down and started the message a third time.

"Gloriazzzzzzzzt's mezzzzzzzzzGlzzzzzzzzzzzzzI'm hhhhh"

He faded away. "I'mzzzzzzzang on—" He seemed to be holding the phone away. In the background she heard a rush that might have been wind. She was about to restart the message when he came back on.

"therezzzzzzzzzzzzzzzan accidenzzzzzzzzzzzzzerezzzzzzzzzzz waszzzzzzzzzzzzzzzvivzzzzzzzzzzI'm finezzzzzzzthing's fine-zzzzzzzzzcallzzzzzzzzzzzhomezzz—"

The machine beeped abruptly, startling her.

"Next message," it croaked, *"received Tuesday—"*

She mashed the stop button.

Silence.

Addled, she replayed the message, listening to its first half. She went through it again, and again, and again: squeezing out phonemes, guessing at blanks, and transcribing in tight block capitals.

GLORIA   IT'S ME   THERE'S BEEN AN ACCIDENT
WAS VIV

Squelching the anxiety ignited by *there's been an accident,* she ran her pen back and forth over the disjoint *was viv.*

Was viv. Wasviv. Wa sviv. Wasvi v.

She couldn't figure out where one word began and the other ended. Or whether it was one word—or two—or multiple words missing innards. She wrote out combinations of letters until the characters disintegrated into chickenscratches, each of which ratcheted up her worry. The list of possibilities contorted into a weird grammar exercise.

I WAS VIVID
HE WAS VIVID
WHO WAS VIVID
WE WAS VIVID, MAN

She blinked and crumpled the paper.

Relax.

Getting carried away wasn't her style; besides, there was nothing wrong—nothing *really* wrong. If anything authentically bad had happened, he would have called her at home.

But he hadn't, and it had been a few days.

Probably he'd gotten out of whatever fix the message implied.

Certain that another message would tell her as much, she fast-forwarded through the rest of the tape.

There were four consecutive hang-ups. Then nothing.

Okay, she thought. Now what.

She went through the second half of Carl's message, using the same process of transcribe and repeat.

I'M FINE   EVERYTHING'S FINE   CALL   HOME

He was fine. Everything was fine. He was going to call her at home. Or: he *had* called her at home.

But—and this was the thing—he hadn't called her at home, not once in the last week.

TWO

"You don't know where he is?"

For the third time, Gloria said, "He's supposed to be in Mexico."

The dispatcher *mm*ed. "But you don't know exactly."

"No."

"And you think there was an accident?"

"That's what he said on the machine," Gloria said.

"Was it a car accident, or—some other kind of accident? Like a skiing accident?"

In Mexico? In July?

"I honestly don't know," Gloria said, pressing her forehead with the heel of her hand. "Isn't there someone I could talk to—"

"Things are real *busy*," said the dispatcher. "Everyone's trying to do, you know, *disaster relief*." She sounded annoyed, as though Gloria was pestering her for help getting a kitten out of a tree.

"I understand that," Gloria said, "but I'm very worried. Try and see it from—"

"Give me his name one more time."

"Carl Perreira."

"You're his wife, Mrs. Perreira?"

Gloria hesitated. "My name is Gloria Mendez. I'm his secretary."

The dispatcher *mm*ed again: longer this time, and suggestive.

"Hello?" Gloria demanded.

"Yeah, *hang on,* ma'am, I'm—hang on." The phone clattered. "Okay, you got a pen? Oh-one-one—"

"Excuse me," Gloria said. "What is that?"

"What's what."

"The number. You're giving me. What is it."

"I haven't finished it yet, ma'am. Oh-one-one, five-two—"

"That's a foreign number," Gloria said.

"Correct, ma'am. You want a gold star or you want to hear the rest of it?"

"Why are you giving me a foreign phone number."

"This is the number for the American consulate in Tijuana."

"He's not *in* Tijuana."

"Look, ma'am, you said you didn't know where he was. I'm giving you what I have here. He's not in Los Angeles, he's not even in this country, I've got no way of helping you locate him at the present moment."

Gloria gripped the edge of the desk. "That's not what I'm—"

"We are *indisposed,* at the present moment. Now I can give you this or I can transfer you to someone else who might be able to help you, 'cept he's going to tell you the same thing as me."

Gloria said, "Okay. What is it."

The dispatcher spooled out the number and hung up.

Gloria smoothed down her shirtfront and her nerves.

The consulate picked up after ten rings. A young man with a surferdude twang introduced himself as Rob and offered graciously to help her. He sounded friendlier than 911, so Gloria kept her temper steady while voicing her concerns.

"Hmm, well," said Rob. "He's in Baja?"

She remembered a map for the desert on Carl's desk. "I don't think so," she said. "I think he's in Sonora."

"There's a consulate in Hermosillo," he said. "You should probably give them a call."

She thanked him, took the number, redialed.

"U.S. Consulate."

Her spiel took longer this time; frustration made her misspeak, correct herself, apologize.

"Miss," said consulate employee David, "please try and relax."

"I'm concerned."

"We'll figure it out. When was the last time you heard from him?"

"Right before he left."

"What's your connection to Mr. . . . uh, Perreira."

Gloria bit her lip. "I'm his wife."

"And he was planning on driving through the desert," David said. "What was this, a boys' getaway?"

"He was traveling alone."

"Aha. And then you got this message."

"Yes."

"You think it was a car accident?"

"I don't know," she said. She hated being force-fed polite conversation. "I don't know anything. He might be hurt."

David said, "If he was taken to a hospital around here, we would've heard about it. If they get an American national they call us. Same thing if he died. We would've been contacted. To my knowledge we haven't heard anything. It happened last week?"

"The message was from Thursday."

"Look, Mrs. Perreira, I'm sure there's nothing to worry about," he said. "He'll get in touch with you. He's probably having so much fun he forgot to call."

She left her number with him. Before they got off, David said, "Didn't you guys have an earthquake this morning?"

"Yes."

"And you're worrying about this?"

"Please call me," she said, and hung up.

Racked and shaking, she went through Carl's desk. His appointment book was blank; he relied on her for his calendar. She dialed his cell for the millionth time and got the same endless ringing. She searched the clutter for anything related to his whereabouts. She didn't have an itinerary; as he did every summer, he'd planned the trip on his own. It was the one element of his life that she did not feel intimately aware of, and its regularity unnerved her a little. "Time to get away," he'd said, fiddling with the muted silver crucifix he kept tucked inside his shirt. That was one clue that vacation was coming: he undid a button, and out came the necklace.

As always, she'd offer to book a flight, a hotel, dinner reservations. He would not have it.

It's something I like to do myself.

What are you freaking out about? she asked herself. Probably everything's fine. You're not his keeper. You should be home, taking care of yourself.

But she was here.

Taking care of him was her version of taking care of herself.

Barb Oberle's mockery notwithstanding, Gloria had to question the logic of devoting herself to a man who had, without rebuffing her outright, also never acknowledged her with more than gratitude. To her, the explanation was obvious: he loved her but couldn't make the words conform to the truth. He spoke and acted monastically because it was, in a way, more honest than bursting forth with imprecise or hackneyed sentiments. Carl didn't burst. Why would he be any different in love?

Barb saw it through a less charitable lens:

"Face it, Gloria. He's gay."

And while Gloria wanted to argue *no,* doubts nagged her.

Was love celibate? Was it most often silent?

She had been holding out for a long time, believing that he would one day turn. Marriage and kids and family, it would all come in an instant. It seemed to her inevitable; she knew him better than anyone, and he her. In her opinion, two people could not have so deep an awareness of one another and *not* call it love.

The only things he did not share with her were his vacation plans.

Which was why his message was driving her insane with worry. It struck at her heart from two angles: first, the pain of ignorance; and second, the pain of knowing he'd kept her ignorant on purpose.

From across the room, the answering machine glowed malignantly.

She grabbed pen and paper and tried it again.

> *Gloria it's me there's been an accident was viv*
> *I'm fine everything's fine call home*

This time around the rogue phrase *was viv* started to take some shape. If she listened carefully, she could detect the sound that came before it. Definitely a vowel sound, something from the back of the throat, not a nasal *i* or an *e* from the cheeks; not a lippy *o*, either. It sounded like an *uh*. *Uh was viv. Uhwasvis.* Or an *ah*.

The Carl she knew was a practical, almost laconic, man. If he had needed help immediately, he'd say so sooner rather than later. Essential information: a phone number, his location, the name of a person.

Uhwasviv.

She listened to the message again, pressing her ear to the speaker.

Beyond the static, in his voice, was an irregular hue. She listened again, reciting the words along with him. *Ahwasviv* slid her, automatically, into another mode; and then a cylinder clicked.

Spanish.

He was saying something in Spanish.

She lunged for the pen and played the message again.

This time the accent gleamed unmistakably.

Of course he was going to say something in Spanish; he was in *Mexico*.

She wrote down the sounds.

ah

uas

viv

ah was ahwas a-uas aguas

Aguas.

And viv? The stem of a word. Could be modified to agree.

That gave her *vivas.*

Aguas Vivas?

Her hands shook as she reached for the phone and redialed the Hermosillo consulate.

"U.S. consu—"

"Hi, I just called? Can you—"

"Hello again. No news so far."

"Is there a place called Aguas Vivas?"

"Aguas Vivas."

"I was wondering," she said. "Because I think that's where he might have been."

"Aguas Vivas? I've never heard of it. Let me—*hey! Sal! Is there a town called Aguas Vivas?*"

Faintly: *nope.*

"He doesn't think so," he said. "He knows the state like the back of his hand."

"Can you check? Is there a map?"

He went to get it and she waited, tapping her foot and squinting out the window at a morning whose arrival she had not noticed. Outside, a couple of kids with backpacks headed to a nearby elementary school. Didn't their parents know that it was going to be cance—

"I have a map . . . here," said David. "With a directory of towns . . . and I—I don't see anything by that name."

"You're sure?"

"Pretty sure. Although"—the phone slipped away from his mouth; she heard him slam a heavy book—"although, you know what, there's bunches of villages around here that aren't on the maps. They're too small, or they're actually part of another town, a bigger town. Sometimes, two places got combined decades ago. All *our* records for the last five years show one name, and meanwhile the villagers are still calling it by the old name."

"Who would be able to tell me that?"

David said, "Well . . . lemme think. There's our local law enforcement. You want their number?"

She got it from him, thanked him again, and reminded him to call if—

"I will, miss. Have a pleasant day."

Fat chance, she thought as she dialed the Hermosillo police department and asked in Spanish for—

"No no," said the guy who answered. "This is the police *academy.*"

She got the right number and called *that* and asked whether they knew if *hay una ciudad llamada Aguas Vivas, por favor?*

The guy on the other end said *Momento, Señora.*

He disappeared for a full five minutes, returning just as she decided to hang up, telling her *Sí, Señora. Hay.*

She asked for the phone number of its police station. It took a while for him to come back with the reply that there *was* no police station; the nearest one was thirty miles away, except—

"Pardon me," he said, "this list is all screwed up, some cretin wrote all over it. . . . I have two numbers here, I'm not sure what they are. You want them anyway?"

She let the first number ring for a solid two minutes before trying the second and being greeted with a drowsy, half-cocked *Bueno.*

"Is this the Aguas Vivas police?" she asked in Spanish.

"This is *Teniente* Tito Fajardo. Who is this?"

"I'm looking for someone—"

"Slow down, *Señora*. Nobody's in a rush. You want to tell me your name?"

"Gloria Mendez. I'm—"

"*Buenos días, Señora Mendez.* You sound perturbed. What's the matter?"

"I think someone I know may have been in an accident. Near your town."

"Oh yeah?" Distinctly, he smacked his lips. "What sort of accident?"

"That's what I'm trying to find out, *Teniente*. It's very important, and I've been getting the runaround from everyone I've talked to so far, so I'd appreciate it if you would *listen*."

Pause.

"Okay, *Señora*. Tell me something and I'll tell you something back."

She played the message over the phone for him.

"You need a new machine," he said. "That tape sounds like shit."

"All I'm trying to find out," she said, "is whether he was in the area."

"This is a big area. We cover a lot of ground. You don't know where it was?"

"I don't even know *what* it was," Gloria said. "It sounded like it might have been a car accident, but I'm not sure."

"That's tricky," said Fajardo. "Like I said, big area, lots of car accidents."

"Were there any involving an American?"

"When'd you say this happened, *Señora*?"

"Five days ago."

"What was the name again?"

"Carl Perreira."

Fajardo sniffled. "Oh yeah? He's your—who is he, your husband?"

"Yes," she said, "he's my—"

"And you said it was a *car* accident."

"I don't *know*," Gloria said. "Did you have a car accident?"

"When?"

"At that time."

"I'm not sure what the question is, *Señora*."

"*Was* there an accident around there this week, or *not*, it's a very simple—"

"*Ay. Señora.* Take it easy."

"Someone may have been hurt, someone maybe God forbid *killed*, and if you can't tell me something then I'd like to speak to your supervisor."

Pause.

Fajardo said, "*I'm* my supervisor. You want to talk to someone, you have to talk to me. Second of all, I'm following procedure here. If you choose to step in the way, then you go ahead and do that, but it's not going to make it any easier for you, or me, or anyone. Now what do you say?"

Gloria made a fist and lightly abused the desk.

"I'm sorry," she said.

"No problem. You sound pretty wound up, is there anything else on your mind?"

No, asshole. "No. Can you please—"

Fajardo interrupted her with a sigh. "Don't start interrogating me again."

"I'm not."

"Okay, just so we're clear about who's running this investigation."

She thought, What investigation?

"Now I can examine the log . . . from this week . . ." Fajardo groaned, as if rising from an easy chair. "I have them down at the office. I'll call you tomorrow morning, if you want."

"I can't wait until tomorrow."

"Well, I'm not going *down* there, so—"

"Please."

Fajardo sniffled volubly. "I'm not sure what to tell you, *Señora.*"

"I'll come there," she said. "I'll drive all night—"

"You don't need to do *that*," he said.

Pause.

He sounded tense when he spoke again. "Look, if you're going to be melodramatic . . . Maybe I have—around here . . . maybe some of the . . . some stuff from . . . when?"

"Five days ago."

"Five days ago, fine. One minute."

She listened as he put the phone down, walked out of the room, walked back in.

"Señora? I think I remember who you're talking about. It was a few days ago. There was an accident involving an American. We don't know who it was, his ID was destroyed, but the car had California plates."

"What kind of car?" she said.

"It was Japanese. A Honda." Fajardo sniffled again. "That sound like him?"

All the hope she'd invented melted into something bilious and acrid. The room seemed to expand, while her insides began contracting to a solitary, fearful speck.

"Señora? Does that sound like him?"

"Yes," she mumbled.

"Well, *Señora*," he said, "I'm sorry to tell you but it was a very bad accident."

She thought, He called me on the phone. How bad

could it have been if he called me and talked. I heard his voice. I heard him. Everything was fine. How bad could it have been. He called me. How bad. He called. How.

"Is he in the hospital," she said.

"No," said Fajardo. "He died last night."

THREE

Reggie Salt said, "They're not going to lie to you, Gigi. If LAPD tells you it's out of their jurisdiction, then it's out of their jurisdiction."

"The guy said that Carl is *dead*," Gloria said. "Doesn't that make a difference?"

"Maybe if someone did something to him," said Reggie. "You said it was an accident."

"That's what the cop down there told me," she said.

"What's this guy's name?"

"Fajardo."

"Mm-hm." Reggie rubbed one eye. "Well, honestly, Gigi, it's up to them. They run the show down there. I mean, they run it badly. But I can't call them up and read them my badge number and have that mean anything to them. They're not gonna care."

Gloria stirred her untouched tea and set the spoon down. Normally, she would've felt qualms about putting a wet utensil on bare Formica, but the table was disgusting enough that a dousing in Swee-Touch-Nee made it cleaner.

She couldn't imagine this place attracting customers unless, like today, it was the only place open for miles.

Reggie was pleased as punch. Frequenting greasy spoons was his favorite way of bragging about his preternaturally low cholesterol. He had once read an article that said blacks were more likely to have heart disease than whites or Hispanics; when he and Gloria got their results back, and his LDL count was half of hers, he took great pleasure in saying, "Science doesn't apply to me."

It had taken her a while to track him down. Yesterday he'd been absorbed in post-quake procedure. They had him commanding a militia unit. Now he was supposed to be downtown on cleanup duty; her panicked phone call had convinced him to stop en route and have breakfast with her.

He checked his watch, took her by the fingers, and daintily stroked from knuckle to nail. "I'm sure this must be real hard. It's always hard."

She wanted to pull back but didn't. He was helping her, and if that required letting him think that he still made her feel good, then fine.

"Do you want to talk about it?" he asked.

"Not right now."

"It helps sometimes," he said. "Just talking about it can be a real release."

Reggie in Sensitivity Mode. Expressing concern in a restrained manner. Being a Good Guy. Skills he had lacked for a long time. Where'd they come from?

She flattered herself momentarily to think she'd had a lasting effect.

Probably not.

After the proceedings, he had come up to her with his tie askew and said, "What the hell was I supposed to know about any of this, Gigi, you never *told* me anything."

It was true. She had never complained, not once. Complaining required energy she'd lacked during their three years. It was easier to divorce him than to lay out every damn time that it *bothered* her, the way he woke her up at night when he came in, the way he left laundry on the floor and crumbs on the counter and his car blocking hers. The way he didn't apologize. Didn't want children.

Now he was eight years on; he had a mustache; he was stroking her fingers and being nice. Maybe the department was giving them training sessions. Trying to rebuild the image of the Los Angeles Police Officer: strong, armed, and therapeutic.

She found it mildly creepy. She thought, You're supposed to be more of a bastard, Reggie Salt.

And then he was. "Well, you can call if you need me. But I have to get out of here. I didn't have time for this to begin with. I'm supposed to be in Watts."

"You don't work in Watts," she said.

"I know, but they like a black man in charge in Watts. It appeals to their sense of order." He drained his coffee and tried to flag the waitress as she disappeared through the swinging doors. He rose, reaching for his wallet.

"A few more minutes." She pointed to the seat. "You can't drive anywhere right now, anyway; they closed Olympic."

"I can." He made a siren noise. "Works great on the 405 at rush hour, too."

She kept pointing to his seat. He smiled and sat.

"I miss your bullshit, Gigi," he said.

"What do I do now?"

"You've called his relatives, I assume. Why aren't they taking care of this?"

"He doesn't have any relatives. He was an only child."

"Was he divorced?"

She shook her head. "Never married."

"No kids?"

"I said he wasn't married."

"You don't need to be married to have kids, Gigi."

"He wasn't like that," she said. "You don't know what he was like. He was quiet. He never—" Not wanting to cry in front of him, she shored up. "You don't know," she said. "You never met him."

"Sure I did," Reggie said. "I came by your office once."

"When."

"I came to drop off a box of kitchen stuff. It was your corkscrew, and a salad bowl . . . remember?"

She did remember: those months: the slow transformation of goods from *theirs* to *hers,* reverse osmosis rendering one life back into two.

"He was in the office when I came by," said Reggie. "You were out getting lunch. I left the box with him."

"Did you talk to him?" she asked.

"I said hello. I think I asked how you were. I think we even shook hands. He seemed like a nice guy."

"He was. He was a wonderful guy." She stirred her tea again.

"If he doesn't have any kids," Reggie said, "he's gotta

have somebody. An uncle or a cousin or something. What was he, sixty?"

"Fifty-six."

"Then there's gotta be someone."

"Nobody I've ever met," she said.

"There's always someone. Call the gu—call his lawyer. Did he have a will?"

Gloria raised her palms: *I don't know.*

"His lawyer can probably tell you everything you need to know. If there's a will, then you follow the will. But don't worry about it, Gigi, it's pretty much out of your hands. You're not responsible for him in any legal way."

She felt responsible, though, in an extralegal way. She could not possibly explain that to Reggie; she couldn't explain it to Barb, either, or the other girls. She could not have even explained it to Carl himself, had his specter arrived and pulled up a chair.

She had never been that blunt with him. Gloria believed that the best way to communicate with someone was to match them. Carl was dry and roundabout and diffident, and she had treated him accordingly. She liked talking with him like that.

For nearly thirty-six hours she had borne the weight of his death by herself, letting the ache build to floodburst. She didn't know how much longer she could maintain a poker face.

Get a therapist Barb would say.

But Gloria didn't want to talk; she wanted to *do*. Anything to feel less passive than she did, sitting here shooting the shit with Reggie while Carl, poor Carl, her Carl, was untended.

A flash: her brother, onstage. He was wearing a crown and a lame high-school rendition of a—

A toga?

A robe. Playing a king. Squaring off against a girl demanding a body.

It was *Antigone.*

Gloria didn't remember the details—it was so long ago, and she had been watching Jesús Julio. But she remembered perfectly the girl's desperation: a desperation like no other: when your loved one laid above the earth, and all you were asking for was the dignity of a burial.

Thinking about the past made Gloria feel twice as wretched. She resented the way her memory showed up at vulnerable moments to amplify the present. The present was bad enough without reverb.

Reggie was talking; she wasn't listening. Blindsided, bound by convention to sit and converse placidly, all the while churning. Only her desire not to need Reggie too much kept her from crying out.

". . . but in the meantime," he was saying, "I'd get it straight from the cop. The Mexican. Find out exactly what happened." He paused. "Gigi? You hear me?"

She said, "He told me it was a car accident and that he couldn't give more information. He said he would mail me the death certificate."

Reggie frowned. "*Mail* it to you?"

"That's what I'm telling you. It's out of whack."

"What about the body?"

She shook her head. "He wouldn't talk about it."

"That's bizarre. . . ." Reggie stroked his upper arms.

"You're sure it was an accident."

"No."

"The cop, did he say the guy was drunk?"

"Carl didn't drink."

"Some people, they never drink," said Reggie, "and then they go ahead and get drunk."

"I never saw him drink," Gloria said.

"Maybe that's why he went to Mexico."

Gloria started to protest but he continued: "It doesn't matter unless he hurt someone, or someone hurt him. If it was a car accident . . . involving another person?"

"He wouldn't tell me. He said there was an investigation under way."

Reggie pursed his lips. "I'm not sure how to read that."

Gloria glanced out the window. Outside, Los Angeles was walking, the blockaded thoroughfares and legions of sunglasses evoking a street fair. Yolky, heavy heat slopped over everything, as though the quake had burst a pipe beneath the earth's surface.

"The cops weren't very helpful," she said.

"That's Mexico for you."

"I mean the LAPD."

Reggie shrugged.

"The dispatcher I talked to was really obstinate. And then in the afternoon, when I called back to tell them what I'd found out, the *other* cop I talked to was obstinate, also."

"They're not being obstinate, Gigi. They're going about their usual business. That can entail being obstinate. Especially on a day like today."

"Where does that leave me?"

"Well, if the guy's dead—"

"He has a name."

A dim *thunk* as the kitchen doors flapped open and the waitress emerged balancing seven plates on one arm. Reggie waved, made a √ in the air, and took Gloria's hand again.

"I'm sure it's hard," he said. "I'm real sorry."

"Thanks."

"You want to talk about it, you let me know. I'm always here for you, Gigi."

She nodded.

He said, "Okay," and got up. "Ten all right?"

Before leaving, he applied a pair of wraparounds to his face, like he was smearing on a lotion. Then he saluted her. A glib gesture, telling her that he cared—to a point. She appreciated that he wasn't going to lie and pretend to get as upset as she was. In a way, they'd become closer—and far more honest—after all the legal ties between them had been severed.

She sat back, rejecting her tea.

"Yo," said the waitress. She ripped the check out of her waistband, slapped it down on the table, and shuttled off with a stack of crusty plates.

Gloria said thanks to her back. The waitress had circled the total, adding her name and a rather ambivalent smiley face. Force of habit, Gloria checked the addition. Including tax and tip, her part of the bill came to about two-fifty. Reggie's came to fourteen.

FOUR

The lawyer Caperco used—not that they used a lawyer regularly—was a fellow named Wes Katz. He kept a plush, dark office on the twenty-third floor of a building in Century City. You could stand at the east window and admire the green-and-gold expanse of Beverly Hills and, beyond that, mammoth banks of encroaching smog. Though Gloria had been there but once, she recalled the room distinctly; Katz had given her plenty of time to look it over, keeping her waiting a half-hour. The walls had been decorated with diplomas and framed news clippings, documents pertaining largely to Katz himself. A few were about his kids: school-paper columns they'd written, things like that. One article announced his marriage to Cheryl Ann Jackson. No photos.

Gloria hadn't liked it at all.

Today he was keeping her waiting again. At least she didn't have to sit in the office, reading the ego-paper.

"They're not sure when the building's going to reopen," said Cheryl Ann Katz, bringing Gloria a glass of water and seating her in the equally plush Katz living room.

Cheryl Ann said, "They need to perform *seismic tests*."

Gloria nodded. So this was where he kept all the family portraits. There was Wes and the boys, probably named Spencer and Josh. Cheryl Ann had apparently been a beauty queen at some point, which Gloria had no trouble believing. The family liked to ski; all around hung images of Vail and Whistler, and one photo could have been New Zealand, with cold-looking sheep off in the distance.

Gloria wondered why the Katzes lived in Cheviot Hills rather than Beverly Hills. Less ostentatious? Maybe they felt that it provided the right kind of down-to-earth community for their organically weaned offspring.

"We haven't even been able to get the car out of the driveway. A tree fell over. It's like living on a farm!" Cheryl Ann laughed. "I don't even *know* how you got here. Where'd you park?"

"I walked."

"From where?"

"I live in West Hollywood."

"Mmm," Cheryl Ann said. "That's some walk."

"About four miles," Gloria said.

"You must have . . . very strong . . . *legs*," said Cheryl Ann, smiling and then blushing fiercely. She stood up like a Trojan soldier. "Mr. Katz will be out in a minute," she declared. She marched into the back hallway and out of the awkward atmosphere she'd farted herself into.

Gloria got up to examine the photos. Cheryl Ann's sash stamped her MISS WEST COVINA 1988.

Mr. Katz will be out in a minute. The automation of it;

the deftness with which Cheryl had seated her; the white white smile. There was no doubt in Gloria's mind that Wes Katz's wife had once been his receptionist.

Was there a first wife? There was. In one candid, she lingered behind the older boy. How'd Cheryl Ann allow that? The queen bee displaced, her portrait remaining like an accusation: *usurper!* Wes must've laid down the law. *That's my son, we're not taking that one down.* And Cheryl Ann, acquiescing. When you steal someone's husband, Gloria supposed, you had to grant some leeway.

It was like watching an ad for a spin-off: *The Katzes Redux!* Now starring Wifey Bigtits!

In a city where you merely had to wait for pilot season for a fresh crop of eager fillies, this sort of banal betrayal was standard operating procedure. Gloria didn't bother to disapprove. In fact, she admired Cheryl Ann Katz *née* Jackson's spunk: Work your way up, marry a Jewish lawyer, send your boys to Harvard-Westlake and Stanford and law school, so that *they* could marry beauty queens and have kids who went to . . .

Truthfully, Gloria was jealous. Not of what Cheryl had acquired—men like Katz made Gloria shiver—but of how she'd pulled it off.

What's wrong with me? Gloria thought.

Then she thought: you sound like you're thirteen.

Then she thought: so what?

Her first impression of Carl—an impression that had not faded in ten years—had been that he looked like Burt Reynolds. Less imposing, to be sure. Lacking Burt's man-on-the-verge-of-punching-you-in-the-face-ness.   Certain features, though: the broad jaw; hair like combed licorice. Naturally arched eyebrows, suggesting constant amusement.

Carl knew more jokes than anyone she'd ever met. They were his primary form of communication.

When I was in high school, I was assigned a locker next to the quarterback. Three weeks later, he blew his knee out. After that, they wouldn't let me near the gym. The other players used to wear garlic around me.

She'd said *I'd like to get ahold of your yearbook and see what I could find.*

I'll have to leave you in suspense. Smiling cryptically, he'd changed the subject.

Their conversations always went like that. She would ask questions aimed below the surface; she would strike hard rock and come up with nothing but topsoil.

It had taken her a while to figure out that he joked because it was easier for him than making straight conversation. Despite appearances, he was—like her—painfully reserved. She had learned to contrive pleasantries without exhuming herself; his strategy was to smother discomfort with wit.

She began to understand this early on, a year into her employment at Caperco, two years after she had married Reggie. Working with Carl enlightened her; her swelling sense of disappointment in her husband was exacerbated by exposure to the kind of personality she really found attractive: Carl's droll calm. She never told Reggie, but one of the cracks that had led to their collapse was the realization—and it had stunned her—that love did not have to be constantly mordant. It could be funny and fun and relaxing and healing. She learned all this from Carl.

Not knowing much about marriage, and hating to quit, she let it drag on. After three years, she'd had it. That seemed to her a reasonable length of time: it was the age at which most children began to speak coherently. If their communication hadn't gotten to a more sophisticated point by then, she figured, it was probably retarded.

I don't know Reggie'd said. *Maybe never.*

She had asked when he wanted to start a family.

I mean, mine wasn't too hot. Yours wasn't, either. Why inflict that on someone undeserving?

She wanted to say *Because we don't* have *to be like that.*

She didn't.

She waited for him to change his mind.

He never did.

If anything, he got more resolute. The more she brought it up, the more it seemed to irritate him. Finally he'd said *You can have a kid, Gloria. It just won't be with me.*

Carl helped her through the dissolution. He offered a month paid leave, which she didn't accept, and warm—innocent—hugs, which she did. He never said much in the way of direct consolation, but that was what she needed. She took comfort in routine, a skill acquired during child-hood. Mere peace and quiet was not to be taken for granted. Carl seemed to understand that, too.

By the time the papers had been signed, she was in love with him.

For seven years, she had been waiting, reflecting his silent kindnesses by caring for him without words—itself a form of therapy for her. She minded his office and his schedule with an exactitude seldom seen outside the Marines. If he came in cowlicked, she brushed it down. She poured his water before he arrived and got him refills before he asked; he liked to have a glass in hand at all times. She took it upon herself to discern what he could and could not eat according to his quirky and orthodox brand of vegetarianism. She called him at home to remind him of weekend church services; she made sure that he was not disturbed when he asked for a moment of privacy, so he could say his personal prayers.

He never spilled over with thank-you's or laid his naked soul at her feet. Her efforts came back rewarded in small wrapped packages: a look, a satisfied yawn, an unprompted smile—his appreciation shining through the chinks of a wisecrack.

You're too good to be working for me.

Then I'll quit.

All right. On the way out, you can also cut off my head.

She appreciated the jokes. But what she was waiting for was a serenade. She longed to see him on one knee.

Any normal person would've assumed they'd slept together. All the ingredients were there: alone together eight hours a day, cramped in that tiny office. They had the same mother tongue, their occasional Spanish more flirtatious than their regular English. It defied probability that they had been in suspension for as long as they had.

Once, they had skimmed the heart of the matter. They had come round to talking about kids, a topic he did not seem to enjoy. He steered the conversation back to her.

You're young. You should meet somebody.

It's not that simple.

Ask one of your friends to set you up.

I'll never find anyone as good as you.

She'd said it half-jokingly, watching for his reaction.

He'd laughed. *So you're looking for an old man?*

You're not old.

Gloria . . . Smiling, shaking his head.

Twenty years isn't that big a difference.

He glanced up. He seemed to have understood her, and he looked frightened.

She started to apologize but he said:

I'd be dead before you knew it.

That, in turn, had frightened the hell out of her.

He went into the next room, and when he reemerged an hour later, he appeared to have burnt off his discomfort. *Besides* he said, picking up as though they had never stopped, *you deserve someone without wrinkles.*

She'd decided to laugh along with him.

And that had been all.

Then why are you kidding yourself?

"Shut up, Barb," she said.

She shuffled across Wes Katz's living room and looked out on the yard. A swingset. A basketball hoop above the garage. Minuscule turds. Did they keep a dog? Gloria hadn't pegged them as a dog family. She looked around and couldn't spot any traces of fur.

Maybe they kept it out back, so it wouldn't soil the Chinese nickel rug.

Actually, she thought, she got a kick out of Carl's wrinkles.

"What did she *do* to you?"

Wes Katz dripped in the doorway. His hotel bathrobe offered her a glimpse of a rubbed-red chest and neck. Wet lines of thinning hair and an aerodynamic chin gave him an aura of great speed, even though he was simply standing there, a dark spot spreading in the ecru carpeting. He gripped the doorposts, as though to prevent himself from flying into the room.

"She's been out of practice a long time, but on her worst day she never made a client *cry.*"

Gloria swabbed sleeve over cheek. "Sorry."

"Jesus H. You need a real drink?"

She said thanks but no thanks.

"*I'm* going to," he said, striding to the bar and producing, in rapid succession, an ice bucket, tongs, and a bottle of Tanqueray. As he reached for a glass, his calves peeked out; they were vermilion, blond, veined. She guessed he played tennis in the off-season.

"My nerves are doing the lambada. Only thing keeping me from Zoloft is—mmhm. Good stuff. Sure you—"

"No thank you."

He killed the drink and poured another. "You should try it. I've been at it all morning. Makes the aftershocks real nice. They begin to feel like a massage chair. Like something you'd get at the Sharper Image. Dwight—that's my eldest, Harry's the shrimp—he's always, Dwight is, trying to get me to buy some dumb contraption from them, a floating pool badminton set that converts to a dog-hair remover. But people *buy* it, *some*one must, because we've been getting those catalogues for years and I've *never* purchased a single fuckin' thing." He shook his head and laughed and sipped his drink. For the first time, he seemed to see her. "You're Perreira's girl, right?"

Her heart caught on that phrase. *His girl.*

Then she realized that Katz wasn't being endearing; he was being a condescending prick.

"Gloria Mendez," she said.

"We met before—"

"Two years ago. I was in your office."

"Oh *right,* right. You had me writing threatening letters to a no-pay in Pacoima. You came all the way over here? The streets are all fucked up. What'd you do, walk?"

"Carl's dead," she said.

Tapping his chin absently. "That's a nice walk to come all the way over here. Something must be up. What's up?"

She wanted to grab his drink and hurl it into one of his second-generation family photos. You son of a bitch, you make me say it *twice*?

He was working his chin, puzzled, as though the universe contained no bigger mystery than why anyone would interrupt his Jacuzzi time.

She said, louder: "Carl's dead."

Katz's eyes bugged out, making him look speedier than usual. "You're kidding."

She told him. When she was done, he poured a new drink and made one for her. She refused it. She was waiting for him to say something useful.

"Jesus H.," he said. "You talked to the cops?"

"My ex-husband is a police officer."

"Who's the attorney who handles Carl's personal affairs?

That's who you should be talking to."

"You do."

Katz shook his head. "I've never seen him in any other context outside of business. Where's the will?"

"I thought you would know."

"I haven't the faintest idea," he said. It came out righteous, and for a split second she could see how Katz would be able to cut an almost patrician appearance in court.

She stood up. "Then I won't bother you—"

"N-n-no, siddown," he said, waving at her, spilling his drink. "No need to run out. D'you know anything about his will?"

"You don't have it," she said.

"Never seen it. That wasn't the nature of our association." Katz licked a drop of gin off his wrist. "Who knows if he even had one. He wasn't that old."

"In that case—"

"If he's intestate, it can be a real headache. . . . Have you called his next of kin?"

"I don't know any next of kin," she said. "I'm not sure there is any."

"Come on," said Katz. "He's gotta have *someone.*"

Same thing Reggie said.

"I've been trying to find someone," she said. "I looked through all his stuff this morning, and—"

"When'd you find this out, anyway?"

"Two days ago."

"Man, you move fast."

"It needs to be taken care of," she said, getting annoyed. "Nobody else is."

"I know, I know. . . ." Katz wandered, skimming dust from the family photos. "I don't really handle this sort of thing. The first thing you do is find his personal attorney. Go through his stuff again. Call his friends. Find family. Nobody's been called?"

"Nobody knows except me."

"They didn't call you from Mexico?"

"The police down there said his ID was destroyed."

"And they didn't report it to the Americans?"

She shook her head.

"Well, it sounds like they're screwing up," he said. "But *that* doesn't really surprise me."

"I've been through everything," she said. "I've been going nonstop for the last two days."

"Well, if you really can't find another attorney, I'm not going to touch it, because quite frankly I'm as clueless as you on this sort of matter. I know an estate lawyer, very considerate fellow. I think he might've been a shrink at some point. Whatever, he'll know what to do. Here," he said, writing on a cocktail napkin and handing it to her. "If there's nobody but nobody, and no will, then the state takes over. They'll send the case to the public administrator."

She asked, "Then what?"

"Then it's out of your hands. It's not even in your hands to begin with." He looked at her, bewildered. "Nobody called?"

"No."

"Well, whatever. One thing I know is, they need proof of death. They can't do anything without that."

Proof of death sounded like a bloody handkerchief, or a

heart in a jar. She felt angry, having to cough up something tangible to validate her grief.

"A death certificate's the usual thing," said Katz.

"The police said they're mailing it."

Katz rattled his ice. "Mailing it, huh? That's weird."

Also what Reggie said. "What's weird about it?"

"Death certificates, usually you have to present some sort of identification in order to—I mean, they aren't *mail order.*" He snorted. "But that's the Mexicans for you."

She felt a strong surge of dislike for this man, stronger than before.

"What about the body?" he asked.

Until that moment, it hadn't really occurred to her that there *was* a body.

He said, "They're going to send it back, or what? They're mailing that, too? It probably costs to have it sent back. The American consulate can help you out with that. Do you know how much money the estate is? I mean, this'll be covered, although—I don't know. Who knows what the rule is, you'll have to talk to them. Or a lawyer. I mean, unless you want him to be buried down there. Is that the idea?"

After firing all these questions, he looked at her as though expecting an answer, and the weight of responsibility lowered itself onto her head: *you know what Carl would want.* A clandestine thrill crept into her chest: she could speak for him, the way you did when you knew someone better than anyone else in the world.

"I . . . I don't think so," she said softly.

"I mean, of course not. Who'd want to be buried way the fuck down there? In some craphole? He's, I bet, got people he'd like to lay down next to, and I'm pretty sure they're not in Cabo or wherever he is. . . . Right?"

"No. Probably not."

"Somebody's got to go handle the body."

"Handle it," she repeated.

"Yeah. Have it sent back." He sucked up an ice cube and spat it out, smaller. "I suppose if you were real adventurous you could go retrieve it yourself."

"Me?" she said.

"It's supposed to be up to the next of kin, but you said you didn't know of any."

"No," she said.

"Then someone needs to step up, take charge. Is there anyone like that besides you?"

Gloria thought for a moment.

"No," she said, "I don't think there is."

FIVE

They reopened the freeways three days later, by which time she had gone over, under, and through everything in Carl's house. The cops kept telling her that she could report him missing if she wanted. Well no, she said. He's not missing. Then what did she want from them? Their indifference, coupled with a growing sense of distress at the thought of his body lying in some verminous Mexican morgue, compelled her to get a good map, check the oil in her '83 Dodge Dart, and set her alarm for three forty-five in the morning.

At that hour, the 405 south yielded to her heavy foot, demanding no impatient lane changes, no leaning on the horn. LAX waved as she passed, giving her a jet-exhaust kiss and blinking farewell. She kept the radio on the lite station until it crackled and became seltzer, and San Diego asserted herself through the airwaves. The scan function snagged on a shock-jock morning show called "Pauly and the Kingpin's A.M. Electric Chair."

Lookee here, happy bluebird listeners, today we're going to

*start things off with a little mental cattle prod, a game we like
to call—*

Name That Loser.

*Yessireebob, we've dipped into the algae-covered depths of
the Pauly and the Kingpin archives, culling a playlist of sound
bites of the most prominent losers who have ever called us.*

And that is a long, long list, my friend.

*Indeed, and if you can Name That Loser based on the clip
we play, you give us a call at 619-576-kay-ar-oh-tee, and you
will receive—*

*Then I, the Kingpin, will come to your house and person-
ally, dude, I will personally—PERSONALLY—shave your
armpits.*

She managed to scrape past the metro area before rush
hour, joining the weary caravan trickling toward the border.
The sun started to bleach the earth. Freeway signs no
longer named a destination, as though the road led to
oblivion. Fluffy suburbs choked out until all that
remained was a handful of houses jutting from the hillside
like exposed bone. Property lines got wider and wider, veg-
etation paler and drier.

You lived down here if you wanted to get away from
Southern California. Gloria thought that was funny,
because just over the border everyone was running *toward*
Southern California.

There was the sign.

BEWARE PEDESTRIANS CROSSING

Yellow, with a black silhouette showing a family fleeing

across the highway, suitcases flying behind as they dashed from an unseen menace. *Pedestrians* wasn't quite the right word. The sign was up for one reason; it might as well have read TRY NOT TO RUN OVER ANY ILLEGAL MEXICANS. A second such sign had been vandalized by someone who'd Magic Markered a sombrero atop the fleeing man's head.

A different message presented itself soon after:

LAST EXIT IN UNITED STATES 1

The countdown began.

LAST EXIT IN UNITED STATES ¾
LAST EXIT IN UNITED STATES ½

They had to warn you every fifteen seconds, in case you didn't realize that you were about to leave all caution behind.

LAST EXIT IN UNITED STATES ¼

A final, frantic sign shouted YOU ARE LEAVING THE UNITED STATES. She envisioned incredulous punctuation: YOU ARE LEAVING THE UNITED STATES?!?!?!

She sighed, rolling down the window as she approached the crossing.

Wiry deputies ogled one another from their respective sides of a towering fence. Their wariness reflected the moods of the countries they represented: vibrating at cross-purposes, like an unresolved chord.

Despite the dogs, and the barbed wire, and the imposing concrete barrier, she made it in and out almost immediately. Mexican border control gave her a perfunctory glance and waved her through without asking for her passport. Really, she thought, they were only pretending to control a border.

As she pulled away, she looked back on a long line of humming vehicles: beat-up pickups carrying bands of stout, muscular men; retiree Winnebagos; rental cars full of hungover sailors on furlough—everyone eager to get to the States. Crossing in that direction took a lot longer. There were more people to keep out.

The sieve hadn't always been that tight. There hadn't been the need, because there hadn't always been *coyotes*— smugglers who, in the course of taking you across, took you for everything you had. There hadn't always been a massive American subindustry of guards and sensors and radar and unmanned reconnaissance flights. Officers with crew cuts, dogs, and flashlights, who drove hundreds of miles every night in search of the destitute and dehydrated.

In her mother's day it had been different. During and after World War II, to alleviate the strain on the American labor force, the U.S. had done what today would be unthinkable, inviting Mexicans across for what amounted to legalized indentured servitude.

Maria Guadalupe Rosales Mendez—Mamá—came at seventeen, in search of work. Instead, she found a husband. His name was Esteban Ortega Alejandres, and they were married by a picker (who doubled as a priest) in San Dolores, Arizona, a shanty-shack pimple on the butt-end of

Nogales founded de facto by hundreds of lonely *braceros*.

Five years of marriage produced two miscarriages and a stillborn. In 1964, he succeeded in giving his wife a living child. Not long after, Esteban Ortega Alejandres was caught under a tractor and crushed to death.

Gloria regretted never having met the man, because he seemed to have been the one bright spot in her mother's early life. Gloria would've liked to have known what a happy Mamá looked like.

The shock had spurred her move to Los Angeles. Gloria could not comprehend why her twenty-three-year-old mother would lug all her possessions (including a scrawny, tantrum-prone boy) five hundred and sixty miles, to a city where she knew no one, could not communicate with fluency, could not easily find a job—except to say that there *was* no reason. It was a blind flight from pain, a purely reflexive gesture.

It was 1966. She'd hitchhiked.

Like the rest of her mother's history, Gloria had gleaned these details in passing. Mamá did not speak about them. But they cropped up subtly, such as when Jesús Julio whined about wanting a bicycle. Mamá would say, "There's nothing wrong with walking, *pillito*."

"I'm too tired to walk."

"You're too *lazy* to walk," Mamá would reply. "Because I carried you too much."

On the final leg of her move, Mamá met a Mexican house-painter who was returning from a visit to his cousin in another shantyville. Distantly, he and Mamá knew people in common: the dispossessed human jetsam that circulated throughout the Southwest, thinning sugar beets and picking tomatoes. By the time they had arrived in Los Angeles, he had agreed to let Maria and her son sleep on his floor.

It was an uneven floor. Weeks of backaches—and indebtedness; she was still unemployed—encouraged Mamá to move into the painter's bed.

Gloria often wondered if Jesús Julio remembered those days. Perhaps the memory of Mamá crawling into the arms of a stranger lingered in his infant brain as a horrible treachery; perhaps therein sat the source of all his future ill will.

It was unreasonable to blame Mamá. She had been scared and lonely and young. If those three discomforts did not justify cleaving to the nearest source of animal warmth, what did?

But Jesús Julio: when he let out a midnight wail, and his mother came from the next room, smelling like turpentine—what did he think?

They lived with the house-painter for almost a year before he left without saying good-bye. Sometimes Gloria blamed him for his caprice, but the truth was that there was no way for him to have known that Mamá was three weeks pregnant with a girl.

At a young age, Gloria decided to exonerate her father by virtue of ignorance.

Forgiving him did not prevent her from obsessing over him. He absorbed her, acting as the source of endless fantasies and nightmares, providing fodder for everyday hallucinations. The broad-backed man in spattered coveralls whitewashing a billboard: him? The hard-skinned band that came once to freshen the lines of her elementary-school playground—was he lurking among them, joking and smoking, unaware that the twiggy girl pressed to the chain-link fence, watching them like they were a double feature, was his? Every encounter with a manual laborer became an opportunity for Gloria to compare features. Perhaps, she reasoned, he had switched professions. She was convinced that eventually her narrow nose and puckered mouth and intelligent forehead would find their originals, and with them a set of acknowledging arms.

She studied the idea of him, and extrapolated his personality, his shape, his history. This, to her, was love: the desire to know all of a person's finest details—even if she had to make them up.

By the time she hit high school, however, common sense began to catch up with her. She realized that her father was likely a nobody, painting fences in some nowhere town, with scant memory of the *chica* he'd banged for eleven months while living in California. The prospect of meeting him began to lose its appeal as she became increasingly certain that she'd be disappointed.

She forced herself to forget that she had ever cared.

It was easy enough. Mamá made sure Gloria had plenty to think about.

Around ten, Gloria began to understand that the definition of "work" she got at home was more exacting than what her teachers expected. She was one of the few girls in school who had to be told to take a break. Even then, she didn't stop; Mamá brooked no sloth.

"You think I get up at four in the morning because I like the taste of dew?" she would holler, clapping her hands as she walked around their two-room in Boyle Heights. She gave Jesús Julio a shake. "You think I like this?"

"*Maaaaamaaaaa . . .*"

"You're lucky I don't wake you up to pray with me. *You've* been snoozing all morning. Take the eggs off before they burn, Gloria."

"*Sí . . .*"

By this point, Jesús Julio would be interring himself beneath the too-heavy wool blanket. "Ohhhaaaa*rrrr!*" he growled as Mamá ripped it away.

"Come on, *pillito,* I've carried you far enough. I'm not carrying you to school."

"Then I won't go," Jesús Julio said, delighted to have found a loophole.

"I won't carry you," said Mamá. "I'll kick you."

After the morning routine, they would all walk to the bus stop. Mamá would stand, waving, embarrassing them both but Jesús Julio more so.

"Shit . . ." he would breathe, settling into his seat.

"Mamá says you shouldn't say that word."

"Well *fuck* that."

Seconds later, he would be talking with his friends, and Gloria would be alone, reading to dampen the histrionics of two dozen preteens. Her homework was done, but Mamá had gotten it into her head that proofreading should continue up until the last possible minute, and that each successive revision would garner additional points. By Gloria's count, she'd earned 235 percent on every assignment from age four to age seventeen.

Life with Mamá had structure, specific appointments for every emotion, including joy. The rules weren't strict so much as they were self-contained: a package deal. You got up because you had to go to school. You went to school because you had to have homework to occupy your night. You needed homework because kids who didn't have it—or didn't do it—ended up as *pachucos*. They joined gangs; they knifed each other for jackets or money or no reason at all. Before you do that, Mamá said, you might as well knife *me* in the heart.

On the weekends, you stayed in. On Friday nights, you went into the closet and you lit secret candles to make the day special. And then you spent the evening reading. No, Jesús Julio, you couldn't go to a movie.

"Why not!"

Mamá slapped him and sat him down. She thrust a book into his hands and forced it open. "Because that is not what we do," she said.

Gloria was okay with rules. She liked a routine, and didn't consider it a big deal.

To Jesús Julio, however, Mamá's tyranny inflicted the equivalent of early death. In a sense, he had more in common with Mamá than Gloria did. They both saw the struggle for dominance as mortally significant. Mamá considered ritual the sole barrier keeping them from the worst degradations: poverty and disdain for the power of the mind. Twice the victim of men, she had decided that the only people worth trying to control were her children.

TIJUANA 3 KM

Gloria buckled down for the passage through. She hated Tijuana; it reminded her of what she and her mother had worked so hard to conquer. Lassitude, corruption, apathy. You could see it in the cracked, garbage-strewn streets. You could smell it from the bars and the rotting plaster of the jai alai *fronton*. Though it was barely eight A.M., you could order glowing drinks by the pitcher. A vendor advertising switchblades and firecrackers and Viagra and *"vitaminas"* scraped soot from his shop window. *Pensiones,* shuttered tight, reverberated with the snoring of Americans too drunk to have made it back last night.

She sped up, blithely ignoring a faded octagonal sign that ordered her to ALTO, rocketing up the *Avenida Revolución,* feeling the tiniest hint of self-loathing, coating that with shame, shaking her head to clear away drowsiness and the thought that she had become a snob.

Mamá's routines held Jesús Julio in check until he started high school. By then she had taken a second job in the dim, ridiculous hope that he would go to college. From seven until four, she cleaned house in Bel Air, and then from five-thirty to eleven, she swept up at the Home of Peace, a cemetery near their house. Gloria saw her for no more than fifteen or twenty minutes a day, during which Mamá was so exhausted she could scarcely speak.

Gloria despised watching her mother crawl to the bathroom; to cope, she strove to make all the suffering worthwhile. She studied her skin off.

Her brother, on the other hand, used Mamá's absence as

a crowbar in the jailbreak of adolescence. He would go out on weeknights and come home incapacitated by drink. He had a record collection too large for a fifteen-year-old with no money. When his friends came by, they would whistle at Gloria as she crouched over the kitchen table with her ninth-hand hardcover edition of *The Human Body*.

"Hey, *chichis!*" they would say, "lessee your human body."

Jesús Julio would laugh. The closest he ever got to defending her was to say to the heckler in question, "Shit, I was going to fuck *your* sister, but I didn't have a nickel on me. . . ."

Gloria didn't take offense. She worried. She saw her brother slipping down the sinkhole Mamá had warned of: talking tough, acting like he weighed a hundred and eighty pounds instead of a hundred and eighteen. He tried to grow a Fu Manchu, an experiment whose failure left him impotently fuming.

"Shut up!" he screamed.

Gloria giggled. "It looks like you have a rash."

"Puta!" He kicked over a chair and stormed out.

She hid the hole in the wicker with a jacket and waited for her mother to come home.

Of course, the jacket fell off the minute Mamá's key hit the lock.

But she was too tired to notice.

She never mentioned it.

In the spring of 1981, the LAPD issued an East LA curfew. A boy not much older than Jesús Julio had shot and killed a patrolman. For the first time in a while, Mamá decided to come home early. They all three sat in the kitchen, eating Cream of Wheat and listening to the radio compete with the cricket that had taken up residence inside their oven.

"Shit . . ."

Mamá had long abandoned policing Jesús Julio's mouth, and he had stopped caring long before that. Gloria tried to get his attention so she could frown at him. She *never* swore; Mamá wouldn't tolerate it from her, a fact she took pride in even as she resented the double standard.

"Sit down, Jesús Julio."

He hopped around, cricking his neck. He looked high, jonesing to strangle something.

"I can't believe we're just fucking *sitting* here."

"Believe it."

"We should be *out there*," he complained, shaking a fist at the wall.

"Doing what?" Mamá asked.

"They can't tell us to stay here."

Mamá said, "I'm happy here," and turned the volume up.

"Fuck!" Jesús Julio kicked the oven. "Shut the fuck up!"

"It's not going to listen to you," said Mamá. "Crickets don't respond to anger."

He stomped out. Gloria waited to see what Mamá would do. Get up and demand an apology. Remark on his immaturity. Cry, even.

She turned the volume up a little further.

Six days later he was gone.

It was as though Mamá had seen it coming and had

already started preparing. He snuck out with friends to cruise after dark; a cop tried to ticket them; Jesús Julio called him a *pendejo loco nigger* and brandished a knife.

Gloria wondered how Mamá knew. Perhaps she had been wrong; perhaps Mamá *had* noticed the whole time Jesús Julio was spinning away from them. Then why had she said nothing? Why sit back and watch all your hard work combust in heatless futility? Maybe she was too tired to care. Or maybe—and Gloria suspected that this was it—maybe he had never truly been hers, from the first shrill moment to the last and fatal tantrum.

Sometimes Gloria couldn't remember his birthday. But she could always recall April 20, the date of his death. He made more sense dead. It was logical, intractable; only his endgame was relevant to understanding him.

As they left his funeral, Mamá had said, "I want you to go to college."

Gloria turned fourteen, fifteen, sixteen. School was a monsoon of tests and accolades. Theodore Roosevelt Senior High had never seen anything like this tight-haired Chicana, racing down the halls in skirts below the knee, sitting alone at lunchtime so she could be with her books. If you had asked classmates what they thought of Gloria, they'd've said,

"Who?"

And someone else might've said, "You mean *la reina de las ranas*."

The Queen of the Frogs, because she loved to dissect. Her biology teacher, Mr. MacCoutry, loved her. He guided her hands and pointed out minute structures while all around her, kids embedded scalpels in the ceiling, smoked pot openly, or simply walked out of class. She stared, enthralled, at a tiny heart, a tiny liver, a tiny set of lungs. Veins suffused with dye curved like paths to treasure. While other students held their noses or barfed from the smell of formaldehyde, she would bend to take it all in, wanting to understand what made life throb. She began to look at her own body with a sort of displacement; at night, she would prod herself, marveling at what lay below.

In eleventh grade, Mr. MacCoutry told her she should consider a future in medicine.

"Okay," she said.

In retrospect, she was sure he'd meant "nurse" or "dental hygienist." At the time, though, she took him at his word. She liked the sound of "Dr. Mendez," and that's who she decided to become.

Mamá approved, and mustered a smile when Gloria ran around the house, waving a scholarship letter from California State University. Gloria kissed her and jumped on the sofa and thought *Maybe things will get better.*

"Miraculous," said Mamá.

Gloria was not too excited to miss the false note. It was the same note that had been keening for years—that crescendoed April 20, when Mamá would call in sick so she could spend the day in darkness and solitude. Gloria hated that her achievements brought not joy but the temporary cessation of pain. She feared that her whole life would consist of creating analgesic successes.

On her first day of college, Mamá came with her to the bus stop. It felt ridiculous, but Gloria allowed it.

"After all this," Mamá said, "I hope you learn something."

After all what? Gloria knew what. *All this* was endless sacrifice calling for endless recompense. *All this* guided her from class straight to the library, leaving no time for soccer games, or mixers, or avant-garde performances of *Twelfth Night; all this* was the momentum of guilt. *All this* was a dead husband, a dead son, a cut-and-run lover; it was thousands of miles and millions of calluses and money. Money. Money.

"What do you need it for?"

"I need books, Mamá."

"Go to the library."

"I need a *bag*."

"You have a bag."

"I need one that doesn't make me look homeless."

"That is an excellent bag," Mamá said. "I got that from—"

"I know. It's from the Swiss Army. I know."

"Then why do you need a new one?"

"Fine," Gloria said. "Forget the bag. I still need—"

"More?"

"I need twenty dollars to enroll in an emergency-medicine course."

"We paid for your classes already," Mamá countered.

"This is extra*curricular*."

"Why do you need more classes?"

"It's good for my record. It'll help me get into medical school."

"They charge you extra?"

"It's a fee for the instructor."

"I know it's a fee for the instructor. If it's not for him, what're they charging you for? Are they going to give you dinner?"

Gloria touched her mother's sagskinned arm. "Think of it this way: I'll be closer to being a doctor."

"Then why do you need to go to medical school?"

"Oh for God's sake . . ." That her mother could be so gung-ho about college yet grapple over every necessary expense blew Gloria's mind. What was the point of saving money? she demanded.

"Fine. Here." Mamá took out a checkbook.

"You don't have cash?"

"I don't think it matters how I give it to you."

"No, you're right, fine. . . ." Gloria waited with her palm open.

Mamá stopped writing. "If you don't want it, I won't give it to you."

"I want it."

"Even if it's a check?"

"I'm not going to beg."

"Are you sure you're going to be a doctor?"

"I'm sure," Gloria said. She was sure.

She had been absolutely sure.

The memory of paper, torn along perforations—

—became gravel peppering vehicular underbelly.

Four hours out of Tijuana, the road she needed forked away suddenly, like a dagger had been driven into the highway. A wretched, pebbly off-ramp presaged a long and uncomfortable drive.

This was the Sonoran desert. Miles of creosote, barrel cactus, empty soil. Beneath outcroppings—they looked like coral, like she was in a submarine—animal life had taken shelter from the midday heat.

She kept one hand on the wheel and traced the map with the other. The route-finding hand made quick dashes to the dial to find a new station each time the music surrendered to talk. Latin pop, all trumpets and Byzantine rhythm, predominated. She got so sick of hacking through hiss and ads that she eventually settled the tuner on an evangelical program.

¡Las puertas del infierno tienen un olor dulce . . . !

She laughed. I bet.

The farther she went, the worse the road got, as though she was traveling back to a less civilized era. Nature, which had been tamed for hundreds of miles, sprung up with a vengeance, attempting to reclaim the road by throwing out weeds and dried stalks. The ground breathed, sulphurous, like a vision out of the preacher's torrid sermon, disturbing the air, making the whole world flicker.

Then proof of humanity erupted in the form of a wooden sign, weathered almost to illegibility, informing her that in 12 KM she could find GASOLINA. She needed it. The last stop had been an hour out of Tijuana, and the needle was dipping into the red.

The gas station confirmed her earlier impression: she was in a time machine. Unmarked gravity pumps straight out of the Eisenhower era grinned at her, elbowing a rubbery hello with their hoses. Green and brown auto-fluid stains turned the ground into combat fatigues. There was a nasty, overcrowded foodmart with mangled ads taped to the inside of its grimy windows; around the building's far side, stacks of decomposing tires nuzzled a saurian tow truck.

Inside, nobody seemed to be on duty. She walked to the back of the building and found the door for the bathroom locked.

"Momento," came a voice.

She went back to the car. Five minutes later, a boy in thin jeans and a Padres cap appeared, smiling and apologizing in Spanish: *perdón, Señora, perdón. . . .* A piece of toilet paper trailed from his shoe. Without asking what she wanted, he grabbed one of the hoses and began filling up the tank.

"I would have done it myself," she said in Spanish, "but I can't seem to get the pump on."

"You have to push this little button," he said. "It's old; nobody knows how to do it except me."

She smiled. Thirteen, he sounded like a geezer. *Nobody knows anymore, these darn kids. . . .* She leaned against the driver's-side door, gazing at the road. By her guess, she had at least another half an hour to go.

"Are you from Aguas Vivas?" she asked.

The attendant raised his eyebrows. "No, *Señora.*"

"You know where that is?"

"Sure."

"You live around here, though," she said.

"Charrones."

"How far is that?"

"Not far," he said. "Sixty-five kilometers."

She nodded, returned to looking at the road.

"Nobody's from Aguas Vivas," said the boy. He finished pumping the gas and rehung the nozzle. "I got to ring you up, wait here." He dashed off, raising a dusty wake. The toilet paper still stuck to his shoe.

She went into the foodmart and found him hammering at a mammoth, rusty cash register like a piano prodigy.

"You can pay me in dollars, if you want," he said. He smiled solicitously. "That's okay. You can do that."

He must've seen the license plates. Or had her accent gotten so bad that she could no longer fake native? It seemed impossible to her that she could be mistaken for anything except a Mexican. This was where she'd come from.

In the genealogical sense.

But she was an American. Always had been.

"What does that mean," she asked, "nobody's from there?" She got out her wallet and handed him a twenty.

"I mean nobody's there," he said.

"Where are they?" she asked.

He handed her a wad of pesos. "They're dead," he said.

She dropped the change into her purse and followed him out as he ran to hold the car door for her.

"Dead?" she asked, snapping her seat belt closed.

He nodded, slammed the door, and ran for the cool of the shop. The toilet paper broke free and caught the wind, twisting up into the blind sky.

SIX

The town was so small that she almost missed it; it came swirling out of the dust, a blip on the otherwise flat vista.

Curiously, there didn't seem to be any houses. The road developed a string of crumbling stores on either side, shed them, and then continued on into the desert. There was neither sidewalk nor pedestrians; no cars, no trees, no streetlights, no stop signs. No intersecting roads. No activity. Just a sorry sandwich of buildings and then nothingness.

All the shops save a few had been boarded up. She cruised past a laundry (closed), a hardware store (closed), a general store with a lurid pink front (open!). The movie theater's marquee had cracked open, revealing the stumps of shattered bulbs. The three-foot-tall neon E of CINE had fallen off, leaving CIN and a gaping patch of pale blue sky. She parked by a shop of indeterminate purpose and got out, hoping to confirm that she was in the right place. In its window, she noted the flaking evidence.

N. CARAVAJAL
PIEDRAS SEPULCRALES
AGUAS VIVAS

The stonecutter's front window functioned as his port-
folio; in it hung hundreds of Polaroids of headstones.
Clearly a man proud of his work, he had handled the pictures with love, keeping them dust-free and pasted solidly
to a piece of gray posterboard. Another posterboard showed
a single stone at various stages of the cutting process: before
it had been sanded, under the chisel, and so on, leading up
to a finished product commemorating the life of JUANITA
RUIZ, 1933–1981.

The window collage also contained testimony from satisfied customers, tearstained gratitude on recipe cards and
notepad paper.

> *You are the very best thank you the Parras family*
> *I am taking a lot of comfort from the beautiful stone*
> *Please I hope you can cut a stone for me to match my*
> *wife's E. Alvarez*

Gloria found this pictorial bouquet both creepy and
touching. And unnecessary. Why bother? A headstone was
an as-needed expense; people didn't usually drop in to
browse.

Then she saw the answer: next to the stonecutter's shop
was another stonecutter's shop. Its owner had also festooned
his window, and an intense rivalry had developed. The
second stonecutter, H. Lopez-Caravajal, appeared to be

winning. He used louder and larger signs, scores of testimonials—neatly typed—and a slew of enlarged photos showing the most minute features of his handiwork. The display seemed to smirk at its neighbor.

In flowery gilt, below his name, Señor Lopez-Caravajal had added

The best anywhere
but especially in Aguas Vivas

Stiff competition. She smiled wryly and touched her fingers to the searing windowglass.

Why did a place this small need two of them?

A gust of wind sandblasted her. She needed a drink and some shade. There didn't seem to be much danger of a parking ticket, so she left the Dodge in the street and headed for the general store.

Midway up the street she saw another sign, handlettered on primered plywood. It had been so thoroughly riddled with bulletholes that she could barely read its command.

BY ORDER OF THE TOWN COUNCIL
NO FIREARMS WITHIN CITY LIMITS

The general store's screen door whacked the counter as she entered; its point of impact was shiny and raw, where wood had touched wood many times before. She mumbled an apology to no one and took a peek down both of the aisles. Canned goods, flashlights, batteries, flimsy nylon ponchos. A smushed pile of tortillas wrapped in plastic; water had beaded inside the bags. She held one up and winced at its moldy underside. Sunlight filtered through disabled Venetian blinds, throwing a fan-shaped shadow across distressed sacks of rice.

An index card taped to the register offered

flores frescas para los muertos

She knocked on the counter. From behind a stack of empty crates, another screen door opened. An ancient man in an apron and no shoes shuffled in, peering at her droopily.

"Yes?"

"I'd like something to drink," she said.

He shuffled behind the counter and produced a svelte bottle of caramel-colored liquid, which he slid across the counter along with a bottle opener in the shape of a chihuahua. She started to take a sip but recoiled from a noxious stench.

"Is this Coke?"

"No, *Señora*. A home recipe."

She took a cautious whiff and again had to pull away. "What is it?"

"Raíz del fango."

Mud root. She'd never heard of it before, but the smell indicated truth in advertising. She put it down and asked if he had anything else.

"You don't want it?"

"No thanks."

He frowned. "I opened it already, *Señora*."

"I'll pay for it. Give me something else, please."

He stared at her a moment, stupefied by her request; then he took the bottle and swigged it half down. He said, "It shouldn't go to waste."

"By all means," she said.

"Only real Mexicans can drink this."

"I'm not a real Mexican," she said.

He smiled. "I know."

She said, "Do you have any bottled water?"

He shuffled to the other end of the counter, keeping his eyes on her, as though he expected her to leap over and mug him. He came back with a brand she'd never heard of. The label said *embotellada en México*. What good was bottled water when it came from the same source as the tap?

Too dehydrated to argue, she twisted off the top and took a long draught. Her insides flushed like growing moss; God, she had dried out. . . . Another sip, twice as long, finished the whole half-liter. When she came back for air, she turned to see the old turkey watching her.

"Thirsty," he said. There was no mockery in his tone; more like wonderment that a woman could absorb so much.

"I've been driving all day," she said. "What time is it?"

He jerked his thumb at the shelf behind him, where a clock nestled between a carton of cigars and a googly-eyed stuffed cactus that had burst its seams. She wasn't even sure what time zone she was in, but by her best guess, she had been traveling for ten hours.

"Welcome to Aguas Vivas," he said. "Who died?"

She stared at him.

"*Someone* must have died," he said. "Or else you wouldn't be here."

"I'm looking for the police station," she said.

"The police station of what?" he asked.

"Aguas Vivas."

"Mm," he said.

She waited for him to ask what the matter was, but he said nothing more.

"I'll take another one," she said, raising the empty water bottle.

"The first one cost you already thirty pesos." He licked his lips and held up his half-finished bottle of home-brew. "And this is twenty-five."

She paid, and he ambled to the other end of the counter, bending with a groan. The back of his trousers strained.

"Can you tell me where the police station is?" she asked, leaning over to see him lethargically stripping shrink-wrap from a case of bottled water.

"What?" He came back up, bottle in hand. "What did you say?"

"The police station."

"Yes, okay, give me a minute." He shuffled around the counter. "Everybody's in a hurry. . . ." he said, handing her the bottle as he passed. He cracked the front door and pointed across the street. "There."

"That's the cinema."

He said nothing, kept pointing like a lawn jockey.

"All right," she said. She wandered across the street, turning back halfway.

"Go on!" he said.

The box office was empty and cobwebbed. The plastic message board listed neither showtimes nor prices; it had been rearranged to read POLICÍA. She gave the old man a thumbs-up. He waved and disappeared into his store.

The theater's foyer darkened as she groped along, finding a light switch hidden behind a pillar. An abrupt blast of fluorescence lit a sepulchral lobby. Frames bereft of posters called attention to their own emptiness. Royal blue carpeting existed as mangy remnants, having largely given way to concrete marred by dried glue. The concession stand had imploded.

Missing was a theater's usual conviviality. No bowtied ushers. No cheery couples splitting up to head for the bathroom. The smell of burnt sugar and butter had been permanently baked into the walls.

The screening room was dark and cool, with five rows of six seats. It had been a real stage once; a medium-sized screen—eerily blank, seeming to glow of its own accord—nailed to the top of the proscenium had converted the place into a movie theater. In front of the screen was a wooden desk and matching chair. A green-hooded lamp cast a moon atop a stained blotter. Feeling as though she had happened upon the set for a play, she made her way down to the desk, circling it from a distance, afraid it would disappear if she touched it. The setup looked like a test site where potential employees could be observed by a hiring committee.

She remembered walking up the beach near Oxnard with Reggie—it had been early on in their marriage, when they still did things like that—and coming across a chrome bed, complete with mattress and sheet, basking by the waterline. Nobody was around for miles, and yet there it was, this stupid bed, sitting there, sinking deeper into the sand as the tide mobbed its legs.

Reggie had glanced at the houses on pilings and said *Well, someone got bombed last night.*

She had not been satisfied with this explanation. Moving a heavy frame and making hospital corners required a concerted effort, *sober* effort, on the part of more than one person. This wasn't a fraternity joke; someone wanted that bed there. An impulse took her by the heart: *Why?* She had been desperate to find out the whole story. She began inventing an explanation, and then another, and another. . . . She wanted to give this disjointed image—bed on sand; indoors, outdoors—a beginning, middle, end. Every suggestion she made, Reggie laughed at.

People do things, Gigi. There isn't always a conspiracy behind it.

She wondered why. She wondered how.

A phone on the desk sent its cord out one of the SALIDAS. She lifted the receiver. It had a dial tone. Feeling inexplicably guilty, she hung up and stepped back and called out *Hello? Hello?*

Shivering, she hurried up the aisle, glancing over her shoulder to erase the feeling of being watched.

Outside, in the heat, she felt secure. She crossed the street and reentered the general store, rapping on the counter and waiting for the old shopkeeper to reappear.

"There's no one there," she said.

"Right," he said.

"Did you *know* there was no one there?"

"*Sí.*"

"Look," she said, "I'm in a hurry."

"I can see that," he said.

"Please tell me where I can find the police."

"The police *station* is over there," he said.

"What about the police*man?*"

He raised a finger. "If it's him you want, then you have to go over to the bar."

She did her best to sound polite while requesting the location of the bar.

"This way," he said, shuffling out the back door.

It led onto a porch overlooking a scrubby yard. Atop a burled table was an aluminum bucket containing a mound of rapidly melting ice and three Budweisers. One chair had been pulled askew, and in it, the old man seated himself. In the other chair—a bamboo rocker on the verge of collapse—a dark man with smooth, juvenile cheeks and a nascent potbelly snored like a kettle aboil.

"That's the policeman," said the old man. He cracked a beer and offered it to her. "Sixty pesos."

"No thanks."

He shrugged and sipped, fixing his gaze on the empty yard.

Gloria looked at the policeman. "Is he going to sleep long?"

"He might," said the old man. "Sometimes he sleeps all afternoon. His wife calls me so I can send him home for dinner."

She cleared her throat.

The old man shot her a look. "What are you doing that for?"

She ignored him and shook the policeman. "Hey. Excuse me." He blinked and snorted and stood up woodenly, stumbling a little as he plucked his shirt from his body and fanned himself. He was shorter than Gloria, his trousers hugging womanly hips.

"I told her not to wake you up," said the shopkeeper.

"Excuse me," Gloria repeated. "I called yesterday. Remember?"

The policeman snorted and swallowed phlegm. "Who are you?"

"Gloria Mendez. I spoke to you on the phone. You're *Teniente* Fajardo."

"We spoke on the phone. . . ."

"Yes," she said. "We did. And I'm here now."

"You came all the way down here?" He sounded baffled.

"I'm here about the body," she said. "I need to bring it back to Los Angeles."

The shopkeeper said, "She's been driving all day."

"The body . . ." Fajardo said.

"I *have* been driving all day," she said, "and I need to get back. So please take me to wherever I need to go so I can pick him up."

"Huh," he said. "Who?"

"The body. Carl Perreira. You told me on the ph—look, is there a problem?"

"A problem?" He glanced at the old man, who shrugged. "No, *Señora,* there's no problem. I have no problem. Luís? Do you have a problem?"

"No, Tito."

Fajardo looked at her. "So unless *you* have a problem, it seems there are no problems here."

"Señor," she said, "I'm here out of respect for the dead."

"I see that."

"—and I wish you'd show some," she said.

Fajardo said, "I respect the dead. Luís? Do you?"

Luís nodded solemnly.

"Where would our little town be," said Fajardo, "without respect for the dead?"

"Wonderful. But can we—"

"I don't know if that's going to be possible, *Señora.*" Fajardo tucked in the front of his shirt. "We're still in the middle of an investigation."

"What investigation?"

"You know," said Fajardo. "When a man loses his life under my authority, it's my obligation to investigate. And I'm sorry to tell you this, *Señora,* but this is a tragic situation." A sense of command appeared in his bearing, as though he had right then decided what to do with her. "Very tragic. Here is not the place to discuss it. Let's step into my office." He clapped the old man on the shoulder and said, "Luís?"

"Adiós," Luís said. "To you, too, *Señora.*"

She turned to make a reply; when she turned back, Fajardo was gone, the screen door squeaking on its hinges.

She caught up to him in the middle of the street.

"Is there someone else I should be talking to?" she asked.

"Not at all," he said. "I'm the only show in town." They reached the theater and he slipped the key into the already unlocked front door. She watched as he proceeded to close the deadbolt and yank at the door, which naturally didn't give.

"What the hell?" he said.

"It was open already," she said.

"How do you know?"

"I came here first." She turned the key and held the door ajar. "See?"

He said, "Too smart for me, *Señora*," and slid past her.

SEVEN

"What can I say to you?"

Fajardo twirled a pencil through his fingers and set it down on the blotter.

"Nothing. Because there is nothing one can say. Trust me, I understand grief. Grief is my business. I want you to understand that *I* understand. I am fully aware of how hard these situations can be.

"And I know how people behave. They try to find a reason, and when they can't—because there is no reason for situations like this—then they start to demand justice. Or they get angry with God, they curse the cruelty of the world. But they're not talking to anyone, *Señora*. You know this as well as I do. When you shout at the sky, you're speaking to the clouds."

He cast a pious eye at the ceiling.

"And to be honest—I'm honest with you, *Señora*, because I get the sense that you're a good woman, and this tragic situation is not going to make you behave like some people behave, like lunatics. . . . But you? No. You're a very controlled person, *Señora.* I can tell. You're his wife?"

"I'm a very close friend," she said.

"I thought you said—"

"You're misremembering."

He frowned. "You drove all the way down here—"

"Yes," she said angrily.

"Okay, okay. . . . How was the drive? Was it hot?"

"It was fine."

"You found the town easily?"

"I had a map."

"Mm-hm . . . good. Well, what I'm saying to you, *Señora,* is that I've seen plenty of grief in my time, plenty of people tearing out their hair about tragedies that they couldn't prevent.

"I knew a couple once, who came to town to bury their daughter. A three-year-old. The mother falls asleep one afternoon, and the girl wanders out onto the porch. There's a stepladder; the father was using it to change a lightbulb. The girl climbs up and falls. On the way down"—he struck the edge of his desk—"her head, on the porch rail. Her face lands in a puddle.

"The day of the funeral, the priest calls me up. You need to come over, he says. We can't get the girl buried.

"It's not what you think, *Señora:* the mother wasn't the bad one. It was the father. He was holding the coffin. *Lying* on top of it. He said he wouldn't let go unless he had a good reason to. . . ."

Fajardo sighed. "I had to pull him off. I didn't want to, but what else could we do? The man demanded logic in a situation where there *is* no logic." He touched his own forehead, brought his fingers away as though setting aloft a bird. "He wanted logic so much that he lost his ability to think logically.

"And where does that get him? Situations like these, *Señora,* they're pure tragedy. To try and find some plan behind it . . ."

He sat back, shaking his head. "It's almost an insult to the deceased."

He got up and paced around. "I use this place as my office. It's cooler than anywhere else in town. I like to come in, and get out of the sun. In the middle of the day, it can go over forty-five degrees outside. In Fahrenheit, that's . . . one-hundred-something? Around that. Very hot, *Señora.* You can die if you're not careful."

He returned to the desk, sitting and leaning to whisper.

"It can be very hard," he said. He opened his palm across the blotter, in the circle cast by the desk lamp. Thus illuminated, it looked like a fat, naked diva in the spotlight.

Gloria kept her fingers laced in her lap.

Fajardo waited. Then he pulled his hand back and said, "I extend to you my condolences."

She nodded.

"It's tragic," he said, "but you have to understand, when a man dies, there are certain steps I am required to take. By law. These matters aren't up to me, *Señora,* because I didn't make the law. It's my job to make sure—"

"What happened?" she asked.

"What?"

"Tell me what happened," she said. "I want to know."

"I'm sure you do, *Señora,* and that's what I'm explaining

to you. The questions of *when* and *how* and *what* have not yet been determined, and it wouldn't be ethical of me to start discussing them with you before I knew what I was saying."

"You're not allowed to tell me how he died?"

"Well, in part, I can tell you, in part—"

"Then tell me," she said, crossing her arms.

"I can tell you the *general* circumstances."

"Fine."

"There's no need to get impatient, *Señora.*" The *Teniente* picked up his pencil and tapped the blotter four times. He opened a desk drawer and took out a tattered log book. He wet his thumb on the inside of his lip and flipped pages. Then he flipped pages in the other direction, lingering over one page as though it needed cryptographic analysis. Finally, he put the log book back in the desk.

"I'm sure this must be very difficult for you," he said, "so I'll spare you—"

"Please don't."

"Okay. Well . . . okay. Here's the information available at this time." Fajardo took the log book back out again and found the page. "Several nights ago, a car skidded off the road approximately five miles out of town. The vehicle rolled over and the gas tank caught fire. The driver, who was alone, was killed either by the trauma of the accident, or subsequent burns to the head and chest. . . ."

As Fajardo spoke, he kept his head down. Having been obligated to listen to Reggie for three years—not to mention his work buddies—Gloria knew what real cops talked like. And this guy, she thought, sounded like a bureaucrat impersonating a soap-opera actor impersonating a cop.

He closed the book. "That's all I'm permitted to discuss at the present time. I'm sorry. This must be difficult for you."

"Why didn't anyone call?"

"Call—who? His identification was destroyed in the fire. And anyway, was he carrying your phone number?"

"I don't know, but—"

"I did what I'm supposed to do under these conditions," he said, "which was to start the investigation."

She said, "What part of the investigation involves drinking beer on Luís's porch?"

Fajardo twirled the pencil, set it down. "Okay. You call me up and start shouting at me over the phone. Today you drive over to my city and start insulting me in person. I don't like the direction we're going in, *Señora*. I'll tell you something: I have seen a lot of grief. It's what I do; I have experience handling it. But nobody who ever came in and started harassing me got helped faster."

"Is there anything being done to—to—*solve* this. . . ."

"That's what I was trying to tell you earlier," Fajardo said. "There's nothing to solve. There's nobody to blame."

"Did you get his license-plate number?"

"Yes, of course."

"Then why didn't you call the authorities in California? You could've gotten his name that way. You could've found out where he worked, or his home phone number. Why didn't you call the American consulate?"

"That's not the way we do things here," he said.

"Someone would have called me, someone would have

done *something*—" She broke off, not wanting to make him into her savior.

"*Señora . . .*" Fajardo oozed, "you're having a rough time. It's pure tragedy." He smoothed his hands across the blotter, as though wiping the case from the table.

"Where's the body?"

"The body is in storage."

"*Where.*"

"At the hospital."

"I need to get it."

"It can't be released yet."

"Nobody's identified it," she said. "It might not even be him."

"You don't want to see it," said Fajardo. "He was very badly burned."

"When can we go?"

He flailed his arms a little. "The hospital is far away, it—"

"Where is it."

"It's a little town, Joaqual, nowhere near here—"

"I'll go myself," she said. She got up and walked up the aisle, hearing his chair begrudgingly scrape the concrete as he got up to follow, saying *wait wait wait.*

EIGHT

She drove, listening to his directions but otherwise not acknowledging him as he feebly protested what he called *a huge waste of time, Señora, huge.* On the way, they passed the accident site, and Fajardo got out with the log book to show her a patch of earth and desert weeds. Flecks of shredded metal and paint dandruff glinted among scorching sand. It seemed that the car had not so much exploded as sublimated, its mist resettling over an area fifty times as vast. It disturbed her to think that Carl's death could be rubbed out so soon, mopped up by the wind and a cleaning crew.

The *Teniente* called the spot an intersection, but the term didn't fit. A single set of tire treads distinguished road from surrounding wasteland. She tried to pinpoint the way back into town, but couldn't, and began to feel dizzy and disoriented.

"It rolled over," she said.

"Yes."

"How?" she asked.

"How did it—? It *rolled,* like this. . . ." Fajardo tumbled one hand over the other.

"I mean what *caused* it," she said.

"He was speeding."

"You saw him?"

"Of course not, *Señora.* I wasn't here."

"Then how do you know how fast he was driving?"

"To roll a car, one has to have a lot of momentum," Fajardo said. "That's physics. The car skidded for two hundred yards. The tracks took a sharp turn back there; one of them left the ground. . . ." He thumbed his belt. "This is all technical, *Señora.* I can give you a lesson in crime-scene reconstruction but it'll cost extra."

"Where did it flip?" She hunched over and examined the ground.

"You're wasting your time," he said. "The tracks aren't there anymore."

"Yes they are; I'm following them."

"Those are our tracks, *Señora.* Let's get back in the car."

"I want to know what happened," she said.

"He was speeding," said Fajardo. "It was dark. Probably he was drunk—"

"Carl didn't drink."

"Then he wasn't a very good driver. The car hit something, and turned over. Or it skidded, and then rolled. He was unconscious when it caught fire, or he got trapped in. Tangled up in the seat belt; that can happen very easily. The driver's-side door was damaged, and he couldn't get out. The car caught fire, and he was burned. . . ."

He continued to offer scenario after scenario, each

presented as fact and then contravened by the next statement—the car rolled, the car crashed, the car lost a wheel.
He was about the worst liar she'd ever seen; she waited for
the right moment to trip him.

". . . and when the fire broke out he was unable to get
away—"

"So he was unconscious," she said.

"Without a doubt."

"Then when did he have time to call me?"

"Call you what."

"He left a message on the machine. That's why I'm here.
How else do you think I knew about this?"

"In that case," Fajardo said, "I guess you didn't understand what I meant."

"I guess not," she said. "Why don't you explain?"

"He was unconscious, yes, true. But not *then*. Not . . . at
first. At first, he was conscious." He drew an X in the sand.
"This is where he was standing. At the time of consciousness." Then he walked five feet away and drew another X.
"This is the position of the front end of the vehicle, approximately, and there may or may not have been consciousness
on the part of the driver. Consciousness is a difficult thing
to determine. What does that mean, really? To be conscious."

She stared at him. "He was *outside* the car?"

"It's possible."

"But not definite."

"I told you," said the *Teniente*, "we're in the process of
investigating."

"But you're saying he might *not* have been unconscious?"

"That's possible, too. It's possible that other things could have occurred. It's hard to tell in situations like this, *Señora*. I, unfortunately, was not on the scene until a while after the death had occurred."

"Someone must've called you," she said.

"Luís called me from town because he could see the flames."

"From miles away?"

"It gets totally dark out here." Fajardo jabbed at the sky. "No streetlights. If you're around tonight, you'll see; it's very beautif—"

"Luís called you, and you came over to the scene."

"Yes," he said.

"And what did you see?"

"By this time, *Señora,* it was many hours after the original accident."

"We got here in twenty minutes."

"No, *Señora*. I was at home. It was nighttime, remember? My house is far away, over the district line. I was asleep when Luís called. I had to get dressed and get in the car. You saw yourself how bad the roads are. And at night you can barely see. I went as fast as I could, and it still took a long time. By the time I got here the ambulance had arrived, and your friend was on the way to the hospital. They took the driver of the car, and I was left to organize the investigation of the scene." He held up the log book. "Which is still in progress."

"On his message, I didn't hear anything like a fire."

"If you ask my professional opinion? It happened suddenly," said Fajardo. "He was getting away from the car, or trying to get away, and he called. . . . He got distracted. The car exploded without warning. He didn't have time to get away from the wreckage of the vehicle, because he was talking on the phone." He clucked his tongue. "What do you think of *that* idea?"

He got distracted. He got distracted calling you, *Señora.* If he hadn't been on the phone, he might've gotten away in time; too bad he decided to give you a ring. . . .

A turkey vulture's yowl caught their attention.

"We can't stay here too long," Fajardo said. "He might eat us."

She watched as the bird descended to pluck at a rodent carcass.

The desolation bothered her. As far as she could tell, the road led nowhere interesting. It made no sense for Carl to be here. She said as much to Fajardo, who shrugged and said, "We get lots of visitors, *Señora.* It's our number-one industry."

"What's there to see around here?"

They got in the car and went another mile. The earth began to lighten, until it glared so intensely that she felt it in her sinuses.

"Look," said Fajardo.

Up ahead she saw something shiny and cool.

It was a lake.

The sight of it made her thirsty. She felt like stripping off her clothes and sinking. The nearer they got, the more fabulous it seemed, the water looming large and ultramarine, downy waves crashing on shores of bone-white—

The road curved up.

The lake disappeared.

The *Teniente* chuckled. "Good one, huh?" he said. "Turn around."

She executed a three-point turn.

"Look back," he said.

She stepped on the gas, and as they descended the rise, the lake reappeared. She made a second three-point turn and sped them to where the water's edge had been. In its place she saw a salty, gritty pit—acres upon acres, surmounting the horizon—studded by thousands of graves. Most were marked with decaying wooden crosses; some were bare; some had pale headstones. No fences, no grass, no heavy gate or chapel. Graves, sheer scale sufficing to delineate sacred space.

He said, "It used to be the Aguas Vivas lake, till a developer drained it and killed the town." He gestured to the desiccation. "Now it's the biggest cemetery in the state."

"What causes the mirage?" she asked.

"Nobody knows. It's something in the sand. They call it *aguas muertas*, which is what people from Charrones call the whole town." He leaned toward her. "Look, why don't we go back to town? You can relax, and sleep off some of the fatigue. . . . We'll go tomorrow. I promise, first thing, I will call and tell them we're coming. We can be there by eight-thirty."

She was exhausted, eager to sleep off her tremulous frustration. Grief had glommed on to weariness, yielding a fragile state she couldn't maintain much longer. And if they turned back, she didn't have to confront the body yet.

"We're going," she said.

Before he could object, she spun the car around and peeled out for the main road, glancing back to watch the earth wash blue and vivid.

NINE

Over the course of the next hour and a quarter, Fajardo continued to spew pseudosympathy, edging closer as she drove, finally daring to slip his arm around her seat. To keep him at bay, she asked for directions over and over.

He said, "I'll let you know when we need to turn," and put his hand on her thigh.

She said, "Tell me about your wife, *Teniente*."

He laughed and sat back, placing his hands in his lap. "She's a wonderful woman. I couldn't ask for a better lady." He stayed put for the duration of the drive.

They followed power lines through midget hills. The road began to behave itself, bringing them to an outpost with a gas station, a bodega, and a near-abandoned trailer park. To Gloria, this scant assemblage did not prove a town, but the sign to her left disagreed, declaring them to be in Joaqual.

A series of three squat concrete-block travesties came up on the left. Number one housed a radio station; number two, a hardware store. Both looked to be in better shape than number three—the hospital. It horrified her to think of Carl being brought here on the brink of death. It would've been easier and more merciful to have left him at the side of the road.

And you couldn't call it a hospital, she decided, as they forced their way through the swinging doors; it barely qualified as a clinic. Bodies, stuffed wall to wall, hacked and sneezed and bled and groaned and complained when other bodies jostled their broken limbs. Arachnoid children scrambled over dilapidated folding chairs and made short-lived castles in the dirt of an overturned plant. A man in torn jeans had a soiled rag wrapped around his hand; between his workboots gathered a pool of blood. Dressed all in blue, a squat woman shoved her way around, giving orders and smacking with a rubber glove those who disobeyed. She had a bad limp and not a crumb of pleasantness. A teenager with code-red acne sat on a bench, picking hopelessly at his face; beneath him, in defiance of the ruckus, snored a hobo with a Jerry Garcia anti-coif.

The din suckerpunched her. Vomit and urine, agony and discord. People plugged ears with fingers as they hollered into cellphones.

One of the kids ran past the hobo, trampling his ankle. He awoke, howling, and got to his feet.

"Chinga tu puta madre pinche—"

He started to chase the kid around, but the woman in blue limped over and flogged him with the glove, ordering him to sit down. He swung at her, way above her head, making an open target of his solar plexus; with surprising grace, she kicked him back against the wall.

"Not your turn!" yelled the woman.

She was the nurse, Gloria realized.

"Wait here," said Fajardo. "I'll see if I can find the doctor." He went over to talk to the nurse, leaving Gloria to squeeze into an unoccupied spot along the wall.

She wanted to feel bad for these people, but all she could summon was a vague, removed pity. The disorder alienated her; the filth made her wary. Once again, she found herself wondering if she had grown too fancy for her own good. If she *had* gone on to become a doctor, was this what she'd be dealing with today? She assumed not. She would have her own practice. *Dr. Mendez.* Radiologist. Neurologist. Surgeon.

At Cal State, she had assumed the same routine she'd used in high school. Study. Study. Study again. Do your homework twice; never worry about what your classmates say. In college, though, gossipers did more than gossip: they actively sought to reshape her into a more normal person.

Do you think you're white?

She remembered a face: skeletal and taut, cheeks sueded and drawn, as though he wanted to suck out her brains. Allan Jarroll-Peña, head of the Chicano Students Union, ran track and rallies, and within her first week, he pinpointed Gloria as a girl in need of a cause.

You act like you're white.

I'm going to be a doctor.

This was 1985. Allan told her the movement didn't need her to be a doctor.

What movement?

Come on Friday and you'll see.

After lab, she went to the steps of the library. She had

never seen people her age act like this before. They picketed and chanted slogans. They seemed so determined that despite herself, she was absorbed.

¡Sí, se puede!

United Farm Workers signs formed butterflies above the crowd, which grew behind her, so that by the time the Legend arrived, she was standing not at the back but smack in the middle. Allan ruled from the top of the steps, whipping the crowd to a froth with a bullhorn. *He fights for all of us, not just for the men and women in the fields!* And the crowd said *sí!* The whole place effervesced as the Legend got up to talk.

We fight for him!

¡Sí!

¡Sí, se puede!

¡Sí, se puede!

Gloria had seen his picture in the paper, and had discussed him once or twice with her mother. She felt horribly out of the loop as she stood behind a boy holding a placard with a quote from Gandhi. She was afraid her naïveté would telegraph all the way up the steps to Allan.

Viva César! Viva La Causa! Viva La Raza!

The Legend spoke for forty minutes about unionization; about the life of a grape picker; about how the cause had been down this road before, in 1967 and in 1973; about how they would never give up; about how he would starve himself in honor of those who did not have the option to starve or not. He mesmerized. Gloria heard him speaking in her ear. When he asked rhetorical questions, she murmured answers.

The rally peaked and subsided, and everyone surged forward to meet him. Gloria got in line and waited for an hour. Allan was smiling at her when she arrived, watching her as she prepared to take her first big, authentic step.

What's this?

Allan elbowed her. *He asked you a question, Gloria.*

She looked at the book the Legend had tapped. *I'm premed.*

Good said the Legend. *Necesitamos más doctores.*

The girl behind her pushed her out of line, and the conversation ended.

After that, Gloria didn't attend any more rallies. She wanted to study and she didn't give a damn about *La Causa.* Allan Jarroll-Peña could phone all he wanted. He was half-white, anyway.

At the end of the semester, she took home four A's and a B+.

Doctor Mendez.

Her mother had taken to calling her that. As in: *You think you can wash your own plate, Doctor Mendez?*

It was March 1986. She was at the kitchen table, selecting classes for next year. Chemistry and organic chemistry concurrently, along with math. Her pen dangled above the course description for a seminar on classical philosophy. She wondered if she could find someone to discuss the material with her. She already knew what Mamá would say: *I don't want to know the meaning of life, Doctor Mendez; I want you to fix my backache.*

Gloria put down her pen and took her plate to the sink. *Muchas gracias, Doctor.*

She rinsed away sandwich crumbs, took a towel, began drying.

You have an exam?

I always have an exam.

Don't expect me to keep track of your schedule, Doctor Mendez. If you want me to do that, you're going to have to hire me as your secretary.

Ha. Maybe if you're lucky. Gloria raised the plate. *You'll have to do my dishes.*

As she reached for the top shelf, the plate slipped. Mamá jackknifed and caught it in one stunningly abrupt movement.

Good reflexes, Mamá.

Her mother, still bent, said nothing. For a moment she remained that way, like a runner in the blocks. Then she fell onto her side: eyelids ruminating, body stiff, lips rictal and undignified. Flash-frozen and clutching the plate.

Looking back on it, Gloria had to congratulate herself on her medical intuition. She'd never seen one before, but her mind had instantly registered a diagnosis: stroke.

A meaty smack brought her back to the present: one of the kids had tripped and bloodied his lip. His mother, busy stuffing a nipple into the face of a wailing infant, paid him no heed.

The nurse said something angry to Fajardo and limped out through a back door.

"She's not happy," said the *Teniente*. "She says the doctor is very busy."

Seeing that the nurse had gone, the hobo took up his hunt for the kid who'd disturbed him. He grabbed a length of rubber tubing from the floor and brandished it like a billy club.

"Isn't that a little dangerous?" Gloria asked.

"Every time I come in here," said the *Teniente,* "that guy is here. He never hurts anyone. He just tries to spit on them."

"Put that down!" The nurse limped back, swinging her glove like a mace.

The hobo dropped the tubing, shrank to a ball, and rolled beneath the bench. He recommenced snoring, one plangent melody among many.

A stained white coat emerged from the hallway, but instead of riding on a middle-aged man, as Gloria expected, it draped loosely across the shoulders of a young Asian woman. Despair rose from her like perfume; she was graying prematurely.

The waiting patients lurched at her like zombies.

"¡No moleste!" she yelled, batting at them, trying get them into line. The nurse acted as bouncer, pressing back the horde with her forearms as she beckoned Fajardo.

Gloria started to follow, but the nurse stopped her.

"Not you," she said. "Just him."

The *Teniente* exited with the doctor.

Gloria watched helplessly. "But I need to—"

"No," said the nurse. "It's not sterile to let anyone—"

She didn't have time to finish; a boy with glasses initiated pandemonium by peeing straight into the air, like some European fountain. The crowd recoiled in all directions, threatening to knock down the four walls. The nurse hurtled toward him and fought to pin his arms down. Gloria gauged her chances of making a break for the back doors, where the doctor and Fajardo had gone, and decided that—in light of the nurse's unflappable brutality—she would wait until the *Teniente* returned.

Ten minutes later, he emerged with a paper bag and a brownish document. Without a word, he pulled Gloria toward the swinging doors. They stumbled into the dirt parking lot, narrowly avoiding a pregnant woman in mid-contraction.

"Ow . . ." said Fajardo. He wagged one arm, wet with the stain of someone's errant cup of coffee.

"What did the doctor say?" Gloria asked.

He handed her a document.

PARTIDA DE DEFUNCIÓN

The spaces for name, birthdate, address, and so on had all been left blank. Only the doctor's signature and the cause of death had been filled out. *Burns third degree* and *blunt trauma head*.

"This could be anyone," she said.

Fajardo flipped the certificate over and showed her a Baggie stapled to its underside. It contained a silver cruci-fix. She did not need to take it out to know it was Carl's.

"The doctor didn't have enough time and information to complete the certificate," said Fajardo. "So you and I can do it now." He took out a ballpoint pen and uncapped it with his teeth. "Name . . . ? *Señora.* Hey. Wake up. If you want to get this done this is the fastest way. Or, like I said, I can mail it to you."

"But . . ." she said. Her head was soup. ". . . the body."

He handed her the paper bag. "Here."

what OH

oh no

Her first impulse was to drop the bag.

In your hands. He's in here.

She opened the bag and took out a small plastic urn.

She held the urn as though it was a beating heart.

"It's standard procedure," said Fajardo. "They're allowed to do it by law. When they have no means of contacting people and the body is badly damaged. The hospital has limited space. You want me to drive?"

She nodded numbly, allowing him to lead her back to the car and place her in the passenger seat. He got behind the wheel.

"Let's get this done, we have a long drive. You want to put on your seat belt?"

She stared at the urn, trying to see through its walls.

"*Señora.*" Fajardo sighed and reached across her for the belt, brushing her breast as he did. He sighed again and flattened the page across the steering wheel. "Name."

She gave it to him.

"Birthdate? Birthplace? Place of employment? Highest level of education attained?"

When they finished, he folded up the certificate and tucked it between her hand and the urn. She had not moved other than to answer his questions; she could not think anything except: in your hands. He's in your hands.

"Are you awake?"

She nodded.

"We should've waited," Fajardo said. "I was trying to help you, *Señora*."

He started the car and craned around to back out. He said, "Maybe next time you'll listen."

THIS IS NOT A PERSON; this is a decoration. A bad one.

Purple plastic. A purple plastic football.

It might work if she wanted to spruce up a nursing home.

She gripped the urn tighter.

For a moment she thought she heard Carl speaking. Complaining about—?

No.

It wasn't him talking.

It was the *Teniente* talking. As he had been for the whole ride.

About the difficulty of his job "out in the middle of nowhere." About the "lack of support," the "long and lonely hours."

"It's not a way to be a man, is it, *Señora*? I mean, you can appreciate this, right?"

Unbelievable that you could carry a corpse like this. So convenient. A custom clearly begotten by pragmatism.

Caveman to wife: *I'm tired of hauling your mother's body around.*

Wife to caveman: *Calm down and have a smoke. . . .*

He storms outside, lights a match, and—presto! A new form of bodily containment is born.

She began to laugh in short sharp bursts. Not her usual

laughter, but the squeal of grinding brakes.

Fajardo, assuming she had heard his previous joke, said, "You just got it, huh?"

She rolled her head, facing him, laughing hard. How stupid could he be?

"Want to hear another?" he asked.

She nodded, biting her lip as another delirious spasm shook through her chest.

"I haven't even told it yet," he said. "And you're laughing already. Good to see, *Señora*. You looked bad there for a while. I was beginning to worry about you. I said, 'When is she going to realize that life is all a big joke?' But you get it, now."

"I get it now."

"That's good." He returned to watching the road. "We'll be home soon. You can have a place to stay in town, and tomorrow you'll be off."

She rubbed the jar. Night had fallen. She could see perhaps twenty feet: see the flash of mammalian eyes caught in the hi-beams. Fajardo seemed at ease, and he had already hit two raccoons.

Aguas Vivas came into distant view, the CIN sign flashing red.

"I let Luís turn it on at night," said the *Teniente*. "He likes to fall asleep to it."

They parked near the theater. Fajardo took her to the projection room, where he unfolded a cot and an army blanket, and invited her to make herself comfortable.

Still dazed, she went to find the bathroom. She rinsed her mouth and face. The paper-towel dispenser had been ripped off the wall, so she wiped away the excess water with her palms, wondering if minute particles of Carl had come off in the process.

Carl particles.

Carticles.

A laugh escaped in the form of a retch. Then she dropped the posture and bent over the sink to let everything drain: a snotty, inelegant, torrent of anguish.

"Señora?" Fajardo called through the door. "You okay?"

"I'm fine," she said.

"You sound like something's wrong."

"Nothing's wrong."

"I'll let you have your privacy."

She waited for him to plod off, then washed up and went back to the projection room to embrace sleep.

The *Teniente* was sitting on the edge of the cot, unlacing his shoes. He had stripped down to his undershirt; his soft, brown, hairless shoulders swelled like bonbons.

"Situations like this . . . Life is hard, *Señora,* very hard, and we have to take comfort wherever we can find it."

"What are you doing."

He stopped fiddling with his laces. "I can keep them on, if you want." He flopped back on the bed. "You look like you're gonna drop, *Señora.*" He patted the mattress. "Better sit down." He began to unbuckle his belt.

She was out of the building before he had a chance to stand.

"Señora!" In her sideview mirror, she saw him careering up the street as he refastened his pants.

"Where you going!"

She rolled up the window, slipping the key into the ignition as he reached her and began tapping the glass.

"Come back inside. You can't leave this time of night, it's too dangerous. There was a woman last year got her throat cut, *Señora,* listen to me. . . ."

She checked to make sure the urn was on the passenger seat. In her pocket she had the death certificate. Dual talismans that she had completed her mission and never needed to come back.

The urn gave her an approving nod: go on. Get out of here.

She started the car and put it in drive.

"*Señora!* I'm not messing around here! Look, we had a misunderstanding, you didn't know what I meant, so—*Seño*—*what the fuck!*"

Her back wheel went over his foot. She thought: Good thing he kept his shoes on.

TEN

She drove all night, plowing through fatigue and getting back at five in the morning. Four hours' sleep was all she could manage before being wakened by the reproachful stare of the urn atop her dresser.

She lay in bed and half-listened to the birds accompanying the clock radio. She had been gone for one day, but everything was different. Los Angeles was largely quiet again. The news was largely vapid again. Carl was in a jar; she no longer knew if she had a job; and she felt like the victor in some sort of perverse scavenger hunt.

She got up, put on a bathrobe and a pot of coffee, and called Reggie Salt.

"You're swift, Gigi." In the background, someone shouted for help. Reggie said, "Hold on," and barked *give him a hand before the fucking thing falls over.*

"Cleanup," he said as he came back on. "All sorts of junk fell off the Watts Towers, and they're putting it all into bags so they can glue it back."

"There was an aftershock this morning," she said. "I felt it in the bathroom."

"Every single time, more shit falls off, and they have to run back to the van for more bags. These guys aren't even city workers; they're neighborhood volunteers. It's like I'm running a summer camp. Oh shit."

A loud clang.

"Is everything okay?" she asked.

"Did you have a question, Gigi?"

She told him about the trip, omitting the part about Fajardo's bad romance. At first she thought Reggie wasn't listening—he kept putting her on hold—but as she finished, he said, "Jesus, what a winner. He put a move on you, I bet, right?"

"No," she said, "but I'd prefer not to have to go down there again."

"You don't."

"I expected to bring back a body."

"I think you got a better deal. Imagine lugging him back in the trunk."

"Cremating him without permission sounds illegal to me."

"Not for the Mexicans," he said. "In fact, it sounds totally in line with what I'd expect. You don't know what kinda procedural quagmire it is down there."

"It's not a quagmire, it's one guy who happens to be an incompetent jerk."

"Don't get mad at *me*," he said. "They're *your* people."

That was one of the things she could never stand about Reggie: the way he felt that because he was black—and had been married to her—he could spit out whatever slur sprung to mind. Like the way he showed up late to everything and said it was on time if you counted in *colored people's time*.

"I'm never late," she'd said to him once. "My history teacher in high school was the world's most chronically late person, and she was Jewish."

"Okay then. Minority people's time."

She had cited his Korean partner, obsessed with punctuality.

"Well then what do *you* want to call it?"

"How bout we call it 'late people's time'?"

By now she'd learned to ignore it. She didn't live with him anymore, and she no longer took it seriously. She said, "They're my people, Reggie. That's right."

THREE DAYS LATER, he drove her to the estate lawyer. She was glad to get out of the house. The urn had been chiding her, wagging its finger every time she passed. At first she kept it in the bedroom, going behind the closet door to undress. Tiring quickly of feeling so chaste, she moved the ashes out into the living room—atop the TV, making it impossible for her to watch *Jeopardy.*

They took Coldwater Canyon to Van Nuys, where the lawyer recommended by Wes Katz kept an office in a building full of low-rent dentists and porn production companies.

"Is this guy for real?" Reggie asked. They were standing in the lobby, waiting for the elevator. He had his finger on the wall-mounted directory. Gloria clutched the urn, which was wrapped in a Ralph's bag.

"I think so."

"Whirlee and Whirlee." He snorted. "It's like a Disneyland ride."

The Whirlee brothers divided their practice. The younger brother worked mornings; the elder afternoons. Since Gloria had scheduled for after lunch, she and Reggie would meet with Steffords.

While they waited, Gloria tried to read *Newsweek.* Reggie kept muttering.

"Steffords Whirlee? What kind of fucking name is that?" She shushed him.

"We're having an interview for clown college."

"Shut up, Reggie."

Steffords Whirlee turned out to be a soporific ectomorph with buck teeth. The lighting in his office was poor, so that at first Gloria didn't notice his comb-over. Which, she surmised, was the idea.

Through the window, she could see across Victory Boulevard into a diner full of lunching starlets, their cleavage hanging in their cottage cheese. Ponytailed men sat across from them, growing apoplectic via wireless networks.

"Wes said he was a good man," Whirlee drawled.

Tennessee? He didn't look like a displaced Southerner; he had the aesthetic of an authentic Van Nuyser. But she supposed that happened to everyone who came out here: your heritage curdled and you got a tan.

"I'm very sorry for your loss," he added.

Everyone kept making it sound as though she'd misplaced her keys.

"Thank you," she said, laying out the death certificate.

Whirlee looked perplexed as he perused it. Before he could say anything, Gloria took the urn out of the shopping bag and put it on his desk.

Whirlee shrank into his chair. "What's that."

"They cremated him before I arrived," she explained.

Turning green, Whirlee pushed away from the desk. "That's really not necessary," he said.

Snickering, Reggie took the urn from the room.

"I'm sorry," Whirlee said to Gloria. "That's a particular sensitivity of mine."

"Ashes?"

"Death," he said. "I have a devastating fear of it."

"You're an estate lawyer," she said.

"My psychiatrist in college thought it might be a good conquering strategy."

"Has it worked?" she asked.

"Not in the slightest." He picked up the death certificate. "This is all you have."

"I know—" she began, but stopped as Reggie reentered.

"I put it by the magazine rack," he said. "We'll get it on the way out."

"Make sure you do," said Whirlee.

Gloria said, "That was all the Mexican police gave me." She showed him the telltale silver crucifix, and gave the thirty-second summary of her southward jaunt. As she talked, Whirlee jotted notes on a piece of hotel stationery.

"Did you contact the next of kin?"

"I tried. I've been calling around for a week."

"And?"

"If there are any, I can't find them. I've called every single client we had. I talked to all our people at the warehouse. I've looked through the office. I went to his house and turned that over. I worked for Carl Perreira for close to ten years, and I never heard him talk about family. He never got a call from anyone except business."

"Doesn't that strike you as strange?" asked Whirlee.

"Of course," she said, "but I got used to it. I didn't see a reason to pester him about it."

"And he didn't have a will?"

"Not that I know of. And not that Wes Katz seemed to know of."

"Maybe there's family he doesn't talk to," said Reggie.

"The law provides a protocol for the distribution of assets," said Whirlee. "There's a set pattern, and whoever they can find from that list is the first heir, or else the money goes into a state fund."

"So what do I do?" she asked.

Whirlee gave her a funny look. "You? You don't do anything."

"Why not."

"Your job is over. Not that you had a job to begin with. You'll turn it over to the authorities. If they decide to accept this"—he waved the death certificate—"and that's a big if—then the machine gets in gear."

"I spoke to the cops before I went to Mexico," she said. "They weren't interested."

Whirlee picked at his teeth, found what he was looking for, swallowed. "Not them. The court. Cases where the decedent is intestate and no next of kin can be found are the responsibility of the public administrator's office."

"What about the business?"

"Sold at auction."

Gloria thought a moment. "I'd like to be involved," she said.

"In what."

"His . . . last wishes."

"That's noble, but I'm afraid it's not really up to you. The public administrator's not going to give it up that fast, because they get a cut of the estate. The city attorney's office takes a cut, too. . . . Everyone does. Are you mentioned in a will?"

"I don't think so," she said.

"Then there's nothing for you to stand on, legally."

"I'm responsible for the business," she said. "He left me in charge. I have a note."

"Saying what."

"'Take care of things when I'm gone.'"

Whirlee stroked his tie. "'Take care of things while I'm gone.'"

"'When.'"

"'Take care of things when I'm gone.'"

She nodded.

"Well," said Whirlee, "unless there's witnesses to it, it's not a valid will, I can tell you that right now."

"I don't want money," she said.

"Then what are you asking for?"

She paused, thinking, that's a good question. She was asking for . . . for the right to cling to Carl's remains as long as possible?

"I just want to be involved," she said quietly.

Pause.

"I'll tell you what," Whirlee said. "I have a friend who's a probate judge. He's old, kind of semiretired. He has a lot of free time and he likes to talk. Let me give him a call and see what he says. Does that sound all right?"

Gloria nodded. "Thank you."

Whirlee shook his head. "Why anyone would *want* to get themselves involved in probate is beyond me. It's not exactly a bucket of fun."

As Gloria and Reggie waited for the elevator, Whirlee's receptionist came out with the urn at arm's length.

"You don't want to forget this," she said.

"No," said Gloria, tucking it at her side.

"Mr. Whirlee won't need to see this again."

"He didn't need to see it the first time," said Reggie.

ELEVEN

"Pardon my *schvitz*," said the judge, "but unless I slip in a game before noon it's impossible to get a court."

He drew his wristband across his forehead and flapped his robe. He was built like a cauldron: short, abdominous, and terrifying in a white V-neck undershirt and wool slacks. He paced around, fanning himself with the Calendar section. "Son of a bitch gave me a hard time, three sets instead of two. Usually it's one-two. Not today. Oh no. I was playing easy on him, my mistake. I can't help it. You beat a man into the ground every day for six years, eventually you start to feel bad for him. He's a terrible player. Terrible. He serves like a *feigelah*. *My* serve gets stronger every week. You wouldn't believe it, but it does."

"I'm sure, judge," said Whirlee.

"No," said Judge Kaplowitz, "you don't believe. I can see the young lady shaking her head. Isn't that right, young lady?"

"I believe you, Your Honor."

"How old are you, young lady?"

"Thirty-six."

The judge shook his head. "Younger all the time, they get. . . ." He kicked his racket out of the way and plopped into his chair, using sweat to plaster his white hair to his scalp. His feet didn't touch the ground.

"I remember when I was thirty-six," said the judge. "You know what year that was, young lady?"

"No, Your Honor."

"Nineteen fifty-four. Were you even born then?"

"No."

The judge winked at her. "I know that, I can add. . . ." He rummaged through his desk. "So how's by you, Steve?"

"I'm doing well, judge."

"You want a rematch?"

"That's kind of you to offer," said Whirlee, "but I think I'd better not."

"The last time we played you didn't win a point."

"That's right, I didn't."

"Don't worry about it, Steve, I still have respect for you as a man." The judge found the object of his hunt: an inhaler. He took two hits and held his breath for a long thirty seconds.

"*Bwhewww* . . . Stuff tastes like garbage. But," he said, "it's better than dying."

"I'm sure it is," said Gloria.

The judge looked at her as though he hadn't expected an answer. "Yes," he said, "yes, young lady, it is. You get to be my age, you can appreciate the reality of death. Not that there's anything wrong with me, of course. But my friends . . . ? Pssh. The gentleman I play tennis with, the one with the *feigelah* serve, he's forty-nine. Last year we made it to the semifinals in the club doubles tournament. Everyone came to watch us play, because we were the oldest pair to make it that far. Not because of him; he was average. But *my* age made us the oldest. My granddaughter came to cheer me on with a sign that said *Kill 'em Kaplowitz.*"

He hopped down out of his chair and seized the racket. "I served," he said, going through the motion, "because he serves like nothing. And there, on the first volley, with everyone watching including my granddaughter, this guy, you know what he does?" The judge frowned. "Son of a bitch says time out. Why is he taking a time out? Because he's having a heart attack." The judge whacked the carpet with the racket and made a fist. "I could've kicked him. If he hadn't been on the stretcher I would've."

"Did you finish the game?" Gloria asked.

"Did I finish the game, no, of course not. You can't play doubles alone. I tried to get another partner, but they said since we registered together, we were both eliminated. I appealed and appealed but they wouldn't hear a word. . . ."

He shook his head. "You want to know the real story, we won three years in a row before that, and they got sick of putting Chester Kaplowitz's name up on the wall in the locker room. So they wouldn't let me find another partner, even though my granddaughter volunteered to fill in. Son of a bitch. I could've won *alone.*"

"It's good to hear that he's back on the court," said Whirlee.

"Oh, he made a full recovery," said the judge. "I wasn't going to let him get away with anything less."

"I hope you're not playing too hard on him," said Gloria.

"Anything's too hard for him," said the judge. "Look at him." He grabbed a picture frame and thrust it toward her. "Look at him, you can see what kind of serve he's got, just looking at his arm."

Gloria was confused. "This is him?"

"At eighteen months," said the judge. "Don't tell me he looks like me. Everybody says that."

"This is your son," Gloria said.

"With that serve, sometimes I think he's my daughter."

"You gave your son a heart attack?"

"Gave him? I gave him nothing. He gave it to himself." The judge snatched the picture back. "My wife God-rest-her-soul loved this picture. She made me keep it on the desk even though I told her, 'Dotty, I don't like it, every time I see it, it reminds me what a bad serve he's got.' But she liked it there, so out of respect for her . . ." He scaled his chair and set himself aright. "My granddaughter, on the other hand, she has a tremendous serve. Like *three* men. It skips a generation."

He put the frame facedown on the desk. "Enough about him, let's talk about this." He opened up a file and took out the photocopy of the death certificate Whirlee had sent. He unfolded a pair of reading glasses, his lips moving as he went over a handwritten sheet of notes. "This gentleman is deceased, Mr. Carl Perreira." The judge looked at Gloria. "And nobody cares except you. Does that approximate the truth?"

"Yes," she said.

"A-huhm." Kaplowitz took out a lapis lazuli fountain

pen, dried his dripping forehead with a tissue. "You retrieved the gentleman's remains?"

"I went to Mexico and got them."

The judge whistled. "That's a hell of a trek."

"Yes, Your Honor. It was."

"You must like to drive."

"I hate it," she said.

"Then you must be very generous, willing to go all the way down there."

Gloria shrugged.

The judge said, "And this is what they gave you. A death certificate that came out of a cereal box and a necklace. This is his necklace?"

"I'm fairly sure it is," she said.

The judge cocked an eyebrow at her. "Would you *swear* on it?"

Gloria colored. "I—yes. Right now?"

"I'm teasing you, young lady. You don't have to swear to anything." He winked again and resumed his business face. "You came back here and contacted Mr. Whirlee."

"Yes."

"Well," said the judge, "that was your first mistake. This man isn't an attorney. He isn't even a man. Are you, Steve?"

"I guess not, judge."

"Steve," Kaplowitz said to Gloria, "I've known since he was a little baby. His father was my friend. A genuine Southern Gentleman, and the only *goy* who would talk to me at the Del Rio. We sued and they had to let us in. But they didn't have to *talk* to us. But your father did, isn't that right, Steve?"

"That's right."

"Which has turned out to be awfully convenient for you," said the judge. He pointed the pen at Gloria. "Not to mention you."

"I know," she said.

"I'm interested in why you asked to see me. If Mr. Whirlee were a real attorney he might have told you that there's nothing I can do for you. Did he tell you that?"

"He did, Your Honor."

"Aha," said the judge. He shook a finger at Whirlee. "There you go again, pretending you're an attorney. Well, Ms. Mendez, your counsel has told you the truth. Mr. Perreira's case is the responsibility of the state, if the state chooses to accept it. But you're here anyway."

"Yes."

"You want to ask me questions."

"In a way, Your Honor."

"What kind of in-a-way questions are you asking?"

"I want to help," she said.

The judge put down his pen. "The probate court system is self-sustaining, Ms. Mendez. It doesn't require any help."

"I know that," she said. "But I thought if there's some way for me to stay . . ."

Pause.

"To stay what?"

"Close. To the case."

The judge arched an eyebrow. "You want money?"

"No, Your Honor. I care about Carl and I feel like I'm abandoning him if I let him fall into the system, with nobody to look out for his interests."

"He doesn't have any interests, Ms. Mendez. He's deceased."

Gloria said nothing.

"You want a souvenir from his house?" asked the judge.

"No."

"What then?"

She gave the judge a hard stare. "I've taken care of him for ten years."

Pause.

Kaplowitz folded back the death certificate. Beneath it was a photocopy of the handwritten note Carl had left. "'Take care of things when I'm gone,'" he read. "This is the last written communication you have from him."

"Yes."

"I assume this refers to his business, Ms. Mendez."

She nodded.

"It's not some sort of suicide note."

She recoiled a little. "No, Your Honor."

"You're appalled by that suggestion?"

"He wouldn't have done that."

"People can surprise you, Ms. Mendez." The judge put down the note. "But I'll tell you something: I believe you. If you tell me you don't think it was a suicide, I'm inclined to take you at your word."

"Thank you, judge," said Whirlee.

"I'm not talking to you, Steve." Kaplowitz's glasses had crept toward the edge of his nose; he pushed them back. To Gloria: "You were close with the deceased."

She said, "We had a good relationship."

The judge nodded at her, and she was sure he was

kneading some sort of obscene meaning into her words. She wanted to say *You don't understand; it wasn't like that.*

"Did he ever promise you anything after he died?"

"We never talked about it."

"Your relationship was purely platonic."

". . . yes."

He appraised her with what appeared to her a benevolent intelligence.

"You miss him a lot," he said.

"We were very close."

The judge was silent for a while. Then he said, "Probate court is a court of equity. Do you know what that means?"

"No."

"It means that the rulings are supposed to reflect not only what's right, but what's fair." He picked up the note. "This doesn't give you any rights, Ms. Mendez, you understand?"

"Yes."

"Your claim is that you've been looking out for Mr. Perreira's best interests, and that you're the person in this world most capable of doing that. Is that what you think?"

"I know so, Your Honor."

"You *know* so," said the judge. "But that still doesn't entitle you to much, and I would be lying if I told you that there was a single jurist in this city who would award you the right to administer Mr. Perreira's estate."

He got up and kicked the tennis racket up into his hands, and began swinging in slo-mo. He looked less comical now, almost delicate. The skin around his wrists was translucent, revealing able veins.

"All the same, it seems pretty unfair to tell you to take a hike. I get the impression—Steve? Do me a favor and give me a minute alone with Ms. Mendez."

Whirlee gave Gloria a look as he exited.

The judge waited until the door had closed to say, "You were in love with Mr. Perreira, Ms. Mendez, is that right?"

She said nothing; the judge seemed to approve.

"All right," he said, "we'll leave it at that."

She started to speak but the judge cut her off: "The court is obliged to appoint an administrator for the estate from the next of kin. If there's no next of kin—as you're telling me—then it's the public administrator. If for some reason the public administrator couldn't take the case, then the court would appoint creditors to administer parts of the estate. If there's no creditors, then the court can appoint any other person." Kaplowitz pointed at her. "That's who you are, Ms. Mendez. You're any other person."

She nodded. Legal code had a way of making a person feel small.

"But if you're that eager to get your hands dirty, then maybe we can give you something to do. Something symbolic. You come to the hearing. You and I will have a talk with the person in charge of the case, and we'll see if we can convince them to appoint you . . . I don't know, what'll we call it. A special consultant. That sounds good to me. How about you?"

She nodded.

The judge went on: "In addition, the administrator of the estate has fiduciary duties. You know what that means?" Without waiting for an answer, he said, "It means that someone's got to be responsible for preserving Mr. Perreira's business while everything gets taken care of, until they can arrange for it to be sold. You claim to know Mr. Perreira's affairs better than anyone, so maybe you can best fulfill that duty. Again, we have to wait and see what the people in charge say.

"I want to make one thing clear: unless there's a will that says so, you're not going to get a penny out of this. But if it'll make you feel better—"

She said, "It will."

After a beat, he said, "It must hurt like hell."

"Yes."

The judge's face wrinkled like a pillow. He drew his wristband across his forehead once more, and Gloria noticed its embroidery: Amherst College.

He saw her reading it and said, "My granddaughter." He opened his desk and took out an Amherst pennant, drawing his fingers across the seal. "She was valedictorian of her high-school class. It's a special place, young lady; they took just nineteen women from California this year."

Gloria said she must be a smart girl.

"Oh yes, very smart . . . valedictorian. Editor of the school paper, director of the play. She worked at a homeless shelter. Feeding those people. The girl is top-notch in every regard. She told me, 'Grampa, I think I might be interested in law.' 'Oh really, Rebecca. Why's that?' She wants to be on the California Supreme Court." The judge cackled. "I told her that's no place for a lady."

"Did she appreciate that?"

"I said, 'You should be on the *United States* Supreme

Court. California, that's bupkus." He used the racket to stretch out his triceps. "Aim high."

"I'm sure she'll go far," said Gloria.

"Goddamn right." The judge trotted over to the couch, propped up one of his potato legs, and attacked the hamstring with a ferocity that made Gloria cringe. "She takes after her mother," he said. He dropped one leg and swung the other up. "Her mother was a terrific gal," he said wistfully.

Gloria didn't ask whether she was dead or divorced out of the family. The judge was in his own head, talking to his knee and grunting as he leaned in.

"You . . . remind . . . me . . . *of her*," he said. Upon release, his foot walloped the floor as though he was a spring-loaded toy. He swiveled his ankles and bobbed on his toes.

Gloria stood in place, unsure if she was supposed to answer him, or thank him, or push away the comparison with modesty. She was about to offer words indistinct when the judge—facing away from her, working on his quads—preempted her by saying, "This is a very unusual circumstance, Ms. Mendez."

"I appreciate it, Your Honor."

He said, "Do you know how old I am?"

"Yes, Your Honor. You're eighty-five."

"Very good," he said. "You know how long I've had this job?"

"No, Your Honor."

"Forty-seven years. I was here before most of these attorneys were born. I think they expected me to die a lot sooner than this, or else they wouldn't've given me the position to begin with. I'm sure that most people would tell you what Steve told you: according to the letter of the law, there's not much the court can do for you."

He stretched up, then straightened. "But I'm not the letter of the law. That's the advantage of being as old as me. Nobody argues."

TWELVE

The waiting began, and the crying came with it.

She knew she needed to start hunting for a new employer, but she couldn't bring herself to do it. It was less than pressing: Carl had paid her overgenerously, her rent was stabilized, and since the divorce, she'd had few expenses beyond the basics. It came as a relief to her when she calculated that she had sufficient savings to live off of for eight or nine months. A job would happen as soon as she felt put-together enough to present at an interview, but that wouldn't happen for—

Not yet, anyhow.

Instead, she continued to put in a full day's work. Without Carl's banter to distract her, she finished by one or two in the afternoon. Too guilty to leave early, she burned the rest of the day, staring idly out the window at the alley where Buck had lived.

She imagined him and Carl together in heaven, chatting about the weather and Buck's big plans for fortune. *I figured it out: I'm going to make shoes that grow along with your*

feet. You buy them once for your baby and then he never needs
shoes no more for the rest of his life.

Sounds like a good idea.

I'm still working out the kinks.

She answered the phone as though business was usual. If
the caller asked to speak to Carl, she explained his death in
the most sterile terms. Everyone was sad to hear it;
everyone was sorry for her loss. Retailers they'd dealt with
for years wanted to know what it meant for Caperco. (She
didn't know.) Manufacturers they had already contracted
from told her that it was too late to stop shipment on those
magic flower tricks, those ice cubes with spiders, those four
hundred cases of plastic rats. (She said thank you and hung
up.)

She found any excuse to call up Barb, or Whirlee, or
Reggie, or the public administrator, a blunt woman named
Maxine Gonzaga. They had placed a death notice in the
paper; so far, nobody had responded.

Two weeks after returning from Mexico, Gloria started
going to Carl's house. He'd left the keys with her, as he did
before every vacation. It, like her apartment, had been
nearly untouched by the earthquake. A few things needed
to be righted, and this she did. She got the place back into
what she remembered as its original state.

Once that was done, there wasn't any reason for her to
be there, but she kept coming. She wanted to spend her
afternoons and evenings surrounded by his minutiae.

Flour jars and toothpicks and paperclips and dust mites.
A vacuum cleaner without a hose. A package of blank VHS
tapes, encased in plastic like plant cells under the

microscope. Items stating his absence; his absence singing her loneliness. To animate his memory, she would move stuff around: rearrange the mugs on their hooks; unmake the bed and make it again; pour handsoap down the drain. Open a drawer and leave it there (*no, he was too careful for that; close it*). Take out the empty trash bag and replace it with another.

She hadn't spent much time there before. A neat, quaint stucco on Saturn, east of Robertson, the house had two bedrooms. In the master, a crucifix was nailed to the closet door. A dark oak dresser with a faux-marble top matched the nightstand. Like her, he had no mirror. The smaller bedroom had a queen with sheets so tight that she doubted it had ever been used.

In the living room, she put the television back on its stand. She cleared a pile of newspapers from the nubby cream sofa, and set the purple urn by a full but fishless tank bubbling its solipsism.

The back room had evolved into storage for leftover work samples. Masks, gags, that horrendous goo: all stuffed into cardboard boxes stacked to the ceiling. The pile swooped up and away from you, its tan, cubic topography suggesting a mountainside broken down digitally. Either sheer weight or dumb luck had kept it from toppling over during the quake. She almost wished it had; then she would've had an excuse to throw it all out.

In one of the boxes, she found a dozen bottles of fake blood. Caperco had once supplied effects for a Z-grade horror movie called *Evil Flesh Orgy of the Damned*. After that, Carl had taken to saying, "I've done some work for the film industry," which made her laugh. Occasionally he would stomp into her office and holler, "Get Spielberg on the phone! Pronto!"

Toothbrush, razor, comb, soap, shampoo, washcloth, towel: the bathroom.

The kitchen had an ugly table, and two ugly chairs.

Otherwise, there were few material enthusiasms. His wardrobe consisted of twenty pairs of socks, twenty pairs of plain broadcloth boxer shorts, seven pairs of pants, and fifteen solid-color button-down shirts. A handful of T-shirts and drawstring shorts for when he went power-walking. A trio of sweaters for the thirty days a year that LA pretended to have seasons. A hideous ski jacket that she made fun of, so much so that he'd taken to leaving it in the car before coming in to the office.

She knew that he read a lot—he had a penchant for bad cowboy novels and World War II-era spy stories—but he had always made it a point of pride that he still used his library card. The only books she found, in fact, were a well-worn Bible and the Houdini biography she had bought for his birthday three years ago, stacked one atop the other on the dining-nook table.

That was it.

It was a modest home, a reflection of its owner. Learning its idiosyncrasies gave her the sense—long held in abeyance—that she had consummated her relationship with him. It wasn't sexual; it was about the quotidian rituals comprising permanence between two people. She mastered the layout of the kitchen and felt as though they had eaten breakfast together. She memorized the flaws in the sofa's fabric and felt as though they had passed an hour in front of the TV. The house allowed her its full run, approving her mission, or at least refraining from judgment.

When these tasks drained her, she would lie down for ten or twenty minutes. At first she tried the sofa, but it was narrow and her arm had no place to go, ending up pinned beneath her and giving her the tinglies. The second bedroom had the queen bed, but she hated to disturb its tautness.

It hurt no one, she supposed, to nap in his bed.

Getting under the blankets seemed like too profound a familiarity, so she would lay on top, catching whiffs of him from the pillowcase. As the days went on—she was a month past the hearing, almost three past his death—the smell got stronger, as though the parts of him locked up in the cloth were being released. As some point, the smell would peak and taper off, before ceasing entirely and leaving one fewer physical trace of Carl Perreira in the world.

Eventually, she started napping under the blankets.

Then she started sleeping there at night.

Not that she slept. A foot-tickling, pot-clanging insomnia assailed her, one which over-the-counter sleep aids did nothing to fix. She would be plummeting into unconsciousness, about to hit bottomless bottom, when acute terror jerked her back up. Forcing herself to stay in bed made it impossible to relax; by three in the morning she would be up, groggy and angry and hurting.

Some nights she would take the Dodge to the Caperco office so she could listen to his final message.

Gloria . . . it's me . . .

REPLAY

Gloria . . . it's me . . .

REPLAY

Gloria . . . it's me . . .

She began to worry about damaging the machine. She made a microcassette copy, which she brought to Carl's house and kept on the nightstand within easy reach.

In the evenings, when his phone would ring, she would jump up, thinking it was him calling to tell her it was all a prank. But it was always a telemarketer, offering Mr. Perreira a better rate *plus* free long distance for a month if he committed to a two-year—

"He's dead," she would say, and hang up.

At first, her friends were sympathetic. But by the second or third time she mentioned Carl's death, she could see their eyes glazing over.

Over lunch, Barb finally said, "Honey, you need medication."

Gloria stopped bringing it up.

With no one to talk to, grief started to push through her surface at odd, humiliating moments. She fought to suppress the urge to explain herself to everyone she met: the checkout girl at Ralph's and the guy at the car wash and the busboy at the Persian restaurant across from the office. She wanted them to understand why she was such a space cadet despite the good weather. She walked down Santa Monica, looking contemptuously at the passersby: They Who Did Not Harbor Constant, Secret Pain.

But Barb's short patience had taught Gloria something, a lesson she'd forgotten since her mother's death: most people—even the ones who liked her—weren't interested in her misery. It was unreasonable to ask a sane adult to feel too deeply for anyone except themselves, or maybe their kids. This was LA, after all.

The judge had said it himself. She was the only one. For the second time in her life, she felt the burden of being the sole mourner.

Late one night in mid-September, loneliness descended on her like a swarm of bees, striking at her jaggedly with an intense claustrophobia and shortness of breath. It was as though she had been dropped into a well. Without realizing what she was doing, she lifted the receiver and pressed keys at random. A man answered with a discombobulated grunt, and Gloria, mortified, hung up.

Trailing her fingers along the wall—she needed to feel something solid and vertical—she wandered into the nook and opened the Bible. She'd looked at it before. In several sections (Genesis 4; Numbers 35; the Gospels on the temptation in the wilderness) a gray finger-smudge marred the margin, evidence of overuse.

Since sleep was what she was after, she decided to skim the most stultifying stuff she could recall from Sunday-morning classes with Mamá at the Church of the Immaculate Sacrifice. She leafed to First Chronicles and read its opening verses.

Adam Seth Enosh
Kenan Mahalalel Jared
Enoch Methusaleh Lamech Noah

Immediately she yawned and moved with grateful torpor to the bedroom. She stripped and slid between the sheets, breathing in the cloud of essence-of-Carl that rose around her head.

The phone rang.

"Hello?" she asked.

"Did you call me?"

Pause.

"Hello? Did you call me?"

"Yes," she said. "I'm so sorry."

"Do you have any idea what time it is?"

She looked at the alarm clock.

4:47 A.M.

"I'm so sorry," she said.

"Don't ever fucking ca—hang on, I'm—"

She started to replace the receiver when a woman came on.

"Hello, who is this?"

Gloria hesitated before saying, "I'm sorry."

"Who is this?"

"I'm sorry. My name is Gloria. I'm sorry."

Shit. Why'd you do that?

"Gloria who? Do we know you?"

"No. I'm sorry, I—"

"You sound upset," the woman said. "Are you okay?"

"No," Gloria said, feeling herself growing hot. "Not really."

It's a woman the woman was saying.

I don't give a fuck if it's the Pope the man replied.

"I'm sorry to bother you—"

I don't give a fuck if it's the ghost of Abraham Lincoln.

"Hang on, I'm going to go in the hallway so my husband can sleep. . . ."

Gloria shook her head, no, no, no; go back to bed, go back and wonder what's wrong with me, don't ask me to explain it to you. Because I will.

"Look," said Gloria, "I'm sorry—"

"Stop apologizing. I'm a graduate student. In social work. What's wrong?"

"I'm—look, this is totally ridiculous. Please apologize to your husband for me."

"He's *fine*. He can fall back asleep like nothing. You sound so sad; please tell me what happened."

Pause.

"My boss," Gloria said.

"Yes?"

"He died."

"Oh," the woman said. "I'm sorry to hear that."

"It's okay."

"Was he . . . sick?"

"No."

"Were you close?"

"Yes."

"I'm very sorry to hear it."

"Thank you."

"Do you want to talk about it? I can give you my work number."

Gloria said, "It's nice of you to stay on the phone with

me like this. I think I'm going to try and get some sleep."

I'm sorry for your loss the woman was saying as Gloria depressed the hookswitch.

SHE OPENED HIS MAIL. The important items—tax papers, Social Security receipts, outstanding utility bills, letters from his mortgage broker—she set aside in a file she was collecting for Maxine Gonzaga. Mounds of paper, the last vestiges of worldly interest in Carl Perreira. It kept coming, rapacious and attention-seeking, came pouring in like flat ants through the mail slot: catalogue clothiers, preapproved credit cards with low LOW **LOW** APRs, Valu-Paks, homeopathic junkmail (*made from real shark's tooth cure impotents erection now!!!*), church notices. Charities wheedling for money.

A *lot* of charities wheedling for a *lot* of money.

Apparently, he had given to all of them at one time or another. *As in the past, your continued support will help us to provide . . .* Those writing to thank him for a recent donation managed to get in a plug for next time. *(. . . and we hope you'll continue to remember us this holiday season . . .)*

A couple of letters threw her for a loop. She would have assumed that his Catholicism precluded support for an abortion clinic, but there it was: *In our nation's current political climate of fundamentalism and intolerance, your generosity has enabled us to protect the Constitutional right of a woman to choose. . . .*

As if to counterweight this, he had also made a donation to the National Council on Abstinence Awareness.

One letter from the Cardinal McIntyre Fund of the Los Angeles Archdiocese thanked him for his extraordinary contribution. Did he know that continued giving was necessary to bolster acts of Christian kindness . . . ?

The receipt was dated the Fourth of July. He'd donated $10,000.

She hadn't known he had that much to give away. It made her wonder what he'd been doing with his money all these years.

Most of the letters came from children's causes. The Make-A-Wish Foundation. Toys for Tots. Big Brothers Big Sisters of Southern California. Some appeared addressed to him personally, as though he had been a mainstay of the organization in question. Out of curiosity, she called one of them—Beth's Room, a clinic for preschoolers with severe learning disabilities.

"That's horrible," said the director, a man with a reedy lisp, when Gloria told him about Carl's death. "That's just horrible. He was like Old Faithful. I'm so sorry to hear this. When's the funeral?"

"It hasn't been scheduled yet."

"Well, make sure and let me know," said the director. "I'd like to meet him at least once, although I wish it didn't have to be like this."

"You've never met him?"

"Mr. Perreira? Never in my life. I've never even talked to him over the phone. Isn't that weird? I knew his name from checks, but I never got to meet him. I tried calling once, to thank him personally, and he never got back to me. He never came to any of the benefits. He was like an anonymous donor, except he wasn't anonymous."

"When you called him up—when was that?"

"Maybe two years ago. I wanted to meet him, y'know? Because it's nice to put a face on a name. And now I guess I can't. How horrible . . . is there anything I can do?"

After he hung up she went to look at the ugly table, where all the thank-you letters were spread. She picked a second charity (the Crenshaw Abused Children's Center) and dialed. Bushwhacking several layers of voicemail, she ended up on the phone with the lady in charge of donor management, who introduced herself as Bette Junger.

"Of course I know Mr. Perreira," she said.

Gloria introduced herself as a friend. "I'm sorry to tell you that Carl died this July."

Bette sighed heavily. "I'm sorry for your loss."

"Thank you," Gloria said. "I was wondering if you ever met him in person."

"We've wanted to, for years, but he never answered our calls or letters. It's not like we needed to bother him; he's been a regular donor since we opened in 1989."

"He sent you checks."

"That's right, every July. This year, too. Oh, shame. It must've been right before he passed on. We got a check from him, and the same set of instructions."

"What were the instructions?"

"'Use it where it's needed most.'"

Gloria phoned a third charity. Yes, Carl was a good man, with an evident love of children. No, they had neither met nor talked. It was tragic that he had died. They were sorry for her loss. Was there anything they could do?

"No thank you," she said.

A fourth, a fifth. They all said the same thing.

She sat at the ugly table, her fingers spread across the letters as though she were extending roots to suck up Carl's largesse.

All the giving. It was his attempt at—what. He had never had kids; was this penance? She had always preferred to think that he didn't *want* kids at his age. It was easier to accept that than to accept that he'd put her off for so many years.

But here was evidence to the contrary: his checkbook bleeding openly. Part of him, at least, loved kids.

So what did that mean for her?

That he didn't love her. That he never had.

Or maybe simply that he was a sucker for a sappy letter.

Meet Roddy, an eight-year-old with an irrepressible zest for life. Just ask him about his favorite hobby: surfing. He knows the best beaches to hang ten, the best wetsuits, and the newest boards. He even does a great Brian Wilson impression.

But Roddy can't go surfing.

Roddy was born with Long QT syndrome, a congenital defect of the heart that . . .

She sat at the ugly Formica table, drinking coffee brewed from Carl's cavernous Chock full o' Nuts tin (the sole food left after she'd cleared out the cabinets) and imagining what it was like to have a child with a congenital heart defect.

First, she had to imagine what it was like to have a child.

Lately, she had been doing her best not to imagine anything. Imagination had become a mugger, leaping out at improbable moments to divest her of peace. When her mind started to wander, she would think of the accident and imagine holding him as he died. She felt an explosion, felt heat melting her skin, felt the shock of air on flesh and fascia and bone. She saw herself—with him—reduced to a cage stewing with liquid organs and an intact heart—a shared heart—that refused to blacken, despite the flames.

THIRTEEN

By her own description, Maxine Gonzaga was overworked worse than a shit collector at a dog show. She was, Gloria discerned, happy to have help. After the hearing, they had met once so Gloria could give a full accounting of Caperco's finances. They took a shine to each other; Gloria liked Gonzaga's crass wit, and Gonzaga complimented Gloria's organization.

"You wouldn't believe how clueless some people are," she said. "You're a godsend."

That was the last Gloria heard of her until a few weeks later, when Gonzaga called to share that Carl Perreira was one elusive son of a bitch. They had gone all the usual routes, and kept running into walls.

"His paper trail stops about twenty years ago," she said. "You didn't know him then?"

"No."

"Neither did anyone else. You're the oldest employee—you're the one employee who worked directly with him—and you have no idea where he came from."

Gloria said she had always assumed Carl was born in Los Angeles.

"There's no birth records. Was he from this country originally?"

"I think so," Gloria said. "But he always said his origins were in Mexico."

Gonzaga said that they were hiring a private investigator. "We do it now and again," she said resentfully, as though it punctured her pride. Would Gloria talk to him?

"If he finds anything," Gonzaga admitted, "it'll be more than what we've found."

Gloria followed her directions to a gray plaster subdivision in Santa Monica. Near an industrial park, the neighborhood was clean and beachy and high-tech; it made her feel like Last Year's Model. She pulled into a narrow parking lot fronting a rock-climbing gym, a tanning salon, another tanning salon, and a travel agency. Lush posters of Fiji and Machu Picchu beguiled her as she mounted the stairs to Fox Investigations.

Frigid contemporary prints and an austere metallic finish to the walls made the place feel like the Submarine Museum of Modern Art. She felt uneasy throughout the hour it took to explain Carl's final days to Aaron Fox, a black PI, imposing in Prada. As she spoke, he stared penetratingly at the smoky glass tabletop, plumbing his own reflection. His talk sounded disinterested to her, as though he was having a different conversation, with someone else, in another room.

But he turned out to be a good detective.

"He never went to Pepperdine."

It was early November. Fox showed her a class roster from Carl's supposed year of graduation. She rubbed the space between Perkins, Douglas, and Perrone, Walter.

"Maybe we got the year wrong," she said.

He showed her rosters from four years before and four years after.

"But he has a diploma," she said.

"Not from there, he doesn't." Fox took out the one she'd salvaged from the office and flattened it on his table.

PEPERDINE COLLEGE

"Pepperdine, two P's, is the one you're thinking of," he said. "Peperdine one P missing is a mail-order certificate that won't exactly get you into law school."

She felt foolish and miffed.

"I'm sure that was the idea," he said. "If people noticed, what good would it be as a fake-out degree?"

She found this logic compelling but ultimately unhelpful, and was equally nonplussed when Fox told her that he couldn't find a single relative, living or dead.

"I've done everything humanly possible," he said. He listed the agencies he'd talked to: the county recorders, civil court, criminal court. He had called the Federal Parole Board; the U.S. marshals; the INS, IRS, and FBI. He had resorted to brute force, scouring old phonebooks from neighboring counties. He had called hospitals and the high school listed on the Peperdine forms. Credit checks and headers were clean, and gave no information older than July 1984; the same went for online genealogical databases.

A review of Carl's phone bills for the last six months revealed that the only numbers he had called were the office and—twice—Gloria's house.

"It's as though he came from another planet," Fox said.

"There must be a—a register, or—*something* that we haven't checked," Gloria said. "He didn't come into being twenty years ago."

"Maybe he did. Was he in the witness protection program?"

"If he was, do you really think I'd know?"

"Did he want to get away from someone? An ex-wife?"

She frowned. "Not that I know of."

"People skip town if they're in legal trouble. Taxes they can't pay, debts."

"It doesn't sound like him."

"Then he was a hermit," Fox said.

She didn't like that word, but its accuracy was becoming increasingly apparent.

Fox said, "He wouldn't be the first one. I once had a guy in East LA who wanted me to surveil his place. He was sure people were trying to break in. He was nuts. Foil on the walls, that kind of thing. Why he trusted me, I don't know. He fired me after I told him nobody had come near him in a month. I did some poking around, and guess what, he's the heir to the Graciano fortune. You know them?"

She didn't.

"They make the jeans," he said. "The expensive ones. With dirt on them."

"I wouldn't know."

"Anyway, the family hadn't heard from him in five years,

since he emptied his trust fund and walked off. He changes his name, drops all his records, gets a shitty apartment, and starts sleeping on a mattress on the floor. Ordering Chinese every night. Paid for everything in cash. I later found out that he kept the whole trust, twenty mil, under his bed. Thing was half a foot off the ground." Fox shook his head. "I don't blame him for being paranoid about a burglary. Point being: If a person wants to be alone, it's not all that difficult."

It seemed to her that Carl had deliberately cut himself up and scattered the pieces broadly enough to prohibit reassembly. His insistence on privacy—which had never before seemed significant—confused and angered her. Didn't he want to make cleaning up his life easy for those who cared about him? (*Those* being *her*, she realized.)

And the blanks in his life made her paranoid about her own. Was she this dissociated? If she died, who would find her body? Who would wrap up her affairs?

Who, if anyone, would grieve?

Maxine Gonzaga had not given up hope that a relative would come forward. There were also heir hunters who located missing kin in exchange for a chunk of the estate— a quarter or more. It was possible that they would dig something up. But for the time being, Gonzaga arranged to inventory and seal Carl's house.

The Sunday following Thanksgiving, Gloria drove over to retrieve the bag of clothes she had left on his bedroom floor.

She decided to take one final look-through, to say good-bye. For all she knew, this was the last time she'd have a right to be here. She gave herself a tour, reliving invented memories: the spot on the sofa where—in her fiction— they first held hands; that time the boxes in the back room fell over; the goddamn bathroom nightlight that always burned out . . . a whole life she had never gotten to live.

It made a good story. Like the bed on the beach. She started out laughing with false nostalgia and ended up crying all over the fucking kitchen.

You have to stop this.

She was afraid of accidentally erasing the line between real and unreal.

Maybe if you wrote everything down, she thought; that would be a good way to keep them separate.

The gigantic Chock full o' Nuts can waited on the counter like a portable nuclear reactor. She lifted it. At the time of the hearing, the container had been almost full. Now it rattled with three or four cups' worth. Had she been drinking that much coffee? One explanation for her insomnia.

She peeled the lid off and took in a pleasant breath. The aroma of coffee made her think of Carl. The office was small, and for the first few hours of the workday, it smelled like Starbucks. She sucked it down all day long; he limited himself to two cups as part of his diet.

The diet.

She smiled.

While she had learned the diet's rules, the guiding principles behind them evaded her. No meat—except chicken on Sundays after church. No fish, ever; the lower on the food chain, the greater respect an animal earned. ("The weakest need the most protection," he said.) No caffeine besides the daily two cups; no alcohol; no refined sugar; grapes, but no grape juice. A lot of bare tortillas. Cranberries were a favorite; he ate them raw.

"Isn't that kind of sour?"

"That's why I like them." He would pop a few into his mouth and wince.

Part vegetarian, part Mormon, part whole foods. If the diet had a name, it could only be Carl Perreirism.

She laughed. She decided to take the can home.

On her way out, she also stopped and collected the purple urn.

HER BUILDING PLUGGED the end of a cul-de-sac in the hilly part of West Hollywood, not far from the Strip. The neighborhood had resident-only parking, which kept club-goers from hogging the curbside from midnight to five. She knew all the cars that belonged there, and immediately noticed the unfamiliar Cutlass Supreme.

It was hard to miss; it was blocking her driveway.

It reminded her of what Reggie used to do.

She left the Dodge in front of a hydrant and got out, clutching the can and the urn. She wanted to get them to safety before she got a ticket. WeHo meter maids were among the most zealous in the known world; their zesty sadism often made Gloria think that they'd be well suited to govern an inchoate African nation. She broke into a jog, squeezing her housekeys like rosaries.

She could tell that the man on her doorstep was a cop.

He might have put on a nice tie, but his shoes were still scuffed. What had once been an impressive physique had succumbed to the pressure of a desk job; as they had for Reggie, promotions in status had been closely followed by promotions in weight.

He had a serious, scholarly expression, which led her to believe that he wasn't your average LAPD investigator. Reggie always bore the faintest hint of a smirk; it drove her crazy. But this guy was sizing her up like a sniper.

He said, "Ms. Mendez?"

"You're blocking my spot," she said.

They went back out to the street.

"I'm Detective Waxbone," he said. "You have a few minutes?"

"Sure." She pointed up the block. "You can go to the lot near the restaurants. On Sunset. I'll be waiting for you inside."

He drove off, and she went back to her apartment, leaving the door open. While she waited she brewed a batch from most of the remaining Chock full o' Nuts coffee.

Waxbone came into the kitchen with his hand in his jacket, as though reaching for a gun. Instead, he withdrew an envelope, which he curved in his palm.

"Would you like—?"

"Thanks." He accepted the mug and her invitation to sit.

"How are you today?" he asked. He sounded stiff, robotic.

"Did Reggie send you here?"

Waxbone blinked, as though scanning her. "No, ma'am. Who's Reggie?"

"My ex-husband. He's a detective, too. He works West LA."

"Uh-huh," said Waxbone. He had a pad and pen out.

"I thought it might be him playing a joke. Detective Reginald L. Salt." She watched him write this down. "You want his badge number?"

He gave her a wan smile, took a hit of coffee, and set it aside. "I'm here about the Carl Perreira estate. You're help-ing sort out the decedent's finances, is that right?"

"As much as I can." She couldn't help sounding defen-sive when speaking to policemen. An artifact not of previous run-ins with the law, but of her marriage.

"Maxine was looking over Mr. Perreira's bank state-ments, and she noticed something strange about the activity on one of the accounts." He opened the envelope and handed her a bunch of stapled papers. "Those are the Caperco business accounts. You managed those, correct?"

"These all look normal to me."

"That's not the problem," he said, taking out another packet. "This is Mr. Perreira's personal checking account." He gave her the pages, embossed with an orange CalFed insignia. "Did you ever handle this account?"

"No."

"Look at the pattern." He showed her. "See?"

She saw.

Carl's balance sat at or near zero most of the time. Every few weeks, it would shoot up several thousand dollars— and then drop back to zero. This repeated itself, month after month, back to when he had first opened the account in 1985.

"Maxine got the records of his checks, and matched them against the fluctuations in the balance. What he was doing was keeping his account empty except for when he needed to pay bills. Then he would pay them all in one batch: his mortgage, his car, his phone, and so on. Whatever was left he would withdraw in cash—presumably what he used for food and gas and so on."

He took out another page. "If you add up all the money he deposited for last year, it comes to a little under forty-eight thousand dollars. That's what he filed as his income for the last year." He showed her the return. "What would you say Mr. Perreira was making, Ms. Mendez?"

"I don't know."

"More than forty-eight thousand dollars a year?"

". . . yes."

"You worked at Caperco; you know how it was doing. Business was good?"

She nodded.

"Uh-huh. Then what would you guess was his estimated income."

Carl had paid her far more than a secretary with a high-school education could expect to get, plus a bonus and benefits. More than forty-eight thousand, in fact, and enough to know that the numbers in front of her were absurdly low.

"I don't know," she said.

"Based on the company's tax returns, and the budgets you gave her, Maxine thinks it was around two or three hundred thousand dollars a year. He didn't have himself salaried, so it's not in the budget. But would you say that two or three hundred thousand sounds like a reasonable estimate?"

She said, "Yes."

"Uh-huh." Waxbone sat back and crossed his arms. "Well, he wasn't reporting that. He was living paycheck to paycheck. But if he was earning more than that . . ." He paused. "Where do you think it went?"

He looked at her with that bookish face of his. An academic face. She bet he had excelled at math. Ending up a cop—had he sold himself short? Or did he enjoy the work? He seemed to want to squeeze her and produce a potable juice-of-confession.

She shook her head and said, "I really don't know."

"Did Mr. Perreira have an offshore account?"

"I don't know."

"Uh-huh. Did he give money away?"

"He gave a lot to charity," she said.

"We know about that," Waxbone replied. "Maxine matched the checks against the account activity. Late June or early July—going back for twenty years—the account spikes. There's one very large deposit, back in February 1991, corresponding to the payment for his Honda, which he bought outright, in cash. This past July he put in more than twenty thousand dollars, and then made a flurry of donations. So when major expenses arose, he had the money to make them. But the rest of the time he must've been sticking it somewhere else, like he was afraid of keeping money under his name."

She noticed him staring at her but resisted the urge to say anything.

"Did Mr. Perreira ever give you large sums of money?" he asked.

"No."

"Either to hold, or as a gift."

"No," she said. "He wrote my paycheck and that was it."

"This doesn't have any legal implications for you," he said, and she understood that he was lying.

She said, "Then why are you asking me?"

"You were intimately acquainted with his affairs."

"You can't prosecute him for back taxes," she said. "He's dead."

"If the *estate* owes back taxes then we have to account for that," he said. "Is there a reason you're getting so upset?"

She started to retort but held back. "Carl and I were close. It's hard for me to imagine him hiding money somewhere."

"Is there someone else he might have been giving money to?"

"I don't think so."

Waxbone nodded. He was sizing her up again.

"Would you like some more coffee?" she asked.

He smiled. "Still working on this one."

She got up and poured herself half a cup.

"Reggie Salt," Waxbone said. "West LA, huh?"

"Except during times of civic unrest," she said. "Then they send him to tame the masses in Watts." She glanced at him, and she could see the machinery behind his skull: *joke input; joke error;* DELETE JOKE.

He said, "I work downtown. I work for the courts."

"You're a DA's investigator."

"Not exactly . . ." Before she could ask another question he said, "Joseph C. Gerusha."

She said, "Pardon me?"

"Do you know anyone named Joseph C. Gerusha?"

"No."

Waxbone nodded. "Because Carl Perreira knew him."

"Who's Joseph—what is it?"

"Joseph C. Gerusha."

"What kind of name is that?" she asked.

"The one on Carl Perreira's mortgage," said Waxbone. Pause.

She said, "What?"

"He's the cosigner on Mr. Perreira's mortgage."

"Who is he?"

"I have no idea, ma'am. We thought maybe you'd know. You've never met anyone by that name? Mr. Perreira never mentioned him to you?"

"No," she said. Her head began to spin. "Why didn't anyone notice this before?"

"Maxine's been slogging through the paperwork," he said. "There's a lot of it. What did Mr. Perreira do before he worked in toys?"

"I don't know," she said.

"Did he have a partner, maybe a business partner?"

"We weren't acquainted back then. He never talked about doing anything else. He was running the company by himself, I think. He told me I was the first person he ever hired, because I was the one person he could stand to be in a room with eight hours a day." She paused for breath, and lifted the mug to her lips. She didn't remember drinking, but it was empty.

"Uh-huh. What about loans?" Waxbone asked. "Debts."

"What sort of debts?"

"Say, business ventures that fell through."

"Not that I know of."

"Did he use drugs or alcohol?"

"Never in his life." She heard herself getting angry again. "And what does that have to do with Joseph Gewhatever-his-name-is?"

"I'm just asking, Ms. Mendez. Did he gamble?"

"I once bought a lottery ticket. He called me a sucker for a month."

"Uh-huh." Waxbone nodded. "So he didn't gamble."

"No."

He kept nodding for a long time, as though a program had short-circuited. Then, without warning, he was on his feet.

"If you remember anything," he said, "feel free to give me a call." He left a card on the kitchen table. "Thank you for the coffee," he said, flashing a token smile and letting himself out.

She stayed against the counter, gripping the mug.

She felt even more wound up than she had when Fox had showed her the bogus diploma. Her understanding of Carl had now developed two large holes, and for that she wasn't sure whether to blame him or herself.

Or why did it require blame? Why couldn't she resign herself to the fact that she had not, in fact, known him inside and out?

Because I *did* know him, she thought.

The last thing she needed was more coffee, but she had to occupy her hands. She ripped open the Chock full o' Nuts can and reached inside for the scoop. The supply was running low; might as well brew all of it.

She opened the coffeemaker and tilted the can, thumping it like a street musician. She held it up to make sure she'd gotten it all, and saw that the bottom of the can had come loose.

It had . . . tilted a little.

Or—swiveled.

The bottom didn't fit.

A disc cut to the shape of the can, turned ever so slightly—knocked free by her pounding—with space around its edges. A few coffee grounds fell into the gap.

She slipped a fingernail under the edge of the disc and tried to pry it up, but it had been tamped down and she broke her nail. Cursing, she wrapped her finger in a paper towel and got out a fork. The disc came free and she saw beneath it a bundle of papers, folded and bound by a rubber band.

She put the can down.

It wasn't money. That much she could tell. She wanted to touch it, but then again, she didn't want to touch it, not at all.

So she poured it out on the floor. Grounds scattered across her spotless tiles, and out fell the clutch of papers, hitting the vinyl like a dead bird.

She picked it up and jounced it. It felt like nothing, air on air. If it was this light, she thought, it couldn't be anything important. As though secrets had mass and gravity.

She chid herself for being afraid of a bunch of papers. From a coffee can.

She unwrapped them.

They were photocopies of financial statements: from an investment bank she'd never heard of, sent to an address she'd never heard of. Joseph Charles Gerusha had his Malle-Vurdham Securities account information sent somewhere in Culver City.

She said, "Oh my God."

Joseph Gerusha's accounts—as of the previous October—totaled ten million six hundred nine thousand four hundred fifty-eight dollars and thirty-three cents.

FOURTEEN

It didn't take much deliberation. She didn't like Waxbone, and she didn't call him before going over to the address listed on the statements, which turned out to be the United States Postal Service's Culver City North office.

Good parking luck gave Gloria unreasonable optimism. She went inside and asked for the manager. While she waited, she watched the post-lunch queue—nine bodies strong—inch along toward the single open register, staffed by a Latina woman about Gloria's age. There were five other registers, each bearing a plastic placard:

STATION CLOSED
PLEASE USE NEXT AVAILABLE STATION

The customer at the counter shook blond out of her eyes as she moisturized her lips. The clerk was weighing and stamping a two-foot pile of manila envelopes. Headshots, Gloria guessed.

The actress left, and the clerk tapped a countertop bell to summon the cavalry, an angular Vietnamese clerk in a loose shirt that would have been formfitting on any other human. The whole line shuddered with gratitude.

As soon as he arrived, however, the first clerk set out a placard—

STATION CLOSED
PLEASE USE NEXT AVAILABLE STATION

—and left.

"What the *fuck*," said a balding man in sharp glen plaid. He shifted a box of yellow plastic bottles to his other arm. "What the fuck is *that*."

By the time a geeky kid with a Bill Gates haircut came to fetch Gloria, the line had advanced two places. The guy in the plaid suit was bouncing angrily from foot to foot. Gloria gave the line a sympathetic glance as she maneuvered behind the counter into the back room, through a clogged maze of boxes and carts, to a door marked V. BIDDLE.

V stood for Vera. She was gelatinous and short of breath; her turquoise eyeshadow and rhinestoned spectacles evoked a 1950s sitcom mother writ large. She manipulated a book of matches with her well-marbled digits.

"No, I'm not going to tell you that," she said happily

when Gloria asked for information about Joseph Gerusha.

"But—"

"There are rules," Vera said. She lit a cigar, puffed, and tapped ashes on a desktop sign that said NO SMOKING. "We have privacy *issues*."

"Someone's died," said Gloria.

"Was it Mr. *Gerusha* who died?"

"Well, no—"

"Then sorry." Vera stoppered her mouth with the cigar and plunged her hand across the table. "Nice to meet you. Have a nice day. See yourself out. Bye now."

Back in the main room, the man in the suit was yelling at the Vietnamese clerk.

"What the fuck is your *problem*?"

An old lady in line mumbled, "Some people."

Gloria didn't know who she meant: clerk or customer. It could have been either. The clerk was moving at the speed of feta cheese, failing to be authoritative in mutilated English. The stress made his poor grammar worse, as the suit loudly demanded to know why he couldn't ship twenty-four containers of nail polish remover to Connecticut.

"Is flammable," said the clerk.

"It's not flammable, it's *cosmetic*," said the suit. "They don't carry this fucking brand back east and every day she calls me up from Yale fucking University. It's affecting her *schoolwork*. You're fucking with my *tuition*."

Gloria decided that he must be an exec from the nearby studio, the one off Washington with the faux-Deco campus crawling with PA's and putzes like this guy. Why wasn't he

FedExing? Why in line at the post office? Most likely a low-level wonk.

The clerk held up a laminated guide.

HAZARDOUS MATERIALS
THE FOLLOWING ITEMS MAY <u>NOT</u> BE SENT THROUGH THE MAIL

An iconic gun; an iconic bomb (complete with sizzling fuse); iconic canisters of spray paint, gasoline, a death's-head bottle of poison . . . The clerk indicated the iconic flame and the Ⓞ and said, "Flammable! Is not possible to send mail!"

"It's for my daughter, fuckhead."

Helplessly, the clerk began swatting the bell and calling, "Vera, Vera . . ."

"Hey. *Asshole.* Are you listening to me?"

"Vera . . . !"

"Hey." The suit dropped the box of bottles, lunged across the counter, and grabbed the clerk by his shirt. The clerk began yelling VERA VERA VERA in earnest. Everyone in line looked flummoxed, superfluous, embarrassed; several of them made their way toward the door. The suit got his hands around the clerk's face, cupping it as though they were in love. *You shithead!* he shouted. *You monkey-fucking wuck!* The clerk flailed for the bell and knocked it to the floor, where it landed with a shortened *tink.*

A one-woman stampede, Vera Biddle whoomped through the back door. She saw what was happening, rushed over to the suit, and began pulling at him like he was a persnickety refrigerator door. The suit turned on her, releasing the clerk. Vera was hollering about the cops—and get out of her post office—and Vin, you stay behind the—

—when the suit reared back and clocked her.

There was an odd silence as she tottered. Then she hit the ground.

Everyone started moving: the clerk scrambled for a phone on the wall; the suit dashed for the door; two men in line leapt to restrain him. Other post office employees were emerging from the back, blinking like troglodytes confronting the sun.

Gloria quickly went behind the counter.

"I'm a nurse," she told the Latina clerk. "You have ice somewhere?"

They went back through the maze, to a kitchenette hidden behind tall bundles of tubed bubble-wrap. The clerk cracked an ice-cube tray into a towel.

"Two minutes on, one minute off, then three minutes on, one minute off," Gloria said. "Then two, then off, then three, then off. Got it? And don't leave her side. Make sure she's surrounded by people. Is she on any medication?"

The clerk shrugged. "Maybe?"

"I'd better go check," Gloria said. "Where's her office?"

IT TOOK HER A MINUTE to figure out how to use the database on Vera Biddle's computer. She copied down Joseph Gerusha's home address, then strolled nonchalantly back to the main room. To her amusement, the clerk was following her ludicrous instructions to the letter, using a watch to mark time. Other employees clustered in little cliques, talking in funereal undertones. Vera was blinking like a slot machine, moaning that her nose was broken. The suit was gone, and the men who had tried to stop him were talking with a lady in khaki pants who was saying to them and to the room in general, "We saw it, I saw it, I saw everything, I'll testify, I could pick him out of a lineup." Vin the Vietnamese clerk stood by a table of packing slips and mailers, worrying a nail with his incisors and contemplating a poster that established the difference between registered and insured mail.

"You can probably stop now," Gloria told the clerk. "You might want to have her head X-rayed, though."

FIFTEEN

The address belonged to a bank in Tarzana.

"How long has Mr. Gerusha kept a safe-deposit box here?" Gloria asked.

The manager, Ed Hicks, didn't know offhand. "I don't remember him, to be perfectly honest," he said. He was pale and freckled, holed up in an office like so many she had been in: carpeting an overzealous emerald, a desk clock with fake brass hands, a calendar with beachscapes.

"Do you know what he keeps in there?"

"Sorry," said Hicks. "I'm not permitted to disclose that. And I'm sure you understand that, even under the circumstances, I'm not allowed to let you see the box without some sort of signed release form, or court papers."

"Can you give me a way of getting in touch with him?" she asked. "Please?"

"Sorry, but—"

"I'm trying to make sure that Mr. Gerusha gets what he's entitled to," she said. "There could be a significant inheritance coming his way. Someone connected to him may have left him a—I mean, wouldn't he want to know that?"

Hicks sighed. "I'm sure he would, but—"

"Or maybe can I leave a message for him, with you?"

"There's no guarantee he's going to get it," said Hicks. "I don't think he ever comes in here. I'm pretty sure I've never met him."

"I just want to send him a letter," Gloria said. "If he doesn't reply then I won't bother him anymore. And I won't tell him where I got his address from."

"Miss . . ."

"Look," she said, "I'm not going to sell it, or send him coupons or anything. It's a *good thing*." She smiled. "I won't even send a letter. I'll send a Hallmark."

After a pause, Hicks said, "A mailing address."

"Thank you."

"That's really all. I mean it."

"That's more than fine. Thank you. Very very much."

He tented his fingers, as though the decision hadn't been finalized. He said, "All right," and began clacking at his keyboard. "It's on Venice, number one-one—"

"Five-oh-seven," Gloria finished for him. "LA 90034. Right?"

"Right," he said.

"That's the Culver City Post Office. Where I just came from."

"Hm," Hicks said. "That's peculiar." He reclined in his chair, as though trying to distance himself from the computer before it did something even weirder. As though a water gun was going to pop out of the screen and nail him.

"One thing I *can* tell you," he said. "Mr. Gerusha has

had a safe-deposit box with Golden State for over twenty years. It was previously at a different branch, which closed and relocated here. But other than that, I'm not sure what else . . ." He trailed off.

"I wish I could do more," he said.

Gloria said thank you and told him they'd be in touch.

THE FUND MANAGER at Malle-Vurdham Securities told her that he had never met Joseph Charles Gerusha in person. They had communicated by letter, which never consisted of anything more than a money order and instructions for deposit. She tried to pump him, but he insisted that even if he did have more information, giving it out would constitute a violation of privacy.

Armed with the list of resources Aaron Fox had used, Gloria began her own private investigation. She found a couple of Gerushas, none of whom knew Carl or Joseph. One J. Gerusha, found on the Internet, turned out to be a retired naval officer living in Tarzana named Jack, who had no idea what the hell she was talking about but was delighted to lambaste her in fragmented and heavily accented English for cutting his prescription benefits how the hell was a veteran supposed to live and did they think he lost a finger at Midway for nothing to be treated like nothing like this like nothing—

"Thank you for your time," Gloria said, hanging up.

She started calling hospitals. They, too, gave her curt negatives. The initial euphoria of having found a trail began to atrophy.

Then she called the coroner's.

"What is this in conjunction with?"

"I'm his . . . wife," she said. "I've been looking for him for . . . a long time."

There was a silence, clicking keys.

They said: oh yes, we had someone by that name.

Gloria dove across her bed for a pen, knocking her bowl of popcorn to the floor. "When was he brought in?" she asked. The receptionist told her. Gloria wrote it down and thanked her, and held up the page like a specimen to be dissected.

Joseph Charles Gerusha had died the week before Carl's disappearance.

IT TOOK SOME HEAVY PERSUASION, but Reggie made a few phone calls on her behalf. He was on a first-name basis with a deputy coroner named Jerome Wurlitzer.

"You owe me," Reggie said. "Again."

She made a wrong turn off the freeway, ending up cruising East LA, past the concrete-and-putty reality of County Hospital–USC Med Center. Stone spheres decorated an open plaza, like an outsize game of Chinese checkers abandoned by the gods. A woman, perched stiffly atop a sphere, kept one eye on a rambunctious three-year-old and the other on a distant window. Gloria wondered what purpose her vigil served.

Bleary-eyed residents thronged near the curb, blowing on lunch-cart java and nibbling greasy panini. Men, women, and a few who were so wrung out as to be sexless.

They looked gutted, as though they'd been forced to chase a pile of laxatives with Drano martinis. It occurred to Gloria that, had things been different, she would have gone through a similar ordeal. Thank God, she tried to tell herself, you didn't. Look at them: eyes like oil wells and skin like coagulated glue. You should consider yourself lucky.

She forced that thought several times, never quite believing it but hoping repetition would make it stick.

The coroner's office was a tan block set behind a broad, hot glob of asphalt. She steered the Dodge through rows of black-and-whites, sheriff's choppers, morbid Town Cars gleaming like obsidian. At the entrance, she crossed through a tornado of bulbous black flies, passing a highway patrolman wearing his helmet, visor down. He nodded at her like Darth Vader.

She expected reboant halls and a ghoulishly scarred Slavic dwarf on call to fetch brains or whatever the mad scientist-in-chief wanted. It wasn't anything like that. It was busy and governmental: like the DMV, minus the air of incipient madness.

Plus a smell.

She could smell it all the way in the lobby.

Rotting flesh.

She gagged a little as she signed in.

The nurse said, "We strongly discourage viewing the body in person."

"I know," Gloria said. "I appreciate it, but I'll take my chances."

"You can make the identification from a photograph."

"My psychiatrist thinks it's necessary for me to do it in person."

The nurse shrugged. "It's your lunch."

Wurlitzer was out, but he'd left instructions with his assistant, who was expecting her. Gloria was directed downstairs to a door marked CRYPT. The stench worsened exponentially, and she had to brace herself against the railing, stopping every few feet to acclimate and have a coughing fit. As she neared the bottom, she heard a voice.

muthafucka on the table gonna get what you deserves
I'ma nigga gonna shoot ya up with all typesa preserves

She opened the door on a secluded corner of the crypt. A young man in donut headphones and scrubs had his back to her. Mop in hand, he jigged to a beat available exclusively to him.

I'ma cut you up nigga, listen what I say
you in the hands of the muthafuckin D-O-A

"*Word,*" he said, spinning with his fist up.

She waved.

"Oh—" In one movement he ripped off his mask and his headphones.

"Hi there," she said weakly. "Gloria Mendez."

"Excuse me." He bowed his head. The change was amazing—instant rectitude, just add water!—and she suppressed a giggle.

His nametag introduced him as EARVIN WILLIAMS, CORONER'S ASSISTANT. A kid, twenty-three or -four. He was white; a razor-thin beard and goatee made him look like a living pencil sketch.

"I'm a friend of Detective Reggie Salt," she said.

He nodded, apologized again. "Jerry told me you were coming."

"I didn't mean to disturb you."

He wasn't making eye contact; he was blushing. "No, I'm—I'm sorry . . . please—uh—please, this way."

He led her down a long hallway busy with cops and ME's conferring through handkerchiefs. Gloria wished she'd brought one: unbelievably, the smell was getting worse. She was amazed to see bodies out on tables. They were all over the place, half-dissected, crammed into corners and blocking the emergency exits. Wrapped in translucent plastic—like carpets—and tied off at each end with crude white twine. She felt as though she had wandered into a hellish sausage factory.

The smell.

It didn't seem to bother Earvin, who took her to a room cramped with cabinets and cartons of gloves. As he thumbed through diaphanous carbon copies—bloodwork, X-rays, toxicity reports, crime-scene photos—she saw that she had been mistaken: he wasn't quite white. Some mix of roots, its proportion unclear. She had once read that race was ceasing to be a meaningful term, as people bred themselves into confluence. Her own experience told her otherwise. Looking at Earvin, she could see that despite whatever saga lay encoded in his genes, he had chosen to be black.

"Do you want to be a rapper?" she asked. She wanted him to relax; he was still looking everywhere instead of at her, licking his lips in agitation.

He laughed and shook his head.

She pressed him: "Do you have a stage name?"

He scrutinized her, chewing his lip. "Okay," he said. "Check it." He pulled up his sleeve. A green tattoo of a chain of skulls twined around his arm. Atop it curved:

"I'm not much of an expert," she said, "but I like it."

He gave her a gratified smile. "What I was doing when you came in? That was freestyle."

"Freestyle?"

"Improvised," he said.

"I'm impressed," she said.

"You think that's good, you should hear my demo." He held up a file. "Here's the gentleman in question." He split the folder and squinted at the page. "Mr. Gerusha. I believe, ma'am, that I remember this individual. He sat in cold storage in County for a long time. Arrived with no ID, except a copy of his birth certificate." He shrugged. "I remember because it was very, you know. Unusual. Or— you know. *Weird.*"

The copy of the birth certificate was of poor quality; the names of the parents had been effaced. All she could make out was that it had been issued in San Diego County on December 17, 1946.

Earvin handed her a smock and gloves. "He's around here somewhere."

They went off in search of the body. Earvin kept having to stop and check for Gerusha's tags. He would open up a bagful of putrefaction and say, "Nope." It looked like he was browsing produce. As she watched him, Gloria wondered how many others could be lost here. At some point, she reasoned, they'd have to run out of space and evict the older tenants. Or was this, for the unlucky few, a semitemporary resting place, until boredom or organizational neuroses brought the oversight to someone's attention?

Her odor tolerance strengthened as they went on. This brought a measure of pride. She could stomach stuff far gorier than medical school would've offered.

The bag containing Joseph Gerusha was tucked into an out-of-the-way, impossibly narrow cubbyhole. Earvin gave a brief speech about what to expect, the difficulty of viewing a loved one, some common reactions, so forth.

"All right," he said solemnly, cutting the twine. "Here we go."

Reflecting later that day, she realized that what had most disturbed her about Joseph Gerusha's corpse was the mold: frosty green-and-white fuzz across a landscape of gray flesh. Like a Thanksgiving turkey eight weeks over the hill. He had not been a large man in life, and had withered post facto. The shrinkage produced a pensive countenance, connoting some inscrutable wisdom reserved for the dead.

At the time, though, all she could think was: *what?*

"You okay, ma'am?" Earvin had one hand on her elbow and one on her back.

"I'm fine." She looked at him. "What did he die of?"

Earvin consulted the chart. "Officially? Liver failure. But honestly, he died cause he just died."

She stepped too close; the smell harpooned her. Wobbling, she reversed, her head cobwebbed with the paralyzing stench and confusing reality of Joseph Gerusha.

Also known as Buck, the homeless guy from the alley.

SIXTEEN

She called up Detective Waxbone.

"Ms. Mendez," he said. "I've been meaning to call you."

They agreed to meet at a place on the east end of Hollywood Boulevard, in Little Armenia. At Highland, a wicked snarl in traffic gave her several minutes to stare at the square spire of United Methodist with its twenty-foot AIDS ribbon. Camera-toting tourists assaulted Grauman's Chinese and the H&H mall, hallucinating celebrities and storming in groups twoscore strong to snap pictures of some poor dazed guy who inevitably turned out to be a recording-studio techie experiencing sunlight for the first time in three days. A yawning dinosaur breached the roof of Ripley's Believe It or Not Museum, surveying the pickings—hookers before they'd dressed for the evening; Scientologists on smoking breaks—and deeming them slim, indeed.

Waxbone had pen and pad at the ready.

"Hello," she said, wondering if he'd write that down.

He didn't. She went up to the counter and got herself a lentil soup and a plate of cracker bread.

"You don't want anything?" she said.

He raised his water glass to her.

Maybe he runs on batteries, she thought.

"You had a question for me," he said.

"I thought you had one for me."

"We'll get to that in a minute," he said.

She involved herself in her soup.

"Ms. Mendez."

Wiping her mouth: "Yes?"

"What was your question?"

"It's not a question," she said. "It's more like a story."

"Okay."

"But I think you should go first." She broke off a piece of bread.

Waxbone stroked his formidable cheek. "Uh-huh. All right. The death certificate you submitted? What was the date of death?"

"I don't remember exactly. Around mid-July."

"July twenty-second."

"If you knew," she said, "why did you ask?"

"You came back to Los Angeles from Mexico when."

"That I remember. I went down to Mexico the morning of the twenty-sixth, and came back the next morning. I was gone for a little more than a day."

"Uh-huh," said Waxbone.

"Why?"

"Mr. Perreira was dead by then."

She stared at him. "I would imagine so."

He dipped into his briefcase and took out a binder, which he opened to face her. "This is Mr. Perreira's final

CalFed statement. It was issued in August, the month after the accident, giving all the activity from June twenty-eighth to July twenty-eighth."

"Okay," she said.

"As you can see, he made a withdrawal on the account right before he left. He took out eighteen hundred dollars. Presumably he meant to use this money on his trip."

"I guess."

"Although that is a lot of cash." He looked at her for a moment. Then he cleared his throat. "Regardless. That left his balance at $8,176. See?"

"Yes," she said.

"What I'm having trouble understanding is this."

He placed his finger on a line halfway down the page.

DAILY ACTIVITY

Date	Description	Amount Subtracted	Amount Added	Balance
07/26	Cash Withdrawal	8,175.77		0.26

He said, "On July twenty-sixth, when this transaction occurred, Carl Perreira was dead."

She said, "I thought his account was kept at zero."

"He deposited a lot before that—here." He showed her the beginning of the month, when Carl had put in close to $20,000. "Then he made the donations. Then he goes to Mexico; apparently, he didn't finish making the payments he'd started. Then he dies, and withdraws the rest of the money." Waxbone sipped his water. "That's the order of events as it stands right now."

"It wasn't him," she said.

"What wasn't him?"

"Obviously, it wasn't him. He couldn't take money out if he was dead."

"Uh-huh," said Waxbone. "I agree."

He said nothing more, and it took her a moment to grasp that he was accusing her. She put down her spoon and said, "Detective?"

"You were out of town on that date?" he asked.

"I told you already."

"Do you have anyone who can corroborate that?"

"You can call Reggie Salt. You can call the Aguas Vivas police. I was in the general store. I also stopped at a gas station." She paused. "I doubt they have a phone."

"Did you have access to that account?"

"No."

"Do you know anyone who did?"

"Besides Carl, no. What are you trying to get out of me, Detective?"

Waxbone blinked: the processing face. "Get out of you?"

"Is there an answer you're waiting for?" she asked. "Something particularly incriminating?"

"There's no cause for anger, Ms. Mendez."

"I'm not angry."

"I simply want to understand this as best I can."

"Good," she said. "So do I."

"Uh-huh. Then we're working toward the same goal," said Waxbone.

"Look," she said, "I can't explain how that happened

because I don't know. I had nothing to do with the CalFed account."

"So you think it's probably a mistake."

"I didn't say that," she said. "I don't think anything. Could it have been a mistake?"

"I checked with the bank manager," said Waxbone. "The date stamp on the transaction isn't entered manually; the computer does it when the customer swipes the card. He said it might be a computer error. I believe the word he used was 'hiccup.' He said, 'They've been known to happen.'"

"Don't they have videotape?" she asked.

"They keep the tapes for three to four months. They were recorded over ten days ago."

"When I go to the bank I have to punch in my PIN. Didn't he have to do that?"

"Yes," said Waxbone. "And he did."

"He punched in a PIN?"

"Well," he said—here she saw him equivocate for the first time—"someone did."

She goggled. "'Someone'?"

"If it wasn't him," he said, "then, yes. Someone. Someone must have."

Pause.

She said, "Are you saying that it's possible it *was* him?"

Waxbone shrugged.

"But he's dead," she said. She added: "His ashes are in my living room."

Waxbone said, "He hasn't been buried?"

"Not exactly," she said, blushing.

"Uh-huh." He nosed at her soup. "It's going to get cold."

"I don't want it anymore."

He snapped off a piece of her bread and chewed it silently. He washed it down with water and said, "Would you mind if we were to drop by your place?"

SHE LED HIM to her bedroom dresser, where she kept the urn. She picked it up and gave it to Waxbone, who said, "Where's the restroom?"

As he held the urn over the tub, he asked, "Have you ever opened it?"

"Of course not," she said. To begin with, she had a consuming fear of spilling ashes everywhere. And besides, who wanted to look at human remains? Only a sicko, she thought, only a sicko would get a kick out of the granulated version of a loved one.

"Would you rather I did?"

She didn't want to argue. She took the urn from him and unlatched the top.

And then she said, "Oh shit," because what wafted out of the urn was the inimitable aroma of instant coffee.

Waxbone leaned over to sniff and said, "Uh-huh." He closed the drain on her sink and ran ten seconds' worth of water.

"What are you doing?" she asked.

"Human remains don't dissolve." He took the urn and sprinkled a pinch into the sink. The ashes cascaded into a brown blob that lightened as it diluted throughout the bowl.

Waxbone looked at her. "See?"

She snatched the urn and went to the kitchen, no longer caring if she spilled anything. Furiously, she opened the cabinet above the coffeemaker, shoving aside the empty Chock full o' Nuts can and finding her favorite mug. Waxbone watched from the doorway as she started to fill a kettle, realized that temperature didn't matter, filled the mug from the tap, added a teaspoon of the urn's contents, stirred, and—without flinching—took a sip of the stalest, limpest coffee she'd ever had.

But it was coffee. No mistaking that.

She poured the mug out and went back to the bathroom, where she vomited.

Waxbone was waiting for her on the sofa. When she came back out, he said, "Was there something you wanted to tell me?"

HE WASN'T ANGRY at what she had to say. He didn't even seem surprised, and she began to believe that he had been following her for the last several days. His maddening stoicism kept her off balance, wondering whether he thought of her as a partner or a suspect. Probably it didn't take much for him to develop this style, she thought. It fit him naturally.

Two days later, he pitched another curveball by inviting her along to inspect the safe-deposit box. Either he liked her, or trusted her, or wanted to trap her by exposing her to a situation likely to produce discomfort.

Or he wanted to thank her for letting him in on her discoveries.

She didn't know. She couldn't figure him out, and at this point didn't feel the need. She already had enough to handle in the Mysterious Emotions department.

Waxbone had a court order. For some reason, Gloria felt a brief rush of omnipotence as he handed his badge to Hicks, the bank manager. Hicks remembered Gloria by name and smiled at her as he led them downstairs.

They arrived at a locked door. Hicks fished a key off a Brobdingnagian ring.

"I've been thinking about it," he said, "and I'm pretty sure that, in all my time here, I've never met him." He started wiggling the key in.

"Is that unusual?" Gloria asked.

Hicks shrugged. "I mean, the stuff people keep here tends to be important, as you might imagine. But you also get people who leave things and forget about them. I'm not here every hour of every day, so he might've come in when I wasn't around. C'mon . . ."

The key had stuck. Hicks yanked it out and tried another. "We have a double system," he said. "This door is deadbolted, then there's the boxes. It makes people feel secure." He tried another key. "The locksmith was here, and the box is already open. I didn't touch anything inside. I've kept the room closed till you got here."

"Uh-huh," said Waxbone. "Good thinking."

He sounded like a lobotomized Little League coach. Gloria supposed some gratitude was in order; he had brought her along. But there was a big difference between appreciation for the gesture and appreciating his affect.

Finally, Hicks found the right key. He said, "After you."

The rows of metal plates made Gloria feel as though she was on trial before some enormous, uniform jury. Their numbers were like sneers. There were two chairs and an oak table, atop which sat the opened safe-deposit box. Its lock had been drilled away; Gloria noticed metal shavings in the carpet.

True to his word, Ed Hicks had left the contents alone. He brought them to the table and then stood back, as though he expected an explosion. Waxbone donned a pair of latex gloves, reached inside, and took out a piece of paper. Gloria read it over his shoulder. It was a birth certificate.

"That's the original of the one at the morgue," she said. This copy was legible; she now knew that Joseph Charles Gerusha's father and mother were Anthony and Katherine Gerusha, and that he had been born in San Diego on December 17, 1946.

"What else is there?" she asked.

Waxbone began taking out all the items, one by one, and laying them on the table.

Stock certificates. Treasury bonds. Corporate bonds. Originals of the Malle-Vurdham Securities statements.

"He's done pretty well for himself," said Hicks.

The detective took out a Social Security card, date of issue February 25, 1947, San Diego, for Joseph Charles Gerusha.

Next came a quartet of photos. They were black-and-whites, unfocused and grainy. A young couple sat on a bench, soda bottles in hand, as they toasted the cameraman. She was dark, with Indian features, wearing a boxy blouse and a baroque pendant encrusted with pearls that looked vastly too expensive for the rest of her outfit. He wore a striped shirt, jeans, and a cowboy hat.

Another photo, sharper: the man and a swaddled mass of infant.

The second and third photos showed the infant up close, held next to the young man's incomplete face.

Next, Waxbone tossed a passport on the table; out fell an old California driver's license. He opened the passport and held the license up for comparison; the faces were the same, matching also the face of the young man in the photos.

"The real Joseph Gerusha," he said. Contrary to all precedent, he smiled.

"No, it's not," Gloria said. "That's Carl."

SEVENTEEN

"You know, you never wanted to see me before he died," said Reggie Salt. "What am I, the default lunch option?"

"You got it."

They were having Thai at the mini-mall on Olympic and Robertson, seated by the window so they could watch the bus stop.

"You look worn out, Gigi."

"I don't like to rest when there's an outstanding problem," she said, accepting a tumbler of sweet iced tea from a fine-boned waitress in a kimono-cum-microskirt.

"That's my life . . ." he said, stretching hugely. "Outstanding problems . . . *mmwah!*" He was broad as a washing machine. She remembered with some amusement the first time she'd seen his penis. It was in line with the stereotype.

And brains, too he'd said.

"I feel bad for people like us," he said.

"Us?"

"The relentless type," he said. "They who need to know the truth."

"This isn't a movie, Reggie."

"Everything in LA is a movie," he said, stealing a swig of her drink.

"Yeah," she said, "but you sound like a preview."

Reggie didn't answer; he was tracking the waitress. "Did you get her name?"

"Ruby," Gloria said. "On the young side, don't you think?"

"I just want a beer," he said. "You're always assuming the worst of me."

"You're always assuming the best of yourself," she said. "Someone has to keep you in line."

They talked and ate for a while. Reggie owned seventy-five percent of the words. She listened and barbed him mildly when his ego got utterly out of control. He devoured his food and started on hers. She had intentionally ordered too much, knowing that if she didn't, she'd end up leaving hungry.

"These're good," he said, skewering another of her shrimp.

"I wouldn't know," she said. "I haven't tasted any of them yet."

Eventually, they got around to talking about the case.

"The driver's license we found," she said, "in the safe-deposit box? It had Carl's picture, Joseph Charles Gerusha's name, and Caperco's address."

"None of the stuff at the bank had his home address," Reggie said.

Gloria shook her head. "Add the Malle-Vurdham account to the stocks, and there's about eleven million dollars in his name."

"Which one, again?"

"Joseph Charles Gerusha."

"Gerusha," he said. "What kind of name is that?"

"Russian," she said. "I looked it up. It comes from the word for 'pear.' Get it?"

"Get what."

"*Per*reira."

"Oh," he said, massaging his forearms. "Very funny."

"That's Carl for you."

"What about his parents? The ones listed on the birth certificate."

"Anthony and Katherine," she said. "I checked up on them: I called the San Diego County Recorder. They died in 1961, in a car accident. Their death certificates and the birth certificate are the only records of them. I called the local schools. Joseph Charles Gerusha dropped out of high school the month after they died."

"And then?"

"And then he disappears," she said. "Somewhere down the line he made investments, and he also developed the name Carl Perreira. Or the reverse. He really was Carl Perreira, who came from God-knows-where, and somewhere down the line he took over this other identity—Gerusha—who was already missing or dead." She paused for breath. "Either way, they were the same person."

"What about the homeless guy?" Reggie asked.

"I'm thinking that Carl—or Joseph—whoever he was—

planted the copy of the birth certificate on him," she said.

"To make it look like 'Joseph Gerusha' had died," Reggie said.

"Yes."

"You think he was running from something."

"I don't know," she said. "But he found the body in the alley the week before. He probably saw his chance and took it."

He looked at her skeptically.

"No, Reggie," she said. "He didn't kill Buck."

"How do you know?"

"The coroner's report said Buck died of liver failure."

"And therefore?"

"Look," she said, "it's been hard enough adjusting to the fact that Carl had two identities. I really don't need to cope with the idea of him being a murderer, too."

"That doesn't mean he didn't do it."

"I'm positive," she said. "Some things he could hide from me. But not that."

"He hid his entire life from you, Gigi."

She felt herself rising to the argument, and pushed her temper down. "I *knew* him," she said. "I knew *something* about him. He wasn't a stranger. You can't spend all day with someone, all day, every day, for a decade, and not know anything about them. That's . . . it's just not possible, Reggie. He lied to me, I admit that. But if he was a killer? I'd know that." She paused. "I would."

He stirred his water, bringing ice chips to dissolution. He didn't want to answer her, but she could hear inside his head: *You're kidding yourself.*

"Ten years," she said.

He looked at her evenly. "People get divorced after fifty, Gigi."

They decided to watch the bus stop for a while.

Finally, he said, "You're letting your emotions get the better of you."

"That's a right I have. I'm not a cop."

"No. But I'll say this, Gigi, you're doing a pretty good job."

"I feel like I know nothing."

"Someone like you can't tolerate not knowing. Unless you've got it a hundred percent, it's always going to bug you."

"What if I never get it one hundred percent?"

"Then it'll keep on bugging you."

She stuck her jaw out. "I'm not going to think about this forever."

"Why isn't this detective helping you out? What's his name."

"Waxbone."

"Waxbone..." Reggie grinned. "My puppy *adores* chewing on his *Waxbone*."

"He's got about as much personality as a dog toy," she said. She grasped her iced tea before Reggie could get to it, and took a long sip. "The public administrator, Gonzaga, she called me up to tell me that work with the estate was being suspended, because they're no longer sure if Carl's dead or not. I finally managed to get in touch with Waxbone, who said that the case is being transferred to the missing-persons unit, and that I could expect to hear something within the next few months." Then, resentfully: "He implied that it's low-priority."

"It is," Reggie said. "They're too busy putting out Amber Alerts."

"But Carl might be alive."

"So what?"

"So they should find him."

"It's not against the law to disappear," Reggie said. "Did he commit a crime?"

"Not that I know of."

"What about taxes?"

"Both Joseph C. Gerusha and Carl Perreira filed tax returns. They each had a taxpayer ID, linked to each of their separate Social Security numbers."

"He wanted to hide his money," said Reggie. "So he used another name."

"Which name is the real one?"

"Does it matter?"

"Sure it matters."

"I don't see why."

"I want to know," she said, "because it's my *job* to know."

"It's not."

"That's my decision, isn't it?"

"Suit yourself."

"You don't think I can find out?"

Reggie shrugged. "If he's taken that much effort to cover his tracks in the first place, I doubt you'll get any further than you have."

"I think he's alive," she said.

"He might be."

She said, "I don't understand why he couldn't tell me."

"Men aren't the sharing types," Reggie said. He groaned softly and tucked in his shirt. "We should come to this place more often."

She looked at her plate, which had been swabbed clean. "Maybe next time I'll get to eat," she said.

"I had four shrimp. I was counting."

"I ordered four."

Reggie laughed and stood up. "Okay, but I only *had* four. . . ."

He went to the bathroom. While he was gone, Gloria waved at the waitress.

"Hi there," Gloria said. "Can I maybe get another piece of bread?"

The waitress nodded sympathetically and walked off.

While Gloria waited she reflected on Reggie's basic message: *grow up and get on with it.* Ten years ago, she'd needed that. It was what had attracted her to him in the first place: a single-minded confidence that promised a life less mired in the past. He refused to let memories encumber him. She admired him for it, in the same way she admired his sense of humor: as something she once loved and now found hilariously frustrating.

He returned, wringing his hands.

"What I hate about the hand dryers," he said, "is that they're programmed to turn off about *three seconds* before your hands are dry. And you feel bad pushing the button again, because it's a waste to run a whole nother cycle for the first three seconds."

"You should rub your hands more briskly," she said.

"I've tried that. It's a rule: they don't work. I think there might be a law about it." He sat down. "You want dessert?"

She shook her head. "Why was he hiding his money?"

"Cause I might get some. Ice cream."

"Reggie. Are you listening to me?"

"Why? I don't know why. There's two reasons I can think of." He raised a finger. "One: someone was trying to get it. That being a person, or the IRS, or a creditor, or whatever." He raised another. "Two: he was planning on taking over the other persona at some point, and skipping town."

"But why would he do that?"

"He wanted to start over," he said. "A new life. You must understand that. Everybody wants to do it once in a while."

"I understand it," she said, "but I didn't *do* it."

"So he had balls that you and I don't have."

"He liked his life," she said. "He had nothing to run from."

"Not that you know of."

"No, no, no . . ." She scraped at the plate with her fork. What Reggie was saying made sense; he was, in fact, articulating exactly what she had been telling herself for several consecutive restless nights. But now she could blame Reggie for blaming Carl, giving her an excuse to revert to Carl's defense.

Reggie perked up. "Here comes Ruby. . . ."

The waitress arrived with dessert menus and a couple of rolls, which she placed on Gloria's bread plate. Reggie reached across the table and plucked one.

"Any kind of ice cream," he said to the waitress. "Surprise me."

GLORIA ARRIVED HOME WILTED, as though lunch had been a ten-mile run. She wanted to take a nap, but her answering machine was blinking red with three new messages.

The first was from a parochial school in Brentwood. She barely remembered sending them her résumé, but she must have, because Ms. Eleanor Landry-Wheelock requested— in her patronizing principal's voice—that Gloria return her call *at the moment of earliest possible convenience, thanks ever so much.*

Gloria remembered: the job description sought an administrative assistant "with room for growth," whatever that meant. She'd sent her cover letter out haphazardly, half-hoping she'd never get called. A new job seemed tantamount to an admission of failure, and so her efforts to get one had been meager: she'd sent out four feelers.

She supposed she should start searching for real soon. It had less to do with money than with the notion that admitting failure might be a good first step toward forgetting.

She took down the number and waited for the second message.

Good afternoon, Ms. Mendez. This is Detective John Waxbone—

She dug in her purse for a pen.

I'm calling, not in connection with the case of Mr. Perreira . . . Although—Mr. Perreira's case . . . I do not,

ahmmm, at this time, there isn't any new information per, uh,
pertinent . . .

He sounded as though he'd been stricken with a computer virus.

. . . although I sincerely wish that there was something for
me to report. As soon as I do obtain new information . . .
Would you mind calling me back as soon as—

She stopped the machine and dialed him.

"Waxbone."

"Hello, Detective, this is Glo—"

"Ms. Mendez," he interrupted. "Yes, hello."

She thought: aren't we quick on the draw?

"How have you been?" he asked.

"Fine . . . is there something you were calling about?"

Waxbone cleared his throat. "I'm glad you asked that,
Ms. Mendez. There is."

She waited, but he said nothing.

"Detective?"

"Uh-huh, yes, sorry . . ."

"Has something come up?"

"Come u—you mean in regard to Mr. Perreira's—"

"Yes."

"I'm afraid not," he said. "I'm calling regarding a—uh, a
different matter. But I assure you, if there was something to
tell you I would inform you. Without delay."

"That's nice to know."

"Am I disturbing you at home?" he asked. "Because if
there would be a more appropriate time for this conversation to take place, we can arrange to have it then."

"Actually, I was about to take a nap," she said.

"Oh. *Oh*. Well, then let's try and, why don't we—"

"But let's talk now."

"Are you sure?"

"Yes," she said.

"But you want to take a nap," he said.

"I'll take it after we're done."

"If it's a bad time—"

"It's a fine time."

"You're sure."

"Yes, Detective."

"Good." He coughed. "Ms. Mendez, I have a question for you."

"Please," she said.

He didn't say anything for a moment. She thought: this is so *weird*.

"Detective?"

"Uh—yes. Uhum, I was wondering," he said, "if you might be interested—"

She thought: oh no.

"—in going dancing with me." He coughed again. "Soon."

"Dancing?"

"Yes," he said. "Salsa dancing. Although—if there's a form you prefer—"

She said, "I don't date police officers anymore."

Pause.

"I see," he said.

"I'm sorry. It's nothing personal."

"That's all right. Have a good day."

"You too, Detective."

She hung up, and started laughing.

Then she felt bad. He was trying, at least. Give the man credit for that. Probably she should've gone out with him once. As a courtesy . . .

And it wasn't as though her door was being battered down. Dancing was classy. Much better than dinner at Sizzler. She couldn't imagine Waxbone doing the salsa, that jerky frame turning into something low and flowing. But evidently, he was the type that defied expectations. Probably he was a state salsa champion or something: Mr. Fire-Hips.

Although—if there's a form you prefer—

Apparently, John Waxbone knew more than just the salsa. Merengue, cha-cha, fox-trot, Lindy Hop, swing, ballroom, tap, hip-hop. The dancing detective. The cop cuts a rug. The funkmeister fuzz.

Patrick Swayze, you have the right to remain silent.

A practical worry nipped at her: nobody in the LAPD was going to give a damn about Carl unless Waxbone did.

Maybe she had made a big mistake.

She was about to call him back and say *on second thought* when she saw the blink of the answering machine. There was still one new message. She got the pen and pressed play.

The first thing she noticed was that the speaker had an accent.

I am look for Gloria Mendez. Please call—

The tension in his voice made her tense. He had neglected to leave his name. She copied down the number. A foreign number.

She dialed in a hurry. The same voice said, "*Sí.*"

"This is Gloria Mendez. You called me?"

"Yes, hello, yes . . ." His English was hoarse and feverish. "I want to find you. I come to the building, no one is there. I ask the building manager, he say you are the person. He says he is dead. I am here half a day, he is dead? Tell me no, tell me—"

"Excuse me," she said. "Who is this?"

"*No* . . ." He sounded anguished.

"Who's dead?" she asked.

He was crying, the receiver bumping his cheek.

"Sir? Are you all right?"

He said, "I am Carlos Perreira. Joseph Gerusha, he is my father."

EIGHTEEN

She insisted that they meet in a public place. He was staying at a motel on Centinela; she gave him directions from there to Rancho Park, describing herself.

She arrived first, and watched as a cab deposited him near the parking lot entrance and he got out, hurrying in the wrong direction. She concealed herself behind the oars of a banana plant. She pegged him at thirty, although he had retained the build of a high-school letterman: jeans adhering to his body, and short sleeves bulging as he raised an arm to shade his eyes. A pair of sunglasses was clawing its way out of his breast pocket. Shaggy bangs intruded on a seamless forehead.

He wandered toward the eastern end of the parking lot, found himself fenced in, and came back. Gloria stepped from behind the plant and waved, causing him to start.

As he approached, the dots on his shirt resolved into tiny pineapples. He had not shaved in a day.

"Sorry—the phone—" he said.

For a moment they stood looking at each other. Then he

handed her a Mexican driver's license. She didn't know what she was supposed to do with it, other than to confirm that he was Carlos Perreira, residing in the Delegación Benito Juárez, Distrito Federal. Born July 17, 1963. He was older than she'd thought. Nice skin, no wrinkles; like brown nubuck.

She gave the license back and gestured for him to follow her.

Rancho Park boasted a double-decker driving range, presently filled to one-sixth capacity. A gang of boys in white polo shirts and blue pants, all wearing yarmulkes, occupied three of the stalls. On the upper level, the golf pro had his arms around a lady in her mid-sixties and was talking her through the basic downstroke.

Don't try and kill it. Just let it fall under its own weight.

Five metal chairs lined the wall outside the shop; she sat and Carlos followed suit. Beside him was a garden hose on a stand. He rested his hand on it and rolled the coil back and forth, its timid squeak playing counterpoint to the marimba of five-irons.

He looked her over. *"¿Usted habla español?"*

"Sí."

"Thank God," he said in Spanish. "I don't think I could do this in English." He patted himself down. "Do you have a cigarette?"

She said she didn't smoke.

"I ran out this morning," he said, "and I could really use one for my nerves."

"I don't think you're allowed to smoke here," she said.

"Shit . . ." he muttered, sitting down. He looked out at

the golfers. "It's the middle of the day, what are they doing here?"

She said nothing. She wanted him to speak first.

He said, "This is what I know."

MY FATHER WAS BORN *in San Diego after the Second World War. I don't know anything about his father, except that he was in the American Navy in Japan.*

But that could be wrong. All of this I learned later, from my grandmother—

Not my father's mother, my mother's mother, but she—

This isn't making any sense. Let me try again.

My father was born in San Diego. He grew up there, but I don't know anything about it. His name was Joseph Gerusha.

At age sixteen, he ran away to Mexico. That's when I start to know something.

This is in 1962. I don't know why he went, but he was serious about running away, not like most teenagers. He went and stayed. He wandered into a church dance in a village in Sonora and met my mother.

The following year, she gave birth to me. She was fourteen. They gave me her dead father's name, Carlos. My father offered to marry my mother, but my grandmother refused to let him in the house. He would sleep in their yard, and my grandmother would come out in the morning, hitting him in the head with a broom and cursing him.

Finally, he managed to convince my mother to come with him back to the United States. He stole a car, and they drove off in the middle of the night.

They made it a few hundred miles, as far as a town called Aguas Vivas.

That's where it happened.

He wasn't a very experienced driver. He ran the car into a ditch at a high speed and it flipped. I was in the front seat. I tumbled under the glove compartment. It was a big car, one of those cars that looks like a typewriter, with the big hood and the high seats. It collapsed on itself when it crashed. The space below the glove compartment was the right size for me. Because of the way the car bent, it created a shell. It protected me. The whole time, the car turns over and over, and I'm in place like a ship in a bottle.

My mother died.

My father panicked and assumed that I was dead, too. Either that, or—this is what I tend to think—he decided he didn't want the responsibility of me. He was seventeen and no longer had my mother to help him. To someone his age, in his position, a baby must have looked like leg irons.

He left me there and ran off.

Someone reported the accident, and the authorities came to look. They didn't realize there was a baby in the car at first, and had towed it to the dump when someone finally heard me screaming. They cut the car open and took me to the hospital.

For a month, I was in the hospital. They didn't know where to send me. Nobody knew who I was. My mother didn't have any identification. Also, I had gotten ill.

Imagine that. I survive a car crash that kills my mother; I survive being trapped in this car, a coffin, by myself; I don't have a scratch—and then, in the hospital, I contract rheumatic fever.

After I got better, they decided to put me in an orphanage, quickly, before something else happened to me, before one of the nurses dropped me on my head or drowned me in the bath. They contacted the orphanage nearest Aguas Vivas—because that's where I was found—and found out that it was in Charrones.

So I went to Charrones.

I was there for almost a year before my grandmother came for me. She'd heard about the accident—in those days, an event like that was big news—but hadn't tried to locate me. She didn't want me, because I half-belonged to the man who killed her daughter.

When maternal pity got the better of her, she came to claim me. We moved to Hermosillo, which is where I grew up.

She had no money, but all I wanted to do was play fútbol *and sit in the library, so our interests fell into line. She left me alone, and she didn't talk about my parents.*

I shouldn't say "never." If she needed to describe a beautiful woman, she would say, "Pretty, but not like your mother." That's how I learned what beautiful meant: I looked at the pictures of my mother that my grandmother showed me, and then I knew.

I have a picture of her. Here.

You can see, she is very pretty. She looked like my grandmother. I think that when my grandmother referred to her as pretty, she was actually talking about herself.

Here's another picture my grandmother kept. Or—not kept. She forgot about it. Otherwise, she would have destroyed it. Every trace of my father she burnt after the accident. Except for this picture. In it, my mother is pregnant with me.

Look.

Is that him? The man you know?

That's how I know what he looks like. Or else I wouldn't have a clue.

The pearl pendant around her neck looks expensive. I'm not sure where it came from; she didn't have money for that. Maybe he gave it to her.

I found this picture between the pages of a book my grandmother used to prop up her kitchen table. One afternoon—I was thirteen—I ran out of things to do, and it was raining, and I took the book from beneath the table to see if it said anything interesting.

It was a terrible book. I remember it clearly, because it was so boring.

The title was Land Without Rain.

It was about irrigation in Mexico. I have no idea why my grandmother had it; she was nearly illiterate. I liked to read, and still I couldn't manage it, it was so full of empty facts and technical jargon. I saw the first sentence and started hunting for illustrations.

Then this photo fell out.

You can hold it for a little while, if you want.

At first I didn't understand what I was looking at. I had never seen my father before. But then I recognized my mother. The bulge in her belly: that had to be me.

It was strange to see myself before I was born. Since I'd never met either of them, I never really understood that I had come from someone else's body. My grandmother had always told me that a vulture had dropped me in her yard.

Look.

Do you see?

My grandmother didn't know I had the picture. I put it in my personal Bible and took it out every time I wanted to remind myself that I wasn't brought by the vulture. My grandmother had no sense of privacy. Nobody did in those days. I remember when I was six, watching our neighbor hike up her skirt and wash herself with water from a bucket.

But my Bible was off-limits. My grandmother never looked in it, and she never found out about the picture—not until much later, I'll explain in a minute.

When I became a teenager, I started to ask questions about my parents.

My grandmother refused to give me a straight answer. She took satisfaction from being able to control the past. My father and mother did not exist; or my father had never existed; or my father, he was a criminal. He was a murderer; he was roasting in hell; and if I got too close to his memory, I would burn, too.

I fought her, diametrically. If she said he was evil, I would say he was the greatest man who ever lived. If she said he'd abandoned me, I would say, no no no: he didn't leave, you drove him off.

I moved out at sixteen and started working. And I started to change my mind about her. I think it was the fact that I had to provide for myself. I began to understand what a burden I had been on her, what a burden my parents must have been. I would send her money—money I couldn't afford to part with—and she would return it with a note: no blood.

I went to visit her, and brought the Bible with the photograph. We sat down and she gave me a cup of café con leche.

I said, "I want you to tell me what happened, but I don't want you to scream, and I don't want you to cry."

Of course she began screaming and crying.

It was a diversion tactic, understand? One she used all the time. She wasn't out to harm me. She wanted to keep me from the shame of my past. To keep me in a shell.

In the middle of her screaming, I opened the Bible and took out the photograph. I held it in her face like this, like a cross to a vampire.

I don't mean that my grandmother was a vampire.

You understand what I mean . . . ? That it was similar, the way I held it.

Okay—good. I don't want to give you the wrong impression.

So—okay. The photo. I held it up, and she stopped screaming.

She said, "Where did you get that?"

"I took it from your house. It was in a book holding up the table."

She tried to grab it, but I ran behind the birdcage.

"I'm not going to give it to you," I said, "because you're going to behave crazy, and we should stop behaving crazy and talk like normal people."

She chased me around the house for ten minutes. She struck matches and tried to throw them at the photo. She set her bed on fire, and I had to beat it out with an old hat. By that point, she was wheezing like she was going to die. She gave up.

She said, "I will tell you everything."

Her version was not a hundred percent . . . unbiased. For example, I didn't completely believe what she said about my *mother. She painted her as a victim, passive, like my father was a snake charmer. I don't know how well my grandmother knew my mother: not well enough to prevent her from getting pregnant, or running away, or getting killed.*

But most of the story made sense. I sifted for facts and discovered that I knew more than before.

When she finished, she yelled, "My table has been wobbling for six years!"

I gave her the book back.

At that time, I was working. My friend helped get me a job in construction. I started off hauling bricks, but I was smart and worked hard. By the time I was twenty-five, I was managing four sites. In Hermosillo, there's a building for the Department of Recreation. It's a local landmark, in the shape of an eagle. And unlike most Mexican landmarks that look like eagles, you can tell this one's an eagle.

I built that.

My boss runs a huge construction company, one of the biggest in the country. He was the contractor for the old stadium in Mexico City. A powerful man named Polaczek. His parents were immigrants. They kept their name.

Construction is corrupt anywhere, but it's abominable in Mexico. Polaczek has a safe in his office, and in it he keeps the list of people he's bribing. I surprised him because I wasn't out to swindle him. I must have seemed naïve. I stayed with him for years while coworkers left to start up their own crooked businesses, or became crooked police officers or crooked building inspectors.

Another reason Polaczek liked me was because I got my projects done on time. I stayed on site until after everyone left.

If workers didn't show up, I went to their houses and woke them up, or tracked them down in the bars. If they didn't come, I fired them. In those days, their union was a mess; I could fire anyone for any reason.

Not showing up is a good reason to get fired. But I'm saying that some people fired their workers to show that they could. That wasn't me.

Polaczek asked me to move to Mexico City, because he was buying out a competitor and he wanted me to run operations. I had more experience than men five years older, and I could balance books as well. Muscles and brains is what he said.

I moved in 1991. That was the best year of my life. I had a girlfriend, a stewardess with Mexicana. I was thinking about getting a business degree. I didn't have much education, but at the time, everything seemed open.

The next year, my grandmother died. She was held up at knifepoint coming home from the market, and she had a heart attack.

After that—

I'm sorry; I'm getting distracted. It's hard to talk about this all at once.

All that matters is how I ended up here.

A couple of years ago, I was throwing a party. Near my office, across the delegación—I work in Cuauhtémoc—there's a wholesaler. While I'm waiting for my paper plates, I pick up a catalogue with a black-and-white picture on the back. It grabs my attention because the guy in the photo is making a ridiculous face. I flip through it. You know how you'll read anything when you're waiting, like the back of an airline ticket.

The plates come out. But they've brought out the wrong ones.

So I wait again, and pick up the catalogue. I play a game, testing if I can remember the prices. As the second plates arrive, I close the catalogue and I look at the man on the back, making that face.

I think, He looks a lot like an older version of my father.

Underneath his picture is my name.

It wasn't a sudden shock. It was more like a needle sliding into my arm.

The man at the counter is snapping his fingers at me. "You want these or not?"

I hold up the catalogue. "Can I have this?"

At home, I tack the man's picture to the wall. Next to it, I put the photo from the book. Like a police lineup, except the goal is to try and make everyone look the same.

When you have my kind of childhood, your imagination can overdevelop. As a boy, I would pretend that every man taller than me was my father. I'd squeeze his face onto their features. I needed to make sure I wasn't having a flashback, or a . . . I don't know, a psychological attack.

That day, I spent three hours looking at the pictures.

The next day, I had them enlarged and put the blowups back on the wall. For a while, it was like I had roommates. I would stay up late, talking to them.

"Are you my father? Where are you? Why do you have my name?"

Without telling people who the photos were of, I brought friends over and asked for opinions: did they think it was the same person? Most of them did. A couple couldn't tell because the age disparity was too great. But none of them said, "No, impossible, two different people."

But I knew it was him.

Before my friends confirmed it. Before I'd blown up the photos.

I knew the instant I saw the name. Because he had renamed himself. After me.

He thought I was dead. By putting my name on a living body, he could bring me back to life.

I understood this, but it took a while to accept it.

And to accept that he was real. I didn't think of him as a person. He was a figure out of a history book. You know about an idea called Jesus, but you don't think he had hair and fingernails, that he went to the bathroom.

Imagine if someone told you that Jesus was your father. And you could get on a plane and see him.

After I decided that it might be true, I had a whole new set of questions. I didn't know if the catalogue I'd seen was current. If I wrote him, would he respond? I didn't know what I would say if he did.

I didn't know if I wanted to get in touch with him at all. What was the point? I didn't need his money; I didn't want an apology. I didn't want anything from him. Some people need to confront their past in order to move on. That's not me.

I did nothing for a long time, and I thought I was okay with that.

Last year, around the anniversary of my grandmother's death, I started thinking.

It wasn't enough.

I called up his company. When the lady answered, I asked

for Mr. Perreira. I said I had some questions about something in the catalogue, and—

That was you?

Oh.

Nice to meet you, in person.

Sure, it was someone, *but I didn't know it was . . . It was you.*

That's strange.

Do you remember me?

Of course not. It was a single phone call. I wouldn't remember it, either.

If you don't remember me, you probably don't remember what you said, either.

Close. You said, "He's on the other line, he'll call you back." That was all I needed to hear. He became real.

It happened when you spoke about him in the third person. Before that, I had controlled him. He was a character in my head, with a past I created, whose words I put in his mouth. It was impossible for him to do anything unless I chose it.

When you said that—he's on the other line, he'll call you back—he stepped outside. He was doing things I had no power over. Even worse: he was controlling me, being too busy to speak, calling me back.

I told you I would call back later.

Instead, I sent him a letter and told him who I was.

A month later, he phoned.

You would think that we had an emotional conversation, but it was mostly practical. He wanted to come to Mexico, but I said: no, I want to see America. He suggested August. I told him it had to be July, beginning of the month, when I could get off work. He gave in immediately. He didn't want to argue over anything.

He had no reason to be that terrified of me; I was equally scared. Scared that he'd turn out to be a nothing, and that my whole life I had been terrorized by a gigantic coward.

I said to him, "You took my name."

"It's a good name," he said. "I wanted someone to have it."

He offered to pay for my plane ticket, but I didn't want him throwing money at me. It was insulting. If we were going to meet, it wasn't going to be about that.

The morning I was supposed to come to the U.S. I got up to take a shower. I was washing my hair, and I started crying.

I don't know what happened. I couldn't move.

I tore up my ticket.

When he called to find out what had happened, I let him leave long messages, which I didn't answer.

A few weeks went by. I went back to work, and I calmed down. I began to regret making a snap decision. It was like the one he'd made. I said to myself, You are not going to be like him. You will not make important choices in the shower.

I called him at home. He didn't answer there, so I called him at work. Nobody answered there, either. I called both places, over and over, and nobody ever answered.

That was five months ago, in July. It was the week of your big earthquake. I read about it and got worried that he'd been killed. I checked the news to find out the names of the victims, but almost no one had died. That's the difference between American earthquakes and the ones we have.

Then I thought: Nobody's answering because the phone lines are down. But even before the earthquake, nobody had answered.

I thought, He went on vacation.

Is that where he was?

Ah. You were on vacation, too.

That's good to know. I got something right.

Why didn't I—?

Because there was no point in leaving a message. I wanted to talk to him. And besides, he begged me not to discuss it with anyone else. He said it would ruin his life. I didn't know if I was going to honor that request forever, but at the time, it sounded fair.

A few weeks later, I called back, and the line had been disconnected. His home phone had also been disconnected. And I knew what had happened: he had run away from me again.

I've been extremely depressed.

It showed at work. My boss told me, "You look like shit." I told him I wanted to visit a relative in Los Angeles, the one who had cancelled on me. It's Christmas in two weeks, anyhow, and business has been slow, so he gave me time off. I haven't taken a break, not in ten years or more.

I got in this morning. I didn't know where else to start, so I took a cab to the office. I had the address from the catalogue and from his letters.

The driver dropped me on the wrong street. I had to walk around for twenty minutes before I found it. This is a bad city to walk in. A guy almost ran me over.

The office was locked. I knocked until some man with a gold bracelet came out of a different office and told me that the person I was looking for wasn't there anymore.

I said, "Where is he?"

"Dead," he said.

I felt like I was going crazy. The cabbie put me in the wrong place, and then I was nearly killed, and now they were telling me that my father had died before I'd had a chance to meet him. That's a pretty upsetting day. Do you see?

I started pounding on the door to your office. I tried to break it down. The guy with the bracelet called the building manager, who told me to call you.

I almost didn't call.

But I did.

NINETEEN

He finished and they were quiet, listening to the drivers and the golf pro's wisdom. The boys with the yarmulkes were long gone, the student was no longer female, but the sounds remained the same: *ping. ping. ping.*

Gloria felt stuffed on words. At first she had not believed any of it. But as Carlos talked, his speech became a waterfall, clean and elegant and sincere. What he said glued together so many broken and aphasic facts; under the pressure of the narrative, Carl's dirty, unshapely history compressed to a sparkling, lucid truth.

Why he prayed all the time.

Why he talked about forgiveness.

Why he gave to children's charities, and to Planned Parenthood, and to abortion clinics.

Why there had been hang-ups on the machine.

Why he went to Mexico every year, and why he had been in Aguas Vivas.

Why he never married; why he was abstemious in so many different ways; why he worked alone; why he didn't want to have children.

Why he didn't want to have children with her.

She could not imagine carrying that much guilt. Guilt laid against his heart so long that tissue had grown around it, incorporating it into his being.

Guilty, he changes his name.

Still guilty, he devotes his money to causes that he hopes will bring atonement.

Still guilty, he immures himself in solitude: payback for the literal prison he had fled.

All in vain.

And then, after forty years, a letter arrives, one that reaches out even as it accuses. The last time Carl saw his son, the boy could not speak; yet here are words. The boy could not write; yet here is his signature.

She imagined Carl's reaction, reading that letter.

The Church. He had given to the Church.

The letter from the LA Archdiocese. Thanking him for his extraordinary contribution of July 4—right before his son was supposed to arrive in Los Angeles.

But then his son doesn't show up.

Carl thinks: my chance has been revoked. My shame tracked me down to taunt me. No matter how much homage he pays to his dead and living son—through a name, or any other means—there is still a dead girl.

So he decides to kill himselves.

Both Joseph Gerusha and Carl Perreira have to die. The latter spent his whole life whitewashing the former. That, in and of itself, is a sin: deluding yourself that the destruction of two lives can be expunged through charity and symbolism.

For seventeen-year-old Joseph Gerusha, suicide is easy. He's been vegetative for forty years, sustained by a Social Security number and a tax ID. Money socked away in case he ever came back to life. When Carl understands that Joseph is never coming back, he pulls the plug and leaves the money.

But eleven million dollars . . . Why not give it all to charity?

Because, she thought, it's blood money: money earned because he was free these last forty years, and not in jail.

The bank accounts, the stocks, the bonds: all of that gets left. That takes care of Joseph Gerusha's financial records. As for the record of his existence: enter Buck.

How did Carl get a copy of the birth certificate without going to the bank? He kept one at home. Waiting for this moment, dreading it but knowing it would come.

Then he sets to work killing himself. He goes to Aguas Vivas, to the site of the accident, and drives a final stake through his heart. He destroys his car. Maybe he sets it on fire, like Fajardo said.

You could see the flames from town, Señora.

But that was a lie. The accident—it wasn't an accident; she had to stop thinking of it that way—had happened during the day. You couldn't see flames miles away during the daytime. And that blank patch of earth: how could they have cleared the wreckage so fast? Fajardo had shown her a bunch of charred weeds and some broken glass, and—distraught and worn-out—she had accepted them.

Fajardo.

What had Carl said to him, when they arranged all of this?

I want my name to die.

That's going to cost you, Señor.

After bribing the *Teniente*, Carl needs something to live on. He comes back and makes the final withdrawal on his savings account. Eight thousand dollars doesn't get you very far in the United States. Not if you have to start over: a new name, a new trade, a new home in a strange place.

A place where nobody can find him.

A place where eight thousand dollars gets you *very* far.

She thought: He's in Mexico.

It made such perfect sense—brought such an agony of solution—that her hands shook, as though she'd dug herself out of her own grave.

It all made sense.

Her first impulse was to hate him.

Him.

Who's *him*?

JosephCharlosGerreira.

She saw sins and twisted steel and confusion, but she saw no person.

He could have told her; she could have embraced him nonetheless. She had no right to judge him. Would she have done any differently?

Yes. She was a woman, and women did not abandon their children.

But the grandmother did.

But . . . the grandmother came back.

But . . . the grandmother was not a seventeen-year-old boy.

She did not want to judge, could not help judging, tried to be gracious in judgment.

She wanted to kill him.

She wanted to absolve him.

It was not up to her to do either.

But everything made sense.

She didn't want to think anymore.

Through the hockey mask of her fingers, she watched the golf pro execute a flawless 140-yard drive, striking a distantly familiar silhouette. She remembered: the insignia of the PGA. She had seen it countless times, flipping through the channels as she avoided all eleven ESPNs.

Reggie liked sports. He enjoying watching college football so he could deride the players' lack of a "mental game." *When I played for SC* he would say. She had to admit, she'd liked having his trophies around; all the spray-painted gold had given their home a sense of accomplishment.

They were high-school trophies; Reggie's college career had been undistinguished, which made him the perfect candidate to mock every play.

Her sport was bowling. You only had yourself to defeat.

She turned to Carlos Perreira and said, "Can we go somewhere?"

AT FOUR IN THE AFTERNOON, you could get a lane at Mar Vista with no wait.

"I put these on?" Carlos said.

"Yes."

"Other people have worn them."

She nodded, punching their names into the computerized scorer.

He dangled the shoes as though they were human lungs. "If you say so."

Once he'd gotten them on, he said, "Actually, they're pretty comfortable."

"They're already broken in," she said.

He hefted a pearloid number 15. She corrected his grip and said, "You go first."

"I don't know how to do this," he said.

"Just knock them all down."

He threw two gutterballs.

"I did something wrong," he said.

"You'll learn. Watch me."

The first game she beat him 126 to 23. She was disappointed with herself; she usually liked to crack 140. When he told her he was impressed, she waved it off.

"Warm-up game," she said.

The next game she threw a turkey and barely missed sparing the following frame.

"God*dammit!*" she yelled.

Carlos said, "If you keep playing like that, I might have a chance."

After eight frames, the score was 142 to 13.

"Why don't you finish for me?" he said.

She did, throwing a strike and a nine for him to bring him up to 41. For herself, she threw a strike before botching her last frame to close with 164.

"You threw two strikes," he said. "Just because you threw one for me, you shouldn't be punished. Count both strikes for you and give me the three."

A third game he chose to sit out. Gloria's three consecutive spares followed by four consecutive strikes blossomed into a 188.

"You're good at this," he said.

"It's been a while," she said.

THE DINER ATTACHED to the bowling alley was as deserted as the lanes. Its designer had begun invoking the late 1950s but given up halfway. The resultant failure partnered framed Bobby Darin LP's with psychedelic spray-paint art.

They took a booth with an unimpeded view of Venice Boulevard. Across the street, three bunned Hispanic ladies, dip-dyed by the mingled glows of KFC and Winchell's, waited for the Big Blue Bus.

"Thank you," Carlos said. "That was a good idea. I was tired of talking."

"I was tired of listening." She slouched against the vinyl. She needed to eat or she was going to keel over.

Yawning, the waitress arrived. A beauty mark swam in the abundant seas of her cheek. "Burger, Coke, fries?" she said.

"A Greek salad, please," said Gloria.

"That's what you want, that's what you get. You?"

In English, Carlos asked for a light beer.

The waitress leered at him. "That's howya keep your girlish figure?" She laughed, more of a growl, collected their menus, and exited.

They said nothing until the salad arrived: an assortment of necrotic greens, toxic slices of red onion, and rancid olives, topped with a slab of "feta."

Gloria jabbed at it. "This isn't food."

"That salad," Carlos said, "is an insult to the long and proud history of Greece."

She consumed a sixth of it before shoving it aside.

"I have to explain some things to you," she said.

She talked. When she got to the part about the CalFed account, he interrupted her to say, "He's *not* dead?"

"No."

"Are you sure?"

"Pretty sure," she said.

"Well that's . . ." He seemed to have no idea how to react. "That's good," he said finally. "Where is he?"

Pause.

She said, "Mexico."

He looked at her strangely.

"Listen," she said.

She talked for another ten minutes. At the end of it, he said, "You're sure he's not dead?"

"I don't see how he could be," she said. "There was a bank account withdrawal the day after he supposedly died."

Carlos said, "I need to think about this."

He went to the restroom while Gloria took the check to the register. The waitress rang her up.

"He's a cutie," she said.

Gloria, who had been rooting in her wallet, raised her eyes. "Excuse me?"

"Your boyfriend," said the waitress. "He's got a nice tush."

"Do you take credit cards?"

SHE DROPPED HIM at his motel. They agreed to meet up the next day. Carlos asked if she had anything that belonged to his father.

"Not much," she said.

"Not much is better than nothing," he said. He made a tight, tendonous fist. "That's all he's given me so far."

SHE WENT HOME and slept solidly for the first time in a while.

TWENTY

At ten forty-five the next morning he showed up in a cab.

"It's difficult to get a taxi here," he said.

They sat at her table. She had spread out every paper trace of Carl she had. "Not much," she said. "Like I said. I'd take you to his house but it's been sealed, and the lady in charge told me they couldn't open it up at the moment." She unfolded the note and handed it to him.

"'Take care of things when I'm gone,'" he read.

"That's the last thing he wrote to me. There's this." She showed him the microcassette of Carl's last message. She hesitated. "Do you want to hear it?"

"Yes."

She pressed PLAY and closed her eyes, hearing the words in her mind a few seconds before they began.

Gloria. It's me.

She had listened to it enough times that she could hear it as though there was no cellular crackle, no tape hiss, no blurred and hurried instructions.

There's been an accident.

No, she thought. There hasn't been an accident.

How could he have said that? Her life had been turned over for months because he could not be honest with her.

Opening her eyes, she realized that the tape had been silent for more than a minute.

"It's not clear," Carlos said. "It's hard for me to understand what he was saying."

"You want to listen again?"

"No." He looked at the rest of the papers she'd spread out. "What are these?"

"I printed out some of his old e-mails, if you wanted to see those."

He started to read. She felt intrusive sitting there, so she offered him a drink.

"Water," he mumbled.

She lingered in the kitchen, emerging to find him staring dumbly at the mess, in much the same position as before.

"Are you all right?"

He nodded once.

She set the water before him and said, "I'm sorry that's all I have."

He touched the glass but did not pick it up. "You're certain he's alive."

"Not a hundred and five percent," she said. "But, yes, fairly certain."

He looked at her. "Because every time I learn something new, I have to adjust." He took a sip of water. "It puts stress on a person, to keep changing his mind. The worst thing is not knowing."

"I understand."

"And you think he's still alive."

"I do."

"The woman who was handling his money—" he said.

"The public administrator."

"Yes. She stopped dealing with his bank and his possessions?"

"Until he turns up," Gloria said. "The police seem to believe that he might be alive. They're not looking very hard, if at all."

Pause.

Carlos stood.

"I appreciate this," he said, gesturing to the table, "but it's not what I want. I appreciate everything you did for him. If he is alive, then I'm going to find him."

"Wait a second." She caught him at the elbow. "Where are you going?"

"I'll find him," he said. "You think he's in Mexico, so that's where I'll look. The last place he was heard from."

"You're going to Aguas Vivas?"

"If that's where to start," he said, "then I'm going. Where can I get a taxi?"

She said, "I'm going with you."

"Thank you, but that's not necessary."

"I was there," she said. "I spoke to the policeman. I know the area. I was the one who went looking for him in the first place. I'm going back there anyway, and we may as well go together."

"You're going back?" he asked.

She nodded.

"When?"

She had decided when she woke up that morning. Before then: she had woken with the decision in place. Articulating it to him made her more confident that it was not only good but necessary.

"Soon," she said.

Pause.

"You should get on with your life," he said. "There's no reason for you to do this."

"All right," she said. "I agree. I'm going anyway. I thought it would be easier if there were two of us. But I understand if you'd prefer to go alone." She held the door open for him. "Be in touch. Tell me what you find."

He didn't move. "You're going whether I go with you or not."

"Yes."

"You really should stay."

"Maybe," she said. "But I'm going."

"The police will find him. It's better for you to stay."

"Then why are you going?"

"I'm his son," he said.

She said, "I was his friend."

He said nothing.

"It's hard for me to understand any of this," she said. "I want to hear it from his mouth. And I can help you."

He licked his lips. "He's already far ahead of us."

"Okay."

"No. You don't understand. I have to leave." He looked at her defiantly, as though he expected her to buckle.

"Tomorrow morning," she said. "I'll drive."

SHE DROPPED HIM at his motel, on the understanding that he be outside and ready to go at five A.M.

Back at home, she packed and called Reggie.

"I'm heading out of town for a few days," she said.

"You deserve it," he said. "Where you going?"

"Baja." It was easier to lie than to justify it to him.

"Well, have a good time. Call me from the beach."

She got into bed at ten. On the cusp of unconsciousness, she woke to an obnoxious honk. By one-thirty, she knew sleep was a lost cause.

She got up, stumbling over the canvas rucksack that lay at the foot of her bed. Her mother had given it to her when Gloria started college: a genuine Swiss Army bag, with a serial number and a sewn-on flag, made of thick, membranous olive-green canvas. It had survived thousands of miles and pummeling overuse; it was the one semi-expensive item Mamá could call hers. She had gotten it from a *bracero* in San Dolores. It still was in good enough shape to hold clothes for a week.

Gloria went through the bag to make sure she hadn't forgotten anything.

Shorts, sweats, T-shirts, a single dress (for what occasion, she had no idea), walking shoes, flip-flops, socks. She'd packed extra panties, thinking: it gets hot; I might be sweaty. Seeing them all laid out on the bed—rolled like cigars—had made her feel old; she owned nothing except gray Hanes.

That was it for clothes. Her passport, her toiletries. Several photos of Carl, for showing around. A paperback she had tried to read three times had been packed, optimistically, before ending up in the trash. Knowing when to quit was as important as persevering.

She set the bag against the wall so she wouldn't trip over it again, and made for the kitchen to fix herself a cup of tea.

She stopped.

She had forgotten something.

Beneath her bed a shoebox collected dust and protected her Polaroid. She couldn't find any film, though.

She was glad to have an errand. No staring at the clock, no need to make tea.

Los Angeles offered a plethora of all-night drugstores. Content to have a goal, in no rush to achieve it, she cruised south past Norm's (parking lot packed with the Volvos of Beverly Hills kids seeking a shot of diner grease), a used-car dealership, 20/20 Video. She pulled into a deserted Rite Aid at the plaza near 18th. Though the route took her far from home, it put her near the freeway, which is where she wanted to go next.

The clerk went cross-eyed when she asked for the film. "I dunno f'we got that. Holdon." He descended to some infernal storeroom, never to return. Eventually, Gloria sought other assistance in the form of a cornrowed girl with bullwhip stick-on eyelashes.

"Where'd Marcus go?" she asked.

"To the basement," Gloria said.

The girl clucked her tongue. "Shit, we got it right here." She reached behind the counter and produced a stack of film.

"I need one," Gloria said.

"Take two," said the girl. "You're gonna run out, and then you'll be sorry."

Point taken. "Two it is."

As the girl rung her up, she wiggled inch-point-five nails—painted like American flags—in time to the piped-in pop. Jackie Joyner-Kersee nails. Gloria hadn't seen those in years; were they back in style?

"Boy is dumb, dumb, *dumb*," said the girl. "Can't never find nothing."

"It's a big store," Gloria observed.

"Shit, *I* know where it all is . . . fourteen-oh-seven."

Another employee, wearing jeans out of a weight-loss commercial (*I used to wear a size 67!!!*), wandered up, squeegee in hand, reading the register over the girl's shoulder.

"Pauline . . ." he moaned.

"What," said the girl.

"We ain't been paid in like *three weeks*. . . ."

"Tuesday." To Gloria: "Debit or credit?"

"Debit, please."

"I ain't been paid in so long, I forget what my *name* on a paycheck look like."

Gloria smiled and punched in her ATM code.

"Man . . ." The boy shook his head and walked off.

"Dumb motherfucker," muttered Pauline.

Gloria liked her. She reminded her of herself as a girl—with a fouler mouth.

"Here you go, ma'am," said Pauline. She tore the receipt from the machine as though surgically removing its tongue. "You want it in the bag?"

"Please."

Gloria started out when the boy who had gone to the

basement came back, his arms full of film of all types. He saw Pauline and Gloria and stopped, mouth open.

"What happened?" he said.

Pauline turned him around and pushed him back. "Put that shit away, we don't need em, they all behind the counter."

"There wasn't none when I loo—"

"You couldn't find your balls, I gave you ten minutes and a flashlight."

The parking lot lamps towered like archangels, spraying their glow through the nighttime mist. From the other end of the lot came the diffuse jellybean cheer of the Toys Я Us sign. Out in front hung desperate banners counting down the TWO WEEKS TILL CHRISTMAS. She paused in the chill air to wonder what she would do for the holidays. Dinner she did alone or at the home of a friend's family, Kathy or Janine or the Oberles. For the last five years, she and Carl had spent the day making deliveries for his church's food bank; at the end of the day, she gave him his new figurines. A nondescript and decent way to celebrate.

What now?

She dumped her stuff on the Dodge's passenger seat and, shivering, turned on the heat. Gruelly dew beaded on the windshield; she pushed the wipers once, started the car for real, and drove to the 10 east.

She let herself be guided toward Boyle Heights.

It was a bad idea on many counts. The last thing she needed before a ten-hour drive was a witching-hour tour of an area where midday drive-bys failed to elicit a reaction.

But it was the Neighborhood.

She took the exit for the Home of Peace, Mamá's old place of employment. Its gates were shut, but Gloria got out to peek at the extravagantly somber tan chapel. Rows of monuments engraved with foreign characters went right up to the cemetery walls. Thirty years ago, it had been crowded. By now, she thought, they must be stacking them up.

Once, when Mamá started there, she had come home and told Gloria, "The Jews wrote the Bible." Gloria, studying, acceded but didn't see what it had to do with her. Her overtaxed mind felt no need to accumulate burdensome factoids.

A few weeks later, Mamá came home and said, "There were Jews in Mexico."

Gloria nodded and went back to her math.

By the end of the year, Mamá was regularly sharing tidbits of information about *The Jews.*

The Jews lived in Spain, and some of them came with the conquistadors.

The Jews were very powerful.

Jesus was a carpenter, but he was also a Jew.

Upon inquiring, Gloria discovered that Mamá had acquired all such information from regular conversation with the rabbi who ran the cemetery. He often stayed late, and as Mamá was the only person around, they would chat. He wanted to improve his Spanish, and she wanted to improve her English. They spoke for fifteen minutes in one, then switched.

"He tells me about the Jews."

"You're not going to learn any useful English that way," Gloria said.

Mamá didn't care. She was happy to have talk. By the time she arrived home, smothered in weariness, she lacked the strength to speak with Gloria for more than a few minutes. At the cemetery, though, the rabbi caught her fresh off her cleaning shift in Bel Air: tired but eager for human contact, after having spent the whole day ignored by Mrs. Walden, who thought it improper to mingle with the staff.

"What do you talk to him about?"

"He wants to know everything. He asked me where I came from. I told him about San Dolores, and about Esteban, and your father. I told him about our trip here, when you were not born."

"Why does he care?"

"Because he's a nice man," said Mamá.

"I don't believe that anyone would be interested in you just because he's nice," Gloria said.

"Muchas muchas muchas gracias."

"You're sure he's not going to do anything to you?"

"Stop. He's curious."

"What did he think of your stories?"

"He liked hearing about hitchhiking. He said it reminded him of the Exodus. I said, 'It only took me a few weeks to get to the Promised Land, not forty years.'"

A month later, Mamá came home laughing.

"The rabbi thinks I'm Jewish," she said.

Gloria slammed her physics book. "That's ridiculous."

"I know, but he said I have a Jewish name."

"Maria?"

"Mendez."

"I know lots of people named Mendez," Gloria said.

"He said it's a Marrano name."

Gloria knew what Marrano referred to, because Mamá had already given her the annotated history of the Jews of Spain, courtesy of the rabbi.

"Isn't that something?" Mamá asked.

"It's something. I don't know what it is, but it's definitely something."

That night was Friday night. They lit candles and read before going to sleep.

Religion had always been a part of their lives, from Mamá's morning prayers to compulsory weekly confession. Gloria hated the latter because she never had anything to say. When Mamá took both her and Jesús Julio, Gloria would emerge from the confessional a good five minutes before he did. It got so that he accused her of cheating. She started making up sins so that she would be able to stay in longer.

Strangely, Mamá didn't make confession. Gloria wondered if her conversations with the rabbi served that function.

Gripping the bars of the cemetery, Gloria pictured him. A black coat to which repeated laundering had imparted a silver patina. His brown beard, veined white. A red tie with tan specks. A shirtfront whose tautness revealed an undershirt. He had disproportionately small feet, encased in loaf-like loafers.

Surely he was dead by now. That's how she thought of everyone Mamá's age.

"Ay, Mami."

To her left, a young man in a do-rag and a skintight

white tanktop was coming toward her, his body undulating like a slinky as he made masturbatory gestures.

Her car was across the street, and he was a good twenty feet off. She made it back with plenty of time, although her hands sweated on the keys.

"Hey, chupame la polla!"

What was he? Sixteen? He stumbled to the cemetery gates and began humping the bars, baying and flopping his tongue sloppily from side to side.

She backed out and put it in drive. As she pulled away, she beeped once and waved good-bye.

That she had acknowledged him at all paralyzed him momentarily. Then he ran into the street. She could see him in her rearview mirror, hip-thrusting and hooting and laughing his ass off, looking like a major success.

TWENTY-ONE

She dozed for thirty-five minutes before her alarm crowed reveille. She bolted up: her neck wet, her head writing irate letters to the editor. Limbs tingling with fatigue, she spasmed through the motions: shower, towel, knapsack, snack bag, car, whoops the map, whoops the camera, you're missing something, toiletries kit under the arm, what are you forgetting, probably your brain, but you can stop in San Diego and buy a new one before you leave the country.

She loaded one package of film into the camera; the extra she stuffed in the side pocket of the bag, which flatly refused to accept anything more. She shut the trunk, did five jumping jacks, and hopped behind the wheel.

Los Angeles was quiet except for dairy trucks. Eastbound on Pico, she passed an emaciated young woman running behind a tri-wheeled stroller. The street shone like a creek. Gloria yawned and stretched and switched off the radio.

Carlos was waiting at the entrance to the motel parking

lot. Like her, he traveled light: a backpack and a briefcase. His shirt was undone three buttons deep; his chest the same color as his face and forehead, and probably the rest of his body. He looked remarkably chipper, as though they were about to set off in search of gold rather than a miserable past.

"Buenos dias," he said, throwing his bags in the backseat.

They went.

At first she thought he wanted to sleep, but then he began asking questions about Carl. How long had she worked for him; what he was like; did he ever seem sad.

"All the time," she said. "Until you said sadness, I wouldn't have been able to identify it. But I think you're right."

"Remorse?"

She thought for a moment. "As though the best of everything was behind him."

He grilled her about his father's hobbies, habits, figures of speech. He seemed genuinely astonished to hear that Carl had taken up regular church services.

"My grandmother blamed my mother's downfall on the fact that my father was a 'heathen.' My grandmother would say to me, 'You marry a Christian; Christians are good to their children.'"

"He became a good Christian," she said.

"Too late," he replied.

Still, he kept asking questions. She found herself speaking with unprecedented candor. She didn't feel ashamed when he asked if she had ever been romantically involved with his father.

"No," she said.

"I hope it's not rude to ask."

"No."

"Because I'm curious," he said. "Why you're doing this for him."

"I had to," she said.

"No. You didn't. So it's interesting to me. When I met you I assumed you were his . . . his girlfriend?"

She half-smiled. "No."

"Or his wife."

Coughing, clearing her throat. "No."

By the time they reached the southern edge of the San Diego area, Carlos had run out of questions.

"This is hard," he said. "Generally you get to know a person over years. Not by crash course."

"It took a while to crack his shell," she said. Thinking, Did I?

Carlos asked for permission to take his shoes off.

"Make yourself at home."

He reclined, propped up his feet, stretched. His shirt strained against his chest.

"Talk about yourself," he said.

"What?"

"You know all about me. I gave a lecture. Your turn."

"It's not that interesting."

"Everybody is interesting," he said, yawning.

"Why don't you take a nap instead?"

"If it's boring," he said, "I'll fall asleep in the middle, and then you can stop."

"I've never given a speech about it before," she said.

"You don't need to give a speech. I'll ask you questions. What's your birthday?"

"January nineteenth."

"Oh?" He sat up. "It's almost your birthday."

"Yeah," she said.

"I'll sing to you."

"That's fine, really."

"What."

"I don't need a reminder."

"Come on," he said.

"No," she said. "Don't."

"How old are you?"

"Isn't that one of the things you aren't supposed to ask someone?"

"I don't know," he said. "I never went to finishing school."

"You're not supposed to ask about weight or politics, either."

"Politics we'll get to in a minute," he said. "Weight I don't need to ask."

She regarded him with amusement. "Thanks a lot."

"I mean, you've got nothing to be ashamed of," he said.

She turned the air-conditioning up a notch. "That's the border."

The signs with the fleeing silhouettes appeared again. The one that had been defaced had been replaced; no more sombrero. The other signs appeared as well, counting down to the moment at which they learned

YOU ARE NOW LEAVING THE UNITED STATES

She glanced over at Carlos. He was reading the signs, wide-eyed and looking vaguely troubled. All the security was directed at him. He was the one the law fought to keep out. She was the one whose rights and services the law protected. If too many of him came across, people like her suffered. Bad traffic worsened. Taxes were hiked in order to support those who claimed benefits without a green card. The demographic chasm that had split California into two distinct entities widened.

She felt bad for Carlos. She felt bad for Mexico, to be treated this way.

At the same time—just like any other Californian—she resented Mexico.

Its citizens *did* pour over in droves. They *did* take her money and her resources. They *did* ghettoize, and neglect to learn English, and take over the radio stations.

That Californians spent as much time talking about Mexico as they did revealed a certain intimacy, even when the issue at stake was *should we send them all home and lock the gates after they're out?* Almost every state election grappled with some sort of immigration-related proposition. People talked about "Mexifornia," and what was going to happen when the inexorable march of statistics proved that they had become not a minority, not a plurality, but the ruling class.

We think about them all the time, she thought.

We? Them?

We.

She was *we.* They were *them.*

When she filled out forms that asked for her ethnicity,

she declined to state. Every time someone spoke Spanish to her on the street in LA, she felt mildly resentful. *I speak English; I was going to be a doctor; I read Chaucer and got an A.*

"Customs wasn't this bad at the airport," Carlos said.

"They're not worried about the ones who can afford to fly," she said.

"Ah." He looked at the fence again. "'The ones.' What does that make you?"

"I was born in Arizona," she said. "You have your passport?"

He dug around in his pockets. "Shit. I left it in my bag."

Mexican border control didn't ask, though. Carlos turned to look at the crossing.

"It's like a one-way mirror," he said.

They headed down the highway, slipping past an accident between an old pickup and a horse trailer.

"Born in Arizona," he said. "That's right, I almost forgot. *Feliz cumpleaños a ti. . . .*" He had an unexpectedly high singing voice; not an unpleasant one, though.

"Stop."

"Feliz cumpleaños a ti. . . ."

"Stop, Carlos."

"Okay," he said. He took a deep breath and launched into different words with the same tune. *"Cuántos años tienes tú, cuántos años tienes tú . . ."*

"If I tell you, will you stop?"

"Sí."

"I'm thirty-six."

"That I never would have guessed."

"You thought forty-six?" she asked.

"Twenty-six. Have you ever been married?"

"Once."

"Kids?"

"No," she said; then, eager to change the subject: "You never got married either."

"I had a girlfriend. Like I told you. That was before my grandmother died."

"What happened?"

He didn't answer, and she started to repeat the question.

"I heard you," he said. He paused again. "I don't talk about it."

"Okay."

Silence.

He said, "I'm the one supposed to be asking you questions."

"Is it a contest?"

"At the end of the trip we'll see who knows the other person better."

"Ask away."

"You were born in Arizona," he said.

"Yes."

He prompted her with a hand.

She sighed. "I'm telling you, you're going to regret this. . . ."

"How much longer is the drive?" he asked.

"Six hours, maybe more."

He crossed his arms and put his feet back up. "Start talking."

At first she left out details, making oblique reference to her brother's death. The further along she went, however, the more loosely her lips moved. She recalled images and events previously quarantined. He was like a therapist: close enough that she could assume he'd understand, anonymous enough for her to offer confession without fear of reprisal. She began to regret lying about her early history.

"My brother—" she said.

"Half-brother."

"Yes. He didn't die of pneumonia," she said. "He was killed."

"I know," he said.

"How."

"Because of the way you didn't talk about it," he said.

She liked when he said that.

"That's why your mother wanted you to become a doctor," he said. "So what happened?"

"I had to drop out. My mother had a stroke."

"Oh, Gloria," he said. "I'm sorry to hear that." Coming from anyone else, it might have sounded glib, but he seemed to mean it. "When?"

"The first year of college. She needed someone to monitor her all day. She didn't have insurance." She signaled, looked behind, and switched lanes. She felt him waiting for her. "She went into a coma, and when she came out she couldn't talk anymore, or walk. She was better than a vegetable, but not by much."

"And you were with her," he said.

She nodded.

"All day," he said.

"All day, every day."

"For how long?"

"Seven and a half years."

Pause.

"That sounds like torture."

"That's one word for it."

"I apologize," he said. "I didn't mean that the way it sounded."

"You're right. It was torture." After a pause, she added: "Expensive torture."

"What did you do?"

"My mother had saved for my education. There was the money she'd saved for Jesús Julio. There was a gift Mrs. Walden gave me when she found out what happened. The man in charge at the cemetery raised a collection. He gave us forty-two hundred dollars." She made a pretext of changing lanes again, so she could stop talking.

He asked, "How did you get along the rest of the time?"

"I sewed for people. I cooked for them. I babysat. Anything I could do that didn't involve leaving the house for very long. Also, I—" She smiled. "It's a funny story. Not what you'd expect."

"I don't expect anything," he said.

"But it's long. . . ." she demurred.

"*How* much further is the drive?" he asked. He made a show of scanning the map, inverting it, *hmm*ing and counting on his fingers. "Well, only four and a half hours left. You'd better hurry."

She smiled. "All right."

He settled back as though preparing to watch a movie.

Gloria said, "The man who ran the grocery was friends with my mother. He was crushed after her stroke. I think he might have had a thing for her. From a distance; he was married.

"After Mamá became housebound, he personally brought us our food. With every order he threw in an extra piece of meat, or some fruit. There was always something we hadn't paid for. He was very generous. And he looked like Santa Claus. Fate loves that sort of thing.

"The first September, after I had been cooped up in the house for six months—I was losing my mind—he sent a package of clay along with our order. It was called Kiddie Klay. You could mold your own saucer. You put it in the oven and it came out glazed, like a real one."

"Except uglier," Carlos said.

She laughed. "Right. It was for little girls; he probably had it lying around, and he stuck it in at the last minute. Maybe he forgot how old I was."

"How old were you?"

"Eighteen."

"And you were your mother's guardian."

"Yes."

"That's a crazy thing to ask of you," he said.

"Nobody asked."

"You had anyone taking care of you?"

"Everyone in the neighborhood worked. A lot of them had two jobs or more, like Mamá. No one could afford to sit around and cook for me. Besides, when I dropped out, it became my full-time job."

"Unpaid."

She nodded.

"So you've done this sort of thing before," he said.

"What sort of thing."

"Like what you did for my father, when you thought he was dead."

"Hardly the same thing."

"It is."

She said, "Give me an apple?"

He rooted in the plastic bag, gave her one, took one himself.

She bit it and pushed juice back in her mouth. "I was in the middle of telling you something."

He smiled. "By all means."

"Mr. Navarro, the market owner, sent me the clay. I stuck it under the kitchen sink and forgot about it completely until the week of Christmas, when I went to find some tape so I could wrap a present for him. I found the box of Kiddie Klay, and I decided to make him something, as a way to thank him.

"That night, after I put Mamá to sleep, I stayed up making him a present. It was going to be a statue of him, but I thought he wouldn't want to stare at a bad version of himself. Since it was Christmas—and Mr. Navarro was very devout—I made him a Madonna and child. With the leftover clay, I made a bird holding a branch in its mouth.

"I didn't think they were any good, but I baked them, wrapped them up, and gave them to him the next time he came by.

"The next day, the day before Christmas, he came back.

"'What's the matter?' I asked. 'Did I forget to pay you?'

"'No,' he said. 'It's not that. I want to know where you got the statues.'

"I told him I made them myself, with the kit he'd given me.

"He thought I was putting him on. He said, 'I don't have time to fool around; I need to go out and get three dozen of them for my friends.' I showed him the package. It had a tiny bit of green left.

"'I used everything except that,' I said.

"When he saw the package, he crossed himself." She laughed, remembering it. "He asked me to make more, but I didn't have any clay left. He said, 'No problem, stay here.' Like I was going somewhere. A half-hour later he came back lugging a crateful of the kits, sweating as he carried them up our front step.

"He said, 'I ordered five boxes of this stuff but nobody bought it. Take it, make me as many of the Santa Marias as you possibly can. I'll give you the clay and four dollars per figurine.'

"I told him I wasn't going to take any money from him.

"'We'll haggle about it later,' he said, 'just make the damned Marias!'

"That day I made six. Each took an hour, although I got better as I went along. I made six more the next day, and he arrived at five o'clock to collect them all. He insisted that I keep the clay. But I told him no money, not a chance, not on my life.

"I found a hundred dollars in the mailbox.

"I guess he showed the things around, because a few weeks later a friend of his—a stranger to me—called to ask if I could make him a figurine for his feast day. I told him I didn't know what Blessed Gonzalo looked like.

"He said, 'Make it look like me.'

"He came over that week and sat while I sculpted him in Kiddie Klay. He was old and it took a long time to do his wrinkles. He didn't complain, but sat there chewing tobacco and talking about . . ." She paused, biting her tongue. "Oh. I know. It was the Dodgers. 'This year, we win.' He kept repeating that. I think he was senile.

"I showed him the figurine before I put it in the oven.

"'There I am,' he said.

"He gave me twenty dollars. I said, 'You don't have to give me anything.' 'Take it,' he said. 'That's what José said it costs.'

"I guess Mr. Navarro told him I had a fee. And he had given me a raise, too.

"Pretty soon people in the neighborhood were coming by and asking me to make them figurines for birthdays and holidays, saint days. The clay was bright, not subtle; when you baked it, it turned shiny, like it had an inner light. That's why it made for good religious figures. I started to receive calls from outside the neighborhood.

"I needed to take care of Mamá, so I limited myself to twenty-five a week. Mr. Navarro wanted to sell them in his store, but I had my hands full already. It was a good sideline; it covered a lot of our rent. I didn't pay any taxes on it, either.

"When I had used up all the kits Mr. Navarro had, he ordered some more. At first he didn't let me pay, but I said, 'It's not a legitimate business if you don't let me buy my own materials.' I was stubborn because I was embarrassed at taking charity. So he became my supplier. He would come up our steps, carrying the crate and dripping sweat everywhere."

She smiled; Carlos did likewise. "He was a big, fat man," she said. "A saint.

"Every year before Christmas I would take a few days and do nothing but make figurines for him, three, four, five dozen. He couldn't possibly have needed that many, but he always made it sound as though he was desperate.

"'Can't you make any more?' he would say when he showed up to collect. 'Next year make sure you start earlier.' I gave him a bulk rate. Sometimes it came out to hundreds of dollars.

"It was fun for a while."

"Why'd you stop?"

"When I moved out of the neighborhood—with Reggie—I wanted to forget everything about it. I made new friends. I wanted to start a real life. I put the stuff away and didn't touch it again until I met your father. The first year I made him two for Christmas. At first I made one, but I didn't want it to be lonely. So I made two. Jesus and . . ." She grinned. "A vampire."

Carlos said, "If the vampire got hungry, he'd take a sip of Jesus's hand."

She laughed despite herself. "I have enough clay piled up in my closet for the next twenty years." She smiled. "I told Carl, after that, I'd have to learn to draw."

She took a deep breath, impressed with her own loquacity.

"Did you ever think about becoming an artist?" he said.

"I thought about becoming a doctor. I thought about

becoming a lot of things. That's all I did: I thought about it. Oh," she said, remembering something else and feeling the good momentum of talking, an unburdening energy, "I also typed for people. I learned to do it in high school. Everyone knew that I needed money. So they made up excuses to bring me things to type. They came when they wanted to send letters home. There was one man who came by every week to write his mother in Guatemala. He was always worried because of the war. He didn't find out she had been killed until he went to visit.

"But usually it was happy news. I got to tell people that they had a new grandson. People gave me whatever they wanted, which was usually fifty cents a page. I did it several hours a day. We had a good typewriter, an Olivetti. I'm not sure where it came from." She paused. "Actually, I think Jesús Julio stole it."

She began laughing.

"I need to pull over. . . ." she coughed, laughing harder.

They rolled to a stop. She cut the engine and had a good two minutes.

"Oh . . ." she said, pressing her chest. "*Oh.* Oh, I needed that. . . ." She flopped back, blinking. "Oh, my God . . ."

"Do you want me to drive?"

"No. No, I'm fine. I'm—I'm terrific." She smiled, and he was smiling, too.

Their next turnoff was that mud-choked excuse for a road. They lurched along as if on camelback, the Dodge's path determined less by her driving than by the guerrilla caprice of rocks and potholes.

"Was your ex-husband religious?" he asked.

"Not at all."

"Because, I wonder how that works."

"How what works."

Carlos said, "There are people who believe and people who don't. Usually they don't have much to talk about."

"Well, we didn't," she said. "That was part of the problem."

"Then why did you marry him?"

The steering wheel twisted beneath her fingers; she brought it back into line. "I'm going to drive off the road."

"You don't have to answer," he said.

"I will," she said. ". . . because I was lonely."

"That's a good reason," Carlos said.

"No. It's not. It's the worst reason to get married."

He nodded.

She said, "After my mother died I spent months lost. When I met Reggie he seemed like the right thing. He was a cop, which gave me a sense of security. I didn't figure out until later that he was a lot less impressive without the gun."

Carlos grinned.

"The divorce helped," she said. "I grabbed myself by the neck."

"So being married was good for something," he said.

"Sure, at least to prove Reggie wrong when he said I'd miss him."

"Where'd you meet?"

"He was investigating my next-door neighbor on a drug charge. It was about three months after Mamá died. He came by to ask me questions and ended up leaving with my phone number."

"You gave it to him?" Carlos said.

"I thought it was part of the investigation."

He laughed.

She said, "You never got married?" Then she remembered that she had already asked, and that he hadn't wanted to answer. She started to retract but he said:

"It's hard for me to trust people. You can understand why."

"I'm sorry."

"You don't need to be sorry, but you need to understand." He shifted. "The year I moved to Mexico City I met a great woman."

"What was her name?"

He smiled. "Gloria."

She twitched slightly. "Whoops," she said, righting the wheel.

"I know," he said. "Funny."

"H—uh—how did you meet."

"A friend. One thing, another, and next thing I know she's telling me we should get married, have children. I went along with it. I *wanted* it. We even picked out a church.

"The night before we were supposed to meet with the priest, my grandmother died. We had to cancel, obviously, and I went north to make funeral arrangements.

"Gloria came with me. The whole time we were traveling, there and back, we didn't say anything about marriage. We didn't talk about my grandmother, either. They had never met, so she had nothing to say. We made small talk. I felt like I couldn't talk to her at all. Alone, with her in the seat beside me.

"One bad day can ruin a whole person. You see them under stressful circumstances, and they perform exactly the wrong way. They say stupid things, they touch you incorrectly; everything they do irritates you. The minute you start to think these things—unless you stop the thoughts immediately—you can be sure that catastrophe is not too far away.

"Soon after we got back to Mexico City, she started talking about rescheduling with the priest. The *last* thing on my mind. I told her I didn't want to have the wedding in that church. I picked a fight with her, the worst one we'd ever had. Both of us made things up about the other one, so we would have ammunition. It ended that night.

"Then I took several years to drink myself into the ground.

"I kept coming in to work in a worse and worse state. I got my job done, but my boss could tell what was up. He finally called me into his office and told me that everything I touched stank of booze. He fired me on the spot.

"That night I drove over to his house, planning on breaking his nose. It might sound ridiculous, but when you've been drunk for a lot of your adult life, something like that makes a lot of sense.

"His wife answered the door, and all the fight went out of me; I started blabbering. She had known me for a while, she knew what was happening. She brought me in, gave me aspirin, and got Eddie. He ordered me to go to *Alcohólicos Anónimos.*

"I said, 'Let me guess, *you* were in it, and they saved your life.'

"'No,' he said. 'But the asshole who ran over my sister *wasn't* in it.'

"There's not much to say except that it worked. For a lot of people it never ends; they have to go every week for the rest of their lives. The instant you remove the safety net they crash. Those people I feel bad for. Their chemistry is screwed up. I'm not like that. I drank because I liked being a tiny bit forgetful. I have a good memory. It's more of a curse than a blessing."

"I know what you mean," said Gloria.

Dust swirled around the car; they were under silent, tan waters.

Carlos said, "I had a good sponsor. He understood that no two drinkers are the same. When I told him I wanted to stop coming to meetings, he said, 'I think you'll be okay.' That was important to hear. And it was especially good to hear from *him,* because he *is* one of those drinkers who will never be able to leave AA."

When he shifted again, his shirt adhered to his back. "My lost decade."

"Yes," she said.

He said, "Like yours."

Pause.

She said, "We'll be there soon."

TWENTY-TWO

They made it to Aguas Vivas at a quarter to three, beating her first time. Having stopped for gas midway from Tijuana, she had a half a tank left. They got out to move their legs.

Carlos said, "What is this place?"

As far as she could see, everything was the same, down to the dust on the shop signs. The street was still empty; the E in CINE, still missing; the stonecutters still at war with each other. She checked their displays to see if there had been developments on either front. *H. Lopez-Caravajal* had made gains. His columns of yellow paper had thickened like a bamboo grove.

"The local industry," she said.

They ambled toward the movie theater.

"That's the police station?" Carlos asked.

"Yup."

"Low-budget operation."

"Lower than that," she said.

"You have to be careful talking to police here," he said. "That's the one rule."

"Things might not be in such bad shape if you had more than one rule."

Carlos said, "You're kind of a racist."

"Some of my best friends are Mexican," she said. "*I'm* Mexican."

"I thought you were American."

"Are you ready? Look tough."

"You're afraid of him," Carlos said.

"Why shouldn't I be? He has a gun and we're about to accuse him of fraud."

"Did he strike you as a man with a bad temper?"

"He struck me as a coward," she said. "He tried to get me to sleep with him."

Carlos burst out laughing. He bent over, hands on knees.

"Is it that crazy?" she said. "I'm a little insulted."

"It had nothing to do with you," he said. "I can just imagine it."

"Wait until you meet him," she said. "Then you'll see how funny it was."

"If you're concerned," he said, "I can pretend like I'm your husband."

"I'm not wearing a ring."

"Boyfriend. Or we'll hide it." He took her hand; she let it happen; they stepped into the shade of the marquee.

Knocking produced no response; neither did repeated calls of *¡Teniente, emergencía!* Behind the theater was a desiccated swath of earth. They went up and down, pounding on the rear doors of adjacent shops.

"Is everyone here asleep?" he said.

"Dead."

They returned to the street and crossed to the general store, wherein she found an empty counter and—she could swear—the selfsame tortillas that had been in stock five months ago, now in the process of liquefying.

Together they stepped onto the back porch. Luís dozed in the rocker. A bottle nestled between his legs; from it a moist penumbra had seeped into the fabric of his crotch. Atop the table, an empty cooler perspired. Five bottles on the floor.

Carlos mouthed *The cop?*

She shook her head and pointed to the store.

Without opening his eyes, Luís said, *"Cerrado."*

"Do you remember me?" she asked.

Luís cranked up one lid. *"Señora.* How was your drive?"

"Not bad," she said.

Luís turned the eye on Carlos.

"I didn't want to wake you," Gloria said. "But there's no one around."

"That's not a good reason to wake me, *Señora.* No one is ever around."

"It's the middle of the day," she said.

"I know," Luís moaned, hoisting himself out of the chair. "You came right as I was starting my siesta. Never mind, we can have it together. You want a drink? The house special?" He grinned.

Gloria and Carlos followed him inside. He shuffled behind the counter and took out three bottles of water, the same Mexican brand she had gotten last time. She imagined an endless supply of no-name foodstuffs stacked in the basement, slowly fermenting and waiting for unsuspecting pit-stoppers.

"You can have this," said Luís, offering Carlos a bottle of home-brew.

"What is it?" Carlos asked.

"A Sonoran drink," Luís said. "To drink it is an act of patriotism."

Gloria set the water on the counter. "This'll be fine."

Luís held the home-brew up. "Nobody wants to drink you," he said to it.

She laid dollars on the counter. "How have you been, Luís?"

"Oh, you know," he said. He spread her money out and counted it, then bent to make change from the cashbox on the floor. "Last time you ran off, you didn't say good-bye." He straightened, slapped a half-dozen coins down. "This time, you can make it up. Before you leave, say good-bye twice."

"I'll make sure," she said.

"You came back for vacation? You like the heat?"

"We're here to see *Teniente* Fajardo," she said. She waited for him to reply, but he sat there like a Weimaraner. "We tried the police station, but it was locked."

"I know," said Luís. "That's because the *Teniente* isn't there. It's his day off."

"How can we get in touch with him?"

"Check the message board," said Luís. "In the box office." He pointed out the door, then peered at Carlos. "Are you the *Señora's* bodyguard?"

"No," Gloria said. "He's a friend."

"Ohh, I see . . . the *Teniente* said you tried to shoot him last time."

"Really. Did he."

"He said you got angry when he refused to kiss you goodnight," Luís wheezed.

"That's not quite how it went."

"I'm kidding, *Señora*. You want some water for the road?"

"We're going across the street."

"Yes," he allowed, "but it's a big street."

WHAT HAD ONCE READ POLICÍA had been rearranged and elaborated upon. The box office sign now informed them that

THE POLICE ARE AT HOME
ANYONE AROUND HERE WHO NEEDS THE POLICE
YOU KNOW WHERE TO REACH ME BUT STRICTLY IN
CASE OF EMERGENCY

Toward the end, the *Teniente* had run out of plastic letters, and improvised.

EN C4S0 DE EM3RG3N(I4

Below the message was a phone number, handwritten on a piece of paper and tacked to the board. Carlos took out his cellphone and gave it to her; she dialed.

"*Bueno.*"

"Is this *Teniente* Fajardo?"

"Hola, Señora."

She said, "Who is this?"

"Turn around."

Luís was standing at the entrance to the general store, holding a cordless receiver and waving.

"Think about it, *Señora.* Right now, I'm talking, and it's going all the way up into space, before it comes back down to you. Isn't it crazy?"

His mouth didn't quite match the sounds. When he started to snicker, she heard it in real time in her free ear, and a quarter-second later in the other.

She hung up and walked across the street.

"You win," she said. "Now tell me how I can reach him."

"He's on his day off," Luís said. "I told you."

"All right," she said, taking out her wallet.

Luís looked offended. "*Señora.* Please. I'm a man of my word. I promised the *Teniente* that he would not be disturbed unless it was extremely pressing."

She put five dollars in his hand. "Is that pressing enough?"

"*Señora,* that isn't even pressing enough to call the plumber."

Ten.

"Now?" she asked.

"Trouble is building," he said. "Maybe it will get worse."

She said, "I'm going to give you ten more dollars, Luís. If it's not pressing enough then, I'm going to have Carlos break your store window. Then we'll all have a reason to fetch the *Teniente.*"

Luís's mouth hung open. Then he cackled.

"I admire the way you think, *Señora*. Just for that, I'll give you a discount on trouble. Five more."

She complied. He took from his breast pocket a notepad with a pencil stump threaded through the coil.

"If I call he won't come," he said, writing. "It's better if you go over to his house." He tore the page out and handed it to her. "You can't miss it. If you miss it, then come back here. We'll have drinks and the problem can be solved tomorrow." He nodded once and shuffled back into the store.

Carlos was standing by the box office.

"What did you do?" he asked her.

"I made threats on your behalf."

"Nothing too bad, I hope."

"Could you break that window?"

He glanced at it. "Probably not."

"Then I was bluffing."

Carlos rubbed his stomach. "It just occurred to me," he said. "We came here unarmed."

"You think that's going to be a problem?"

"No," he said. "Unless it is."

TWENTY-THREE

Out of the desert swelled a pimply clutch of structures, the color of the earth but more so. Tract housing—fifteen units—was laid out like an unraveling nautilus. At the far end, Fajardo's place staked its claim to acres of cacti, chaparral, yellow gravel. Some of his neighbors had cultivated gardenettes, lining front steps with pink and white carnations that probably required replanting every ten days. The *Teniente* had made no such effort. His house was the most run-down, with the dingiest plaster and the largest cracks in the poured-concrete walk. In the driveway was a decrepit purple pickup truck that had not been washed since birth. A garage door hovered four inches ajar.

The sun was sinking; bad roads had slowed them. She remembered Fajardo making excuses for his tardiness at the scene of the accident. Now that she'd driven it, she could almost believe him.

To the far northwest were hills covered in a red-and-white suburban lichen. This, she assumed, was Charrones. What were these houses doing out here? Too remote to be convenient to the city, they smacked of planned community gone wrong. Gloria wondered if Fajardo had gotten the land cheap as part of an agreement to live here. Wasn't that how they got these places started? But then the developers went under, or discovered they'd built atop a fault line, or couldn't sell one for profit. Too late for the suckers who'd packed up and plunked down in the midst of a wasteland, doomed to reside in an aborted dream.

On the porch, two planters filled with white stones flanked a shattered watering can. A blond baby doll with one arm missing lay supine and expectant, as though awaiting a transplant. There was also a single flattened slipper, striped blue; some animal had tried to make a meal of it. The concrete, once painted red, had faded, leaving sickly pink archipelagos, islets of raw and pockmarked gray.

Inside, a woman was screaming.

The door was unlocked. A cluster of votive candles, beaded rosaries, icons, and flimsy copper etchings covered the foyer's semicircular table. Over this presided a mirror and a large brass crucifix. Beyond was a gloomy room in which a gaunt woman held a child of uncertain sex by its underwear. The mother was the one screaming; the kid flopped around in noncompliance. Gaudy commercial music scored the scene.

Gloria called out, "Hello?"

Jerked as though prodded in the belly, the woman released the kid—who toddled off—and came forward into the light, brushing a stray brown vine behind her ear. She wore several large and cheap rings, navy leggings, and a loose T-shirt that said FREEDOM USA. She was gaunt and pretty in a long-faced way: all cheekbones and deep sockets.

She gave them each a once-over, then addressed Carlos in a brittle voice: "Yes?"

"We're here to see *Teniente* Fajardo," he said.

"Are you."

"This is Gloria Mendez; my name is Carlos Perreira."

The woman cocked her head at him. "Well, that's good to know," she said.

"Are you his wife?"

The woman sneer-smiled. "In fact, I am."

"Nice to meet you," Carlos said.

"Oh, yes. Nice to meet you. *So* nice to meet you."

"Is the *Teniente* around?"

The woman cantilevered her bony frame in the doorway, a pose at which she appeared practiced. Gloria suspected that this was not the first time she had had to protect her husband from unexpected guests.

"Tito is resting," she said. "He cannot be disturbed."

"Well," said Carlos. "That's too bad."

"Yes," said the woman. "How sad. Good-bye." She started to close the door in their faces, but Gloria stopped her gently.

"We've been driving a while," she said. "Can I use your bathroom?"

The woman looked at Carlos, who said, "She'll be quick."

The TV jingle ended, replaced by soap-opera dialogue. A crash from a faraway room: kitchen utensils hitting a dirty floor. The woman closed her eyes and sighed.

"Follow me," she said.

Carlos waited on the front step while the woman led Gloria into a living room that had surrendered to toys. Secondhand action figures and plastic balls tripped them; waterlogged picture books were stacked under the recliner and by the radiator. The box from a child's tricycle supported the TV. An oppressively loud organ gargled the *telenovela* pathos of a stubbly hero caressing a doe-eyed brunette in a halter top.

Consuela, I love you.

Juan, no! We can never be together, your father will disinherit you.

Consuela, I don't care. Taking Her in His arms, He lowered Her to the floor. *¡El amor es más fuerte que el dinero!*

The woman, who had stopped to watch this scene, snorted.

From another room, a boy began crying, "Maaa. Maaaaaa." The woman bit her lip, as though trying to decide whether the term applied to her or not. In the midst of this, a crusty-faced girl of two tottered in, chewing on a sock.

Ma, ma, ma, ma . . .

"Adela," said the woman. "That's not for eating."

The girl kept working at the sock as though it was a recalcitrant piece of taffy.

"Mamamamamama."

"Take it out of your mouth, Adela."

"Mamá! Mamá! MAAAMAAA!"

The woman's head swung toward the cries. She howled *Shut up shut up shut up shut up!* Then she smacked Adela

hard enough to spin her. After a bewildered silence, the girl
began to wail, the crust atop her upper lip moistening
afresh. Her mother picked her up and hauled her out.

"Mamá!"

A moment later, the woman swept back in, en route
toward *Mamamama*. Came the sound of two slaps, yelps,
two more slaps, silence, and then a final slap.

Reentering, she gave Gloria a vacant, perplexed look.
"You're still here."

"The bathroom?" Gloria said.

"There." The woman went off in the other direction,
back toward the crying boy.

Gloria turned the corner and came upon abutting doors,
the first of which turned out to be a closet that, when
opened, released the stench of mothballs.

As she opened the second door, she heard—

ssssffffffffffffssssck
ssssffffffffffffssssck
ssssffffffffffffssssck

The little girl, Adela, was seated cross-legged on the
floor, chewing on her toes and sniffling.

Behind her was another girl, strapped into a narrow bed
and connected to an oxygen tank. Her eyes bulged and
deflated as she breathed.

Adela saw Gloria and waved.

Gloria waved back and stepped out of the room.

The third door was the bathroom. She parted its blinds
with two fingers and looked out on the backyard. A
kidney-bean patio reflected a waning but spectacular
sunset. The concrete—same red as the porch—had dulled

to a uniform and watery rust, as though it had once been the site of an ancient bloodletting ritual. Ill-formed hedges died to the left; otherwise, the patio afforded a full view of the flat and rocky earth.

The *Teniente* was there, snoozing shirtless in a beach chair. His butt was on the edge of the seat, itself at the edge of the concrete. Barefoot, grubby at the calves, he looked ready to slide into the dirt for a swim. A dish of sweat clung to the small of his back. All around him was a worshipful throng of prostrate Budweiser longnecks.

Gloria used the toilet and went back to the toy room. The woman was waiting for her. Gloria thanked her and saw herself out.

Carlos was shaking his head when she came out. *"Que desmadre . . ."*

"This way," Gloria said. She led him around the side of the house, past a storage shed and a pile of manure, coming out onto the patio where Fajardo was asleep.

"Teniente."

Fajardo stirred, turned on his side, fell back asleep with his head dangling over the back of the chair.

"Wake up, *Teniente.*"

Fajardo sat up and twisted to squint at her, running his tongue over his lips. He looked back and forth between her and Carlos, seemingly entranced; mouth-breathing.

Like dormant machinery conquering inertia, he came to life: feeling around for his shirt, which he found slung over the chair. He forced his head halfway through a sleeve before realizing his mistake. He wiped his hands on his shorts and his nose on his hands. He tilted back the box of

Budweisers; bottles collided with a glassy flam. He unclipped a bottle opener from his waistband, rinsed his mouth with beer, and spat. He took a swallow, reoriented his chair to face them, and crossed his legs.

"Why are you at my fucking house," he said.

"Nice to see you again, *Teniente*."

"It's my day off."

"I know," she said.

"If you know, then you know I don't see people today."

Carlos said, "We didn't call in advance, because we didn't want to disturb you."

"Is that right, *mijo*? Cause that's exactly what you're doing: disturbing me." He turned to Gloria. "Neither of you are supposed to be here, unless it's an emergency. I bet you got my address from Luís, senile fart. . . . Well, I'm not going to talk to you, so you can fuck off."

Carlos said, "We can come back later—"

"Hey, *guey*. Shut up. I wasn't talking to you. And you're not coming back later, or tomorrow, or anytime. You're *tres-pappi*"—he drunkenly mangled the Spanish *traspasado* until it came out right—"trespassing. So leave."

"We drove all the way from Los Angeles to see you," said Gloria.

"I'm flattered. Now you can drive all the way back. Have a pleasant trip and try not to run off the road."

Carlos started to go, but Gloria said, "We're not leaving, *Teniente*."

Fajardo stood up, staggering a little, on the cusp of—she couldn't tell what. It scared her, and she had the urge to run. Carlos was pulling at her with his eyes. But she did the opposite of what her brain said to do, did the reckless thing, and stepped forward.

"It's late," she said. "You wouldn't want us driving back now, would you?"

"It didn't stop you last time."

"But you were right. I should have stayed. I should have listened to you."

Fajardo smiled broadly. Then he said, "Okay." He disappeared around the side of the house, and came back dragging two rusty beach chairs, which he forced open.

"I changed my mind," he said, placing a hand on Carlos's shoulder and pushing him down. "Make yourself at home." He offered a chair to Gloria, who needed no such encouragement. He sat, took a sip of beer, and said,

"Normally, Luís is trustworthy. He wouldn't give out my address unless you made him *think* it was an emergency. And if you make him think that, then you *lied* to Luís. Correct, *Señora?*"

"Correct."

"This is an unfortunate technicality of the law, and I regret to have to tell you about it this late in the day. But it's my job to enforce the law, and so here it is. And it is this: When I am not in town, Luís is my deputy. So, when you told him you had an emergency, what you were doing, you were *lying*—to an officer of the law."

He belched. "That, you see, is illegal."

"I guess so."

"What do you think, *guey?* Was that illegal?"

"If you say so, *Señor,*" Carlos said.

Fajardo laughed. "If I say so? You're going to take my word? You trust me?"

"You're a policeman, *Teniente*. I have to trust you."

"You sure do, *guey*. And my word is the law." Fajardo got up. "The court is in session," he said.

"Court?" Gloria said.

"You commit a crime, *Señora*, you have to pay up."

"Now's not the best time, *Teniente*."

"You don't get to call the shots here. You're on trial. You are dealt with at the whim of the state."

The thought of *Teniente* Tito Fajardo representing the state conjured for Gloria an image of him in Napoleonic garb, with his hand stuffed into his vest.

"Could we reschedule?" she asked.

Fajardo wagged his head in six directions, meaning *no*.

"Pure justice is blind," he said. "What's blind mean? Blind means when you can't see. And when can't you see something? When it's moving very fast. Therefore: the faster justice moves, the purer it is. So let's get on with it."

He hammered fist on palm. "I declare you *guilty*," he said, swooning close to her. He gave off a mild, sweet odor—sugar excreted through his skin, like molasses on leather. He was drunker than a poet.

"Your sentence can be served right here," he said.

"I don't think there's any need for that," Gloria said.

"What kind of law do we have if we apply it selectively?" The last word, *selectivamente*, came out as an inebriated haggis of *sl's* and *tv's*.

"I think we were doing just fine before," Gloria said.

"*Pffft.*" The *Teniente* straightened up priggishly. "You

confess, then you deny. What is a policeman supposed to do, eh, *guey*? Tell you what. You're a man, be a man. You serve time for both of you." Deftly he reached for his pocket, whipped out a pair of handcuffs, and attached Carlos to the arm of his beach chair.

"Solitary confinement," Fajardo said. "The electric chair!" He did a celebratory dance, humming and downing the rest of his drink. *"Yo soy el policía, yo tengo manillas rápidas. . . ."* He cracked another Bud and stuffed it into Gloria's hand. The last one he offered to Carlos, who said, "No thanks."

Gloria set the bottle by her side. Fajardo didn't notice; he was settling into his chair and shifting to face the hills.

"You don't know what you're in for," he said, pointing to the horizon. The sunset was almost gone. "The view is"— he started to say *preciosa*, but couldn't manage the double sibilant, settling instead on *linda*.

"We saw it from the road," Gloria said.

"Nnnn . . ." When Fajardo shook his head, his whole body came along. "You haven't seen the *good* part."

She started to ask what the good part was, but he shushed her, kept shushing her each time she moved or spoke, for a solid five minutes, until the sun had long bowed out.

"Watch," he breathed.

Slowly, the clouds changed, growing brighter as the rest of the sky darkened. For a minute and a half, the contrast intensified: pink cloud bruised heavens, yellow cloud navy heavens, then—surreal and luminous—pure white on coal black.

And then it was over. The clouds darkened rapidly, reciting the same litany of colors as the sky of ninety seconds prior. Celestial buckshot pierced the black, cueing the cicadas. A weak floodlight came on and turned their faces to masks.

"There," Fajardo said. "Now isn't that better?"

"Very nice," Carlos said.

Fajardo looked at him. "You've really never seen that before, *guey*?"

"Never, *Señor.*"

"Well, you're missing something." The *Teniente* glanced at Gloria's bottle. "Not thirsty? I'm sure your friend would appreciate it, since he's serving your time."

"I'm happy to suffer in silence," said Carlos.

"You are a knight, *Señor.* You were born four hundred thousand billion years after your time." To Gloria: "Where'd you pick him up?"

"We have some questions for you, *Teniente,*" Gloria said.

"Questions are for schoolchildren and for . . . for . . ." He cracked his knuckles, in search of a finial for his apothegm. "For *women,*" he said. "*Siempre. Where* is the money? *Why* are you late? *Why* don't you give the boy a little toy, a little *thing*? What do you want for *dinner*? What do you want to *night*? What makes you think you can stick it *there*?" He laughed and laughed and cursed as he spilled beer on himself.

"I *am* a woman," Gloria said. "That means I'm entitled to ask."

"You're a woman? I thought you were a snowman." He finished the beer and reached for hers. "May I?, thank you."

She said *Go ahead* as he finished his first draught. He pointed the neck of the bottle at her. "You should know better than to waste this stuff, *Señora*. It's not cheap."

"You buy American beer," she said.

"Nothing else. You expected me to be a 'Corona drinker'?" Fajardo belched. "I don't use Mexican beer."

"No?" she asked.

"No way, *guey*." Fajardo was looking at Carlos. "You know why? Because it's made from water that my kids *piss* in. I get enough of that changing diapers, I don't need to *drink* it for relaxation, *guey*."

"You change diapers?" Gloria asked.

"American beer is clean," said Fajardo. "Yes I change their fucking diapers. You give me no credit, *Señora*. All you ever give me is heartbreak. . . ." He dabbed at his eyes with the hem of his shirt. "How the cuffs treating you, *guey*?"

"They're not bad."

"Not too tight?"

"No."

"Do you feel like you're serving your time?"

Carlos said, "I'm serving it."

"Yes but do you *feel* like you're serving? Do you feel reformed?" Fajardo rose up, wiping his mouth with the back of his hand. "You need to feel like it's going to deter you from committing future crimes, *Señor*, or else what's the point of jail?" He grabbed Carlos's wrist and clicked it one notch tighter.

"How about that," he said, breathing into Carlos's face.

"It's fine."

Click.

"Now?"

"Fine."

Click.

"Now?"

Carlos's jaw bulged. "Now it feels pretty bad."

Fajardo smiled, kissed Carlos on the nose, and loosened the cuffs a couple of notches. "Your duty to society is almost discharged," he said, collapsing into his chair.

"You remember the first time I came here, *Teniente?*" Gloria said.

"Mmmm? Oh sure," said Fajardo. "Sure, I remember the day. It was a spring day in summer. The birds were chirping and the skies were blue. I was young and full of life. The Revolution was in full swing. The violins were playing. The beer was cold and the nights were hot. The— *bbrehhhck.*" His belch finished in laughter.

"You remember why I came?"

"You needed to get laid."

"No, *Teniente.* I was looking for someone."

"An American. *Hombre numero uno.*"

"Sí."

"But instead you fell in love with a Mexican." Fajardo sat up and smiled at Carlos. "Where are you from, *guey?*"

"Mexico City," Carlos said.

"Oh yeah?" Fajardo sounded interested. "What part."

"Benito Juárez."

"No shit. I used to work around there. I was with the police." Fajardo took out his badge. "I still *am* with the police." He let the badge slip from his fingers; it settled beneath his beach chair. "Life in the police can be very dangerous. You know?"

"I'm sure," Carlos said.

"What do you do?"

"I'm in construction."

"Oh *interesting*," said Fajardo. "*Construction*, huh? Then we probably have a lot of friends in common. You guys are all a bunch of fucking crooks. Who's your boss."

Carlos hesitated before saying, "Eduardo Polaczek."

Fajardo's face doubled in size. "*Yeah?* Really. I'm sure you're mistaken, *Señor*, that would be crazy, if that was true."

"It's true," Carlos said.

"Eddie Polaczek's your boss," laughed Fajardo. "Eddie the Animal. Eddie, Eddie, oh Eddie . . ." He stamped a foot. "I know that guy, he's a fucking *animal*. He's anima*l-istic*. You know what that means?"

"Yes."

"You have a sophisticated vocabulary. Like a computer teacher."

Carlos glanced at Gloria, who mouthed *okay okay*.

Fajardo said, "You live in the capital, you work for Eddie the Animal. Kids?"

"No."

"I didn't think so. You don't look like a family man, like me. *I* have kids."

"We know," Gloria said. "We saw them."

"You went in the house?" Fajardo rubbed the damp from his forehead. "You met my wife?"

"Her, too."

"Then you know the whole family. Now you can come for Christmas. Bring candy for the kids. They like it. Buy it in bulk."

"I'll see if I can make it. I want to ask you something, *Teniente*."

"You don't have any kids, either, do you, *Señora*?"

"It's about the man I was—"

"Do you?"

"No. Listen—"

"To tell you the truth," Fajardo interrupted, "you're not missing much."

Gloria said, "You lied to me, *Teniente*."

Fajardo sat up. Like a tank gun, he rotated toward her.

"I did?" he asked.

"Yes, *Teniente*."

"No I didn't."

"You haven't heard what I'm going to say yet."

"It doesn't matter what you're going to say, because I never lied to you about anything."

"The man I was looking for? You told me he was dead, *Teniente*."

"Gloria," Carlos said, "take it easy."

"He *is* dead," said Fajardo.

"That's bullshit," Gloria said.

"Gloria—"

"You told me he died in a car accident," she said. "You gave me an urn."

"*You* insisted," Fajardo said. "I wanted you to rest but you hit the road in a state of grief." He was sobering up fast; she could see him fighting for control. He stood, waving an admonitory finger. "It was against my better judgment but I let you go. People are unpredictable when they're bereaved, especially women, it can be hard—"

"Those weren't his ashes in the urn."

"If you don't believe me, try and put them back together. You'll see, it was him."

"It was coffee, *Teniente*."

Fajardo's mouth sawed. "Okay," he said. "Okay okay okay. You've been out in the sun too long, *Señora*. You're starting to hallucinate. It happens to the best of us. It's a common thing in the desert, if you get dehydrated. People start to hallucinate. You remember the mirage I showed you? The water?"

"That's not a hallucination," she said. "It's a trick of the light."

"Yes a little, and no a little. Trust me, I've seen that mirage about nine thousand times, and—sometimes?— sometimes, it's realer than others. You don't watch your fluid levels, it makes the illusion a tiny bit more convincing." He clapped his hands. "You need a drink. I'm going to get you a beer." He started toward the screen door.

"Alcohol dehydrates you worse," she said.

Fajardo gave an aggravated grunt. "Have it your way. . . ." He stepped off the edge of the patio and picked up a gnarled, heavy piece of deadwood. Leaning on it like a prospector, he stared into the blank expanse. There was a silence.

"That glowing monster is Charrones," he said finally. "That's where Elisa wanted to live when we came here." He scratched his arm and spat, then looked back at the house nervously, as though he expected his wife to be behind him with a rolling pin.

"At least we have the view," he said. "I'll send you a postcard, *Señora*. You can put it on your wall. I'm tired and I want to enjoy my night off. Go home to America."

"Teniente," she said, standing up.

"If you want to know something then ask from your mouth, *Señora*, not your ass. I'm not going to stand here on my night off and answer stupid questions about ashes."

"Did you put the coffee in the urn, or did someone else?"

"I thought we were past this."

"The body—"

"Was cremated."

"And it turned to coffee?"

"May*be*," said Fajardo. "Maybe he was the reincarnation of Juan Valdéz."

"I put the ashes in water—"

"Why'd you do that?" Fajardo looked disgusted. "That's sacrilege."

"To see what they were. And they dissolved."

"So?"

"So human remains don't dissolve."

Fajardo shrugged. "I don't know anything about that. But I guarantee, he's dead as a rock."

"He's not," she said.

"Oh for *Christ's sake*," said Fajardo. "You can't roll over in your car and have it explode and get burned to nothing without being pretty dead."

"You never saw the accident."

"I worked in reconstruction, I know how these things look when—"

"But you didn't *see* it happen," she said.

"Of course not. I was *at home*. On my *day off,* in fact." Fajardo stepped back onto the patio, looking irate. "Like to*day*. I'm not doing this any more, *Señora*." He folded up his beach chair and began tossing empty bottles in the box.

"His bank account had a withdrawal made on it after you reported him dead."

Fajardo waved a dismissive hand. "In the police academy they have a technical term for that kind of thing. It's called 'who gives a fuck.'"

"You're going to have to answer eventually," she said. "I'll go to the next highest authority, and—"

"Why don't you stop talking right now."

"I told you—"

"You come here, waving nonsense in my face, it doesn't mean anything to me. Not a thing. Your friend is dead, tragedy, have a good night." He put the box under one arm, the chair under the other, and started around the side of the house.

She said, "This is his son, *Teniente*. He's looking for his father."

Fajardo froze, then turned and looked at Carlos. "You?"

"*Sí,*" said Carlos.

The *Teniente* dropped everything and came toward them. "You, *guey*?" He grabbed Carlos's face and forced it into a pucker. "I don't know, *Señora*. There doesn't seem to be much family resemblance."

"I thought you never saw him," she said.

"I'm guessing," Fajardo growled. "What a sad story. You lost your father. How'd you end up with *Señora Preguntas, guey?*"

"I'm a friend of hers," Carlos said.

"Are you fucking her?"

Gloria said, "Jesus," and stepped toward Fajardo, who pushed her back.

Silence.

"What's your name?" Fajardo asked.

"Carlos Perreira."

"Don't be a smart-ass or I'll throw you in jail."

"It's on my ID."

"Give it to me."

Carlos fished out his wallet and handed it to Fajardo, who spent a moment pawing through it. When he finished, he dropped it in Carlos's lap.

"That's the dumbest story I ever heard, *mijo.* You need to come up with some garbage better than that. Now pay attention, *Señora.* Your friend got drunk and ran off the road. He killed himself. He's lucky he didn't kill anyone else in the process. *That's the story.* And if you want my opinion, he deserves to be dead for behaving like a reckless shithead. Get out of my house."

Gloria said, "I can call the Los Angeles police and have them explain it to you."

"Do whatever you want. They won't interfere with my investigation."

"What investigation."

"*This* one. The ongoing one I'm conducting into the death of your friend."

"You're conducting an investigation."

"Of course. The case is not yet closed. I never close a case if there are still leads," said Fajardo. "They deserve to be followed up on, to the last detail."

"When have you been doing that?" she asked.

"I'm *doing* it, right now. This is my investigative style. I'm pondering all the options. And I advise you, *Señora,* not to stick your fingers in. You interfere with a police investigation, I can arrest you." He grabbed her arm and pulled her out of the chair. "You know what? Until now, I've never considered you as a suspect."

Carlos said, "Wait—"

"But I don't know why not," said Fajardo. "After all, you were close to the man, you seem to know a lot about his death, you keep hounding me with crazy theories. . . ."

"Señor." Carlos got up, clumsily trailing the beach chair by one wrist.

"What the fuck do you want, *guey?*"

There was a moment of silence before Carlos said, "Let's everybody calm down."

"Good idea. Go over to the corner, and calm yourself down. Stick your hand up your ass and have an adventure while I ask my suspect, the *Señora,* some questions."

"I think we've overstayed our welcome," Carlos said. "We'll leave."

"No you won't," said Fajardo. "*Now,* you're going to stay. Because I'm conducting an investigation."

He yanked her toward the house and Carlos lunged. The *Teniente* released Gloria and threw two quick punches at Carlos, first a low backhand that clipped him in the neck and then one that landed full-on in the eye. Gloria scrambled for the piece of deadwood and whacked Fajardo in the back. It didn't do much damage, but it did throw him off balance, and when he turned in search of her, Carlos swung the beach chair, connecting with the *Teniente*'s head; the impact gave off an aluminous *ping* reminiscent of the driving range, knocking him from the patio. Carlos took her by the arm and they fled around the side of the house.

She clambered into the front seat and gunned the motor and threw it in reverse and was about to go when Carlos yelled *Wait wait wait wait wait*; he'd gotten stuck trying to get in with the beach chair attached to his arm. She said *forget it* with an urgency she knew would be justified in a few seconds, and sure enough, Fajardo came around with a gun and shot off the passenger's-side mirror, and she slammed on the gas and the car whipped back, jerking wildly as she wildly jerked the wheel, Carlos hanging halfway out, the beach chair sparking and spitting gravel as they fishtailed and Fajardo shot at them again, missing, but once was enough to convince her that even drunk, he wasn't a bad shot, and she put the car in drive and followed the spiraling road out to the potholed, unlit highway, and Carlos shouted for her to slow down and she did, enough for him to get the goddamned chair into the car.

She looked at Carlos. He was breathing hard and bleeding. His shirt was torn and his elbow scraped to hell. He looked as though he'd run across hot coals.

She said, "I think we're onto something."

TWENTY-FOUR

For several hours they wandered in the dark, their head-lights slicing out a path. Gloria spotted what she believed was the outskirts of Joaqual; somehow, they had come around and approached it from the south. Bosomy hills alternated with little valleys, and the Dodge rose and dipped as though they were riding gentle surf. The road took an eastward turn, and they came through a narrow pass cut into a pile of boulders, each one the size of her apartment, passing finally into a desolate nook filled with the dim green neon of a motel. It was situated smack in the middle of the valley's flat bottom, like an abandoned doll-house. They could no longer see the town; they could barely see anything, save the lime-tinged thrust of stones and cacti.

The night manager at the motel had a beard designed to hide his carbuncular past. It didn't work. Hair sprouted in patches of variegated density, giving the effect of Spanish moss. The skin beneath was so badly bitten as to suggest an intricate—and beautiful—repoussé pattern on the inside of his cheeks. He was missing his right upper canine.

He had left one earplug in. The other dangled at mid-chest, piping Mexican rap at an unbelievable volume: bumps and whines and a guy yelling about cars and *putas*. If he keeps that up, she thought, he'll go deaf by thirty. She marveled sadly that—given the disadvantages puberty had bequeathed him—he didn't act to preserve what he had left.

He looked past her at the parking lot, where Carlos was trying to get the chair out of the car.

"Second-floor room is okay?" he asked, a little too loudly.

"Two, if you have enough vacancies."

"We specialize in vacancies." He pushed a registration form across the counter. "You can have all eighteen of them if you want."

"Is there a hospital near here?"

"In Joaqual," he said. "But it's closed."

"There's nowhere else?"

"Tejaces."

"Where's that?"

"A hundred miles that way."

"What do you do if someone gets hurt?" she asked.

"Tell them to wait."

In the parking lot, she found Carlos standing outside the Dodge, the chair under his arm. For the first time since the fight, she got a good look at him. The light from the motel lobby disclosed scrapes along his cheeks and arms; one dried gash had nearly bifurcated his eyebrow. It was ghastly enough to look like a stick-on prank Caperco would sell; it made her breath catch.

But he was smiling, which relaxed her.

"I'm beginning to like this," he said, fingering the links of the handcuff, the tubing of the chair. "I've never cared much for jewelry, but I think it might catch on."

The neon advertised in Spanish a SWIMMING POOL, which Gloria thought was a lot more business-savvy than the more honest LARGE DIRT PIT. Like a lot of things in the region, it had been arrested midway to completion. The motel's L curved around it like a shrine to indolence. Along the second-floor exterior balcony, moths made a mecca of a bare bulb. Gloria and Carlos's rooms were adjacent, two doors down from a communal bathroom, where they went to clean him up.

"I think he was wearing a ring," Carlos said.

She dabbed at his eyebrow, and he winced.

"Sorry," she said.

"You're doing fine. It would hurt worse if you weren't." He was sitting on the toilet, the beach chair leaning against his thigh, a cigarette in his free hand.

"I'm worried about this getting infected," she said.

"What, here? This place is a palace. You could do heart surgery here." He flicked at the pile of bloody tissues resting on the edge of the sink. The porcelain was skinned with black crud. Filth on the mirror tanned their reflections. Probing the wound, Gloria wondered if they should have gone to the hospital instead.

"It's cleaner than my grandmother's kitchen," he said.

She wiped blood from his nose. "Don't slander your grandmother."

There was no garbage can in the bathroom, so they gathered up the tissues and threw them out in Carlos's room. Gloria was tempted to dump them on the floor. A little color, she thought, would add a festive feel to this dump.

There was, otherwise: a bed wide enough for one person, and a lone men's shoe filled with sand, positioned in front of a mousehole. She told Carlos to keep pressure on the cut and said, "I'll be right back."

The night manager perked up when she walked in. He removed the earplug again.

"Let me guess," he said, "you want another room."

She leaned on the counter. "I need a hacksaw," she said, "and some iodine."

She could see him trying and failing to put those two objects together in a meaningful way. He shrugged and turned toward a back door. *"Mamá!"*

Out came a prune in a flannel housedress. With mottled ankles and meat-curtain arms, she bore no resemblance to her gangly son—except that when she said "You want something?" she displayed a blank in place of her upper-right canine. As though she and her son had both been in a fight with the same bully.

"Do we have any iodine?"

"What you need it for."

"My friend cut his face," Gloria said.

"He cut it shaving?"

Sure, why not. "Yes."

"Why's he shaving at this late hour," the old woman asked.

Gloria regretted having opened the door to conversation.

"He has a thick beard," she said. "He shaves three times a day. Sometimes four."

The old woman looked at her son. "You never shave."

He squirmed. "Iodine, *Mamá*."

"We don't got it." The old woman hawked and started out. "Tell your friend to be more careful," she said, slamming the door.

"I got something you can use," the manager said. He reached under the desk and pulled out an unlabeled bottle of sallow syrup. The liquid clung to the glass as it sloshed.

"What's that."

"Tequila." He set it down. "Here you go if you want it."

She looked at the bottle, at him. "Why would I want it."

"Alcohol kills the germs."

Uncorking it, she took a whiff. It was, to be sure, alcoholic.

"What do you need a saw for?" asked the night manager.

"I'm performing an amputation."

"What part?"

"You'll find out in the morning, won't you?"

He pointed to the bottle. "You probably going to want that for yourself, then."

She wavered. It was too late to get to the clinic tonight. Tomorrow they could go back; she wanted to talk to the doctor, anyway. She put her hand out to take the bottle, and he blocked her.

"Twenty dollars."

She stared at him. "He's hurt," she said.

"Fine," he said, "forget it." He put the bottle under the counter and said, "I don't think I can help you with the saw, either."

She offered him five. He did nothing, and she started out.

"Fifteen," he called.

"I'm giving you more than it's worth," she said. She held out the five. "Take it or I'll tell your mother you're drinking on the job."

"*Señora,* she bought it for me in the first place." He took the money, gulped a third of the tequila, and gave it to her.

"I still don't have a saw," he said.

On her way back to Carlos's room, she grabbed her toiletries. He was sitting on the bed, his shirt rolled up, inspecting a plum-sized scrape covering one prominent stud of abdominal muscle.

He saw the bottle and said, "What is that?"

"Tequila."

He gave her a reproachful look. "You know I can't have that."

"It's to sterilize the wound."

"That's not going to work."

"It'll do something."

"Yes, it'll give me hepatitis."

"Sit back."

She perched on the bed, tipped the bottle against a clean tissue, and began stanching the cut, lightly at first then with gradually increasing pressure.

Carlos said, "It doesn't hurt much."

"Good."

"You do this like a professional."

"I had a course in emergency medicine. In college."

"They teach you how to dress a wound with tequila?"

"The first thing they teach you is, 'You're the first line of defense.'"

"Meaning?"

"The hospital is where you go to fix the problem. The techniques you learn are to make sure the person doesn't die between the restaurant and the ER."

"What restaurant."

"The restaurant where your friend is choking. It was an example. That's mostly what we learned, choking." She folded her legs under her and leaned in closer. "I know how to perform an emergency cricothyrotomy."

"A what?"

"I don't know the word in Spanish. When you cut a person's neck so they can breathe."

"*Traqueostomía.*"

"Not that," she said. "That's a long-term procedure, for a permanent breathing tube. This is a quick thing when someone's got a blockage and the Heimlich doesn't work. You make a short incision in the membrane . . . here." She traced below his Adam's apple; his neck was smooth and warm. "You hold the airway open with a special device," she said. "If you're really stuck you can use a drinking straw—what."

"You're funny."

"What's funny?"

"Not funny," he said. "Enthusiastic."

"It's what I wanted to do."

"I know," he said. "I think it's charming."

She picked up a fresh tissue. "I'm surprised I remember any of it."

"I think you would have made a great doctor." He put out his cigarette in the sink. "I would even let you do that thing on me. The Christ-o-whatever."

"Cricothyrotomy. You wouldn't have a choice; you'd be unconscious."

"Well, if it ever happens I give you blanket permission, in advance. Although let's try the Heimlich first."

"Agreed." She applied more tequila.

"Ow. Do you think I look like my father?"

She stopped working for a moment. "A little."

"My grandmother said I look mostly like my mother," he said. "But of course that can't be completely true. After I saw his picture in the catalogue I started examining myself to figure out which parts belonged to him."

"They may not be things you can see."

"No. Sense of humor, or . . . the way he thought."

"He was very dry."

"I'm like that. Is that what you hear, when you talk to me?"

"Some," she said. More than she wanted to admit. She added, "But you're not the same person."

"No." A pause. "It's strange. He's with me, whether I want it or not. That's part of the reason I wanted to see him. I'm carrying him around all the time as it is; I might as well see the real thing." He shifted closer to her. "What about your father?"

"My mother never talked about him."

"She never remarried after the first man."

"Mamá?" Gloria laughed. "No."

"What did you think of that?"

"What did I *think* of it? I didn't think anything of it. It was a fact of life. I had a mother and she was herself, and there was nobody else in the equation."

"Another thing we have in common," he said. "One of many."

She nodded, and tipped the liquor against a new tissue. "This stuff stinks."

"You don't need to tell me. It almost ruined my life."

"Is that what you drank? Tequila?"

"It's more a question of what I *didn't* drink. Though I didn't like tequila much."

"Neither do I."

"What's your drink?"

"I don't have one." She got a new tissue. "I've never been drunk."

"Never?"

"When I met Reggie he spent the first month trying to get me drunk, and I spent the first month trying to get glasses out of my face." She finished with the big cut and moved on to its retinue of scratches. "He told me later that the reason he got interested in me was because I fought him so hard."

"I know marriages that run that way."

"Ours didn't. It didn't run at all. We had opposite styles. He would try to raise my temper. He thought it was romantic. It reminded him of the early days. You know, when conflict and flirting are cousins. But after three years, I found it very, very boring."

She smelled the bottle and shuddered. "I've had tequila once. At a wedding for Reggie's friend. Someone gave it to me by mistake. I thought it was apple juice."

"You didn't smell the difference?"

"I took it without thinking. It only took a sip for me to realize."

"And?"

"Not for me." She spilled more from the bottle. "When we're done with this, you can have the rest of it to yourself. I give you my half."

When he did not respond, she said, "I'm sorry. It slipped my mind."

"I'm allowed to talk about it," he said. "I'm just not allowed to drink it. Like I said, tequila's not my favorite. Although I'd drink it before Budweiser."

She smiled. "Well, now you've met him face-to-face."

"Son of a bitch." Carlos fidgeted. "Did you see the way he turned? He went from joking to crazy in thirty seconds."

"He's one of those people, the worse you catch them in their own lie, the angrier they get."

"'Those people'?"

"Men," she said.

He laughed again, stopped short. "Look at that," he said.

"What. Oh my God."

At his flank, a zag of blood was spreading through his shirt. He lifted it up. Another cut: not deep, clean, but in need of attention.

"Where'd that come from?"

"I don't know. Maybe it opened up when I moved."

"It's going to ruin your shirt."

"It's ruined already," he said. He tried to roll up the fabric, but it slipped loose. Then they tried to take the shirt off, and it wouldn't fit over the beach chair. The cloth bunched around his hand, so that the chair looked like it was wearing a turban.

"Either we can rip it," she said, "or we'll get it off when we remove the cuffs."

"By the way, any idea of how that's going to happen?"

"I'm thinking about it," she said. "Here, sit still."

She wet a tissue and smoothed over the cut on his side. It looked worse than it was, because of the frightening location and the blood. She was thankful for his clean skin. He was hairless and had no body fat. Touching him was like polishing marble.

"We can do it tomorrow."

She looked up. "What?"

"Get the cuff off. I'm gonna have to sleep with it." He jounced the chair. *"Ay."*

"Careful . . ." She took out her toiletries bag, rooting past a toothbrush mummified in a tissue, travel toothpaste, floss, ibuprofen, nail clipper . . . There: Band-Aids. She had enough to cover the worst cuts.

As she applied the final one, he clapped one hand against his knee.

"Bravo," he said.

Smiling, she tossed the tissues and bandage backings in the trash.

"You'd better pour the tequila down the drain," he said. "I don't want to be tempted in the middle of the night."

"I'll take it back to my room," she said.

"A few years ago, that wouldn't have been enough. I would have broken down the door."

Her room was fancier, with a dilapidated chest of drawers and a cracked picture of a ship that struck her as bizarre, given that they were far inland. She chucked her bag on the bed and put the bottle in the top drawer. Her hands trembled from all the scrubbing and careful motions of first aid.

She reopened the drawer.

She uncorked the tequila and took a swallow.

It wasn't as bad as she remembered. Citrus and menthol. She braced herself and took another sip—a big one. Too big.

Hacking, she recorked the bottle and put it in the drawer, thinking, Now what did you go and do that for?

She wiped her mouth and her tearing eyes and searched her bag in vain for a cough drop to kill the fog in her throat. She tried swallowing repeatedly, but it stuck there like skunk spray.

She cleared the bed and flopped down. The mattress was as yielding as a block of oak. After a few restless minutes, she got up. Limbs tingling. Jesus. Was it that fast? She had barely eaten anything today. This is what college kids did, she thought. Normal ones who didn't plan on becoming doctors when it made more sense for them to become secretaries.

She didn't like the path her thoughts were on, so she went back to Carlos's room. He answered in his boxer shorts. The chair was attached to his wrist, wearing its headdress.

"You look absurd," she said.

"I can't get it off," he said, tugging at the shirt.

"You won't be able to tear through that with a single hand," she said. She got the nail clipper from her toiletries bag and used the point of the file to create a hole in the sleeve. This she widened, cutting through threads and a band of ribbing to free him. She threw the mangled carcass to the floor like a gladiator.

"Ta-da!"

He looked at her. "You're drunk."

"Did you see what I just did?"

"What did you *have?*"

"A sip."

"It must have been a big one."

She snapped the nail clipper closed and tossed it in the air like a six-shooter, missing it on the way down.

"Whoops."

As she bent to pick it up, she noticed his boxer shorts agape; she could see—

—nothing, she didn't see anything, she stood up.

He was shaking his head.

"Can we talk about tomorrow?" she said.

"You have to go wash your mouth out first."

"Why?"

"I don't want to smell it on your breath."

The water in the bathroom tasted worse than the tequila. She rinsed twice and spat, careful not to swallow it. It was chilly outside; she rubbed at gooseflesh as she stood waiting for him to reopen the door. She heard him dragging the beach chair and giggled.

He opened up and said, "I feel like I have a Siamese twin."

She breathed at him. "Better?"

"Better," he said, sliding his arm around her waist and bringing their hips together. "Now I can do this."

He tasted like the southern sun.

TWENTY-FIVE

Reggie would sing doo-wop in the shower afterward. She'd be in bed, covered in sheets up to her neck, modest as an ear of corn, feeling nevertheless naked, and she would hear him moving around: the vacuumy squelch of soap in armpits. All the while singing the old Cadillacs song.

Gloooria
It's not Mariiiie . . .
Glovorii-ya-ah-ha-ha
It's not Sheriiiie . . .

When he got to the line *she's not in love with me*, he'd stick his head out of the bathroom and croon directly at her. Sometimes he'd stop and say *Are you in love with me?* And she'd say *I don't know.* He would step into the doorway, flopping his penis around, looking like a kid who'd brought home a perfect report card.

How about now.

She would pull up the sheets yet tighter, so that you could see the soft contours of her abdomen. *I'll think about it.*

He would laugh and jump back in the shower. *Gloori-ahhhhhh!*

She had learned to expect the clamor, expect the exact conversation, expect to be called upon for a witticism. Even now, she expected it all; she was pulling the sheet up around herself in preparation. She could hear water and smell steam. She anticipated the song and the question: did she love him or not.

But this time she was alone.

Carlos had taken her travel shampoo and gone down the hall to wash. Trailing the beach chair.

"If I stay in long enough it'll rust off," he'd said.

She hadn't bothered to reply that aluminum doesn't rust. She hadn't said anything. She'd curled up in the sheets and given him a wave good-bye.

She let her mind wander: over the wad of bloody tissues in the garbage can, the shoe across the room, the desert outside, the starchy horror of the pillowcase—focusing on every stimulus until it lost resolution, became grain and granule. She went clear of everything except the throb in her belly, a remnant of pleasure, absorbed by her body's forgiving inner walls.

She felt good.

Telegrams kept arriving from various parts of her body: ribs, ears, the webbing between her toes.

HEY GLORIA STOP WHAT THE HELL TOOK SO LONG

STOP ANYWAY THANKS A MILLION STOP LET'S TRY
NOT TO WAIT TEN YEARS NEXT TIME OKAY STOP

It startled her to think that before Reggie, there had been
a drought going back to college. Charlie DiScala was her
chemistry study partner. She'd slept with him for the
same reason she'd gone to the UFW rally: it seemed age-
appropriate. When she discovered that he was uninteresting,
that he wanted to be a dentist, and that she didn't have time
for him, she'd confessed her wantonness and gone back
to her books. He was promptly forgotten, as the memory
of sin before marriage was displaced by the atomic weight of
magnesium.

A dentist.

You had to have a low opinion of yourself to aspire to
dentistry. Why endure all that schooling to do glorified
masonry? It was almost as bad as psychology.

Allan Jarroll-Peña had ended up a psychologist.

A research psychologist, to be precise. His expertise was
the interactions of groups with mixed racial constituencies.
She knew this because one day at work, in a rare moment
of distraction, she'd gone on the Internet and typed his
name into a search engine. He came up on faculty at the
University of Wisconsin.

. . . I am also the advisor for Students for Progressive
Agriculture, having for years devoted myself . . . In my spare
time (what spare time?!?!) I enjoy playing the French horn and
taking care of my fantastic Yorkies, Emilio and Button. . . .

After Charlie, there had been nobody. Something
about screwing—at home or out of it—while her mother

languished half-dead in the living room felt obscene. Not to mention that waking hours spent cooking, cleaning, typing, sculpting, and wiping up Mamá's shit hardly left Gloria feeling sultry enough to take on the town. Most of the Hispanic men her age worth dating had moved out of the neighborhood, leaving behind gangbangers and drunks and shy church-freaks who annoyed her to no end.

Reggie had showed up at exactly the right time. He was attention, male attention, normal male attention. He *wasn't* from the neighborhood, which meant she could leave expecting never to talk about it again. She moved into his West LA duplex after three weeks and married him after nine. Gloria could admit now that he could've said basically anything and gotten her to sleep with him. He could have been a traveling salesman. Or a painter. He could have been anything except familiar.

After their first time together, while he was showering, she went into the kitchen where he couldn't hear her and wept with relief.

Once the euphoria of touch rediscovered had passed, however, the pleasure she took from sex began to thin and grow brittle. They had stylistic conflicts. She couldn't let go unless it was completely dark. She instituted a lights-off rule, which Reggie hated. To get around it, he would start kissing her neck while she read, hoping she'd forget the bedside lamp and go along. She never did.

In time, she came to envision sex as a retreat into herself. When he complained that she was tuning him out, being passive, she had no response, because it was true. She didn't trust him a whole lot, a condition that worsened as their marriage hardened and set.

It didn't help that he wouldn't shut up. In mid-act he would squeeze her buttocks and say things like *your ass should be in a museum;* or he'd sink his face in her cleavage and say *your tits smell like tomatoes.* And so on and so forth, drowning her in overtness and cliché. By the end, he'd be hollering *oh! yeah! fuck! shit! yeah!* It embarrassed her so intensely that on the worst nights, she would cramp up, unable to go on.

Finally, she'd had enough and cut him off, mid-metaphor.

Your pussy is like a wood-burning stove—

Reggie.

What?

I'm having trouble concentrating.

He'd said nothing. When he finished, he rolled over and said *I didn't know it required that much concentration.*

It does for me.

He'd gotten up, pausing midway across the room as though wine had been flung in his eyes. *Did I say the wrong thing?*

That had happened close to the end.

Tonight she'd surprised herself. After Carlos's first kiss, she had taken over. The beach chair hobbled him. He kept saying *Careful* or *dammit* or *oops* until she told him *it's not there, there is no chair.* At one point, he raked the wall, putting a scratch in the plaster. *They'll never notice* she said, urging her breast into his mouth.

She couldn't afford to get hung up. She'd been holding

back her whole life, and it didn't make sense to act like a nun.

Tonight she hadn't acted like a nun.

She smiled wider and shifted in bed; mild soreness. They had not been prepared. Her *system* hadn't been prepared. *All right all right all RIGHT*, it had said, *you didn't exactly WARN us*. When push came to shove, though, she had been ready enough.

He was gentle. His hands were not what she would have expected from a man who made his living with wood and nails. She reminded herself that he was a manager. Years ago, probably, his skin was rawhide. She was glad to have gotten him now rather than at that stage. She needed tenderness. Although a vision of him in a hard hat, tool belt, hammer hanging from a denim loop, and workshirt rolled to the elbows . . .

Hands that buttery. Didn't calluses keep up for years?

Maybe he used lava soap.

The Lava-Loving Latin Lover.

Charlie DiScala had, if she was remembering correctly, an Italian father and an Irish mother. Reggie was black. She had completed a North American sexual trifecta.

Congratulations!

She felt a weird kind of patriotism, as though allowing a Mexican man inside her earned her a medal of valor.

Once they got past the nuisance of the chair, he'd said almost nothing. The little he did say served largely to communicate his desire to please her. He sounded like his father; she had moments when she closed her eyes and imagined that it was him. Or him. Or them: an amalgamation: familiar warmth wearing novel flesh.

Guilt and joy arrived all at once, jostling each other in the doorway, and she was sobbing. An act adulterous converted, through circumstance, into an act of reverence; making love to the past; a homecoming.

TWENTY-SIX

It had been years since she'd had another person beside her in bed. The mattress slanted under his weight. Every half-hour or so he turned, maddeningly retrieving her from the edge of sleep. By four A.M., the tequila had cleared from her system, leaving her staring down a whopper hangover. She went back to her own room to lie in bed and watch the light traverse fissures in the plaster. At quarter to seven, she got up and dry-swallowed three aspirin.

By seven-thirty, she had groomed and dressed. She went to hunt down some coffee. The front desk was unattended and locked; on the inside of the smudged glass door hung a piece of paper that said BACK LATER.

She walked across the parking lot and got her first eyeful of the cup in which the motel sat. Across the plain, saguaro cacti clumped like families, maternal bodies sheltering shorter ones with juvenile purple flowers. An uncle-you-don't-talk-about cactus growing horizontally had let its own eccentricity get the better of it; it had broken under its own weight. The upright plants behind it said *See, see what happens when you act like that?*

There were no highway markers, no speed limits, no lanes, no turnoffs. The road had been beaten out of the earth but never maintained; the Dodge's tracks marched singly through its dirt. Arroyos filled with rocks and patrolled by neurotic lizards ran along its sides. Had she deviated by a foot on the drive in, they would have been hamstrung. She thanked whatever saint was responsible for preventing auto wrecks.

In the middle of the highway, a bird alighted on a withered husk. A worm was pinned in its mouth.

No. A snake. A tiny, motionless snake.

Dead already, and it wasn't even eight.

The desk clerk hadn't arrived. She crunched over to the Dodge and rubbed frost from the windshield into her chapping hands. It wasn't going to help in the long run, but it felt soothing and she went with it, a strategy she decided on for today.

She wanted to call Barb Oberle but couldn't get any cell-phone reception. She made a note to try from Carlos's phone later.

What would she tell her?

Guess what I did.

Barb would probably know from her voice. She'd say *Thank God, I was worried you'd explode.* An idea with some scientific support. Weren't they at the right age, supposed to be hitting their sexual strides? Gloria wondered if she had tired him out.

Barb would say *I hope not; he'd better be ready for another round.*

Gloria smiled. She wondered what married sex was

like—really like, after ten years or fifteen or forty. (Reggie didn't count.) Was Barb happier than the others? Or bored? It seemed impossible to be both, but that was the sense Gloria got. Sometimes it was like Barb was talking about her son rather than a peer.

He used to leave the toilet seat up. But I got him trained.

Gloria could think of countless little ways in which Kenny had reshaped his wife, as well. Barb's aversion to drugs went up in smoke when he began pressing high-quality hashish on her. Gloria had once found a fantastic collection of pipes while fetching a pair of scissors from Kenny's office.

In actuality, the Oberles had trained each other. *That* was the fate of most married couples: mutual housebreaking.

Her attraction to Carl had been different. She knew, instinctively, that their union would have been more respectful, more restrained, more adult.

Well yeah, more adult, Barb would say. *He's got two decades on you.*

What would she say now? With the taste of Carlos still lingering in Gloria's mouth?

Paging Dr. Freud. You better get your casebook.

Gloria laughed.

She wanted to remember this moment as clearly as she could.

Back in her room, she dug out the Polaroid. She took a test shot out the window: click, flash, whine, wave. Beautiful.

Carlos did not stir as she entered. On his stomach, head

twisted out, the cuffed hand dangling, chair halfway beneath the bed. Squash-faced, with fish lips and a chubby right cheek. Boyishly smooth all over. She framed him and let rip.

He still didn't move. What a sleeper. No wonder he hadn't had trouble, while she'd spent the whole night in disarray. She was like the princess and the pea. She wished she could relax, like him.

Look at him.

The photo got most of his face, but it wasn't very clear. She stuck it in her back pocket and tried again. That one came out better.

As she geared up for a third, he began to wake.

"Nnnnn."

"Good morning."

"No, no, no . . ." He sat up, reaching for her. Or—she thought he was reaching for her. He wasn't; he was reaching for the camera, which he eased from her hands and set on the floor.

"Sleep," he said.

"One more," she said. "You look nice in the light."

"What time is it?" he asked. He checked her watch. "Ohhhh . . ."

"I didn't sleep so well," she said.

He patted the bed. "Make it up now."

"I'm not tired. We have to get going soon. I thought I'd do something creative."

"It's too early," he said. "Come back to bed."

"I'm dressed already."

"Get undressed." He tugged at her leg.

"Let me take one more."

"No," he said. "I don't want any."

"Why?"

"I don't like them."

"Come on . . ." She knelt to pick up the camera and he caught her by the wrist.

"No pictures," he said.

After a moment, she nodded, and he let go. She picked the camera up.

"Gloria."

"I'm turning it off."

He watched her do so, then got out of bed and went over to his pile of clothing, facing the wall to dress. His limbs looked bony and hard; his ribs poked through as he yawned.

"It's cold," he muttered, stepping into his jeans. The beach chair rattled as he moved. He raised a shirt above his head, but he realized he couldn't get it on.

"We have to get this fucking thing off," he said.

"Okay," she said, looking at her own wrist, red with his thumbmarks.

"I'm starving." Then he said, "You took a picture of me."

"You told me not to."

"The first one. You took one while I was asleep. It woke me up."

"I didn't mean to."

"Give it to me."

"Why?"

"I told you, I don't like pictures of myself."

"It doesn't make you look bad."

"That's not the point." He licked his lips. Softer: "I didn't mean to snap at you. It's a sensitivity of mine. I'm self-conscious about it. It has to do with . . . drinking. Self-image. You know what I mean."

She nodded. She had no idea what he meant.

He approached her, massaged her shoulder with his free hand. "I'm sorry," he said. "I should have said, 'Good morning.'" He bent to kiss her wrist.

"Good morning," she said, staring at the back of his head.

"Can I please have the picture? It would make me feel a lot better."

She reached into her pocket and took out one of the two photos. He inspected it.

"It is nice," he said. "Thank you." He kissed her on the forehead. "You're very understanding." He walked back across the room and began slipping on his socks.

"So what's the plan?" he asked.

She said nothing, thinking.

You're hungover and crabby. You wouldn't want to be woken up like that, either.

"I'm sorry," she said.

"About what?"

"About the photo."

"The ph— forget it. I'm up now, and I'm ready to go. You had a plan for us, right? That's what you said last night."

"Yes," she said. She squeezed the camera. "You're right. Let's go."

*

THEY HEADED NORTH for Joaqual, pulling up to the series of squat banalities, of which the hospital was the third. Carlos pointed to the hardware store.

"They can probably get it off," he said. "Drop me off and I'll come meet you at the hospital."

"You don't want to come?"

"Who knows how long it'll take," he said, pulling a new polo shirt from his bag. "It's more efficient this way." He kissed her hand. "I'll walk over when I'm done."

"Okay."

"And I'm sorry about before. I can be a bear before I get something to eat. Let's stop soon?"

She nodded. "I'm sorry, too."

"I can foresee a career ahead of you."

"Career?"

"As an alarm clock. You wait with the cam— hey . . ."

Laughing, she shoved him out and drove on, looking in the rearview as he strode half-naked toward the store, his body gleaming.

SHE FOUND THE CLINIC in a state of quiescence: you could negotiate the waiting room, get a seat, read in semi-peace. Kids lay across their mothers' laps, conked out or whimpering as they weathered the agony of infected ears and strep throat. A greenish man in a shiny black suit was doubled over. The hobo she recognized; he was asleep in the corner, molded around the potted plant, twitching his dreams.

The nurse was nowhere to be seen. Gloria asked a frowsy woman where the doctor was.

"We're in line," said the woman. "You have to wait till after us."

Gloria found a seat and picked up a tattered newspaper. She glanced at the lead story, a swarm of statistics and hieroglyphics about the ammonia content of genetically modified grains. The article implied that these figures were highly significant. It was a trade journal for horse ranchers. She put it down.

An old man emerged from the back room, hobbling on a cane fashioned out of sanded two-by-four. He held aloft a Baggie of white pills and announced, "I am cured."

A woman with a flushed child said, "Good for you, where's the doctor?"

The old man shrugged. "The doctor is not in," he said, and exited.

The rest of the room burbled angrily. The frowsy woman got up in a huff and disappeared through the back doors, returning a moment later.

"The doctor's office is locked," she complained.

The group seemed to have heard this before. They all got up, collecting their reading and their knitting, righting woozy children and urging them to get up, come on, we can go get something to eat, yes we're coming back, stop arguing.

One of the smallest kids began crying.

The greenish man stayed bent over.

The frowsy woman said to Gloria, "We're still in line, so don't try to get ahead." She exited, again in a huff.

They all must know the order, Gloria thought. Which meant she, too, could leave and get a cup of coffee. Her head was reading her the riot act.

As she exited the clinic, the dirt parking lot was to her right. To the left, a vacant field. Beyond that jutted the rear end of the hardware store: a tall, open lumber shed. Men used axes and handsaws and a single radial saw to cut the wood to uniform lengths, twining the pieces into ziggurats and hoisting them onto the back of an idling flatbed.

All at once, the workers dropped their stacks and retreated into the shed, as though they'd been paged by the pied piper.

Curious, she walked down the concrete ramp to her left, to get a better squint over the field. As she turned the corner, past the rear wall of the clinic, she heard hacking.

It came from the frail Asian doctor. She was on her haunches, leaning against the wall, sucking on a long column of ash. Her free elbow propped open the clinic's rear door. She stifled another cough and turned in Gloria's direction.

"Shit!" she said, getting up. Her arm slipped and the door closed. "Oh, crap," she said to it. To Gloria, in Spanish: "I didn't see you. "

"I speak English."

The doctor's face widened. "Really?"

"My whole life," Gloria said.

"Thank you." The doctor placed the hand with the cigarette against her forehead; she was a smoldering unicorn. Her hair had picked up more gray since the summer. "You don't know how nice that sounds. Sometimes I think I'm forgetting. Or I can't figure out what to say in Spanish, and I have to like, draw it to the person—listen to that. Draw it *to* the person, I can't believe I just said that." She looked at Gloria. "You speak *English*. . . ."

Gloria smiled. "You should call home more often."

"When? I'm here all day. I'm asleep the other six hours, plus there's the time change." The doctor snorted. "Forget it. I'll see them all in two weeks when I'm done. Or—no I won't, not really. I won't see anyone, ever, cause as soon as I get back I have to finish my residency, and I'm pretty sure it's not going to get any less, you know, *time-consuming*. Then I'm a doctor and I'm going to be doing *that*, and I'm pretty sure I won't have much time to talk to anyone once that gets going. So this pretty much is the last normal conversation I'm ever going to have."

"I'll try to make it a good one," Gloria said.

"Don't worry, my standards are low."

"Why'd you come here if you're so unhappy?"

The doctor pulled and coughed. "I wasn't unhappy before. I'm only unhappy now. I *thought* it would be a nice change of pace, and besides it's a good thing to do, you know? A lot of people I know have done this program and found it really rewarding. I mean, it *is*, but sometimes I'm just like: 'of *all* the places in the world . . .' The program has a branch in Kenya, and who knows when I'm ever going to be *there*. I took Spanish in college, so it seemed— you know, *logical*, to come here. But it's been a *nightmare*. The place has no staff except *me* and these two GP's, who found out I was coming and then like *halved* their schedules, so you know what that means for me. The place has no money. People come in with serious diseases at an *advanced stage*, and they think I can treat them on the spot.

I send them to Tejaces, which is the closest thing to a real hospital for like nine light-years. A lot of them refuse to leave unless I've given them *something*, some *pills*." She scoffed and hurled the cigarette away. "I'm treating *liver cancer* with aspirin, I mean for God's sake . . ." She hopped after the butt to stomp it out.

"What about your nurse?" Gloria asked.

"I haven't had a nurse in three months."

"There was one the last time I was here."

"Lola? She quit to open up a faith-healing place. When were you here?"

"I was—"

"Are you a patient?"

"Not quite," Gloria said carefully. She had to be delicate here, to soften her up a little. "I'm a nurse myself, so I understand."

"Yeah? A bilingual nurse." The doctor had a masculine laugh. She patted herself down for another cigarette, but found none. "You want a job?"

Gloria smiled. "I might. I have a question about the facility, actually."

"I don't really have time, I have patients to fool." The doctor checked her watch and pulled on the back door; she had locked herself out. "Shit."

"It won't take long."

The doctor sighed. "All right. Follow me closely."

They went around the corner to the front of the clinic. As they came through the lobby, querulous patients congealed around them. The doctor fought them off gently and headed for the back room, yelling in Spanish *Get in line, get in line, one minute.* Gloria felt like the friend of a movie star, tagging along at the Oscars. By virtue of her proximity to the doctor, she, too, was being mauled and groped. The frowsy woman yelled at her *Wait! Cheating bitch!* as she slipped through the double doors.

They were in a narrow hallway blocked by a gurney. Atop it was a pile of fetid linens. Gloria recognized the smell: unchecked disease: the smell of her mother.

The doctor barked her shin on a pair of crutches leaning against the wall, sending them skittering. For a moment, Gloria thought the floor was dirt; then she saw that it was incredibly grimy concrete.

There were a few unmarked doors, and one with its legend nearly scraped off but still legible: OFICINA DEL DOCTOR. The doctor explained that she had to share it with the other physicians—not that it mattered, since they never bothered to show up.

The room was hexagonal, tiled on all sides, with show-erheads at regular intervals along the walls. The floor slanted toward a patched-over drain.

"The building used to be squash courts," said the doctor.

Gloria didn't ask why there had been squash courts in the middle of the desert. She had gotten accustomed to a rapid rate of camouflage.

"I need to go back out there soon," said the doctor as they sat. "For all I know someone's arresting as we speak."

The room was a parody of third-world health care. A soiled examination table; a knee-high cabinet missing one door, holding a tray of hypodermics and what looked like a stockpot (for boiling needles?); jars with tape, cotton balls, unwrapped gauze pads. And then Gloria noticed two brand-new things: a compact, shiny defibrillator, and an oxygen tank with a pristine nonrebreather mask.

Neither of them sat. The doctor said, "I'm Naomi."

"Gloria."

"What can I do for you?"

"I had a friend who died in an accident around here this past July. He was brought to this clinic and then cremated."

"It's the law," said the doctor. "If no one comes forward in forty-eight hours, a clinic without storage facilities can pay to have the body taken somewhere with a morgue, or cremate it. When I first got here the physician I was replacing told me not to bother paying for transportation, since nobody will pay us back. On the other hand, the state subsidizes up to three hundred pesos for disposal. The guy who comes charges one hundred fifty. He comes with a van, and brings us back the ashes. I don't ask what he does."

"What about the other one hundred fifty pesos?" Gloria asked.

"What?"

"The state gives you three hundred pesos for every body, but it only costs one hundred fifty. Do you get the rest?"

"We don't get it unless we spend it," the doctor said, fidgeting. She was obviously in need of a cigarette. Veins marbled her straw neck; her eyes looked as though they had been proofread.

Gloria took out a photo of Carl. "This is him."

"I've never seen him."

"A policeman from Aguas Vivas brought me here to

claim his remains. This clinic issued a death certificate. I'm wondering if you wrote it."

The doctor stared at her. "I don't have to answer that."

"No, you don't." Gloria waited, then said, "When I got back to Los Angeles the police discovered that the ashes were fake."

"You were here when?"

"Last July. I wasn't allowed past the waiting room. I came with *Teniente* Tito Fajardo. He went in and came back out with an urn and the death certificate."

The doctor idly rolled a pencil back and forth across her desk.

Gloria said, "I'm not looking to get you in trouble. I want to find out what happened to him. He was a friend of mine and I'm worried."

Pause.

The doctor said, "The only reason we're having this conversation is because you speak English. And because you're an RN."

"I appreciate it."

The doctor rubbed her eyes. "I've gotten used to doing things differently. If it works, I'll do it. If I'm stressed enough, I'll do it even if it doesn't work. Dr. Harvey—I replaced her—she told me to go with the flow. That's the Mexican way." She sighed. "I'm going to tell you and then you have to leave."

Gloria nodded.

"I hadn't been here like, more than a couple of weeks. It was one of the first nights I was alone on shift. A madhouse. Go with the flow.

"The policeman came in here and told me to give him the form for a death certificate. I said, 'For who?' He said, 'I already sent the body to be cremated.' I said, 'You're not supposed to do that,' but he said it was normal procedure and that I had to issue him one, or else he was going to arrest Lola."

"The nurse?"

The doctor nodded.

"He *said* that?"

"He said it. And that would've been like, the end. It was much worse than if he'd threatened to arrest me. Lola was running the show. I kept screwing up, mixing up words, I was so nervous. I couldn't believe my ears. I didn't think he was real, I was ready to call the actual cops, because I'd heard that people dress up as cops. He looked pretty nervous himself, like he wanted to get it over with as fast as possible. When I hesitated he said, 'You need money?' Then he wrote down a number. At that point it was a no-brainer."

"You gave it to him."

"Of course I did."

"How much did he give you?"

"A thousand dollars. Cash." The doctor coughed, pounded herself lightly on the chest. "You have no idea how far that goes here."

Gloria looked at the the defibrillator and the oxygen tanks. The doctor followed her gaze and nodded confirmation.

"But it was worse than that. We didn't have any *antibiotics*. And besides, I didn't know what he wanted the certificate for. He couldn't *kill* anyone with it. The worst he could do was like, commit insurance fraud, and I'm not a big fan of insurance agencies anyway. I'm from Ohio. My malpractice is going to cost like ninety thousand dollars a year and I have *loans* to repay." She took out her lighter, flicked and closed it. "That's what I asked myself. What was the worst he could do."

"I'm sorry," Gloria said, meaning it.

The doctor waved it off. "Look, I made a call, and I don't regret it. It was the right one. I'm sorry for whatever happened to your friend. If something is screwy, report the policeman. He's out of joint, that guy. He came in once before, asking for azithromycin for a sick kid. When I wrote down his phone number I caught him looking down my shirt."

Gloria said, "That sounds about right."

"I need to go back out there."

"I appreciate it."

The doctor bit her lip. "We keep the hundred-fifty."

"What?"

"The extra hundred-fifty pesos. We file it with the state as though it costs three hundred, and we keep the extra for supplies. I got three hundred for filing your friend as a cremation. I don't remember what happened to that money, that money in particular. Wait, I lied, I do. I paid for part of those crutches in the hall. Some kid had a bad fracture. His girlfriend's brother beat him up with a shovel. I almost had to send him to Tejaces for surgery. I set his femur with tape and plywood from the hardware store. He actually healed." The doctor sounded amazed. "It was ridiculous."

Gloria said, "I'm glad the money was good for something."

"It was." The doctor went to the door. "Stay as long as you want," she said, and left. It sounded like a request.

CARLOS WAS SHIRTLESS, waiting by the Dodge with his arms behind his back.

"I went in," he said, "but you weren't there."

"I was talking to the doctor."

"And?"

"First let's see."

He displayed his hands. The chair was gone, and the chain had been cut, but the cuff was still on his wrist, dangling three links.

"I came in trying to be discreet," he said, "but as soon as I showed the guy behind the counter, he called over everyone in the store, 'Look at this!' It wasn't so bad until he got everybody cutting lumber to come inside. *That* was bad."

Gloria laughed.

Carlos said, "They started debating the best way to get it off. One guy wanted to use a metal file. Someone said, 'He'll be here for three weeks if we do that.' Another genius suggested we burn it off with acid. They settled on a hacksaw. They had to be careful so they wouldn't slice up my hand. It didn't matter, because it was a piece of shit: the blade broke. I had to pay for it."

"I hope you protested."

"I'm not going to argue with thirty lumberjacks," he

said. "One guy started talking about his friend who escaped from prison and tried to cut off his shackles by laying them across train tracks. 'He got sucked in,' the guy said. 'He was ground beef.'"

Gloria made a face.

"Then everyone started asking *me* how I got cuffed in the first place. 'Are you a criminal? What did you do?' I said, yes, I was arrested by the Coast Guard. This is how they punish you."

"Didn't they have a power tool or something?"

"They had a reciprocating saw, and a bandsaw, but the owner didn't want to use them. I can't blame him, because without a metal-cutting blade it would destroy his equipment. Not to mention possibly cutting off my hand. Finally someone got the idea that you could use an ax. At least that way I wouldn't have to lug the chair around. They put it across a big block of wood, like a beheading, and the largest guy there chopped it off. The ax got damaged, so they made me pay for that, too."

He reached beneath the car and brought out the chair and ax.

"Why aren't you wearing your shirt?" she asked.

"I was going to put it on," he said. "But I thought you liked me better this way."

She smiled. "You must be cold."

"It's ninety degrees, Gloria. But whatever you want." He pulled a polo out of his waistband and put it on. His hair rose in a cowlick—Carl's cowlick. She ironed it down.

"So that's my morning," he said. "What did she have to say?"

"Who?"

"The doctor."

"How do you know it was a she?"

"It was a guess. I'm very progressive."

"She happens to be a she. Get in the car, I'll tell you all about it. We need to talk to the *Teniente*."

"Okay. But let's do a little *planning* this time." He picked up the beach chair. "We can give this back. Maybe that'll put him in a better mood."

"What about the ax?"

"You want a souvenir?"

She said, "There are plenty of other things I'd rather take home."

TWENTY-SEVEN

Lunch was chicken with rice and beans at a roadside stand on the outskirts of Joaqual. On the ride, she filled him in. Carlos whistled when she told him about the money.

She sipped water *embotellada en México.* "Whoever paid Fajardo off is getting a raw deal. I'm ashamed at how many stupid things he pulled right in front of me. It worked because I was tired and confused. Although that's no excuse."

"Everybody makes mistakes."

"I'm careful," she said, sipping. "So, here's what I've been thinking—"

He interrupted her with a kiss on the shoulder.

"What was that for?"

"Because you're so careful," he said.

She smiled. "We don't have much leverage."

"We could bribe him."

"Besides that."

Carlos said, "You want to kidnap one of his children?"

"Be serious a minute. The man shot at us."

"I don't think he'd do it again," he said. "He was drunk. He's probably afraid we're going to report him."

"We could."

"To who? And why would they believe you?"

"We have a witness."

"The doctor?"

"Mm."

"She's not a witness to the shooting," Carlos said. "She's a character witness."

"She's a lack-of-character witness. But if she understood what was being covered up—"

"*We* don't know what's being covered up."

"We don't?"

"No."

"I thought we did."

"We don't. Not for sure." He lowered the sunshade and looked in the mirror, fingering his lacerated eyebrow. "This isn't looking so bad anymore."

"I forgot," she said. "We can go back and have it stitched up."

"It'll heal. You handled it fine. Although—do you think it'll scar?"

"It might."

He frowned. "Son of a bitch . . ." He leaned in to look closer.

"Carlos?"

"Mm . . ."

"What do you think is being covered up?"

"Hm?"

"You said you don't know for sure."

"Well—no. We don't. Son of a bitch . . ."

"Don't touch it."

"He'd better not have given me a scar."

"Carlos, did you hear what I asked?"

"About—"

"About our theory."

"Yes," he said. "So . . . yes."

"Do you have an opinion?"

He didn't answer.

"Carlos?"

"I'm a little preoccupied at the moment," he said. He sounded irritated. She glanced over and saw him fingering the cut again.

"Don't touch it."

He closed the mirror with a petulant sigh.

"It'll heal," she said.

"Yeah . . ."

"So are you going to answer my question?"

He looked at her. "Hm?"

"Fajardo."

"Yeah," he said. "Yeah. I've been thinking."

"And."

"And . . ." He sniffled. "What if we're wrong? We came without any preparation. How do you know Carl—my father—how do you know he's not in the United States somewhere? He might be hiding out in another city."

"Fair enough," she said. "But the *Teniente* knows something, or else he wouldn't be trying to scare us off. So we should find out what that is."

"What if he really is dead, though."

She looked at him. "I thought we were going with the theory that he was covering his tracks."

"We were." His voice was an alloy of skepticism and indifference; it flustered her.

"We've been going with that assumption the whole time," she said.

"Yes, we have."

"Do you think it's wrong?"

He waved vaguely, turned to the window.

"Carlos?"

"I don't know . . ." he said. "Maybe."

"Then who made the bank withdrawal?"

"What if he made it, and then he died."

"You think he went down to Mexico, called me, went back to the United States, went to the bank, took out money, went *back* to Mexico, and then died? By accident?"

"I don't know."

"That doesn't make any sense."

"How do you know he called you from Mexico the first time?"

"I—"

"This whole thing might be a false trail. Maybe he's somewhere else, alive or dead."

"All right," she allowed. "But then where do we start looking?"

He didn't answer. The Dodge passed through a mosquito convention; carcasses peppered the windshield. Gloria tried unsuccessfully to summon wiper fluid, creating smears out of specks.

"I can barely see," she said. "And we're almost out of gas."

He was quiet, slumping.

"Are you feeling okay?" she asked.

He angled away from her. "This is a godforsaken part of this country."

"I think there's something beautiful to it."

"Bare bone," he said. "That's all it is."

She wanted to say: that can be beautiful, too; but that sounded morbid and academic. She edged the car toward the exit for the gas station.

"I hope he's dead," Carlos said.

She didn't say anything.

"I wouldn't be sad at all," he said. "I'd throw a party."

"I hated my brother, but it hurt when he died."

"He didn't do to you what my father did to me," Carlos said.

"You're right."

"Don't tell me I'm not allowed to be angry."

"I'm not."

"I'm allowed to hate him."

"I'm not saying you're not." She paused. "Then why come with me in the first place?"

"If he is alive, I want to tell it to his face."

"When you talked to him on the phone, did you tell him that?"

"Of course not."

"Because I can hardly blame him for running, if he thought you were just going to devour him."

"You're defending him."

"I'm not," she said. "I see it your way. I see it his way, too. I don't think there's anything wrong with that."

The gas station she'd used last time was largely unchanged. The wind had dislodged a few shingles from the overhang, but the gravity pumps, the columns of tires, and the decaying tow truck fit snugly into her memory. Inside the foodmart, the same boy was manning the desk, paging through a magazine. Gloria cut the motor.

"Don't be angry," she said. "I knew your father for a long time. It's been tough relearning him."

"He abandoned me. I grew up poor. I wouldn't have ended up in construction, drinking myself to death, if I had been raised by my father in the United States."

"Carlos . . ."

"It's a pretty simple matter of economics," he said. He looked past her. "The kid is coming."

She saw now that it wasn't the same boy as last year. While the shape of his face was eerily correct, this boy was younger, eight or nine.

Gloria rolled down the window.

"Hola," said the boy. *"¿Como estáis?"*

"Good," said Gloria. "And you?"

"You want gas?" he asked, already picking up the nozzle.

Carlos touched her arm before she could respond. "We can do it ourselves," he said to the boy. "Give us a minute and we'll do it."

The boy looked unconvinced. "It's hard to get it to work," he said.

"We'll call you if there's a problem."

The boy shrugged, hung up the nozzle, and retreated to the foodmart.

Carlos rolled up the window. "I don't want to argue. But

I'm getting kind of tired of driving around this shitty coun-tryside."

"We've been here a little more than a day."

"I know," he said.

"If your patience runs out that quickly—"

"It's not that," he said.

"Then what is it?"

Pause.

He said, "Last night I had a dream. It won't sound so bad now, but believe me . . ."

She waited.

He said, "We were in our motel. Except it was fifty sto-ries high. We knocked on all the doors. All the rooms were empty, except for the last one, which is where we found him.

"He was on the bed. He couldn't see us. He looked exactly like me, older. What I'm going to look like in thirty years. His chest was a cupboard. It had handles. He opened himself up and he was hollow.

"I swung at his face but my hand went through like it was nothing."

He flopped back, red. "It's hot," he mumbled, opening the window again.

"That sounds awful," she said.

"It was a bad way to wake up."

She said, "You don't look that much like him."

"It's a dream, Gloria. You can't *refute* it."

After a long silence, he said, "I'll pump the gas. You want to get something to drink? Get something for me, too. Water, no soda."

She tried a smile. "Watching your weight?"

He smiled back, and—like a flag unfurling—there was something between them again. "I'm always on my guard," he said.

"The word is *careful*," she said.

The foodmart greeted her with air, not cold but at least moving. Moisture tickled her all over, running along the bottom edge of her brassiere and the inside of her elbow. She stood by the refrigerator case, letting its breath wash over her.

As she brought bottles up to the counter, she saw what the boy was reading: an old basketball magazine entitled *El Jam.* On the cover was an in-your-face action shot of a large Chinese man blocking a shot.

"Do you play?" she asked.

His eyes rose over the page. "Yes."

"With your brother," she said.

He put the magazine down. "You know my brother?"

"I was here before. There was someone who looked like you."

He nodded.

"He works here, too," Gloria said.

"We all work here," he said.

"How many of you are there?"

"I have five brothers," he said. "And three sisters."

"Wow . . ."

As she took out her wallet, he watched her clinically. "How old are you?"

"Thirty-six. How old are you?"

"Seven years and eleven months. Do you know math?"

"A little bit," she said.

"You do?"

"I think so."

"What's twelve times thirty-seven?"

"I don't know," she said.

"Four hundred forty-four. What's fourteen times eighty-nine?"

"I don't know."

"One thousand two hundred forty-six. What's seventeen times ninety-nine?"

"Six."

He made a disgusted face. *"No."*

"What is it?"

"One thousand six hundred eighty-three," he said. "That's the *easy* one."

"My mistake."

"Ask me one," he commanded.

She tossed him some simple multiplication; he knocked it away like batting practice.

"Harder," he said.

Bigger numbers he zinged right back. She didn't know if he was correct or not, but his bracing confidence impressed her.

"You have some brain," she said.

"That's right," he said. "I do. You're from America."

"Yes."

"I'm going to America."

"Oh really? When?"

"I'm going to be a farmer," he said, as though that answered her question.

"You are, huh?"

"My father's a farmer."

"Does he mind that you work at a gas station?"

He looked at her oddly. "He owns it."

"The gas station?"

He nodded.

"Oh," she said. "I thought he was a farmer."

"He's a *farmer*," he said deliberately. "*And* he owns a gas station."

Carlos entered. "That pump is *slow*."

Gloria said, "Ask him a math question."

"Math?"

"Hard," said the boy.

"What's five times five?"

The boy rolled his eyes.

"Try something harder," she told Carlos.

"Harder than that? All right. What's one hundred twenty-eight divided by eight?"

"Sixteen."

"Is that right?" Carlos asked Gloria.

"I don't know."

From underneath the counter, the boy produced an LCD calculator. He laid it on the desktop and punched in $128 \div 8$.

16

The boy said, "Another."

"Uh . . ." Carlos picked up the calculator. "Five hundred, uh . . . thirty-seven, divided by . . ."

"Forty-six," Gloria said.

The boy closed his eyes for a moment. "Eleven point six seven."

Carlos showed Gloria the calculator.

11.67391304

"How'd you do that?" Carlos asked.

"When I'm bored," said the boy. He stopped there: sufficient explanation.

"Well," Carlos said, "good job." To Gloria: "We need wiper fluid, and I think some oil."

The boy hopped off his stool and fetched two bottles and a funnel. He started to go out to the car, but Carlos detained him. "You got a restroom?"

"Around the back."

"I'll do this myself. You can sit here and do math with my girlfriend." He winked and went back outside with the bottles.

The boy hopped up on the stool and resumed chatting as though they had never been interrupted.

"I'm going to America when I'm older. I could go now but it wouldn't be useful."

She didn't know what that meant, but didn't have time to ask; he said:

"We had a drought for three years. The river dried up. We all went to work. My sisters are at home. He has a handcuff, how come."

She realized he was referring to Carlos. "It got stuck there by accident."

"Okay," he said breezily. "Do you like America?"

"Yes."

"Do you have a TV?"

"Yes."

"Do you watch it a lot?"

"Sometimes," she said. "Sometimes I watch it too much."

"What does that mean, too much."

"Never mind."

"Do you know Yao Ming?"

"Who?"

He held up the magazine.

"Nope," she said. "Sorry."

"Do you ever see movies? What's the best thing about America? Can you give me a picture? I want to play the drums, are they expensive? Is California in Los Angeles? Why did you come here?"

She answered each question faithfully. When she corrected his geography, he repeated the new information to himself as though girding himself for an exam.

"Los Angeles is a city," he said. "California is a state. Los Angeles is *in* California. Los Angeles is a city. . . ."

"You have states in Mexico. It's the same thing."

"I know the states," he said. "Aguascalientes, Baja California, Baja California Sur, Campeche, Chiapas, Chihuahua, Coahuila, Colima, Durango, Guanajuato, Guerrero, Hidalgo, Jalisco, México, Michoacán, Morelos, Nayarit, Nuevo León, Oaxaca, Puebla, Querétaro, Quintana Roo, San Luis Potosí, Sinaloa, Sonora, Tabasco, Tamaulipas, Tlaxcala, Veracruz, Yucatán, Zacatecas, plus the Federal District. That's alphabetical order. I can do it backwards, also."

"That's very impressive."

"I know the land," he said mysteriously. "I'm going to be a farmer in America. When I get there, I'll memorize the states. What are they?"

"I don't know them in alphabetical order," she said. "I probably couldn't do them out of order unless you gave me an hour to think about it."

"Here's the ones I know," he said. "Texas, Arizona, New York, Canada, Hawaii, and California."

"You're on your way. I hope you've been practicing your English."

"You want to hear?"

"Sure."

He got down off the stool again and went to a metal stand with bags of pork rinds clipped to it. Approximately his height, it made a perfect imaginary microphone, around which he undulated in an unsettlingly erotic way.

"Now—for the first time!" he said in English, accented but still identifiable; it came out like *por de beers time.* "Never before seen in one collection!" He made the gesture of flipping back bangs (his hair was blunt-cut, but the motion was perfect), took a deep breath, and began to sing.

I'm all out of love
I'm so lost without you

She couldn't contain herself; she emitted a chirp that caught him off guard. He stopped and said, levelly,

"Air Supply."

She said, "I didn't realize. Please, keep going."

He did, hopping from one great power love ballad of the 1970s to the next, a catalogue of songs that made her hit SEEK. Foreigner, Heart, REO Speedwagon . . .

And I can't fight this feeling anymooooore

"And this collection is not available in stores!" he said, resuming the narratorial pseudobaritone. *Note abay-la-bul een storss.* "But only by calling this toll-free number *Now.*"

He finished off with a few more snippets of music and ordering information, after which she applauded.

"If I'm not a farmer," he said, "then I'll become a singer."

A nerve twisted in her heart. She pitied him as much as she admired his gusto.

"Sounds like a good plan," she said. "What's that noise?"

The boy pointed. "From the bathroom."

"It sounds like a person."

"*Sí, Señora.* Your friend is talking in the bathroom."

"You can hear that?"

"It comes through the wall."

"I can't hear what he's saying."

"You can't hear the words unless the person is very loud," said the boy. "Sometimes I hear people fart."

She laughed. "You're too smart to live in the United States."

This lit him up. He rocked the stool. "My cousin has a friend who takes you across."

"Across the border?"

"I don't have enough money yet," he said. "But I will."

She didn't want to ask how this friend of a cousin took you across. Crowded you thirty in the back of a lettuce truck; put you on his shoulders and staggered across the rapids of the Rio Grande; led you on foot over barbed wire. She was reluctant to break his spirit; yet she didn't want it broken by someone harsher, who would not leave a margin for repair.

She said, "It can be hard."

"Okay," he said.

"No," she said. "It can be *very* hard. Even when you get there, it can be tough to make a living. It's expensive."

He sat, taking it all in, nodding sagely.

"It's difficult for a Mexican to get citizenship, and—"

She stopped. What was she doing?; she was talking to a *child*.

"It's hard," she summarized.

He rubbed his chin. For a second, she imagined he had a goatee.

"How come you speak Spanish," he said.

"My family came from Mexico."

"They did it," he said. "So I can, too."

"A long time ago. My mother worked her whole life and never got anywhere."

He said nothing.

"Even I don't have much," she said, at once regretting that. To him, she probably looked like a millionaire. Humiliated by his placid and forgiving stare, she added,

"Although you never know. Maybe you can become a mathematician."

"If I can't become a farmer, or a singer."

"You could become a singing mathematician," she said lamely.

He looked puzzled. "What's that?"

Out of the corner of her eye, she noticed Carlos replacing the pump.

"I think we're almost done," she said. She handed him thirty dollars and told him to keep the change.

"No, *Señora*. My father says I'm not allowed to do that."

"I'm not giving it to you for free," she said. "It's for the concert you gave."

For the first time, he smiled. *"Gracias."*

"De nada."

She started out.

Then—obeying a whim—she turned back to the counter.

"Since you have such a good memory," she said, "do you know if you've ever seen this person?" She showed him Carl's picture.

He took one look at it and said, *"Sí."*

The shock made her guts contract. "You have?"

"Sure," he said.

"When?"

"A long time ago," he said. "The summer."

"Here?"

"Sí," he said, sounding alarmed by her vehemence. She lowered her voice:

"Tell me what happened."

"My brother was working. I was in the back"—he pointed through one wall of the station—"playing with the tires. I made a house. When I heard a car come in I went to look, because I wanted to know if it was a Mercedes. But it wasn't."

"What car was it?"

"A truck."

"What color?"

"Purple," he said.

"What else do you remember?"

"The truck left them here, then they borrowed the tow truck. The man bought a bottle of water."

Carlos honked. She waved for him to come inside, and said to the boy, "Them? He was with someone else?"

"Yes."

"Can you describe them?"

The boy rubbed his nose. "He looked like the man in your car."

"Gloria." Carlos appeared behind her. His arm around her waist felt like the restraining bar on a roller coaster, preventing her from tumbling out of the world.

"I almost forgot to give you this," he said to the boy, handing him the funnel.

"You have a handcuff on by accident," the boy observed.

"What?"

The boy pointed.

"It's not an accident," Carlos said. "It's my bracelet."

"Men don't wear bracelets."

"I do."

"*She* said it was an accident."

"Well," said Carlos, "she's not right about everything."
He laughed again. "We'll see you later," he said, steering her
outside.

They got in the Dodge. She started the engine while
Carlos checked the map.

"Cute kid," he said.

TWENTY-EIGHT

Before he died, Gloria's brother had shown evidence of one skill. The ability to act was hardly a rarity in Los Angeles; but looking back, it seemed to Gloria remarkable that a barrio boy whose fate was multiple gunshot wounds could mimic gentility on a stage—gentility as well as love, sorrow, wisdom, patience, strength. When the curtain went up on Jesús Julio, he flaunted all the qualities he lacked in real life, so authentically that Gloria heard her mother crying after his shows.

In some ways, though, it made perfect sense. He had always been an actor. The roiling emotion that manifested itself as colic in his infancy and abruptness in his death found, at select moments, an even-keeled outlet.

In eighth grade, one of his teachers—a woman whose optimism rendered her impotent in the Los Angeles Unified School District—contrived to mount portions of Oscar Wilde's *The Importance of Being Earnest* for the school's end-of-year graduation cantata. This event was regarded, by students and teachers alike, as a hazing that junior-high-schoolers had to endure before they could go to Theodore Roosevelt and pretend to be grown-ups. Like being forced to chew ten packs of gum in order to earn a cigarette.

Somehow Jesús Julio ended up cast as Jack. Gloria remembered the day he came home with the script, because he picked a huge fight with their mother before stomping out of the house and down the block to the park.

"Go tell your brother I'm not making him dinner," Mamá had said.

Gloria found him hunched, script in hand, atop the monkey bars. She watched him from a distance as his lips moved. He seemed to be vibrating. His intensity took her by surprise. She had seen him fly off the handle; she had seen him punch the wall. This was different: all the fireworks were going somewhere, from his head to the page and back again. She imagined that he would burst into flames.

It is a terrible thing for a man to find out suddenly that all his life he has been speaking nothing but the truth.

She called his name, and he almost fell off.

"What do you want," he said.

"Mamá said she's not making you dinner."

"I don't want any fucking dinner."

"Mamá says—"

"Yeah, I know Mamá says not to say that. Fuck off, I'm busy."

He went back to mumbling. She stayed until he noticed her.

"I said *fuck off*," he said.

"What are you doing?"

"I have to study this thing," he said.

"For what?"

"Graduation. Go away."

On the walk home, it occurred to her that although he had scorned whatever was in those pages, he was reading them—by choice. She had never seen that before.

In the weeks that followed, budding stage fright brought out his worst. He would snap about anything, then yell about being too busy to deal with this goddamn fucking shit before grabbing the script and stalking off to the park, where he would alight atop the monkey bars and study lines until the orange of sunset crossfaded to the orange of sulphur lamps.

Mamá told Gloria that she would be happy after it was over. Not happy, *relieved.*

Gloria agreed. She was tired of going to fetch him.

Ladies and gentlemen, I present to you the class of 1978. The same teacher who'd settled on drawing-room comedy served as mistress of ceremonies.

What was her name? Gloria couldn't remember. H-something.

Harcourt. Miss Harcourt. Angora and ironed hair. She had probably gone to some teacher's college. She talked like a saxophone with a sinus infection.

Our theme this year is One Big Family. Because we here at Hollenbeck Junior High School are One Big Family. And now that we've brought our parents and siblings here to share with us, our One Big Family has gotten even Bigger. . . .

Next came the principal. The valedictorian, a Japanese

girl with braces. They gave out awards. When a pair of Russian Molokan twins shared the prize for most-improved student, a skeletal woman with severe cheekbones wept freely.

Gloria zoned out, playing imaginary tic-tac-toe on the argyle sweater of the man in front of her. She looked around the auditorium and saw nothing inspiring. A violet science-fair banner, somehow untouched since 1974, flaunted its own longevity.

As Mamá waited, she played with the buttons on her jacket as though she wanted to yank them off—something she never would have done consciously. It was her only good outfit, a silk-and-lace suit that had never really been in fashion but was in excellent condition. Her Bel Air employer had given it to her, along with a load of outgrown children's clothes that Gloria avoided, and regarding which Jesús Julio said, "Fuck that shit."

The jacket, however, got lots of use. Mamá wore it to church. In fact, that night was the first time that Gloria had seen Mamá wear it elsewhere.

"And now for the entertaining portion of our evening," said Miss Harcourt. "Selected scenes from Oscar Wilde's classic comedy *The Importance of Being Earnest.*"

Everyone sat up; havoc had arrived.

Because of the length of the text and the brevity of her time slot, Miss Harcourt had resorted to a narrator to fill in missing information—no mean feat, considering that the play had been reduced to eight minutes. Year after year, this constraint had the effect of diluting the story to absurdity. When the stage hands whipped out a couple of stock chairs and a table, and one of the graduates came forward to begin *Our scene opens in the opulent morning-room of Algernon Moncrieff,* the mischief began to froth. Someone threw a paper airplane that crash-landed in the third row. A guy at the back started barking and making obscene noises until he was escorted out to a smattering of applause.

"Why are they doing that?" Mamá whispered angrily.

Gloria had her hands on her head. All she could think about was what a monstrous tantrum her brother would throw that night.

Jesús Julio's first line was *I am in love with Gwendolyn, and I have come to propose to her.* He came onstage careening into the furniture. Everyone jeered and hooted and heckled, and Mamá began pulling at her buttons frantically.

"What is he *doing*?"

After a few anguished moments—throughout which Mamá repeated *what is he doing what what what*—Gloria discerned that Jesús Julio was bumbling and puffing himself up like a fool *on purpose.* It took the crowd longer to get it; they had such rock-bottom expectations that his fluid ineptitude seemed genuine. But then he made a huge show of dropping a teacup and catching it—then dropping it again, and catching it between his legs—then dropping it a third time, and catching it behind the back as he squatted—and it dawned on people that what they were witnessing was not eighth-grade mediocrity but some sort of comic genius.

Three hundred and ninety seconds later, he bowed, and

for the first time in the history of Hollenbeck Junior High School, the graduation cantata got an honest-to-God ovation. Jesús Julio, breathing hard, smiled to nobody in particular.

"Here!" shouted Mamá, waving.

"Here!" Gloria shouted, standing on her chair.

He did not see them, or pretended not to. He came home that night happy, with a yearbook full of congratulatory signatures (*I never knew you could do that* wrote his math teacher). Mamá had prepared a cake that said PARA EL MEJOR ACTOR.

He wasn't hungry. He went straight to sleep, leaving Gloria and her mother to eat a tenth of it before dumping it in the trash. Mamá was hurt but counted her blessings: it might not have been a joyous night, but it was a peaceful one, and for that she and Gloria gave thanks.

His decline over the next few years deflated their hopes for newfound maturity. He cursed out teachers and broke into lockers. His relationships with administrators, secretaries, the coach, the nurse, were bad or nonexistent. Everyone wanted to kick him out except Mr. Fabian, the drama teacher, who unleashed Jesús Julio's freshman year Shylock on an unsuspecting fall night.

> *The villany you teach me, I will execute,*
> *and it shall go hard but I will better the instruction.*

When he stood before the court of Venice, sunk into a legal trap he himself had laid, he neither shouted nor groveled. He maintained the pitch-perfect resentment of the first three acts, a scarcely concealed murderousness that became strangely piteous. He said: *You may hate me, but look what hate makes you.* Watching him, Gloria felt ashamed of herself, and she knew that the rest of the audience felt the same.

His performance was good enough to prevent him from being expelled for poor grades. He ignored the requirement to attend summer school, and Mr. Fabian begged for and secured his readmission.

Sophomore year's *Romeo and Juliet* firmed up his reputation, and *Antigone* the following semester cemented it. The latter performance occasioned a meeting between the vice principal and Gloria's mother, at which the suggestion was put forth that she enroll him in acting classes instead of regular school.

To which Mamá replied, "You're crazy."

After Jesús Julio died, she felt guilty for not having listened. But Gloria knew it was an exercise in self-loathing. He was destined to mess up. Acting classes would not have prevented it—probably not even delayed it.

Nevertheless, Gloria also wondered why, if he was destined to flush his talent down the toilet, he had gotten so much of it.

And why had she gotten none. She was a bad liar, always had been. Until this moment, it had never been a problem.

But now she was trying to act calm, and she was failing.

"Who were you talking to in the bathroom?" she asked Carlos.

"What?"

"In the gas station," she said. "I heard you talking through the walls."

His face bunched up like it had this morning, when she'd taken his picture.

"You did," he said.

She hastened to add, "I didn't hear *what* you were saying, just that you were talking."

"I was talking to my boss."

She steered them back onto the north-south road, back to Aguas Vivas, passing the turnoff for the cemetery-cum-mirage.

He looked like the man in your car.

That didn't mean that he was the same person. Lots of people looked alike. The boy was a veritable facsimile of his brother. It could have been any middle-aged Mexican man. To a seven-year-old kid, they probably all appeared the same.

Ask me another one.

Not this kid. This kid had a maximum-security memory.

If the kid was right—and she couldn't stop thinking that the kid *was* right—then Carlos had seen his father. But that didn't fit.

I hope he's dead.

I wouldn't be sad at all. I'd throw a party.

She needed time to work this out. She suggested they go back to the motel and check in again for the night.

"Now?" he said. "It's—"

She slid her hand over his crotch. "I'd really like to."

*

HIS BODY WAS LESS SUPPLE this time around; in his face
was a detachment that made her seize up. He kissed her as
though searching her mouth for lies.

Probably it would turn out to be a big mistake, she
thought. She held that notion long enough to feel a jolt of
pleasure.

But her instincts revolted. She thought, He's in me and
I'm afraid.

She went on seesawing, and was nowhere near orgasm
when he started to clench his buttocks and tell her to come
along with him. She closed her eyes and faked it almost
good enough to fool herself.

He rolled off her. "Any more of this and I might have to
take you back home." He turned on his side. "Are you
hungry?"

"Sleepy."

"You're not hungry at all?"

"I need a nap."

With a grunt, he sprung to his feet. He scratched his
shoulders and made a pigeon-chest, letting out a satisfied
brrrmmhhhmmm.

"I'm going to take a shower. Then we can eat. Does that
sound good?"

She murmured assent. The urge to sleep was genuine, and
she bit her tongue to ward it off while he collected his clothes,
his towel, the shampoo, his room key. He said, "Back soon,"
and closed the door softly on his way out.

She counted to thirty, then went for his bag, unsure of
what she was after until she saw his cellphone. Her fingers felt huge as she mashed buttons, bringing up by

accident the games menu before she found the outgoing-call list.

She redialed the last number. It rang twice.

"*Bueno.*"

She knew the voice, but she wanted more than a single word. She waited.

"*¿Hay alguien allí?*"

She hung up.

It was Fajardo.

She jammed the phone back in the bag, smashing her wrist into something hard. She parted a stack of boxer shorts and three pairs of balled-up socks, and there it was, a gun.

He had a gun.

He had a gun in his bag.

She'd been having sex with him, and there was a gun in his bag, on the floor, five feet away.

He'd said to her *We came here unarmed.*

But—

He had a *gun.*

Her first thought was to put it back. As though she had uncovered a secret so vile that her trespass humiliated her.

If you put it back, she thought, then he'll have a gun.

Then take the bullets out.

But she didn't know how. She didn't know anything about guns. It was newish, not a revolver one but one of the other kinds. An automatic. Or was it a semiautomatic? A toggle on the side she guessed was a safety. How did you get the cartridge out?

She didn't even know if it was loaded.

She regretted never having listened to Reggie. *One lesson, so you know how to use one; everyone should know, specially a woman.* She thought weapons were disgusting; she supported gun control. And now she could hear Reggie saying *I told you so, Gigi, I fucking told you so.*

Pointing the thing away from her, she looked at the butt. She was pretty sure that it would be hollow without a cartridge. It wasn't. So it had been loaded at some point. The question was whether the cartridge itself had anything left.

She hefted. Heavy enough; there must be at least a few shots left. Or was the gun itself the weighty part? How much did bullets weigh? How many bullets were there per cartridge? If they were two ounces apiece and there was a dozen of them, that was a pound and a half. Could it weigh that much? No. Less. Fewer. A quarter of an ounce, ten shots.

Two and a half ounces.

Impossible. A quarter of an ounce couldn't do anything.

But a BB weighed next to nothing, and it could put an eye out. A girl she remembered from Hollenbeck got shot in the stomach with an airgun and bled to death. Maybe a quarter of an ounce was about right. A difference that small she wouldn't be able to detect by feel alone.

If it was a weight and number in between—

This was ridiculous.

Stop thinking and do something.

She supposed she could fire a test shot.

She almost did.

The other thought she didn't have the time or clarity to consider was: he had a *gun,* for God's sake, and therefore he had lied. Which, she supposed in some abstract way, made it possible that he would hurt or kill her. He who five minutes ago had been kissing her.

She tried to think if she'd given him reason to hurt her.

You had to ask questions. Questions about the bathroom. Questions about the plan. Acting stilted in the car.

Taking his picture.

She bet he knew.

Of course he knew.

So, now, what was the goal?

To avoid getting killed.

She started toward the door, but he was coming back up the hall.

Into bed; gun under the pillow. She became driftwood, opening her mouth and breathing noisily. The weapon poked hard and tubular under her face, like the bed was getting a boner. She hoped she appeared convincingly like "sleep." Hoping the spirit of Jesús Julio lived in her at this moment, though it never had before.

The door opened.

He hesitated on the threshold.

Watching her.

Being considerate of her nap.

Or sighting at her head?

He padded to the far end of the room. She opened one eye. He was leaning out the window.

He checked his watch and turned back; she closed the eye.

Humming "Guantanamera," he sat by her and stroked

her hip. She pretended to mumble and sniffle, conjuring up a spoonful of drool, which she let out as she shifted away from his touch.

She heard him chuckle.

He touched her again, tenderly, on the arm.

Was she wrong?

"Gloria," he whispered. "Gloria."

A bad mistake?

Maybe he carried a gun for protection.

Is that what he'd say?

She'd almost believe him if he said it, he was touching her so sweetly.

"Gloria."

He wanted to wake her. Sure he did, he was hungry. That was the arrangement. She napped, he showered, then they got food. But he felt bad disturbing her. She could tell by the reluctance with which he called her name, skimmed his fingertips across her earlobe.

"Gloria."

She faked a yawn and said, "Nnmm."

"Do you want to sleep?"

"Mmhmm . . ."

"I'm going to find something to eat," he said. "I'll take the car."

On the one hand: a chance to get rid of the gun. On the other: no way to leave.

He withdrew his hand. "I'll bring you dinner, okay?"

She peeked as he went to the door. He stopped and turned and went to his bag.

no no no no no no no no

He took his cellphone out.

He said, "I'll have this with me in case you need anything. Can you remember the number if I tell you?"

"Mmm." Lucky, she thought, that paralyzing terror sounds like drowsiness.

"Gloria? Are you awake?"

"I'm awake."

"Can you remember the number if I tell you?"

"Yes . . ."

He told it to her twice.

"Repeat it back so I know you know," he said.

She obeyed.

"Okay. I'll see you soon. You sure you don't want anything?"

"No thanks . . ." She yawned again, scratching at her breast.

His hand was on the doorknob when his phone rang.

"I'll take it outside," he said, exiting.

The door started to close and she heard him say, "Did I call when? I was in the show—oh shit—" And then he stuck his foot in the closing door, reentering the room and saying "Did you—?" but she was already up on her knees, gun in hand, muzzling at the center of his chest.

"Wait a second," he said.

"Shut the door and step back against the wall."

"Gloria—"

"Shut the door."

He seemed to be judging whether she would shoot him, and what he accomplished by staying.

He let the door close.

"Against the wall."

Stepping forward: "Gloria—"

"Don't. Don't."

"You're misunderstanding."

She moved what she hoped was the safety into what she hoped was the open position.

Right on both counts.

"Okay, I'm back. See? I'm back."

"Put your hands up."

"Are you kidding me? *Gloria*—"

She edged the gun at him and he broke off, raising his hands. The handcuff slid halfway down his forearm, chain tinkling.

"This isn't safe," he said. "You don't know how to handle a gun."

"Yes I do."

Outside, the crickets began to fiddle.

"Can we talk about this?"

"I think that's a great idea," she said. "You tell me who you are and why you have a gun in your bag. Then I'll tell you what *I'm* going to do."

"It's hard to talk when you're pointing that at me."

"Don't look at it."

"It's hard to do that when—"

She gestured to the floor. "Lie down."

"What?"

"Get on your back," she said. "Put your hands above your head. Move slowly or I'll shoot you."

"Gloria, please calm down."

"Go," she said. "Keep your hands high."

He slid along the wall as though painting it with his back. Then he knelt, reversed himself—"I'm going to turn over, don't do anything"—and sprawled like a starfish.

"Happy?" he asked.

"Not yet." She propped her elbows on her knees and trained the gun on his midsection. His hand was four feet from her ankle. She told him to scoot toward the wall.

"You're getting all excited for nothing," he said, worming sideways.

"This thing in my hand isn't nothing," she said. "If it's nothing, why are you so afraid of it?"

"You're taking this out of context."

"Put it back in."

"You're not going to believe me."

"I suppose we can just sit here, if that's the way you'd like it."

"Gloria. I want you to put that down."

She held it out at him and he shrank back. It was kind of like having a remote control. He was in the crook of the wall, his left foot resting against the old shoe covering the mousehole.

"Talk," she said.

Pause.

He said, "My father is dead."

"He's your father?"

"Yes, he's my father."

"I don't believe you," she said.

"I told you you're not going to—"

"Talk."

The crickets were loud and grating.

He said, "He's my father. That's the truth. How else would I have known everything about him, if he wasn't. Everything I've told you is true except for the end."

"Starting when?"

"I never came to Los Angeles. I did find my father through the catalogue, and I did arrange to meet him. I did feel nervous and I did want to back out. But we met in Aguas Vivas."

"Why?"

"It's where my mother was killed. On the road near the cemetery. Where her car went out of control."

"Was the *Teniente* there?"

"No."

"What were you planning on doing?"

"Talking to him."

"That's all?"

"I was angry and I wanted to tell him that."

"You came to kill him," she said.

"No," he said.

"You're lying."

"You have to listen," he said, his voice breaking. "It's not that straightforward."

"Shit," she said.

"It wasn't—I didn't plan anything in advance—"

"Get back down."

"I'm down."

"Don't do that again or I will, I swear I will."

"I can't do this lying in the middle of the floor."

"Try."

"I can't. Please. I'm trying."

"Try harder."

Silence.

"He came to meet me and he said he was sorry. He wanted me to forgive him. That was the first thing out of his mouth. 'Please forgive me.' No *hello*. No *it's good to see you*. Atonement, that was all. On order like fast food.

"Was I supposed to say: It's not your fault, you didn't mean to do anything wrong? It *is* his fault. It's *all* his fault. He shit on my life, then went off to lead his own.

"I wasn't a person. I was a way to achieve peace of mind.

"Even if he'd asked in a way that made it clear he felt *bad*, I couldn't reverse forty years that fast. I barely knew him. It was the most arrogant thing in the world. I could have killed him right then. And it would have been justified.

"But I didn't. I said, 'Maybe at some point.'

"We drove out to the site of the accident. We got out of the car and stood on the side of the road for an hour. It was hot as hell. I could barely stand it. But he didn't move. He didn't cry, he didn't say anything. He watched the ground like it was going to open up and speak to him.

"Finally he said, 'I want to start at the beginning. I want to put my feet where they were, put them facing in the right direction this time, so that instead of running from you, I'm coming to save you. I'm leaving this spot again, but I'm taking you with me.'"

Carlos snorted. "Like it was that simple. It made me want to scream. It was so *childish*. Can you imagine the narcissism?"

"No," she said. "I can't."

"Then you never knew him. Because that's what he was really like. If you think you know anything about him you're kidding yourself. You knew the version that flattered him." He got up on his elbows. "That version *edits me out*."

She said nothing.

"Don't sit there and call me a liar."

"I don't believe you," she said. "I don't *not* believe you, either. I want you to keep talking. Tell me what happened after you went to the roadside."

"We went to go to my mother's grave." He shook his head. "He wanted *her* to forgive him, too. He threw himself on it, sobbing and hitting himself, screaming, 'I'm sorry, I'm sorry, I'm sorry.' It was like he was raping her. It was revolting and I told him to get off her. He said, 'Not until she forgives me.' I said, 'She's dead, she can't.' And he argued. He dared to argue. 'She would forgive me. She loved me. I loved her.'

"If he loved her—if he loved me—then why did he leave us there? He was full of shit and I told him so. I could have killed him then, too." There was something strange in his voice. "I didn't kill him, though. I grabbed him and threw him to the ground. I said, 'If you want to be forgiven, you can spend some time living in the dirt, like I have for forty years. If you want to know your family, get used to being low.'"

Carlos sat up. "He started crying. He said, 'I'm bad. I'm horrible. I'm a horrible person.' 'Yes,' I said, 'you are.' 'I deserve to suffer,' he said. 'Yes, you do.' 'I deserve to die.' I wasn't going to argue with him. He started to cry harder. It was pathetic. I told him, get up. You're not helping me. I don't give a shit about you crying. You can cry all day and all night, it still won't help me or her. So get up.

"I turned to go back to the car and there was a shot.

"At first I thought he was shooting at me. But he had the gun pointed in the air. He started walking toward me, holding the gun out. He got close to me," he said, drawing himself up on all fours, "and put it in my hand. He took my hand and brought the gun up to his own head, so that I was holding the gun, and he was holding the gun, and both of us had our fingers on the trigger." Inching forward. "Do you understand? He put my finger on the trigger. Then he pulled it. He shot himself in the head with my finger. I didn't do it. It wasn't up to me. He wanted me to do it because he thought he'd earn forgiveness that way. But like he always was, he was selfish; he didn't bother to think what it would look like. It would look like *I* did it. So I had to bribe the *Teniente*. We had to bribe the doctor. We had to cover it up. Because of what he did. All he wanted was to forgive himself and so he shit on me again. I had to cover it up, Gloria, because of the way it looked. It looked like I did it, but I didn't. I didn't do it, Gloria. Do you understand? Look at me, Gloria. I didn't do it. Gloria? Look at me. Look at my face. I'm telling you the truth. I didn't do it. I would never do a thing like that, I'm not like that. Look at me. Look at my face. Look."

He went for the gun.

The first bullet went through his shoulder. She was up and kicking: kicking back across the bed, kicking up the sheets, kicking up blood, kicking at him as he came at her. He pulled her from the bed and her body slid down against his and the muzzle landed in the hollow of his throat and she shot him and she shot him again and he strangled on muck and his neck was a hole and his body thrashed and then moved involuntarily, like an animal.

TWENTY-NINE

Had he been less muscular, she might have attempted to get the body down the hall, down the stairs, and into the trunk of the Dodge. His density—as well as her common sense—forbade it. It was staying here no matter what, and so she organized her thoughts around that reality, forcing herself to focus on what she was doing rather than why she was doing it.

Rolling him under the bed took several minutes. His head had nearly come off; reaching for it made her fingers curl in protest: *we will not touch that no no no.* And he was still bleeding. She'd had no idea how much blood a single body held. It slashed the walls and the ceiling in violent, astonishing stripes; it coated her and got into the carpet. She hoped it didn't soak through and drip on whatever was below.

She bent his legs so they wouldn't stick out.

In the bathroom, she ran hot water over a bunched-up pillowcase. She used the remaining shampoo to clean the walls, scrubbing until the stains thinned enough to be indistinguishable from the smudges left by smoke and God-knew-what else. She had seen enough Court TV to know that she wasn't going to remove every last scrap of DNA; the better strategy was to get away as soon as possible. The carpet she barely bothered with, except to sponge the wettest spots. And to pick up the—

There was flesh.

She gagged. Put another name on it, a different concept to mask the palpable awfulness of it, warm and singed in spots and ragged in a way that no human tissue should ever be.

What was the word?

Giblets.

Her mother used to make a dish with fried livers; that's what she was cleaning up. Not vein and tendon and fat— what fat?, where did that come from?; he *had* no fat?; but there it was, yellow and soft like a puddled candle—but some exotic dish, there was nothing to be sickened by, nothing, she was okay, she made it through the crypt, she made it through the clinic, she made it through years of Mamá's incontinence; she would make it through this but no, no, no way.

She bent over the windowsill and threw up, narrowly avoiding the hood of her car. She wanted to wipe her mouth, but there was nowhere clean, not her skin or her clothes, so she had to live with it, acid under her tongue and burning her throat. She crammed the linens into a plastic bag, which she tied off and left at the foot of the bed.

She went to her room and got a towel, fresh clothes, and

soap. Blood had dried all over her, as though she'd had a massive attack of Gorbachev. Her creasing skin caused it to flake like red dandruff.

What if it attracts attention? she thought.

Like the gunshots aren't going to attract attention.

Nobody had come to investigate, but she didn't want to bank on that holding out.

Under the hottest possible water, she scoured crust from her body. The drain clogged with small brown clumps as she raked her fingers across her scalp. She had to rinse three times before the water ran clear.

She dressed in her room, grabbed her bag, his bag (heavy with the gun), and the bloody stuff, and crept down the stairs to the parking lot. It was almost dark. Across the gravel, the light was on. The shape of the night manager bobbed; he had his back to her.

She put the bags in the trunk and got behind the wheel.

As she nosed to the mouth of the lot, she glanced at the lobby. The night manager waved.

She parked and got out.

He greeted her and removed his earplugs.

"Going to the disco, *Señora*?"

She looked at herself. She hadn't noticed what she'd put on: a loose purple rayon shirt and black leggings. She resembled a contestant on *Dance Fever*.

But—

But he hadn't heard.

"My friend is sick," she said.

"Too much tequila?"

"Is there a drugstore near here?"

"In Charrones," he said. "That way."

"I don't want him woken up. I'll pay for the extra day now." She gave him money and said, "Do not disturb— tomorrow morning, either."

"I get it, *Señora*. You don't want me to check on him?"

"No. Let him rest."

"Cause this is a full-service motel."

"That'll be fine. Give him quiet. Tell your mother, too; tell whoever's on staff. No disturbances." She gave him another ten. "Clear?"

"Sure." He replaced his earplugs and retreated to the office.

She drove slowly northwest, past the junction for Aguas Vivas. An irate driver passed her with a honk and a flash of his brights. Consulting the map, she saw that she had gone too far; she made a three-point turn on the highway and retraced fifteen miles, locating at last the turnoff to the cemetery. Past its fringes, the road kept going. She drove for thirty minutes into the desert. Moonlight limned the mesas, squatting on the horizon like half-note rests. When she had gone far enough, she veered off, hoping her shocks and tires would be kind. She found a spot behind a thicket of cacti, lowered the windows a quarter of an inch, and locked the doors. The seat reclined with a squeak. She closed her eyes and went to sleep.

SHE COULDN'T.

His face and *bang bang bang* and gushing, sticky and

reeking, not unlike a very rare steak. All night long she yearned for water; her own saliva tasted bitter.

What if she had made a mistake.

But there had been murder in him.

But she had never killed anything before.

She kept opening the door, falling half out of her seat as she retched and retched, bringing up nothing but bile.

Just before sunrise, she emerged from the deepest rest she'd had in three days: a semi-drowse that left her sweaty, hostile, and stiff. The car had steamed up. She got out and let it air, unlacing the knots in her lower back by swiveling her hips. She crossed her legs and touched her toes; crossed the other way and stretched again. It was a desert dawn: frosty but promising fire.

His face; the gun; the hole in his throat. She wiped imaginary drops from her thigh.

Look at me. Look. Look.

She had come that close to listening to him.

Look at me.

Self-defense.

Please, Gloria, please please please please.

Reggie would say *You shoulda shot him sooner.*

She locked her fingers behind her back and bent over. She felt about to snap. Carlos's arms were twice the circumference of hers. He could probably bench-press her.

Yet here she was, while he leaked into the floor.

She felt like a rag.

And, bizarrely, she felt invigorated.

She guessed that right about now, the night manager was telling his mother *Oh yeah, they said to go on in the room first thing in the morning*. How long was it before Fajardo's phone rang?

She and the *Teniente* had to have a talk.

DEW HAD SETTLED along Aguas Vivas's single thorough-fare. She parked in front of the stonecutters' shops and got out, looking for a place to wait.

A loud, metallic whine made her jump.

It came from *H. Lopez-Caravajal*—the successful one, with the typed testimonials. His lights were off.

She checked her watch. It was seven A.M.

The noise stopped and was replaced by the tap of a chisel.

She knocked. A moment later, the shade covering the front door slid aside, and a wrinkled eye socket appeared, level with hers. The shade swung back into place, and the door opened.

"*¿Sí?*" The speaker was lost in darkness.

"I apologize for bothering you. I'm waiting for *Teniente* Fajardo, and I wanted to know if I could sit inside. It's cold out here."

The stonecutter stepped into the light. He was her height plus two bristly gray inches. Compact and weath-ered, with an ancient Indian face, he seemed unlikely in work pants and a white shirt. Goggles and a mask hung round his neck, and glittering powder covered his entirety.

"You can come in," he said. He sounded like a delicately bubbling kettle.

She thanked him and followed him down a murky

corridor with an uneven floor. She equilibrated herself by touching the walls on either side of her, nonetheless tripping as her feet caught the corrugations of rough-hewn planks.

She felt his hand on her elbow, shepherding her into a dim room with a desk, an ailing vine in a wicker basket, a calendar. Two chairs and a chipped ceramic dish with wrapped caramels. One wall sported glossy photos of extravagant headstones: rich color prints crackling at their centers. Except for those, she could have been in the waiting room of a podiatrist.

"*Teniente* Fajardo never arrives before nine," he said, leading her through the shop. "I can hear his car. I am Hector."

The waiting room opened on an antechamber with a sealed case of *cerveza,* a towering file cabinet, and the door to a water closet with a freestanding metal sink.

Beyond was a third room, infinite and dank. At its far end was a garage door. It smelled like a cave; preternatural mugginess and an oozing floor gave her the impression that she was being digested. Stacks of raw stone—gossamered and drenched in alabastrine residue—rose ten feet. It was a wonder he could get to the pieces on the bottom. She guessed that they had been there since the beginning of time. Then she saw a mini-forklift with battle-scarred tusks. In some way, it resembled its proprietor.

At the center of the room was something like an operating theater. A metal table supported a hunk of yellow granite the size of two copulating cereal boxes. Beside it lay a series of chisels. Dangling from a hook at the edge of the table was a handheld grinder, its cord snaking off into the unknown. A gooseneck workman's lamp hovered above it all. Eddies of dust and wetness wound round one another, negating one another and disappearing, agglutinated, into the gaping maw of a ventilator fan.

"Don't let me interrupt you," she said.

"It can wait," he said, indicating the stone. "She isn't going anywhere."

"Do you mind if I have a look?"

He invited her to the table and traced for her the beginnings of a name. "This lady was an amateur singer," he said. "So I will put musical notes on it."

"How old was she?"

"Ohh, old. A hundred and two."

"She lived in Aguas Vivas?"

"Nobody lives here, *Señora*. She lived a hundred miles away. But this is the biggest cemetery in the state. Everyone is buried here."

"So I've heard. And just the two of you to do the stonework."

He smiled faintly.

She said, "It sounds overwhelming."

"It's not so bad," he said, gesturing around the shop. "Most people can't afford stones. Most of the time they take a wooden cross. I enjoy the chance to cut; it is like a hobby to me. The real work is the cemetery itself."

She cocked her head at him.

"I manage it," he said.

"The whole thing?"

"For forty years." His face snagged; he did a speedy fingertip count and corrected, "Forty-one."

"Do you have anyone helping you?"

"I hire men to dig and do the heavy lifting. There is the priest. But I am the office."

"No help from him?"

"Him?"

"The other stonecutter."

"Nestor? He is no help at all."

"I admire your work ethic."

"I get along," he said. "Would you like a drink?"

She followed him back into the antechamber and watched as he dug out a beer. Ingrown nails, opaque from many years of close pressure, burrowed stubbornly at the tough plastic.

"I can have water," she said.

"It's good beer," he said. "My nephew works at the factory."

She smiled apologetically. "It's early. . . ."

He shrugged. "All right." He ducked into the bathroom, reemerged with a mug of tap water. He then went back to clawing at the beer. As he did, she glanced over the file cabinet. Its five drawers were marked with the first three letters of surnames: Aba-Del, Dem-Jua, and so on.

"What's this?" she asked.

"Unnh . . ." He'd made some headway: a hole big enough to get three fingers in. He took out a bottle, held it up, and then unceremoniously stuck it back in, where it resumed its place neatly among its peers.

"I have saved myself work for later," he said contentedly. He looked at her hand atop the cabinet. "That? That is the cemetery."

"It's smaller from up close," she said.

Hector's grin ambled across his face, left to right. "Everything I need to know is in there. People say I should have a computer."

"Who says that?"

"Commercials. No worry, *Señora,* I don't listen. I think their opinion is biased."

She ran a finger across the cabinet's top; it came away dusty. "You have in here—names?"

"Everyone recent." He eased open one of the drawers, heavy with files stuffed with index cards. Rubber bands bound the cards in bricks of fifty or sixty, each of which had a dated tag taped to it. He took out ABRILO 1999, put the rubber band around his wrist, and displayed the top card. Stapled to its back was a photo of a headstone.

"I keep a record," he said.

"All of them?"

"*Sí.* How else is a man supposed to improve, unless he thinks about his work?" He tapped his head. "I can't remember everything. That is why God invented cameras. And I keep records for the families of the dead. So that they do not have to remember all the time."

He began flipping through cards as though showing off his grandkids.

"This stone was huge," he said, handing her a card and the attached photo. On the card was written a man's name, some code (she guessed it was the location of the plot), his date of burial, and cause of death. The stone was gray and square, a hulking monument to a man she assumed was proportionally shrimpy.

Hector said, "I stopped cutting such big stones fifteen years ago, because they hurt my back. But I liked his daughter. She was very broken up."

"You keep records of how they died," she said.

"A side interest," he said. He smiled sheepishly, took the card from her, replaced it, flipped to another. "Aha. This was the first time I made a circular stone. The first time in all these years."

Another card. "*This* fellow had a great affection for his dog. His wife asked me to carve a picture of it on his stone. It took three months. You can see the detail involved. I worked at night to finish it. Then after I had it set, she called me up and asked me to redo it. She said I did the wrong dog. I said, 'You gave me a picture, how could I have done the wrong dog?'

"As it turns out, they had two dogs. He loved one, and she loved the other one. She had given me the wrong picture by mistake. She paid me to do it again.

"Then I showed her the new stone, she said, 'I don't want it anymore.' Why not? Because it made her jealous. She decided he had loved the dog more than her, and she did not want to let it win."

He shook his head. "At least she paid."

"Sometimes they don't?"

He smiled as though she'd asked an absurd question.

She said, "What I mean is, I'm surprised you remember who paid and who didn't."

"Sometimes I remember that. Sometimes I do not. It's not the most important thing about a person."

"What is?"

"I remember most if they had an extremely sad story, or an extremely happy one."

She told him she wasn't sure what constituted a happy story when it came to dying.

"People go as they lived," Hector replied. "If a person was full of life, a clown, someone who made you cheerful, then their death can do the same.

"An example: my father. He was a funny man. He knew more stories than you could imagine. Enough to fill a library. When I was a boy I used to wonder: he wasn't big enough to hold all of those words. Where did he keep them? Once I asked him.

"'In my closet,' he said, 'is a box with every single story in the whole world.'

"I wanted to see this box, but he said I could only have it when he died, because it was a secret passed from his father to him. He said not even my mother knew about it.

"Shortly after that he did die, of cholera. I went into my parents' room after the funeral. My mother was weeping on the bed. I asked if I could look at the secret box in the closet where he had the stories. She said, 'There is nothing in there except shoes.'

"I didn't expect her to know about it. I waited until she went to the kitchen, then crept back into her room.

"I expected to see more than a pile of old shoes.

"But that was all.

"As you can imagine, I was disappointed. I decided that he must have made everything up. The box of stories was itself a story. And therefore, if I wanted to retain anything he had told me, I would have to re-create it myself.

"That night I started to write down everything he had told me, from the time I could remember remembering. It wasn't much. I was young, and it was difficult for me to think about him and copy down the stories at the same time. I wrote six pages before I quit for the night. By that time the sun was coming up, and I was exhausted.

"I did this for several days, until I ran out of memories to trap. It felt miserable, as though I had lost him a second time. I then decided that it had been a mistake to try, because it was worse to do a bad job than to do nothing. If I had been honest with myself, I would have known that it was impossible. By the end of that week I had thirty-five pages. To see my father reduced to a bunch of paper, this thin . . .

"It made me understand ignorance.

"A few days later a package arrived. My mother said it came from some cousin of my father's she had never met. 'They've sent you candy,' she said, 'you're not allowed to eat too much.'

"Inside were layers of food: a jar of candied oranges, some chocolate, pistachios, things I had never tasted . . . stacks and stacks. I ate all the way to the bottom.

"There I came to a piece of wood with my name written on it.

"Beneath it I found a wooden box, cracked like the surface of the moon. It had a hinged top, with a clasp and a lock. At first I couldn't see how to open it. I held it up. There was an envelope taped to the bottom, with a note from my father. It said:

"'Write it all down.'

"Out of the envelope fell a key, which opened the lock. Inside I found all his stories, written in his hand, wrapped in paper. And beneath that was another packet of paper, with stories *his* father had told. There were seven of these packages, going back before the beginning of Mexico. And there was one piece of empty wax paper, folded up to accommodate my stories.

"I did not tell my mother this."

Hector sat back. "It was the happiest day of my life. But he couldn't have done it while alive, because it would have ruined the surprise."

She hesitated to ask, "Do you have a son?"

"Not yet," he said.

His optimism warmed her. She said, "I'm sure he'll be happy to get the box from you."

"It's a responsibility as much as a privilege."

"Yes."

"When I became manager of the cemetery, I discovered that my tendency to record is very strong. Stronger than in my father. Stronger than can be held in a single box. It needs more space. So in addition, I have the cards," he said, tapping the cabinet. "Another expression of the same urge."

"It must comfort the relatives to know that their loved ones are being remembered all the time."

"I suppose," he said. "But most people never think about it. They like to forget. If they remembered every good thing, they would never feel surprise, which is the cause of happiness. And if they remembered every bad thing, life would be unbearable."

He shrugged and said, "The cards serve a practical

purpose, to record the location of the plot. It isn't possible without a map. Except for me."

"How big is the cemetery?"

"Six hundred eighty-two acres," he said modestly.

Its immensity flabbergasted her. "And how many spots are still open?"

"Most of them. We will have space forever." He put the cards back in the file. "They die in regular numbers. Sometimes more, if we've had a bad winter. There was an influenza epidemic three years ago and they came by busloads. But otherwise, they die the same, steadily. It will never be full."

"You have funerals today."

"Burials are in the afternoon." He grinned. "The priest is a late riser. I work in my shop in the mornings. After ten I am on the site the rest of the day."

That explained why she'd never seen him before.

"When you knocked," said Hector, "I thought you were someone from a funeral party, and you got lost. The priest meets them at the front gate, but sometimes they miss it. Then I saw you were here too early, so I was curious to talk to you."

"There is someone buried there I'm interested in. She died a long time ago."

"How long?"

"About forty years," she said.

"Your first visit has taken a while."

"I never knew her," Gloria said. "I'm curious."

Hector appeared to appreciate that. "What's her name?"

"Perreira."

"That's a common name, *Señora*. Who Perreira?"

Gloria turned her palms up helplessly.

"Let's see," said the stonecutter. "You don't know her, you don't know her name, and you think she died forty years ago?"

"Well . . . yes."

"You're sure she is buried in Aguas Vivas, though."

"N—well. I—I think she is."

He raised squirrelly eyebrows. *"Señora?"*

"I'm not sure," she said.

"Aha," he said. "That sounds not likely."

She agreed.

"Therefore," he said, "it is extremely interesting. We'll have a look."

He led her to an unlit corner of the shop, occluded by a plastic tarp. It closed behind them, and for a moment they were alone in the dark. She heard key gawkily penetrate lock, and they passed into another antechamber, the mirror image of the one in Hector's shop—sans beer.

"What is this?"

"The place of business of Nestor Caravajal," he said.

"What?"

"My neighbor."

Confused, Gloria said, "Is he here?"

"No."

The front room of the second shop was identical to Hector's front room, but instead of a desk and office accoutrements, it was a labyrinth of file cabinets—themselves identical to the cabinet in Hector's antechamber.

He said, "This is the rest of the past."

"Are you partners?"

"No, *Señora*. Half-brothers."

Nestor Caravajal. And Hector's name? She stretched back, and caught it. He was Hector *Lopez-Caravajal*.

"I don't understand," she said. "If you're brothers—"

"Half."

"Half-brothers, if you're *half*-brothers, then—you share a workshop?"

"It was more economical," Hector said.

"That seems like an awkward arrangement," she said.

"Mm." He nodded. "It was while Nestor was still alive."

"He's dead?"

"*Sí.*"

"Then why is his shop open?"

"I keep it open," he said. "In his memory."

Gloria stared at him. "But I saw your window displays. You're in competition."

"*Sí.*"

"How can you be in competition if he's not alive?"

Hector said, "In my own shop I work for myself. But Nestor's shop, I work for him." He touched his chin. "It's incredible," he said. "The quality of our work is virtually the same."

Against her better judgment, she asked, "Does he get a lot of customers?"

"Unfortunately no. It hasn't been a good ten years for him."

"If you ask me," she said, "it would be more efficient to combine the businesses."

"In a certain way," he said. "But you cannot have a free

market without competition. That is a monopoly, and that I could not allow." On that note, he opened the nearest cabinet, JUE-QUI 1960–1965; the smoke of incinerated time billowed out.

"Besides," he continued, leafing through files, "competition is necessary to keep prices stable." He took out bundles of index cards. Some of them had been tied with twine rather than rubber bands; there were far fewer photographs.

"In the very old days," Hector explained, "I saved the camera for significant, or highly artistic, work. See—"

He offered the card of a man who had died of a gangrenous infection. Attached to it was a black-and-white snapshot of a headstone with baroque engraving.

"Very nice," she said.

"Thank you. That was a supreme effort. I cannot do that kind of detail anymore. My hands are failing. Soon, my eyes will fail. Soon after that, my hearing will fail. Soon after that, I will lose my sense of taste and my sense of smell. Soon after that, I will die." He said all of this as though he savored its predictability.

"When you die, who's going to manage the cemetery? Cut the stones?"

"My son," he said.

She nodded.

"You are think I'm too old to have a son," he said. "It's all right; sometimes I think that myself."

"Then what's your answer?"

"If, when I die, I have no son?"

"Yes."

"Simple," he said. "Time will stop."

He cracked his knuckles. "I will look through this stack. You look through that one. Tie it back up when you're finished."

She took the cards and started to flip through them, lives reduced to three lines in spidery purple ink. It was like watching a highlight reel of the region's populace as it stampeded off the edge of existence. At first she tried to pay close attention to the details. It seemed to her the respectful way to proceed, giving each name a moment's pause. They were people, not typographical obstacles.

Her reverence held out for the first five minutes; then it all began to blend. Names were promptly chucked into the mental wastebin if they failed to match the PERRIERA template. After the better part of an hour, she was ready to resign.

Then Hector said,

"Here is a Perreira."

He gave her the card.

Perreira—Carlos	*A, 116, 8*
Fecha de Muerte	*13-7-1963*
Causa de Muerte	*tuberculósis*

"Not a woman," he said. "But it is from the right time."

There was no photo attached. The blankness burned like an open sore.

"Do you remember this person?" she asked Hector.

Beneath his eyelids, his pupils moved. "Oh. Of course."

"Who was he," she said.

"A baby boy."

"Was he from here?"

"Yes."

"What about his parents? Who were they?"

"His mother—" Hector began. He looked at her strangely. "You know *Teniente* Fajardo?"

Gloria said, "What's that got to do with him?"

"Ay ay ay," said Hector. "You want to know about his parents."

"Yes."

"Let me find you the card," he said, "then you'll understand."

He went through the same pile in which he'd found Carlos Perreira and a dozen or so entries later came up with another one.

Fajardo—Gloria	*A, 138, 25*
Fecha de Muerte	*17-7-1963*
Causa de Muerte	*suicidio*

Numb, she said, "I don't know what's going on."

"This"—the card in her hand—"was the *Teniente's* sister. This"—he held up Carlos's card—"was her son. He died, and then she—" He stopped. "As it says."

"Who was the father?" she asked.

"It's a sad story."

"Please," she said.

"This was a long time ago. Right when I started to be the manager of the cemetery. Before that, the cemetery was not a cemetery. It was a lake. You would not know it if you saw it now. But once it was full of water.

"It began when a speculator bought up land a few miles away. He wanted to build his own town.

"The speculator—his name was Gaspar—he was originally from Aguas Vivas. His family was wealthy and moved to the United States when he was a child. He attended university. I don't know what he read, *Señora,* but it was an education you could only get in America.

"He returned to town and announced that he had seen the future of Mexico, and it did not include villages like ours. Everyone had to move to cities or else they would be left in the past, while the rest of the country modernized.

"Nobody understood what he was talking about. Mostly people ignored him. But then he started paying people to move. He offered what was at the time a large sum of money. Almost everyone accepted.

"They all moved to his new town, Charrones. Gaspar promised them a large park and a stadium. People imagined it as the biggest town in northern Mexico. They all bought houses, hoping to cash in. Gaspar had already bought all the land; he sold them their new houses. More expensive houses than the ones they had sold to him. In this way he forced them to trade up, without forcing them. A clever plan. It was a combination of his sleight of hand and their greediness.

"He then imported a group of American laborers. It seemed needless to haul them to Aguas Vivas when there were plenty of locals in need of a job, who would work cheaper.

"He had two reasons.

"The first was this: he thought Americans worked harder.

"And this: Americans were willing to do things that no local would do.

"He wanted to prevent people from moving back to Aguas Vivas, or reestablishing a town outside Charrones. And the best way to do that, he had decided, was to make Aguas Vivas unlivable.

"The Americans didn't care. They did what they had been paid to do. I'm sure they did not give it one second of thought. Why should they have? The land meant nothing to them, as it did to us. They could not have understood the importance of the village. So when Gaspar told them to demolish all the houses and drain the lake, they listened."

Hector sniffled. "Gaspar—he's different. He, I can say, was not a good man. Because he should have understood what he was destroying. He had been born there. But he ignored that impulse.

"The other reason why I can't blame the Americans who worked for Gaspar: they were young, they could not know any better. For example, the father of this baby."

"He was one of the workers," she said.

"Yes."

"Do you remember his name?"

"No, *Señora*. He was just another American. It's hard for me to see it clearly, but I can't imagine he was older than seventeen."

"His name was Joseph," she said.

Hector nodded. "I believe you. He was a handsome boy. He met a girl."

"Gloria Fajardo."

"*Sí.* She and her family continued to live in Aguas Vivas after most of the people had moved. Gaspar tried to buy their home but her father refused to sell. He was the police constable. From one of the oldest families in the village. He had an emotional connection to the lake, to the buildings, to the house. They stayed after Gaspar made it impossible for them to get anything without traveling for hours. The girl hated it, and was angry, and so she became pregnant from one of Gaspar's workers.

"Eventually the work was done, and all the Americans went home. Except for the boy. He decided to stay and help raise the baby. He lived in the house with her family. Her parents despised him, and made life miserable for him. He tried to win their acceptance. He dropped his name and took a Spanish name."

"Perreira," she said.

"It seems so," he said. "That's the name his son had, so I suppose that's what it was. Gloria's father, the former police constable—when everyone left, you see, there was no need for a policeman—would come into my office, bored out of his skull, and complain to me about it. I told him it was none of my business. I didn't want to become involved in their family troubles.

"It was hard for me to believe the boy would stay more than a week, he was so hated by her parents. But he stayed for almost a year."

She said, "He left when the baby died."

Hector glanced at the card. "Tuberculosis. I had forgot; this is why it helps to write things down."

"When he left, he went back to the United States?" she said.

"I assume so. I assume also that he tried to convince the girl to go with him. But her father would not let her go. A few days later she hanged herself in their house."

He shook his head. "She was a nice girl."

She said, "My name is Gloria, you know."

Hector smiled. "That is an interesting coincidence."

"If the *Teniente* is that girl's brother, he's much younger than she would be."

"Tito was a child when she died. I would be surprised, *Señora,* if he remembered any of it."

"What happened to the family after that?"

"They left Aguas Vivas and moved to Mexico City."

"And then the *Teniente* came back."

"I hadn't heard from him for over thirty-five years until he showed up with his family and said he was the new police chief. It was good to see someone moving back. I had been alone for years."

"Why are you still here?"

"Gaspar hired me to take care of the new cemetery. This is how I come to be here." He paused and said, "Actually, there was one person I forgot. Luís. He's been here since before I was born, and he also refused to sell. So he was here, as well, and Nestor and me." He leaned in and spoke conspiratorially: "But having Luís around was as good as having no one. We don't speak. An old family feud."

Outside, a car rolled past. They both turned toward the sound. Moments later, a door slammed.

Hector said, "You look sad, *Señora.*"

"I am," she said.

"It's a sad story." He scanned the file cabinets as though soliciting confirmation. "Maybe if you think about it long enough," he said, "it will cease to make you sad."

"It's possible," she said.

"Or maybe it will make you sadder."

"That's possible, too. But I'm still glad you told me."

"Your interest is flattering. These people rarely get a chance to speak."

She started to hand him the record of Gloria Fajardo's death, then said, "May I borrow this for a few hours? It will help my conversation with the *Teniente*."

Hector nodded.

"I'll bring it back," she said.

"I know you will," he said. "That is why I decided to let you take it."

THIRTY

Gun drawn, she made her way through the movie theater. She found Fajardo at his desk, breathing steam from a mug. He rolled his eyes up at her.

"The lady who runs the motel is going hysterical," he said.

"If it was up to me, I wouldn't have left him there," Gloria said. "He was too heavy to move."

He nodded. "I saw your car."

"You want to give up your gun?"

"Come on, *Señora*. We can talk."

She stopped in the aisle, aiming at him. "Go on."

He put his hands up and stood behind the desk. "You can take it off my belt."

"I don't want to touch you," she said. "Move over there."

He came around and stood down the aisle from her.

"Turn around," she said.

"What are you going to do?" he asked. He sounded honestly afraid.

"Just turn around."

He obeyed.

"Put the gun on the ground. Good. Now step over it, go over there—where I can see you—and lie down."

"*Señora,* the floor hasn't been washed in twenty years."

"Go."

Muttering, he did as she said. She took his gun and put it in her pocket, where it sagged like a hernia. Next she opened all his desk drawers. A couple pints of anonymous liquor, a stack of porno magazines, a book on home carpentry with an unbroken spine. A few bullets; those she tossed into the seats.

"This is my office," he complained.

"I'll buy you a broom. It needs a cleaning anyway." She stood over him and frisked him. "Don't get too excited."

He frowned but said nothing.

"All right," she said. "Get up and go back to the chair."

He did, keeping his hands over his head. "Can I at least have my coffee?"

"Sure, *Teniente.* We're friends here."

"Would you like some?"

"No thanks."

"I can't function without it," he said. He leaned over his mug and let himself be poached. He was paler than usual; he had been sapped of his former bluster. "You're being very professional about this," he said.

"It's either that or we have a shoot-out."

"We can't have a shoot-out, *Señora.* I don't have a gun."

"That's the idea." She put his sister's index card on the desk and turned it to face him. He stared at it, then cradled it like a poker player.

"Hector told me," she said.

"Good." He bent over the steam again. "I didn't want to have to explain it."

"What about Carl?"

"Which one?"

"The one I know."

He blew and took a sip, grimacing at its heat. "I think my sister called him José."

"I call him Carl."

"He's dead," said the *Teniente*. "You probably already knew that."

"Did you kill him?"

Fajardo looked weakly offended.

"Who did?" she asked.

"Carlos."

"Why?"

He didn't answer. He kept blowing at his coffee and taking painful test-sips.

"What's Carlos's real name?" she asked.

"That *is* his real name," he said. "His last name is Margain."

"Who is he?"

"My cousin."

"What did he want from Carl?"

Sampling his coffee, he could finally get it down. "Money."

"And I'm sure you didn't want any of it," she said.

"I didn't care. I didn't want anything to do with him."

"He's dead," she said. "I'd like you to account for that."

Pause.

Fajardo said, "We're being honest with each other, aren't we?"

"I hope so."

He nodded. "It was a mistake for me to move back here," he said. "The problem is, I was too young when my family left. I didn't appreciate what a shithole it is. For years all my father talked about was how picturesque the town was, how full of life the people were. It was a fairy tale.

"But I was a kid. Kids can't see through that stuff. Some people grow up and don't learn to see through it. There's plenty of people out there in the world who believe in the Tooth Mouse.

"My father, though. He had no excuse. He should've known that after everyone moved and the water was gone, the place would be ruined. Even *if* the village was nice to begin with, it certainly wasn't anything like that by the time we left for Mexico City.

"And the truth is, it was *never* that nice. Before my mother died, she told me, 'Your father likes to shine the past.'

"I was fourteen when she said that. I didn't really understand what she meant until I came here and saw my father's bullshit firsthand." He assumed a paternal mien. "'Oh, you go back, Tito, a beautiful place, with blah blah milk and honey. The family land. Generations since there wasn't one of us pissing on that plot. Everybody knows us. Ladies in the streets bow as you pass, they all know your name and respect you.'"

Fajardo smiled grotesquely. "Now I see it for myself, every day, in full color." He lifted an arm toward the theater's rotting walls. "Isn't it fantastic, *Señora*? Don't you see the lights? Don't you hear the villagers, busy going to the market? The town council hosts parades every day; did you notice them? Even when it rains, they have parades—because it *never rains*."

"If you knew it was this bad, why come back?"

"Elisa wanted to get out of the city. She thought the pollution hurt Pilar. It did. Have you ever been to Mexico City?"

She had not.

He said, "At the end of the day I'd blow my nose, and the snot would be *black*, like I had an oil well in my head. My daughter has cystic fibrosis, *Señora*.

"I have a friend works for a congressman. For a small fee, he got me this job."

"Why not someplace nicer?"

"Nicer? Where?" he said. "Aguas Vivas was the place to go. My father . . ." He sought a word.

"My father," he concluded.

"Once you saw it, you could have left."

"You don't understand. When I first got here, I thought it *was* beautiful. I took a look around and I could *see* all the things he had described. Crazy but true. I plastered his lies over everything. Like hanging a painting over a hole in the wall."

He finished the coffee, set the mug down, pushed it away.

"Listen," he said. "After this conversation, I would prefer if we—you and me—could stop thinking about any of this."

"It's really up to you," she said. "It depends on what you tell me."

Pause.

"Okay," he said, and began to speak.

A little over a year before, Carlos Margain had come to stay with the *Teniente* and his wife, as he did when he was broke and out of work. A frequent occurrence; he was an actor.

"Or—he *wanted* to be an actor," said Fajardo. "For a while he studied at the theater school at INBA. He went to study in the United States, a year at a university program. I think it was expensive. Is Massachuse expensive?" He didn't wait for her to answer: "I'm sure it was, or else he wouldn't have gone. He only likes overpriced things. His parents are rich."

"What about your side of the family?" she asked. "Where's your expensive education?"

"Money doesn't spill when you guard the bucket. My aunt and uncle are the most vigilant people you'll ever meet.

"Carlos and I grew up close, though. We spent a lot of time together as kids. He's never been serious about acting. He doesn't like to work. Being an actor allows him to do nothing and call it preparation."

This time when Carlos had come to stay, he had been in trouble. His parents had finally decided to cut him loose, and had stopped sending checks.

"He deserved it," Fajardo said. "I mean, he's thirty-three."

"That's how old he is?"

"'That's not what he told you?'"

"Forty-one. I thought he looked too young."

"He looks too *old* to be thirty-three. He drinks a lot. He's had his nose broken twice in fights. The bastard looked even more handsome afterward, but that's not his doing."

This time around, Fajardo had agreed to take Carlos in for two weeks.

After he spent two and a half months in front of the television, Fajardo began contacting other relatives in the hope of finding someone else to take him in. More than a bad houseguest, Carlos was becoming a danger.

"No matter how many times we told him not to," the *Teniente* said, "he would smoke in the house. Once I asked him to give Pilar her medication. He forgot, and then gave her three to compensate. She almost died.

"But"—a harlequin's laugh, one that degraded the laugher—"but it's impossible to say no to him. He does things that would drive any normal person crazy. Outrageous things. And then he says something charming, or pathetic—whatever the situation calls for—and you forget why you were mad.

"When we were kids he threw a friend's cat out the window. The boy's mother called Carlos to scream at him, and he convinced her that he'd been trying to prevent it from committing suicide. She ended up sending him a thank-you note.

"He exploited me and my wife. He kept us off balance by telling us different stories. We would end up arguing with each other over who had given Carlos the wrong instructions. Meanwhile he would go off and watch TV. I saw it happening, *Señora,* but there was nothing I could do about it. He's persuasive."

"I know," she said.

By the fourth month, Fajardo decided to drop the ax. He told Carlos straight-out that he would have to leave.

"He became a bull. Indignant as hell. He said he was a guest, whether I liked it or not. Not only that, but he wasn't going to lift a finger around the house anymore, because every time he tried somebody got angry at him."

"Why didn't you throw him out?" Gloria asked. "You're a cop."

"That's what Elisa said."

"Well, why not?"

"He's my cousin, *Señora.*"

"So what?"

Fajardo's mouth pinched. "It seemed like a better idea to set him up with a job. That way he wouldn't have to sponge off us, and we would be free of him. I wanted a permanent solution, *Señora.* Throwing him out would only work until he came back."

"Nobody made it your responsibility in the first place," she said.

"I told you, *Señora,* we're close. I am the family he comes to when he needs help. And . . ." He hesitated. "He made it my responsibility. He decided to come to me, and then it was out of my hands. It's not good to argue with him, *Señora.*"

Gripping the mug tightly, Fajardo added,

"He holds ugly grudges."

For the first time, she felt good about having pulled the trigger.

The next month passed without change. Carlos took up in front of the TV.

"Like a squatter in my living room," said Fajardo. "He got up to get food, or to go for a jog. He liked physical fitness and spent a couple hours every day running and doing push-ups. To maintain his body, for when he got a movie role.

"Elisa once tried locking him out. He pounded on the door for two hours. Of course she relented and let him in. He walked to the couch as though nothing had ever happened. 'I guess you didn't hear me,' was what he said.

"There was no end in sight. I was afraid she was going to murder him in his sleep."

"She should've," Gloria said.

"But I was trying. I was working on a job for him. You probably can't understand how hard that is, *Señora*. Around here we have terrible unemployment. And I found him a couple of offers, *good offers*. He turned them down. He said he wouldn't take a job unless it made him happy." Fajardo's mouth twisted sourly. "We don't think like that here, *Señora*. But try convincing him of that. He said it was unjust. He called it small: he called it the Mexican way of thinking. That all we're good for is cleaning some asshole's house in the United States.

"One semester at some university and he won't work anymore.

"But *injustice* was bullshit, because he never worked before, either. He called it a protest instead of what it really was: laziness.

"I suggested he join the police academy. He laughed and told me that was for people with no imagination." The *Teniente* looked morose. "How could I argue with that?

"A friend who runs a construction business in Aguascalientes was looking for an assistant foreman. I did some readjusting of Carlos's work history, and spent hours on the phone, pleading that he was a hard worker, a smart guy. To get me off his back, my friend agreed to meet him. The day that Carlos was supposed to go, he claimed he was too ill to travel. He stayed in bed all day."

She asked, "What's your friend's name? The one who runs the business."

Fajardo looked at her funny. "Why?"

"For the record."

"Eduardo Polaczek," he said.

Polaczek liked me because I got my projects done on time. I stayed on site until after everyone left. If workers didn't show up, and we needed them, I went to their houses and woke them up, or tracked them down in the bars.

"Don't let the name fool you," said Fajardo. "He's a genuine *hidrocálido*."

"Did they ever meet?"

"Are you kidding? Eddie wouldn't answer my calls after that."

Polaczek had a safe in his office, and in it he kept the list of people he's bribing. I surprised him because I wasn't out to swindle him. I must have seemed pretty naïve.

"He said his name the night we were at your house," she said. "It set you off."

"Did it? I don't remember anything from that night. If

you say so. He probably thought I wouldn't notice because I was so drunk."

"He told me that that was the name of his boss. Polaczek."

"He went about as far as the bathroom to get that job," said Fajardo.

"I bet his illness lasted twenty-four hours, followed by a miraculous recovery."

"Elisa was furious. He had seemed willing to take the job."

"What a shame," she said, meaning it.

But, she thought, *you're* the one who slept with him.

That was hardly the same sort of gullibility; she hadn't known him for years; it took her only three days to figure out that something was wrong with him.

But you *slept* with him.

"Did he ever have a girlfriend?" she asked.

Fajardo looked at her. He kept looking at her for a while, and for a second she thought he knew. She wanted to say something, to switch tacks; she said, "Or a wife?"

"No, *Señora*. Nothing like that. He fucked a lot, but women were never his strong point. Once he had fucked them."

Despite her raging curiosity, she told herself that this was a bad topic. What happened next, she asked, doing her best to seem nonchalant.

He said, "One night, middle of July, I received a phone call. A man had broken down out near the cemetery. The highway there is rough, as you know. I was tired and I didn't want to go, but there was nobody else to do it. The attendant at the station is a kid. I drove over in a bad mood, expecting to have to change a tire for some idiot.

"From a distance I could tell it was going to be worse than that. The car had gone off the road, into a rut. When I got closer, I saw how bad it was: one of the wheels had buckled, like the axle had given out.

"The man was on his cellphone. He hung up when he saw me and introduced himself as Perreira. He said, 'Thank God you're here, I'm almost out of batteries.' He was American but he spoke Spanish well. I also noticed that he didn't look drunk. I wondered what could've distracted him so that he'd run off the road that carelessly.

"Then I noticed his face.

"There aren't words for it," said Fajardo. "It was like opening an oven, all the heat coming at you at once.

"He didn't recognize me. The last time I had seen him, I had been a baby. But I knew his face from photos of my sister. I could hardly breathe. I shook his hand and answered when he started asking about his car, what could he do, he needed to get back to California, what a mess, sorry it was so late.

"The car was going to need to be towed to Joaqual. The repair would take a while, if it was worth doing at all. There was a tow truck at the gas station, but it was better to come back in the morning. It was already after sunset, and by the time we got the truck out, with the bad roads, we would be working through the night. I offered my house to sleep, and he agreed."

"You didn't tell him who you were."

The *Teniente* thought for a while. Then he said,

"I wanted it to stay buried.

"When we got home, Pilar was on the sofa. The man looked so concerned I thought he would cry. He asked if he could help out. I told him I couldn't accept money from a person encountered in the course of duty."

She gave him a wry smile.

"I'm not saying I don't like a gift every now and again," he said, "but there are rules. We don't live in chaos, *Señora*. And anyway I didn't want his money."

"You resented him."

"What does that mean? I was too young to remember my sister. I suppose I resent the effect he had on my family. After she died my parents stopped speaking to each other. You could blame some of that on him. But you'd have to stretch to call it His Fault. He didn't *help,* but I can see plenty of other people who deserve as much blame as him, or more."

"That night, Carlos talked to him?"

"They talked about where he was from—Los Angeles. Carlos wanted to know if the man was involved in movies."

Gloria said, "He said, 'I've done some work for the film industry,' right?"

"It isn't true?"

"It was a joke he had."

"Aha," said Fajardo. "Carlos took it pretty seriously. He tried to get him to list his credits. The more he played it down, the more Carlos wanted to know.

"That night my wife and I were talking in the kitchen. I told her I thought our guest was the American who'd gotten my sister *embarazada*; I would bet the house on it.

She wanted me to confront him and ask for money. She didn't know he had already offered. I said no. She got exasperated and went to bed." He laughed shortly. "That's Elisa. We gave up a long time ago talking about things we don't agree on.

"The next morning I got up early to deal with the stranded car. Carlos was up before me. That never happened. Never. I wondered if he was genuinely sick.

"But he was up, and alert, and waiting for me. He was cheerful. He sat in the kitchen while I woke up the guest and gave him something to eat."

Fajardo frowned. "I tried to give him something to eat, anyway. He kept turning me down. He wouldn't take any coffee, either. I offered to let him call home, but he didn't want to do it on my bill, and his phone was dead. Carlos jumped in and let him use his cellphone. He tried his office a few times, but never left any messages. I think he was embarrassed to explain the situation to a machine. He told me his secretary was on vacation, and that nobody would miss him if he got back soon enough.

"The first thing we needed to do was get the tow truck. As soon as I said that, something truly bizarre happened: Carlos volunteered to go. He said he knew how to do the towing.

"'You have more important things to do, Tito,' he said.

"I should have known then that something was wrong. I told myself that he was putting on a good face in front of the American movie producer. And if that meant he wanted to help, then it was my lucky day.

"I took the truck and dropped them at the gas station.

The plan was for them to tow the car to Joaqual, and then for us all to meet up.

"After they left, my wife found money in Pilar's bedroom. He left fifteen hundred dollars in cash, along with a note. I think it said *use where you need.*"

"I went to work, expecting to get a call about two o'clock.

"At four-thirty Carlos called and told me to come out to the cemetery." Fajardo tried to sip, found his mug empty. "You're sure you don't want?"

She shook it off.

In silence, he poured a cup; in silence, he returned to his seat. He blew, sipped, cleared his throat, and went on.

"I found him sitting on the hood of the tow truck. The first thing he said was, 'We need to put him somewhere.'

"He had overheard me talking to Elisa. If this was the American who had been cursed at every family gathering he'd ever been to, he had a tool for blackmail.

"They were driving from the gas station to the car, and Carlos started threatening him. He never had any foresight. He could never understand why 'I know who you are' and that type of bullshit didn't work. The man denied everything, of course, so Carlos got more aggressive.

"I wasn't there for the conversation, so I don't know exactly what was said. My guess is that he started bringing up real events from the past, and that it upset the man enough to start an argument. . . ." He waved his hands. "You can figure out what happened."

"How did he do it?" she asked.

"He wasn't prepared to hurt him. It was spontaneous.

It—" Fajardo stopped, his brow furrowed like wallpaper gone wrong.

"What," she said.

"It was messier than that."

"I shot a man through the neck last night," she said. "I think I can handle it."

"All right. Then listen."

The man got out of the tow truck and Carlos ran him down.

But he didn't die. He tried to crawl away.

Seeing this, Carlos beat him to death with a chain from the back of the truck.

Speaking through her fingers: "What did he look like?"

"It was very bad," Fajardo said.

His skinny arms, his back, his bowlegs, his head, his face, his face, oh his face, his poor poor face, illegible. It made her want to cry. Not cry; she had gotten past crying; she had cried enough for three lifetimes; what she felt was rage: spitting, spraying rage; one that seeks the closest target. She took Fajardo's mug and hurled it against the wall.

Silence.

Having jumped out of his chair, he stood watching her like a lion tamer.

She said, "I'll get you a new one."

He nodded.

"Sit," she said.

Pause.

He sat down.

She said, "I didn't know you could kill someone with a chain."

"After the first five seconds," Fajardo said, "he was probably unconscious."

She took a breath. "What happened next."

He was still eyeing her warily.

"Don't be melodramatic, *Teniente*. I'm not a vigilante."

"You wouldn't have any reason to be," he said. "*I* didn't kill him."

"You helped."

"That's not the way it was," he protested. "Carlos threatened me. He threatened my family. My daughter. Then he began pleading: I had to help him; we were cousins, weren't we? Then he switched back to intimidation: if I didn't help him, he would implicate me; it was my fault for having led him to believe that this guy had money. I was frightened. I can admit that, *Señora*. He scared the shit out of me, he could change moods so fast." Fajardo snapped his fingers. "Like *that*."

She nodded. "So, you helped him."

"Call it whatever you want. He did it, and left it for me to wipe up."

"You could have said no," she said.

"Are you crazy? He might have done something to us. And let me ask you another thing: what good would it do to put him in jail and have him hate me? The man he killed was an American. The crime took place on my territory. I had the right to decide whether to pursue the investigation. And you know, *Señora,* your friend was no saint. My parents—my sister—he was hardly innocent of . . . of, of . . ."

He trailed off. "Fucking hell," he muttered.

"You helped him," she said.

"I helped him. Fine."

"Then what."

"Carlos searched the car. He couldn't find anything except old maps and a catalogue with the man's picture on it. That's how we knew he was the right person: the name said everything. Then we buried the body."

She hated that word. "Where."

"Off the highway. Near the cemetery."

"Well *that's* good," she said. "At least he's *near* a cemetery."

Fajardo toyed with his badge.

She said, "What did Carlos do after you buried him?"

"He decided that he might as well get as much money out of it as possible. He went to Los Angeles and removed most of the money from the man's bank account."

"How could he do that?"

"Please, *Señora*. Your border control is a joke. Friends of mine go across all the time looking for work. Once you've done it a few times you get the hang of it. And if you get sent back, you try the next day. As it happened, Carlos made it across that night. He took the bank card and went."

"There's a PIN on the account," Gloria said. "He must have gotten that from somewhere."

"It wasn't hard to guess."

"What was it, his birthday?"

"No," said Fajardo. "His son's."

This, more than anything else, made her want to cry. Instead, she said, "What did you do with the money he gave you?"

"I used it to pay the doctor."

"She told me you gave her a thousand. And he left you fifteen hundred."

Fajardo looked at her. "My daughter, *Señora*."

She decided not to argue the point.

"While Carlos was in California," he said, "you came along."

"That's when you faked the death certificate."

"I had to improvise when you showed up. I wasn't expecting anyone to come so soon. I told him I would cover whatever story he invented, and no more."

"Oh *I* see. *That's* why you tried to climb into bed with me."

"That's another, another—a different thing. Let me say—"

"I don't want to hear it."

"My wife," he said. "My wife—"

"That's the point, *Teniente*. Your wife."

"She's depressed. She hasn't come near me for years. Not since Pilar. She's tired all the time. It's unnatural, *Señora*. We're hardly married anymore." He stopped, shrugged. "Take it how you want. We're being honest with each other here, I'm apologizing."

"I don't care," she said.

"I'm not saying you should care," he said. "I'm *apologizing*."

"I know."

"Then why don't you—"

"Because I don't forgive you," she said.

Looking threadbare, he withdrew into his chair. "I'm apologizing anyway."

She said, "Finish the story."

"Carlos came back from Los Angeles disappointed. He was convinced that the American was a Hollywood mafioso, with swimming pools full of cash. He said, 'I'm going to bleed that motherfucker, Tito. For the family honor.'

"I told him about your visit. I hoped he would understand how badly he had screwed up. But he just got more excited. It made him think there was a *lot* more money waiting; 'If the guy is important enough to be looked for . . .'"

She thought: Important to me.

"He tried to talk me into a scheme where I would pose as the dead son. He had an absurd story: I had been abandoned, I was looking for him, whatever."

"You were an alcoholic," she said.

"What?"

"That was part of the story. You were an alcoholic," she said. "Right?"

"I don't remember. It's possible."

Or perhaps, she thought, that had been a detail added for her sake.

My lost decade.

Yes.

Like yours.

She started to laugh. She had written the script for him, giving him her own lonely history. He had ground her heart to pieces, reshaped it in his own miserable mold, and spooned it right back into her mouth.

Another thing we have in common. One of many.

"Shit." She laughed. She was remembering the diner in the bowling alley, when they sat down to eat and he ordered *a light beer.* A light beer for the recovering alcoholic. She felt like an imbecile and so she laughed and said *shit shit shit.*

"*Señora?*"

She wiped her eyes. "This is turning out funnier than I expected."

"I'm glad you think so, *Señora.*"

"I do," she said.

The *Teniente* told her about the plan Carlos had constructed for claiming the estate. "It had no substance other than a bad sob story," he said. "I refused to go."

"You didn't stop him from doing it."

"My permission didn't mean anything to him."

"You gave him enough information to create a complete history."

The *Teniente* gestured dismissively. "Everybody in our family knows what happened. Everyone in Aguas Vivas knows. Ask Luís, he'll tell you. Ask Hector."

"He did tell me."

"There you go. The story is public domain, *Señora.* What Carlos did to it—the embellishments—those are all his."

"Who gave him the photo?"

"What photo."

"He showed me a picture of his mot—of your sister, Carl, and their baby."

"He probably took it from my house, or my father's house. I have no idea."

"Did he promise you money?" she asked.

"He said he would give me something for Pilar if I backed him up."

"Which you *did*."

"I didn't," Fajardo said. "I didn't do anything. I let him go off to California and I prayed he wouldn't hurt anyone. I hoped maybe he'd end up in jail."

"You backed him up when we came to your house."

"He didn't warn me. He came to make sure I didn't confess to you. I probably would've, if he hadn't been standing right there. What did I care? When you showed up at my house, I was off guard, not to mention shit-faced. And I was sick of him trampling my life. He almost sent my daughter into a coma." He stood up and paced. "You see what I'm talking about? I never agreed to be a part of this. He *made* me a part of it." He paused. "When I shot at him, I meant it."

"No," she said. "You didn't."

He gave a defeated smile. "He's still my cousin, *Señora.*"

"Now you don't have to worry about shooting him."

"I guess not."

After a pause, she said, "You're welcome."

They sat in silence for a long time.

"What do we do now?" she said.

"I don't see why we have to do anything."

"What about Carlos?"

"Nobody will miss him."

"What if somebody does."

"In that case," he said, "I reconstructed the crime scene and determined that it was a suicide."

Silence.

She said, "Then what do I do."

"Go home, *Señora*. Do you have a job?"

"I need a new one."

"Go find one. Let my cousin rest and your friend rest and let's not talk about it anymore."

Pause.

"How do you feel about it?" he asked.

"What."

"Killing him."

"I thought you didn't want to talk about it."

"I don't," said Fajardo. "But I'm curious. I've never killed a person before."

She said, "To tell you the truth, it feels like shit."

"If it's any consolation, he wasn't a good person."

She looked at him. "You've never killed anyone, have you?"

"I just told you, I haven't."

She said, "Then shut the hell up."

THIRTY-ONE

Before she left town, she stopped at Hector's shop. He came to the door with his goggles on, fly-eyed, covered in the particulate by-products of grinding, endowed with a sheen, his belly and his cheeks catching light from all directions. He tipped his beer to her as she gave him the index card and thanked him.

"My pleasure," he said. "How did your talk go?"

"About as well as it could have," she said. "And the stone?"

"You want to see?"

Intense spotlight filled the work table. She could see the precision of Hector's lines, and told him so.

"Soon it will all be gone," he said. He waved the card. "Time to put her to sleep." He started toward the door to Nestor's shop.

"Would you mind getting the location of her son's grave?" she asked.

He nodded. "One moment." He ducked underneath the tarp.

While he was gone, she examined his work in progress. From a distance, the stone appeared uniform, like a bowl of clotted cream. Closer, it resolved into chunks of corn and sand—some blotches the size of an obese postage stamp; others collectives of tightly packed cells yielding a block of one color—a complexity that increased as she moved in, swept away dust, put her eyes five inches from the surface. Here, yellow wasn't yellow; it was everything from gray to green, black flecks to nacreous scintillae, resplendent and refractive.

And if she kept going, would more appear? Would she set free an unimagined spectrum? Or would the pattern on the surface appear and reappear in itself, fractal and fugue-like?

And if she went deeper?

And beyond that? To some essentiality?

Or perhaps there was no essence. Perhaps it was—down to the smallest part of the smallest part—an iteration, a code for a code for a code.

She would never know. This was as deep as she could go, as much as she was ever going to see.

"How does it smell?"

She straightened up to see Hector smiling at her.

"I drew you a map," he said. "The family was not prepared to bury two people so soon. They did not own a plot. This is the lot number. Then the row, then the grave. You won't see anyone there. That lot filled up thirty-five years ago. The funerals taking place today are in three hours, half a mile away from there."

She turned the map so that the road out of Aguas Vivas came up from the bottom of the page.

"It is close to the highway. Go in the front gate, and

follow the signs—no. Do not do that. Here." He slid a pencil from his shirtpocket and rubbed out his first route. "The fastest way is to park at the side of the road and walk down." He made an X, wrote *Gloria;* by a second X he wrote *Carlos.*

"Very easy," he said. "No fence."

She stuffed the map in her pocket, so she didn't have to look at her name juxtaposed against his. "Thanks."

"There's a problem, come back and I will give you super-good directions. I'll come out there with you."

"I would hate to bother you again."

"Not a bother, *Señora.*" He smiled crookedly. "I enjoy visitors."

She started to tell him to say good-bye to Luís for her, then remembered the feud. Instead, her parting words were, "I'll find it."

As she got in the Dodge, Hector stood in the doorway, waving his meaty paws beneath the powerful nine-thirty A.M. sun. He was one of those men who didn't sweat. He wiped dust from his forehead like water.

"Drive safely!" he called.

Somehow she had expected a less prosaic send-off. But what did he know? To him, she was another tardy relative. He had stones to carve. It didn't get much more concrete than that.

She wiggled her fingers at him as she drove off. The air felt pleasant in her palm. She kept her arm out the window until she reached the highway, imagining that enough speed would lift her off the earth.

*

SHE STOPPED FOR GAS. The attendant on duty was a grown man with a blinding pate and a mustache that easily could have served as a prosthetic tail for a marmot. He filled up the tank without speaking.

When he gave her change, she said, "You have very smart boys."

He blinked as though she had poked him in the navel. "Yes. They are."

"Say hello to them, will you?"

"Who're you?"

"Yao Ming."

HECTOR'S MAP INSTRUCTED HER to stop a few hundred yards beyond the turnoff. As she drove up, she watched the ground go blue and wet and alive, then drain in an instant.

She got out. It was, she knew, the spot at which Carl had gone off the road. On one side of the highway was the vast Aguas Vivas lake bed, now home to the dead. The other side was a barren expanse, hillocked and patchy like a badly made bed. Somewhere out there was Carl. She had to smile. He had the whole desert to himself.

The boy's grave was closest to the road. She stumbled down the embankment. It was hot and getting hotter by the minute. She gave herself a little burn when she accidentally placed a hand on a passing headstone. Sucking her thumb, she consulted her map and saw that she was standing in front of the plot.

No—that was someone else.

Here it was. A stone the size of a paperback novel. She knelt to read it.

Carlos
1962–1963
Dios lo quería

God loved him.
Or else *God wanted it.*
She didn't have much conversation to make. He was, after all, a baby.

It felt wrong to leave without saying anything at all, so she cleared her throat and scraped the barnacles off a lullaby.

For you I would walk all morning
For you I would sew all day
For you I would cook all evening
For you I will pray all night
My morning will come to greet you
My day will wrap you in clothes
My evening will fill your belly
My night will bring you dreams

His mother's grave was a hundred yards away; her stone slightly bigger.

FAJARDO
GLORIA BEATRIZ RAMOS
Febrero 1947–Julio 1963

Gloria tried to imagine carrying a baby at sixteen. At that age, she had been studying and planning for college. She had not yet decided to become a doctor. Time had gone slower then, because it had lacked an endpoint.

She talked to Gloria for a while, told her about José. She kept calling him Carl, then apologizing. She talked about his diet and his business and his charities. She talked about his sense of humor and his devotion to the church. She laughed and said *He was so funny;* she recounted the horror of his final phone message.

She left out the last five months. They had more to do with herself than with him.

She talked until she ran out of descriptors and anecdotes. By that time, her head was starting to throb with sunstroke. It would be late by the time she made it to California.

"That's all I know," she said, and left.

IN HER REARVIEW MIRROR, she watched the cemetery sink underwater.

THIRTY-TWO

She needed time to decompress. She didn't want to see or speak to anyone, but to iron out the trauma as best she could on her own. She ignored the messages on her machine, two of them from the principal at the high school and a couple more from the girls, wondering where she was. It soothed her to know that at least a few people kept tabs on her.

Despite crippling fatigue, she spent the first nights clutching at her blanket and clawing at the bed, covering her head with a pillow to drown out the echo of shots; the peppery stench of burnt skin and gunsmoke; the warm splash. She would go to the bathroom and race back to bed, afraid of the shadows made by branches, and the wind chimes her landlord insisted channeled good chi to the building.

It wasn't guilt so much as horror that she had led herself within a nail clipping of being killed. She had always prided herself on sound judgment. What had changed?

Not the sex. Not her intelligence. Certainly not that he had a convincing story.

It was, she decided, boredom. Coupled with loneliness. You need a hobby, she told herself.

The trip seemed to have taken a year, not a few days. Time meant something else in Aguas Vivas, where it was infinitely slow and infinitely hot.

But in Los Angeles, it was almost Christmas. People were either chipper or homicidal, or both.

When she felt ready, she called the school back and said regretfully that she would have to withdraw her application. She'd decided to seek a different sort of job. One at a big company where she could be anonymous and have conversation with her coworkers without making too many friends. She didn't intend to stay there for the rest of her life.

Most of all, she needed a job that wouldn't interfere with night classes. She had contacted nursing programs and requested applications. She intended to make good on a few promises.

"MS. MENDEZ?"

Waxbone didn't sound ruffled or hesitant. Gloria thought it was brave of him to call. And tenacious. Beneath the plastic lurks Don Juan.

"I hope I'm not bothering you."

"Not at all, Detective. I was going to call you this afternoon."

"Uh-huh. What about?"

"I reconsidered your offer."

"You—you did?"

"It's been a while since I've done any sort of dancing," she said. "You'll have to give me a lesson."

"That's . . . Thank you. Really?"

"Yeah," she said, "why not."

"I'm glad to hear it, Ms. Mendez. Very glad. Although that's not what I'm calling about."

It was her turn to feel clumsy. "Oh," she said.

"No no," he said. "I'm grateful that you've changed your policy."

"Policy?"

"About not dating law enforcement. You've . . . I guess the expression is that you've made my day."

"Yeah," she said, thinking: maybe the policy should be renewed.

"I'd be privileged to show you the basic steps," Waxbone said. "People are often intimidated by dance, particularly Latin dance, which has an element of sensuality that makes people squeamish—reluctant to abandon themselves to the rhythm, so to speak. But if you can get past the initial feeling of self-consciousness—"

"Detective."

He wasn't listening: "—a rewarding experience. Many call it liberating. And the salsa isn't actually that complicated a step. It's a very relaxed hip motion, with the hand—well, I'd have to show you. Before we hit the club I'll give you a tutorial. I remember the first time—"

"Detective."

"Uh-huh?"

"What *are* you calling about?"

Pause.

"It's regarding Mr. Perreira. Missing persons called me this morning. They got a call from the consulate in Sonora, who had a call from Mexican police. I'm sorry to tell you this, but his body was found." He waited. "Ms. Mendez?"

"I heard you." But Fajardo had agreed: it was all beneath the earth; there was no reason to tell anyone. "What did they say?" she asked.

"The authorities there believe that he was the victim of a carjacking. The perpetrator left Mr. Perreira's identification but took the contents of his wallet, including his bank card. It seems probable that the withdrawal on the account was made . . ."

She already knew the truer version of everything he was saying. But he didn't know that she knew. And she didn't want him to know, because that incriminated the stuffing out of her.

"What about his ATM code?" she asked, hoping that sounded like the question of someone oblivious.

"The perpetrator obtained it somehow," he said. "Thieves can do very sophisticated things with computers nowadays. With increasing use of the Internet, identity theft is fast becoming . . ."

It had to be Fajardo, she decided. It worried her a little. The *Teniente* wasn't too slick under pressure.

". . . transported back to the United States," said Waxbone.

"What?"

"His body."

"Oh," she said.

Waxbone began talking about a funeral. She wondered what it would be like, grieving after grief had passed. She supposed that some of it would return, the residue that could not be wiped from her heart until he was in the ground.

"In the meantime," he said, "I'll get in touch with Maxine Gonzaga and let her know what we've uncovered."

What *who's* uncovered? she thought.

"To be honest, Ms. Mendez, I'm not sure of the protocol for this situation. They might have to go back to the beginning of probate again. The public administrator's office will likely need more of your assistance. You've been extremely patient throughout this process, and I hope you'll continue to be." Waxbone cleared his throat. "And I hope—although I, I hope your offer to—uh—that your offer still stands."

"You mean to go dancing?"

"Uh-huh. Uh, yes."

She pursed her lips. "Sure, it still stands."

"I appreciate it."

"No problem."

"Should we make arrangements now—"

"I'll give you a call."

"Uh-huh. You have my number?"

"Yes."

"Well, good. Good. Thank you, Ms. Mendez."

"Detective? If we're going dancing, you can stop calling me that."

"Uh-huh. What would you rather—"

"How about Doctor Mendez."

"If that's, uh-huh, if that's what you'd prefer, then—"

"I'm joking, Detective. Call me Gloria."

"Gloria. Okay. I'll do that. Gloria."

"And I'll call you John."

"That sounds good."

"All right?"

"All right," he said.

"Good-bye now, John."

"Take care, Ms. Mendez."

A COUPLE OF DAYS later, Maxine Gonzaga called.

"There's a guy out in Tarzana named Jack Gerusha," she said.

Gloria distantly remembered calling him, getting excoriated and hung up on. "What about him?"

"He's in a nursing home," said Gonzaga. "Want to come?"

The Goldest Years Retirement Lodge was a glistening brick of chunky peanut butter along a flat drag of strip malls and scabby Lincolns three half-lives gone. Heart-stopping heat gave way to the lobby's air-conditioned forty-eight degrees.

"Is 'goldest' a word?" Gonzaga asked as they waited for the desk nurse.

"Not one that I know." Gloria rubbed her arms. "I thought old people were always cold."

"I thought they were always hot."

"But what about poor circulation?"

"The proof is in front of us," Gonzaga said. "It's a god-damned igloo in here."

It was lunchtime. They walked through a dining hall full of tables set in sixes and dressed in pale blue polyester. The residents spewed bits of cottage cheese as they chatted. The place looked like a high-school cafeteria, complete with gossipy, murmuring cabals. There was a doddering table, a lively table, a table of women who all dyed their hair in pastels, solo diners glaring at everyone in sight. Gloria smiled at the men and they leered back. One of them said "Why hello there, pretty lady" and was promptly smacked in the shoulder by his tight-lipped female companion.

Jack Gerusha was sequestered in the corner like a rajah. He had his own nurse, who spoon-fed him Jell-O and dripping gobs of peach. Unlike the rest of the residents, who all gripped flimsy plastic utensils, he had an actual place setting, and it appeared to be sterling silver.

Maxine identified herself and introduced Gloria as her partner.

"I'm Celia," said the nurse. "Say hello, Mr. Gerusha."

Gerusha held up his right hand, missing its pinkie. Grinning deliciously, he curled down two of the remaining fingers.

He was flipping them off.

Then he saluted, sat back in his chair, and instantly fell asleep.

Celia shrugged. "He can be a grump."

They moved a few tables over. Gloria glanced at the old man's neck. He hadn't shaved—or been shaved—in at least a week.

Gonzaga said, "Nurse Richards told you we were coming?"

"Yeah, about a relative of his. I didn't know he had any relatives."

"Who admitted him here?"

"He did. He got tired of wiping himself." Celia's mouth turned up at one corner. "So now I get the privilege. He could've gotten a private nurse, but he likes having people around to yell at. Three months ago he was living on his own. Then he had a minor stroke. He's been heading downhill, forgotten a lot of his English. Oh—and he likes to make crank calls. When telemarketers call he gives them hell."

"Was he married?"

"No. No family. No kids. He had a brother who died a long time ago."

"What did he do?" Gloria asked.

"Jewelry, I think. He doesn't like to talk about the past, and he can be hard to understand, so I've put it together from things he says in passing. He talks to himself sometimes. He has a boxful of stuff that he spends hours talking to."

"He talks to inanimate objects?" Gonzaga asked.

"They're in his room," Celia said. Seeing their willingness: "We better go before he wakes up."

Even with little exposure to nursing homes, Gloria could tell that Gerusha's room was cavernous. She remarked on this to Celia, who said, "It used to be two rooms. He paid to have the wall knocked down. Jill said he might be inheriting some money?"

"Possibly," said Gonzaga.

"He doesn't need it." The nurse opened the nightstand and withdrew a wooden box with a label that said REAL FLORIDA CLEMENTINES. It contained several dozen black velvet boxes. The first one Gonzaga opened contained a magnificent pair of earrings: large, rose-colored pearls set in antique gold.

They reminded Gloria of something. They reminded her of the photo of young Joseph Gerusha and his female companion, Gloria Fajardo.

Her pendant: enormous pearls.

Celia started opening the other boxes. They all contained pearls—scores of pearls, licked vainly by golden flames. Gorgeous, pristine, edible-looking pearls, some the size of grapes; many adorned with staggeringly elaborate diamond or ruby accents. Pearls, like tiny balloons; the rotten fruit box a pirate's hold split open.

"Gol-*ly* . . ." said Gonzaga.

"I know," said the nurse. "And who knows what he's got in the bank."

Gloria wondered how Gerusha could keep this stuff here. The staff seemed nice enough, but it would take an inhuman effort to resist pocketing it. Especially considering that he was such a curmudgeon. Then it occurred to Gloria that he might have arrived here with more loot than she was seeing.

"When I called and spoke to him a few months ago," Gloria said, "he made it sound like he was poor. He yelled at me about Medicare."

"He's not poor," Celia said. "He's just unbelievably cheap."

Beneath the jewelry boxes was a neat stack of postcards. Gonzaga picked it up and began sifting through, handing them to Gloria. Brittle and acidified, they traced a weird route from Hawaii to Fiji to Japan to various spots in Micronesia. Back to Hawaii. They were written half in English and half in Russian, and addressed to somebody named Ahtoh in San Diego, California.

"Who's that?" Gloria asked the nurse.

"His brother."

"Ahtoh?" said Gonzaga.

"I think it's pronounced Anton."

"In what country?"

"I think he was Russian from way back," said Celia. "That's what he's implied."

"But he was in the U.S. Army."

"In Japan. I think that's where he brought the pearls back from. South Sea pearls? That's what they're called."

"Is Anton still alive?" Gonzaga asked.

"He's the brother who died a long time ago," said Celia.

"In a car accident," said Gloria.

Gonzaga and Celia looked at her.

"How do you know?" asked Gonzaga. "Is that right?" she asked the nurse.

Gloria said, "The birth certificate at the bank had Joseph Gerusha's parents on it. Anthony and Katherine. They died in the sixties—sixty-one. Around then."

"We can ask him," said Celia. "He doesn't remember a whole lot. And you saw his attitude. But it doesn't hurt to try."

Jack Gerusha was still out when they reentered the

dining room. The women all pulled up chairs, and Celia roused him.

"Mr. Gerusha, these ladies would like to ask you a question."

Gerusha snorted and rubbed his forehead. "Fock off," he said.

Gonzaga said, "Mr. Gerusha, did you have a brother?"

"Where is angel?" he asked, snapping his fingers at Celia. Rolling her eyes, she used a paper napkin to wrap his silverware. She tore off a strip of paper and tied a little bow around the head of the fork. Thus ensconced, it did in fact resemble an angel—albeit one stained with duck sauce and fruit syrup.

"Here you go," she said. He smiled and slid it into his breast pocket.

"These ladies want to know about your brother, Mr. Gerusha."

"Fock."

"Was he named Anthony?" Gloria asked.

At the mention of the name, Gerusha's face slackened. He looked at her like she was an apparition that had risen through the floor.

"Was Joseph his son?"

Gerusha frowned. *"Vor,"* he muttered.

Gloria looked at Celia for help, but she shook her head.
"Vor."

"What's that mean?" Gonzaga asked.

"Maybe it's Russian," Gloria said.

"Mrs. Bakhov speaks," Celia said, indicating one of the dyed ladies. "One sec."

While they waited for her to return with an answer, Gloria asked Gerusha, "Anton was married to Katherine?"

The old man's face loosened again. "Katarina," he said dreamily.

Gloria opened her purse, took out a picture of Carl, and held it for Gerusha to see. He stared at it a while, his head bobbing slightly.

"Yosif," he said. *"Vor."* Then his face softened to something like mourning. He sighed heavily and began muttering: slurred and trilled and salivary.

Celia came back. "She said *vor* means thief."

Gonzaga said, "He stole something from him?"

"Jewels," Gloria said. "After his parents died. He stole things from his uncle."

"He must have stolen a lot," Gonzaga said. "Eleven million bucks' worth?"

"I'm sure it wasn't worth that to begin with," Gloria said.

"So how did it get to be that much?"

"There's twenty years of his life unaccounted for," Gloria said.

"Katarina . . ." said Gerusha. He stiffened and got up. Celia went to help him. He batted at her angrily, took possession of his walker, and clomped toward the door.

"Sorry," Celia said.

"It's okay."

Gloria and Gonzaga watched her follow him across the room. He dragged a limp left foot.

"Do you really think that's what happened?" Gonzaga asked.

"It could be," Gloria said. "Or else I'm being too imaginative."

"I'll look into it. I can contact the VA; they might have records of his family. We can trace connections to Anton—Anthony, or whatever his name is." Gonzaga sounded eager. "You know what, we could be on to something here—the whole picture. There could be a lot of people we haven't found yet. Someone who knows more about this than we've been able to determine. I think . . ."

As she talked, Gloria gave occasional signs of agreement. Gonzaga wanted to start from the beginning; she thought they could figure it all out; the whole thing would be theirs.

Gloria wasn't sure she wanted to know any more.

Maybe Carl was a thief. Or maybe the money—or was it jewels? or both?—had belonged to Carl's father, and the uncle was the duplicitous one. Maybe it was none of the above, and Carl had gotten his money in some other way.

Maybe there was a way to tell, and maybe there wasn't.

As she watched the old man walk away, it occurred to her that she had finished here. She didn't want to know. The ignorance that had fired her days and tormented her nights was rapidly fading to a reminiscence, an experience she could already see framed. And she knew that it meant the end of her love. Because love is the desire to understand, and recovery is contentment with questions.

She felt okay.

Gonzaga, on the other hand, was busy spinning conjecture into theory into line of investigation. She wanted Gloria's help, and—

"I'm not sure I'm going to be of any use to you. This time around."

Gonzaga stopped short. "What?"

"I said, I don't know if I can help out."

"You're not interested in finding out?"

"I am," Gloria said. "Sort of."

"You wanted to be involved before."

"I know."

Pause.

Gonzaga shrugged. "If that's what you want."

"I am interested," Gloria said. "It's just that I have to get back to my own life."

Gonzaga nodded. "Okay."

"You'll still let me know what you turn up?"

"Yeah."

"Anything I can help you with—if you can't find the answer on your own—feel free to give me a call."

"I will. Thanks for coming out. And for all your work."

"Thanks for putting up with me."

"Nah. You were a big help."

"You don't need to thank me," Gloria said.

"Someone does," Gonzaga said.

Gloria shrugged. "Not really."

They got up and headed back toward the lobby. Gloria had to resist reaching into her pocket to play with her new pearl earrings.

"LONG TIME NO SEE," Reggie said, sliding into the booth.

They were at the Original Pantry. He had gotten

through a session at Metropolitan, and was still wearing his court demeanor: fat and sassy, smug to be on the right side of the law.

"Guilty or not guilty?" she asked.

He gave her a look: *Get real.*

"What did he do?"

"Hit his wife in the face with a plate cause it wasn't clean enough." He glanced at the tabletop and began picking at a wart of dried jam. "Hurt her pretty bad."

"She pressed charges?" Gloria knew that wives seldom did.

"She tried to drop, but the ADA went ahead anyway . . . this won't come off." He used his fork to chip at the jam until it sailed away.

"I shouldn't eat at this place," he said.

"We could've met somewhere else."

"Nahh . . ." He ran his hands over his gut. "Wouldn't pass it up for anything. I love it here."

Their waiter was shaggy and hoary, with knuckles like pipe joints and eczematous elbows. As he took their orders—buckwheat hotcakes and ham for Reggie, toast for her—his eyes watered as though he was on the verge of exploding with elderly contagion.

"You got it," he said, and tottered off.

Reggie watched him go. "That guy was alive on the third day of creation."

"I hope he doesn't breathe on your food."

"What about your food?"

"I ordered mine for show," she said.

He laughed, slapping the table. "Well, I'm sure *some-one*'ll get to it. . . ."

She asked about the trial, about work. As always, he had a lot to say about nothing, and she let him go on as long as he wanted. The waiter returned, armed with plates, which he hammered down like he was playing bop-the-mole.

"Hash browns," he said, tossing them to Reggie.

"Thanks," Gloria said.

"That's all you want, huh?" the waiter asked her. "Maybe I get you some butter?"

"No, thank you."

"Enjoy it," he commanded, and ambled off. She watched his bony rump pump beneath the bow of his apron strings.

"Irreplaceable," Reggie said. He was already a third of the way through his ham, chewing like a beaver, blotting sauce from his lips. "You sure you don't want some?"

She tossed the toast on top of his browns. "I'll pass."

"Suit y'self," he said. "So, what's been going on? How was your vacation? Give me the full monty."

"Not bad."

"Did you water-ski?"

"No."

"Swim?"

"Nope."

"Tell me you did more than sunbathe," he said.

"Not really," she said.

"What a bore," he sighed.

"I met a man."

That got his attention. "Yeah? Who."

"It's nothing," she said.

"What? Come on, that's hooey."

"Really. It's nothing."

"*Gloria . . .*" he said reproachfully. "Pictures?"

"They didn't come out."

"Aw—come on . . ."

"Sorry."

She could see him trying not to care; it gave her a huge kick.

"I'm real glad," he said finally. "That's great news."

"I didn't sleep with him," she said.

Reggie sat up as though goosed. "*Gigi.*"

"That's what you wanted to know, right?"

"No. No. Listen—no. I did—I—how could you assu— I mean, *seriously . . .*" He looked like a cartoon character, with his eyes rolling. "What do you take me for?"

"Then forget I ever said it," she said.

"Hey, you can do whatever you want. I'm not your guardian."

"I know."

"You can sleep with him, not sleep with him, you can do whatever you want. You can do it with female dwarves for all I care. It's not my business."

"I know."

"But—if you're telling me anyway, then—and I have to say it once, I'm not going to mention it again—I think you made the right decision. Not to sleep with him. It's not my affair to stick my nose in, or whatever, but I'm not in favor of that."

"Sex? You used to be."

"I'm in favor of *that*," he said. "Don't you worry about me. What I'm not in favor of is, you know. Rushing things. With a stranger."

"He wasn't a stranger. We got along."

"Please, Gigi."

"What."

"How well can you know someone after a week?"

"How well can you know someone after a year?" she asked.

"Better than after a week," he said.

"You think so?"

"I do," he said. "I do."

She thought for a minute about *Teniente* Tito Fajardo: fervor and detachment, righteous conviction and laxity bordering on malice, self-doubt and vainglory. She thought about Carl and his mismatched selves. She thought about Carlos, and Reggie; about her brother and her mother. It was a good thing she had never become a psychologist, like Allan Jarroll-Peña, because if she thought honestly, she couldn't assemble any of them into a coherent whole.

And her? When she had told Carlos about herself, laid out her life in chapters—what had she given him? She thought: not even a representative sample. Because new parts of her bubbled up into consciousness every minute. But she was feeling good about it. Excited to meet herself tomorrow.

She wanted to tell Reggie everything. It was some story.

The other patrons were clearing their throats and straightening their papers, talking to one another, talking, talking.

One fewer story didn't hurt anyone.

"It's really not very interesting," she said.

Reggie groaned. "Forget it. I don't *want* to hear, if you're going to make it a pain in the ass."

The waiter staggered past, shedding a grease-stained bill between their water glasses.

"I have to go in a minute," she said.

"Oh yeah?"

She could tell by the way he said it that what he meant was: *another date?* She said, "I'm meeting Barbara."

"You gonna tell *her* about your vacation?"

"Maybe."

"All the details?"

"Maybe."

"More than you told me?" he asked.

"Probably."

He shook his head. "You guys . . ."

"'Guys?'"

"I mean women," he said. "*Guys* as in *women*."

"Well," she said, "then we're not really guys. Are we."

He stared at her, then cracked up. "I guess not."

"Thank you," she said, smiling.

"You should've been a lawyer."

"Yeah."

"I mean it. You should've been a cop."

"How'd I get demoted that fast?" she asked.

He shot her a faux scowl and picked up the check. As he looked it over, he bit his lip. "Ah—you know what, Gigi—?"

She already had her purse on the table.

"I'll pay you back," he said.

"On me," she said, handing him a twenty.

She had never seen him quite so dumbstruck.

"Yeah?"

"I'll take care of it."

"You sure?"

She said, "That's how it always is."

ACKNOWLEDGMENTS

Many people enabled the creation of this book by sharing their expertise with me. Thanks to Benjamin J. Mantell, Jeff Forer, Michael Rosen, Larry Malmberg, Jed Resnick, Terri Porras, and Maribel Romero. Special thanks to the Honorable Leon Brickman (Ret.). Any errors or stretched truths are mine and mine alone.

My agent, Liza Dawson, has been a model of confidence and cheer; additionally, her editing proved invaluable. Her friendship is a gift for which I am eternally grateful.

All of that praise applies equally to my superlative editor, Christine Pepe. Thank you for everything.

Thanks to Amy Brosey for her sharp eye and her respectful pen.

Thanks to my siblings and my grandparents.

Ema and Abba: you inspire me. Ema in particular gets full credit for handing me the seed that grew to become this book. *Ha'omer davar b'shem she'amro mevi geulah le'olam* (Talmud, Megillah 15a).

Mom and Dad: for being my first and best writing

teachers. For always smiling when I said, "Read this." For bankrolling my indolent derrière. For dogged encouragement, vision when others were blind, immaculate selflessness, and infinite love.

My wife, my wife, my wife.

*Now turn the page to read an extract
of Jesse Kellerman's next tense thriller*

Trouble

Available from Sphere hardback in January 2007

ONE

THURSDAY, AUGUST 19, 2004
COLORECTAL SURGERY, WEEK ONE.

Jonah Stem heard a scream.

He was walking to Times Square at two forty-five in the morning to buy new shoes. The staid, sturdy Rockport Walkers that had survived two years of theoretical medicine had finally succumbed to its uncontrollably runny realities. Befouled beyond repair, they made a squishing noise and left a trail, like overgrown snails. Salient among the novel qualities they had come to possess was the stink of human shit.

Shoes were shoes. Their destruction didn't bother Jonah per se, except that it acutely underscored his own incompetence—something he didn't need to be reminded of these days, with people lining up to do it for him.

For this mess, as he did generally, Jonah blamed himself. He knew the rules; he'd read the Book, heard it from the

Ghosts of Third Year Past. Once your day was over, the only safe strategy was OTD—Out the Door—ASAP. If you lingered and got caught, you were SOL. Particularly on surgery. Surgeons—surgical residents, rather—didn't especially care that your day had been over for twenty minutes. (Attendings didn't especially care about you at all.) When they needed you, you went. The best way to avoid being needed, then, was to get out of the building supersonic fast.

Instead he'd dawdled. He had twelve weeks here; it paid to take the time to learn his way around. Asking too many questions—even innocuous ones like *Where are we meeting* or *Where's the bathroom*—made you look unprepared. It primed the pump for getting pimped, because while the Gods of Surgery might forget your name, forget that you had other obligations, forget that you were a person with a beating heart and an independent will, They always, *always* remembered your weaknesses. They took note of who copped to ignorance, and on that person They pounced, eager to impart Their full-tilt-no-holds-barred balls-to-the-wall medical pedagogy until he sobbed and sniveled like a little pants-wetting baby girl.

Jonah liked hospitals at that hour, the alleged end of the workday, when patients finished their early dinners and settled in for TV and Toradol and complaining. Midtown-St. Agatha's—a thrumming snuffleupagus of sterile linoleum, wheelchairs, high-rising paperwork, hypoallergenic pillowcases, accident victims, cancer victims, moans, kidney stones, sample closets, graywater mop buckets, insurance fraud, viruses, bacteria, prions, fractures, lesions, lacerations, nociceptors firing and relaxing—took a breath. A place like St. Aggie's was never truly silent, but like all large medical institutions, it seemed to hiccup at around six thirty P.M., granting an illusion of peace; an idea of what peace might be, if you weren't imprisoned in a goddamned hospital.

He meandered varicose corridors, shucking the stickiness, the soreness, the self-pity. He was here to learn. He was going to be a doctor; he spent years toiling to earn the right to be so abused. He had taken college courses and review courses. He had spent hours glued to books, had bushwhacked the MCAT and pummeled the Boards. All to get here. Finishing work feeling like a used condom was a *privilege*. Who cares about the antiseptic smell; the harsh, bluish lights; the overenthusiastic pastels, like chunks of Miami air-dropped smack in the middle of Manhattan. He felt better, and then there were fingers snapping in his face.

"Hello. Are you there."

This was how they were. You accepted it or you dropped out. You found ways to cope. You imagined yourself in a different milieu—say, at a party—where you had the asshole in question beat by at least thirty yards

You totted up your victories. One: hygiene. Residents didn't get out much, and this one in particular suffered from excess cerumen production, which two years ago Jonah would have called by its more descriptive, real-world name: a Colossal Avalanche of Earwax. Advantage, Stem.

Two: style. The resident's spreading waistline had succumbed to an infestation of beepers and PDAs, phones and Blackberries, making him look like Batman minus the pointy ears and award-winning physique. Advantage, Stem.

Three: charm. Obviously, he had that locked up; look at the guy, poking him in the arm and ordering him downstairs with that imperious smirk, advantage, St—

"Stop staring at me like you're deaf." The resident's badge bounced as he gesticulated. His name was BENDERKING DEVON PGY-2. He had a hare-lip, currently twisted into a sneer. "I know you can hear me."

"Sorry."

"We need hands."

Jonah loved that. The rest of his body, including his brain, was irrelevant.

His shift was long done; he didn't belong to Benderking's team; he needed to get home for his four hours of sleep. But this was his third day on the service, and he wanted to make a good impression; so he smiled and said *I'm there* and jogged along toward the OR. Unless a doctor asked you to wash his car or fellate his poodle, you did it, and you did it with love.

As they hurried downstairs, Benderking gave him the essentials: Caucasian F 37 stomach pain. After an unattended hour in the ER, the nurses find her flailing around, tachycardic, hypotensive, pushing 103°, respiratory distress, distended. Eighteen months status post gastric bypass, she had experienced a weight loss of one hundred and twenty-five pounds plus. Like setting a person down after a twenty-year piggyback ride.

Through the double doors and there she was: loose skin flapping, the skin she no longer fit, a drab pink wedding dress she could not remove.

The room was madness, everyone running to prep as

they waited for the surgeon, pausing only to engage in the choicest OR pastime: yelling at the medical student. Jonah fetched a gown and gloves, and the scrub nurse yelled *you contaminated it, get another*, even though the items were still sealed and sterile, as though he was uniquely, grotesquely infectious. He shuffled to and from the supply room, dutifully shlepping another gown, another pair of gloves.

Into this squall sailed a gray-haired, gray-skinned, epicene man in his sixties: Gerard "The Slice" Detaglia. He wiggled his pianist's hands and said, "Shall we dance?"

Scrub-in. Detaglia buffed each side of each finger with five strokes from a Betadine sponge. This behavior—carried out with a priest's solemnity—marked him as decidedly old school; surgeons under forty favored instead a quicker but equally effective chemical rub. But Jonah wasn't going to make the same mistake as yesterday, when he'd used the rub while the surgeon sponged, and the rest of the team shot him a look of horror, and he instantly gleaned that he'd screwed up.

They were everywhere, these laws that nobody told you about but that ensured a beatdown when you broke them. Which you did. You couldn't help breaking them. *Nobody had told you about them.*

The guiding principle of medical education was that people learn best under threat of mortification.

Standing at the back of the line, waiting for his turn at the sink, Jonah reflected that there was truth to this proposition. As soon as he'd committed the scrub faux pas, a new rule—*do as the surgeon*—had automatically appeared in his brain, produced by the same mechanism. that spurs skunks to spray, anemones to contract, birds to wing at the sound of a gun. He knew; and he wouldn't mess up again.

The Gods of Surgery were jealous and punishing, and he had sinned. As a third-year, he could not be expected to do much more than suture, retract, suction. Like any apprentice, his real purpose was not to help but to validate the hierarchy. As every doctor before him had suffered, so must he.

The team backed into the OR, hands elevated and dripping. The scrub nurse passed out towels to Detaglia and the residents, leaving Jonah to fend for himself. In the end he didn't have time to find one, and was still wet when they gowned and gloved him, leaving him squirming and humid inside two layers of latex.

"*Medical student.*"

Another way they kept you in check, by never using your name. Obey unthinkingly, Nonhuman. In this case, the scrub nurse was giving him the light handle covers and saying *Get on with it already.*

He obeyed.

Strangely, surgery went much faster with the stereo off. Detaglia dove through skin, fat, muscle; he commandeered his nurses like a pasha; they moved at his bidding and flirted shamelessly. After an hour of retracting, Jonah's forearms blazed with pain. *It's worth it, you're going to be a doctor; Doctor Stem, Doctor Doctor oh Doctor, Christ it hurts it hurts stop shaking everyone is looking at you.* They weren't, of course; they weren't paying any attention to him. He had to stop thinking this way. If he was going to make it through the year—*day three*—he'd have to thicken his skin.

He had never been the hypersensitive sort—at least, he didn't think so— and this was the wrong time to start. He tightened his grip.

The patient's innards bulged in the wrong places, embarrassingly so, and prying her open felt intrusive, like barging into someone's bedroom before they've had a chance to pick up their underwear. As Detaglia worked, Jonah thought of the scene in *Raiders of the Lost Ark* when they spring the Door Best Left Alone and everyone within a mile turns to fondue. He forced himself to look. *Get in there, see what's going on, you can't learn unless you stare it straight in the face.* Many of his fellow students—had they bothered to listen to Benderking—would have checked out mentally by now. But Jonah had a strong, almost Victorian sense of Duty, and having committed himself to being in the room, he wanted to *be* there. It was disgusting, but that was life, sometimes you did things you didn't want to do. He was further gripped by the notion that he'd paid tuition for this, and dammit if he wasn't going to learn. He wanted to barf. He blinked. *Look.*

As he leaned forward to observe the incision, the peritoneum burst, and a blast of bloody guts spilled across the table, his chest, the floor, his—

His shoes.

He looked down. In his haste, he'd forgotten to don booties.

The Slice sighed and said, "Oh, heck."

The organs Jonah knew from books and labs were robust, smooth, warm. This lady's reminded him of a Brunswick stew; they resisted categorization: poking through, tearing, melting. She leaked. Shit and bile and cells, all curdling in a vile juice. The terminology Jonah used to organize the situation—acute mesenteric ischemia, bowel infarction—did not capture its true disorder, as her shocked body ceased to respect its God-given blueprint.

And she hemorrhaged. Blood slickened the floor. The circ nurse mopped like a fiend, snarling at Jonah to express her displeasure. *Medical student would you get out of the goddamned way. Medical student please lift your goddamned leg please. I'd like to pick that up medical student but I can't because you're in my goddamned way.*

He contorted to accommodate her, struggling not to lose his grip.

Worst of all was the smell; the body gave off gas like a downed zeppelin. The stench reminded him of a frathouse, Sunday morning circa ten thirty A.M. The sheepish, post-bacchanalian miasma of *seemed-like-a-good-idea-at-the-time:* putrid meat and stale flatulence, comically magnified. To prevent himself from passing out, Jonah focused on the irreparable damage done to his shoes.

It took five hours to remove eighty percent of her intestine, which came out black and kinked, like a harvest of seaweed. When Detaglia revascularized the little that remained, the tissue flushed pink, the cardinal color of life rushing to reclaim its seat. Jonah was impressed. Everyone was impressed. The Slice was known as a clutch hitter, but this was special. Assuming she did not die overnight, the patient might go on to lead a full and rewarding life. With a colostomy bag.

"Well," said Detaglia, glancing at the red biohazard sack,

heavy with guts, "she wanted to lose weight."

By the time Jonah had ditched his scrubs, it was half past two. Rounds began at six A.M. If he went home, he'd get at most ninety minutes of sleep before having to hop back on the subway. He should have asked for the day off but considered it gauche, not to mention spineless, to start taking liberties with his schedule after three days on the job.

The thought of being on his feet for another eighteen hours—in those shoes—made his skin crawl. This was New York, though, capital of late-night solutions.

He hit the street.

It was hot out and he could hear traffic skating the West Side Highway. Except for the hospital, Eleventh Avenue above 50th consisted of auto dealerships proffering luxury vehicles unsuited to Manhattan life. Above the locked-down driveways of body shops, broken windows glinted scaly and blue-black, fish netted in an oil spill. Near the pile of dirt and pigeon waste that was DeWitt Clinton Park, someone had left a toilet—tank, bowl, the works—out on the sidewalk like a Dadaist sculpture. He gave it a title: *My Life Is Poop.*

The moon was stingy; the streetlights weakly flickering.

———

That was when he heard the scream.

Coming from 53rd Street, it had an operatic quality: a pure, shrill, hellish beauty.

Following it around the corner, he saw a woman on all fours. Behind her stood a man in a flaccid overcoat several sizes too big. He seemed in no particular hurry, slumped casually against a Dumpster, watching her crawl away.

oh my God he stabbed me

Despite the pressing heat, she was dressed in a down jacket and dark stockings. She jerked like a windup toy, listing to avoid her left hand, her left arm dripping with dark black blood. Screaming and screaming and screaming. The jagged hull of an adjacent demolition site reflected her voice at unexpected angles.

please help me

please help me

please help me

She looked straight at Jonah, her face incandescent with fear, striped by swinging hair, a pale sheet of need. *Help me help me.*

She was speaking to him. *Help me.*

Later he would come to understand that most people would have walked away. A few would've called the police and waited, watching from a distance. But to Jonah the situation presented itself quite differently. What he saw was the man, the woman, the moon—and he felt not only disinclined to leave but an overwhelming obligation to stay, as if the woman's voice—*help*—was in fact the voice of God, funneled and filtered and broken but no less imperative: a moment chosen for him.

And he was going to be a doctor.

He did not think.

He ran forward, waving his arms. *Hey.*

The man glanced up and immediately reconfigured himself in agitation: he shifted from foot to foot, rolled his shoulders, scratched at a tangled beard and tugged gnarls of incoherent hair. He muttered to himself. Shirtless beneath the coat, its sleeves dangling past his hands, making him look childish and lost. Jonah recognized the man's state; he knew it intimately, embraced it regularly; and he felt a wash of calm. He knew what to do.

He said *Please look at me.*

The man looked at him.

Jonah said *Nobody's going to hurt you.*

I'm dying screamed the woman.

Without turning around, Jonah said to her *You're going to be okay.*

dying

dying

I'm dying

Can you do something for me? Mister? Please. Take a step back.

The man grimaced with impatience, like Jonah had jumped a cue. He sidestepped and Jonah stepped to match him.

Okay, hang on. I don't want to—

The man tried a second time to go around him, and Jonah came forward—

—listen I don't want to nobody wants to
and everything accelerated.

Hair and heat and suffocating body odor; a wrenched limb; down; the ground; and then, for the second time that night, Jonah bathed in a great deal of blood.